FINDING IMMORTALITY

BILL CONRAD

First Edition

interviewingimmortality.com
bill@interviewingimmortality.com
www.facebook.com/Interviewingimmortality/
www.goodreads.com/author/show/17088207.Bill_Conrad
www.amazon.com/Bill-Conrad/e/B074FFPZX9

This is a work of fiction. Names, characters, places, and incidents either are the product of the author's imagination or are used fictitiously. Any resemblance to actual persons, living or dead, businesses, companies, events, or locales is entirely coincidental.
Limits of Liability and Disclaimer of Warranty:

The authors and/or publisher shall not be liable for misuse of this material. The contents are strictly for entertainment purposes only.

Printed and bound in the United States of America
ISBN: 978-1-7340387-2-9

TABLE OF CONTENTS

A REVIEW OF THE PREVIOUS BOOK,
Interviewing Immortality 1

ONE 5

TWO 7

THREE 21

FOUR 39

FIVE 65

SIX 79

SEVEN 105

EIGHT 121

NINE 141

TEN 167

ELEVEN 197

TWELVE 247

THIRTEEN 267

FOURTEEN 301

FIFTEEN 325

SIXTEEN 341

SEVENTEEN 359

EIGHTEEN 377

NINETEEN 389

TWENTY 429

TWENTY-ONE 441

TWENTY-TWO 449

EPILOGUE 455

ABOUT THE AUTHOR 459

DEDICATION 461

A REVIEW OF THE PREVIOUS BOOK

INTERVIEWING IMMORTALITY

My name is James Kimble, and two years ago, I wrote a book based on my life. I titled it *Interviewing Immortality*.

My story began right after I turned 31. I had recently completed my divorce and still worked at Best Buy, the electronics retail store. In my spare time, I wrote books, and on weekends, I went to book signings to promote my *Grime* book trilogy. All in all, my life had not been that exciting, but I felt modestly happy. I only had one problem; my humble life contained a big lie. I had plagiarized my best-selling book, *Grime: The Big Hate!*

Of all the places for my hum-drum life to come crashing down, it was during a book signing in the small town of Sandy, Oregon. A well-dressed woman walked up to me and gave me the scare of my life. After I recovered, I vowed never to set foot in that town again.

I was getting ready to drive home that evening when this same evil-looking woman came right up to me, grabbed me, tied me up, put a hood over me, and drove me away. It all happened quickly, and I felt scared beyond belief. That night, she restrained me in a bedroom and then, to my surprise, fed me a delicious breakfast. She told me her name was Grace and admitted to being over 500 years old.

This crazy woman then demanded that I write a book about her. However, this would be difficult because I hurt my hand in the scuffle. As soon as I agreed, she took me to a clearing in the woods. I could see two men secured in filthy cages. Without explanation, Grace began inflicting excruciating pain on one man and then cut him open. Imagine how shocked I felt to see a living person tortured to death. Then to my horror, Grace removed three of his organs and inserted them into her own body in a procedure she called a "harvest." Without a word, she cut into my body and placed the remaining harvested organs inside me! Did this hurt? More than a little. When we returned to her house, I became dreadfully ill.

The next day, the woman said these new organs would miraculously prolong my life and bring other great attributes. The downside was that I would have to "harvest" every six months to maintain a long life.

Bright and early the following morning, I woke in pain and had an undeniably hostile urge. I had convinced myself that I wanted to see the other man who was locked in one of the steel enclosures. After communicating with this prisoner, I determined that he was an evil man, and then I did the unthinkable. I killed him with an old hammer. Me, an ordinary guy … I killed a man in cold blood! I then used Grace's methods to place his organs inside my body without fully comprehending my gruesome actions.

After a good night's sleep, I woke up feeling fantastic; in fact, I felt livelier than ever. Grace and I ate breakfast and retired to the living room. I was eager to get started on her biography and began peppering her with questions. Grace instead diverted the conversation with questions about my life. I told her about my divorce and my writing. Grace was unimpressed and forced me to confess that I had plagiarized the first two books in my Grime series. I had never revealed this fact to anybody, and my admission was heart-wrenching.

After I came clean, I earned some respect in Grace's eyes. She began opening up with recollections of her own life, starting with her Russian childhood and family. At age fifteen, she unexpectedly met none other than the beautiful Pharaoh Cleopatra. The Egyptian queen became fascinated and impressed with this young girl and shared her secret of immortality. Like me, Grace was horrified by the concept and physical pain of the harvest, but the procedure's aftermath vastly improved her mental and physical abilities. She also excitedly embraced her immortal existence.

As I absorbed all this background information, Grace's pet mountain lion, Heathcliff, caught my attention. What a fantastic, sleek, and enigmatic animal. Plus, this cat could communicate mental images to me.

Then, as suddenly as my ordeal with Grace began, it ended. I had to quit my job at Best Buy because of my dishonesty, but the harvest abilities allowed me to become a *Portland Tribune* newspaper reporter.

ONE

There are some basic rules to writing a book that I will now impart to you, the reader.

1) After you murder somebody, DON'T WRITE A BOOK ABOUT IT! This is common sense. Writing a tell-all book leaves a well-documented trail for the jury to follow.

2) Change the facts if you are foolish enough to write a book about your crime. For example, one fact you should never reveal is your actual name.

3) If your book includes an accomplice, you must change any facts about them. Skipping this simple step will transform you from author to corpse.

4) And finally, no matter what, DON'T WRITE ANOTHER BOOK! Even a dead person can follow that logic.

To continue living, those are essential rules to follow. Yet, I ignored my sage wisdom and wrote another book. I hope that after reading following pages, you will understand my reasons.

TWO

I survived her wrath! It is impossible to understand how wonderful it feels to be alive until a person comes within inches of death.

After my harrowing *interview*, my life returned to normal, and I found a new job at the *Portland Tribune*. My boss, Lloyd Stevenson, assigned me to be his new "people person." The job involved selecting a popular, controversial topic, explaining the facts to a local person, and writing up their reaction. My workdays lasted three hours, and the stories wrote themselves. Easy money!

As you may recall, a 500-year-old woman who called herself Grace forced me to undergo a painful procedure called the "harvest," which required me to place an organ (a prepared human pancreas!) into my body. This life-prolonging procedure nearly eliminated aging and improved my mental and physical abilities. The effect lasted six months. If I stopped harvesting, my newfound abilities would subside, and my body would return to its standard aging rate.

The harvest effects were profound, especially on my mental abilities. My memory, logic, intuition, and mathematical skills were far better. Plus, I could calculate the passage of time with extreme accuracy.

Before my harvest, I could not run one block without collapsing in exhaustion (which was pretty sad). If you asked me to touch my toes, my hands stopped at my knees.

I began taking karate lessons, practicing yoga, and going for hour-long runs. My body became so flexible that I easily touched the ground with my palms. My allergies, digestive issues, and tinnitus were all gone. Plus, the six ugly moles on my face fell off, my bald spot disappeared, and my skin took on a youthful complexion. I require less sleep and am much stronger than before, but I cannot build muscle mass beyond a certain point. To top it off, I lost 32 pounds without even trying. Women began turning their heads when I walked by, and I got asked out on dates. Obviously, that had never happened before.

My personality and interests also changed. I now have a deeper appreciation of classical music and famous artwork. Plus, I have taken a keen interest in physics, biology, and astronomy. The change also gave me endless patience to listen to intelligent people. My political views switched from passionate liberal to balanced neutral. Overall, I went from being an arrogant introvert to a self-confident extrovert with a winning smile. Everybody noticed how much I grew as a person, and they all liked the new James Kimble.

My life's direction also underwent a substantial change. Before the harvest, I applied the minimum effort in everything. On weekdays I got up at the last possible moment, drove to work, did a mediocre job at Best Buy, went home, watched television, and fell asleep. I slept in late on weekends, watched uninspiring television programs, and fell asleep early. I had no real interests, and only writing provided limited pleasure.

Now, my mind challenged me to get the maximum out of every day. I wanted to learn every subject, taste every type of food, and experience every sort of activity. As a result, I had a robust overall drive to be a better person and diligently accomplish every task with pride.

However, not all the changes in my life were positive. I had never been paranoid, but now I began to view unfamiliar people with great suspicion. I am acutely aware of my security and carefully scout my surroundings before entering a new location. I find it essential to have at least one knife, and occasionally I carry a concealed gun. Also, I act more aggressively, and it takes a lot of effort to keep this overcompensation in check during disagreements.

What was I going to do with my life? I had a plan! I would knock out *Interviewing Immortality* and leave harvesting behind. However, the last line in my book contained a contradiction within this boastful taunt, "It is still a choice: kill or let nature kill me."

I want everyone to know that this statement was stupid, selfish, and arrogant. I do not know what I was thinking when I wrote it. I, James Kimble, stopped a man's beating heart! And for what? To touch my toes and get hit on by women? Killing a human being is by far the worst deed any person could do. My callous actions haunt my soul every waking moment, and I have guilt-filled nightmares. No matter how great my life had become or how long I would live, taking another person's life for my petty personal benefit would never happen again. My deplorable actions brought me great personal shame, and I had no valid excuse. Did I deserve to rot in jail? Absolutely! Would I confess my crimes? Well ...

Another aspect of the harvest is the foresight to see the long-term consequences. The life I took belonged to a man of ill repute, and I could not change the fact that he died. Therefore, I chose not to confess my crime. My logic was that my writings made the world a better place. I understood this reasoning was a selfish cop-out, but this delusion allowed me to sleep.

My plan started with me quietly appreciating the harvest effects before removing my harvested pancreas. I would return to the small-time author's life, buy apartments for income, and write in my spare time. Unfortunately, I could write nothing of substance without the harvest abilities, and therefore, my time as a column writer and reporter would soon end. I accepted this fate with positive dignity.

I would never murder again, and this would allow me to live with a guilt-free conscience. My parents raised me to be an upstanding man, and I vowed to behave for the rest of my life. If anybody asked, I would tell them I created *Interviewing Immortality* as a publicity stunt, and this explanation would end the conversation.

Despite my meager *Portland Tribune* salary, I applied for a loan on a four-unit apartment complex. It was inconceivable to think a bank would give a loan to somebody like me, but I had an ace up my sleeve. My harvest-powered mind figured out precisely what the loan officer wanted. I completed all the forms without errors, prepared a flawless report of the project finances, had excellent references, and spoke with extreme confidence.

The dilapidated apartment complex I purchased had endless issues. There had been a kitchen fire in unit number two. None of the electrical outlets worked, teenagers had vandalized every room, and the old faucets shot out brown water. Fortunately, I had an informal agreement with my roommates, Dave and Craig. They helped me fix up the apartments in exchange for reduced rent. However, while we did quality work, we neglected to have our work inspected by the city.

Over five weeks, we made the apartments look spotless. Then, I used my contacts at the *Portland Tribune* to produce a professional advertisement and rapidly located four paying tenants.

There is an unusual aspect of loaning money, wherein the further you are in debt, the more money banks want to lend you. This concept may seem counterintuitive, but I made every payment on time (bank profit), fixed up my apartments (adding value), and rapidly gained paying tenants (documented income). The bank appreciated my professional attitude and good business intuition. A month after my fourth tenant moved in, I got a loan on a three-unit apartment complex and then a five-unit complex. Easy money! Of course, Grace had recommended apartments as an excellent long-term investment.

While my harvest abilities were still present, I began writing *Interviewing Immortality.* My process began by entering the handwritten notes in my *Dawson's Creek* notebook into my laptop. Unfortunately, when I wrote those notes, I had an injured hand from the scuffle when Grace captured me. Even without an injury, my handwriting was terrible, but now the result looked like incoherent chicken-scratch gibberish. My translation efforts took over two weeks, and I often guessed while unraveling my cryptic labyrinth of misspellings.

The resulting notes were an awful nonsensical account of my interaction with Grace, along with my incoherent thoughts of the moment. It took eight days to develop the best format for *Interviewing Immortality*. Incidentally, I originally titled the book *A Graceful Interview*. Get the pun?

I sent a sample chapter to my publisher, Bethany, and to my delight, she liked it. However, we disagreed about the format. I wanted a balance between my story and Grace's. She suggested I focus on Grace's history. Nevertheless, I stubbornly insisted on my original format, as I believed readers would empathize with my reactions.

While I wrote my book, I came clean on my Facebook page. I told all my online followers that I had not written *Grime: The Big Hate* and had only written half of *Grime: Just Cause*. My followers posted many angry comments, and many unfriended me. I also got comments from authors who said I would never be welcome in the writer's community. The Facebook group Writers Helping Writers permanently banned me as a member. As an aspiring author, this negative onslaught was agonizing.

I chose not to respond to most of the angry comments but sometimes stated, "Guilty as charged." For the first two weeks, nobody respected my honest approach, but a strange thing happened. The public forgot. I had my five minutes of shame, and I climbed right back on top.

New readers picked up my *Grime* books and wanted a connection to me. Others wrote comments like, "Yeah, whatever. His book reads well, no matter who wrote it." One wrote, "The guy worked at Best Buy and did what he had to do. What were you expecting?" Another wrote, "James legally purchased the original work and changed it. His only mistake was not crediting the original author. Get off his back!" I could not believe this defensive reaction and would never have written such forgiving comments.

Bethany contacted the family of the original author (Jack Dunkin), diverted the remaining *Grime* series' profits, and stopped printing the books. Out of respect (more likely fear of a lawsuit), they printed 10,000 copies of the unmodified book under its original title, *An Oxford Tale of Mischief.* The publishing company promoted the book as a "rediscovered masterpiece." Upon its release, many bookstores prominently featured it in their front window. I found it strange that Bethany did not publish the book under Jack Dunkin's pen name, Edmund Summers.

A few days after *An Oxford Tale of Mischief* came out, critics dealt it scathing reviews. Readers believed the story had already been explored (with my version), and *An Oxford Tale of Mischief* was not worth the price. As a result, fewer than 2,000 copies moved off the shelves.

I've spent a lot of time contemplating the low sales, and I now understand that my poor attempts to "freshen" *An Oxford Tale of Mischief* succeeded. I equate this to remaking a classic story in a campy style—for example, Mel Brooks's excellent movie *Robin Hood: Men in Tights.*

Jack Dunkin's family detested the low sales, and they have been threatening my publisher with a lawsuit. As for me? I had closed that dishonest chapter of my life, and it felt great to be free.

My harvest abilities allowed me to convert my written notes into a book in less than four weeks. Before I proceed any further, you may remember my simple "rules of publishing" from the beginning of this book. Let me take this opportunity to explain the reason behind breaking rules one and two. I published the book under my name and provided all of Grace's details for a straightforward reason. She terrified me! I slept with a kitchen knife under my pillow, and I felt over-the-top petrified of that murdering psychopath! She asked me to write a book, and boy-howdy, I vowed to complete her request at any cost! I looked into those eyes and saw what my fate would be if I failed.

As for the consequences? Honestly, I did not think about what would happen after I published *Interviewing Immortality*. Bethany wanted me to change more facts and use a pen name. I feared Grace so much that I ignored Bethany's sound advice. Even with all that has happened since then, I believe I made the right decision.

Fortunately, a few bookstores agreed to "give a second chance to a disgraced author," and Bethany printed 1,000 copies. Right after the book hit the shelves, nothing happened. Honestly, the lack of interest stunned me. I expected some kind of response because I had written a nonfiction book that stated, "Hey, world, there is this woman who has lived for 500 years by killing people, and here's the proof."

One would think that the media would have taken some notice. At least an article in "the lighter side of things" of the *Portland Tribune* would have proclaimed, "Immortals are real. Who would have thunk it?" Even the *Portland Tribune's* response (on the last page of the Entertainment section) had two sentences: "Our own James Kimble has written the book *Interviewing Immortality*. Check it out." I could not believe the complete lack of interest in my truthful account.

The craziest reaction came from my *Grime* fans. A bunch of them bought *Interviewing Immortality* on the first day. Their dedication deeply touched me. In the evening, they posted many comments like "The fourth book in the *Grime* series lacked continuity." Really?!

Sales quickly tapered off, but I only felt relief because I had satisfied my obligation to Grace. To celebrate, I took the afternoon off and drove to a local park. After walking around, I ate tasty lasagna and took a nap. That evening, I looked forward to resuming a quiet and safe "Grace-free" life. It did not matter how many copies of the books were sold. I slept peacefully from the moment my head hit the pillow until the sun hit my eyes.

Well, a few people read *Interviewing Immortality,* and ten days later, there was a knock on my front door. When I cheerfully opened it, a sharply dressed police officer asked, "Are you James Kimble?"

"Of course," I answered with a smile.

"We have questions."

The officer threw me into the back of a police car, and I found myself in a dingy room at the Portland Police Department. After an hour of staring at the poorly painted green and white walls, a man dressed in a sharp black suit came in and said, "My name is Detective Camron. Is that silly book true?"

I could not believe what was happening, but I should have been expecting a visit from the police. Let's recall that Bethany had voiced "major concerns" over my truthful choices. I will go even further. My harvest-powered mind should have applied basic logic to the situation. When a person writes a book about killing somebody, the authorities automatically take an interest. For me, there should have been absolutely no surprise reaction, but I felt dumbfounded.

At my core, I consider myself a good person, but I did not know how to answer Detective Camron's basic question. As I looked at him in stunned confusion, I began thinking of my situation and knew I had to shrug it off. My mind began focusing, and I went over the possible answers that would improve my situation.

Detective Camron possessed a striking figure. He stood six-feet-three, was in his early 50s, had thick black hair, a crazy red dice tattoo on his neck, a robust build, and boundless confidence. I knew my predicament placed him in a superior position. He leaned over and propped his head up with his hands to get as close to me as possible. I calculated we had been staring at each other for 43 seconds. I then contemplated how easily my mind figured out the exact time. This timekeeping harvest ability inspired me to understand that I had the upper hand.

I knew Detective Camron did not have enough evidence to place me under arrest. I also knew Grace would have covered up my crime with a bunch of red herring evidence. Feeling confident, I changed my stance and looked at Detective Camron for 37 seconds while waiting for my confidence to unnerve him. Twenty-eight seconds later, he began looking unsure. When I felt the moment to strike was right, I stated in a matter-of-fact voice, "It's a prank. A publicity stunt to publish my book as nonfiction. I didn't commit any crime, nor did I witness anything illegal."

Detective Camron did not expect this positive response and looked at me with confusion. Twelve seconds later, his confidence returned. With a crafty smile, he said, "A judge granted a search warrant, and officers are tossing your place. You better start telling the truth!"

A lot happened in the next sixteen seconds. I felt horrified; my *Dawson's Creek* notebook was at home. It contained everything about Grace, and I knew she would not be happy to the details I left out of the book made available to the police.

As suddenly as my horror came, it ceased. I knew the awful handwriting in my notebook was indecipherable by anybody but me. Also, my laptop was under a pile of dirty clothes in my car because our washing machine was broken again. My valued copy of the Cleopatra scrolls, the mint oil, and harvesting equipment were all in a safe deposit box under a corporate name. My two cobras were the only evidence connecting me to the crimes described in *Interviewing Immortality*. However, I knew possession of dangerous reptiles was illegal without a license.

I stared back at Detective Camron and nodded. He did not know what to make of me or my confident smile. At that moment, I recalled Grace's fantastic ability to stare deeply into a person, and for some strange reason, I attempted this.

I began by looking deep into Detective Camron's eyes and forcing him to remain still with her eye-dagger staring technique. The effect started working, and I sensed his fear. For the next 68 seconds, I used every ounce of mental strength I had to hold him in place while he broke into a cold sweat.

I let up and leaned back. Detective Camron stared at me in horror. His hands shook, and I thought he would fall over. It took him great effort to stagger out of the room. I smiled with smug satisfaction, knowing that somebody had been looking through the one-way glass, and they were now yelling at Detective Camron. This episode took me to a new level of personal satisfaction.

Sixty-one minutes later, the door opened, and another man came in. He asked questions while pounding his fists on the table. I sat there looking at him with a silly grin while appreciating how my body and mind performed. The best part was that I knew my confidence was genuine and not an act. *I am truly better than other people.* Eventually, the man confessed that they did not have any evidence against me—victory at its finest!

When I got home, I found chaos. First, I saw the police had confiscated my roommate Dave's gaming computer, which upset him no end. Also, they took all my writing material and music compact discs. It amused me to see they had also taken my old desktop computer. It stopped working two years ago, and I had forgotten all about that pile of junk in the back of my closet.

To my great dismay, they took my two cobras. I had named them Bud and Kelly from the television show *Married ... with Children.* I had no intention of using the snakes for harvesting, but we enjoyed having them as pets. Unfortunately, the police had left a document with Dave informing us that those snakes were dangerous and that the Humane Society would euthanize them. This disheartening circumstance hurt, and I called the police several times to beg for their release.

The document also said they would return our property after the investigation, which could take up to six months. The news upset Dave because he had paid to attend a large online gaming tournament that weekend.

That evening, when Craig came home, he wanted to know what happened to Bud and Kelly. He held a shoebox with two mice he found at work to give to them. When Craig learned what happened, he felt relieved because he took his new MacBook to work that day.

After we cleaned up, I got my laptop computer out of the car, made a backup of all my files onto a flash drive, and put it in my safe deposit box. I then encrypted my laptop files with the most complex password that the encryption software would accept: #_1_HIT-*BillieJeanIsNotMyLover*-August/29/1958! Yes, I admit it, I'm a huge Michael Jackson fan, and I celebrate his birthday every year.

After this disruption, our lives returned to normal. Dave purchased a better gaming computer, and Craig purchased a king snake on Craigslist. Yet, every day, I feared a call from the district attorney's office, getting arrested, or having the door broken down by a SWAT team, but nothing happened.

Five months after meeting Grace, the harvest effects were wearing off. This decline dulled my mind and reduced my advanced motor skills. However, I expected this eventuality and planned to remove my harvested pancreas when it no longer provided benefits.

THREE

A t this point, my life story should have read: "I removed my harvested pancreas and returned to an uneventful existence." But, instead, I can trace everything back to one phone call. Grace told me that the most significant harvest gift is the ability to comprehend the passage of time. She certainly hit that nail on the head.

Two months after repairing my four-unit apartment, I rented unit number three to a married couple, Cynthia and Darin. They smiled when we met, and they paid their rent on time. Occasionally, the other tenants complained about their loud arguments, but the complaints were infrequent. The couple had an amazing boy, Julius. Even though he was only twelve, he stood five feet eight and could run faster than anybody I had ever met. Every time my roommates and I went over, we played soccer with Julius at the local park. He had a bubbly personality, a huge amount of brown curly hair, and a funny way of rolling his l's when yelling "Goal-lll!" I liked Julius and thought of him as my nephew.

On an overcast Wednesday morning, Cynthia called to complain about the hot water in their shower. Who could have known that this one call would change so many lives?

We had replumbed the entire apartment building during the remodel, which got rid of the rusty pipes and improved the water flow. At the top of the stairs, the maintenance room contained a large water heater, and I set the temperature control well below scalding. The apartment nearest to the heater had a hot shower. Unfortunately, Cynthia and Darin's apartment was the furthest from the water heater, but their water seemed warm enough.

On the way to work, I stopped by to check the temperature. Cynthia answered the door in a foul mood. She was five-feet-four and had recently cut and dyed her black hair red (probably by herself). Today Cynthia wore pink camouflage jeans and a shirt calling for a recount of the last mayoral election. I tried to be nice and told her the water felt warm on my hand. This gentle remark was met with an insult, so I agreed to call a plumber in the evening. Cynthia promptly cussed me out for not immediately fixing it. I swore back at her and then left. As I drove, I regretted my diatribe and realized that the lack of a harvest deeply affected my mood.

That evening, I met with a plumber in the maintenance room. He did not like our remodeling effort and informed me it would cost $4,320 to bring the plumbing up to the Portland building codes. This fix included installing temperature regulating valves in each apartment shower. These valves physically prevented the heated water from scalding a person. He said that I could be liable for any injuries if I did not install the valves. I thought the plumber was trying to scam me, but I agreed to have the valves installed. That evening, I spent an hour looking up the Portland building codes, and he was correct. My mother would call this a blessing in disguise.

Over the next three days, the plumber installed the new valves and changed pipes, and I paid him with my credit card. I wondered how many months it would take to pay off my balance. Later that evening, I got a call from all four tenants complaining of cold showers. I called the plumber, and he told me that the city building codes stipulated a maximum 102°F temperature on apartment showers. Also, by code, he had installed a lock on the maintenance room door and put a locked, secure cover over the water heater controls. He also installed a new temperature and pressure (T&P) relief valve, which physically prevented the water heater from exceeding 120°F.

I passed along the news, and the four tenants said they disliked "lukewarm" showers. Of course, Portland gets cold in the winter and I related to their feelings, but I followed the laws.

❖ ❖ ❖

Two weeks later, sales of *Interviewing Immortality* took off because I gained a new fan base. In high school, I had met a few Goth students. They smoked, wore black clothes, and talked about how bad their lives were. I never understood their fascination with death and despair. Now, the Goth community had found a new hero. Grace's "death to the dregs of society" lifestyle appealed to them. While Grace had negative traits, she dwelled on the positive aspects of her life, and I cannot picture her wearing black clothing, smoking, and listening to depressing music.

Grace was a sophisticated woman who stood five feet four with soft brown eyes, brown hair, and a dancer's body. She wore custom-tailored clothes and took great care to maintain her stylish appearance. Each word she spoke conveyed intent and intelligence. Overall, I considered her attractive, sophisticated, observant, and wise.

One fine Tuesday morning, my phone blew up with interview requests, and my Facebook page overflowed with comments, questions, and requests. *Is Interviewing Immortality fiction? What death chant did Grace recite when she harvested? Did she listen to the Goth band Evanescence? Please post a detailed harvesting instruction video. How many nose piercings does she have? What does she mix with the blood of her victims before drinking it? What is her favorite brand of cigarettes?*

Bethany loved the attention and wanted me to tap into this exciting market. Lloyd enjoyed having a column written by a "famous writer." He arranged an exclusive interview that appeared in the Arts and Entertainment section. I did not appreciate this sudden fame and would have preferred to slip into obscurity.

Because of my celebrity status and increased book sales, Bethany translated *Interviewing Immortality* into Russian. As I had predicted months ago, the Russians went ballistic. From reading a few translated posts, they all took my book to only contain facts, and they loved the connection to their rich historical past.

Unfortunately, this sudden interest had an unexpected result. A Goth teenager in Abilene, Texas, read *Interviewing Immortality*, and he convinced his father to read it. Texas Ranger Theodore Garrison disliked the August 1936 account of Grace shooting six Rangers. He checked into the archives and discovered that deputy James McCaw and five other Rangers had gone missing at that time. Seven days later, two ranchers found their shot-up bodies. This tragic event was big news at the time. Hee He retrieved the original case file and learned that my account contained details hidden from the public.

On Sunday morning, I heard a knock on the front door. I knew Detective Camron would be on the other side. I opened the door with a smile, and he took me back to the interview room. Detective Camron and Ranger Garrison pounded me with questions while I sat in the same grubby chair. Clearly, they could not read my notebook handwriting and demanded that I tell them everything about the murdered Texas Rangers. Also, they wanted to know the whereabouts of the woman I called Grace.

"I would like to know that as well," I answered with a hearty laugh.

My flippant comment did not go over well, and I quickly learned that Texas Rangers do not appreciate wisecracks.

It had been five months and ten days since my harvest. My abilities had faded, which meant I lacked confidence, and my word choices were not the best. I tried unsuccessfully to do the dagger stare with Detective Camron and then lied, "My Uncle Joe used to be a Texas Ranger. When I was a teenager, he told me a story about an unsolved shooting. I did some research and used this information in my book. This whole thing is a big publicity stunt. You're wasting your time."

They asked if they could see my shoulder where I had allegedly inserted a harvested pancreas. I slid my shirt down to reveal my shoulder. When I wrote *Interviewing Immortality*, I changed/omitted four key aspects of the harvest process. The general location of where to place the pancreas is one of the altered facts. The officers looked surprised, and I did not know if I had convinced them or not.

Two hours later, they let me go but told me there would be further questions. I did not like their accusation, but I knew Grace had done a superb job of covering up the crimes. Nevertheless, the experience still unnerved me. I realized I would never be free from suspicion.

The next day, everything returned to normal. I estimated I would have to remove the pancreas in four weeks. While it wouldn't be an exciting life, I would still lead an honest one without murdering people.

That Friday, at 10:19 p.m., my phone rang. Somehow, I knew it would be bad news. The call came from a tenant in my four-unit apartment, and they informed me of a massive water leak. My roommates and I jumped into my Toyota. As I drove, Craig called the plumber and asked him to meet us there. We arrived to see loads of people outside the apartment, the fire department, and the police.

I introduced myself as the apartment manager, and a police officer named Gerry escorted me inside. He was a muscular individual with pepper-gray hair who needed to lose twenty pounds. Fortunately, Gerry was friendly and really seemed concerned about learning the truth. He showed me where somebody had broken the maintenance room door to access the water heater. Inside, I saw the smashed temperature controls and the T&P valve spraying water. I asked Dave to shut off the main valve.

Officer Gerry then led me to the ambulance to see Cynthia and Darin. The skin on their arms had turned bright red, and was apparent that hot water had severely scalded them. I felt horrified to witness their pain with the guilt of knowing my amateur plumbing had caused it.

"The shower burned the crap out of me!" Cynthia screamed.

I apologized seven times while saying I would pay for their medical bills. The paramedic tried to calm the pair down while treating their severe burns. As he proceeded, I wondered why they were taking a shower at the same time while fully dressed in dry clothes. When I asked about Julius, Cynthia flippantly guessed he was at the local soccer field. I told Craig to locate him and escort him back to our location. It did not dawn on me to ask why they allowed their son to play soccer past 10:00 p.m.

The paramedics tried to treat Cynthia, but she refused their help. So, they asked her to sign an "against medical advice" form, and while grabbing the clipboard, her wound accidentally brushed up against the paramedic's arm. This action aggravated Cynthia, and she howled in pain. The paramedic again tried to calm her down, but he saw a red mark on his white uniform and asked, "What the heck?!"

The paramedic ran a cotton swab across Cynthia's burn, and it turned red. She screamed and covered her arm. Then, the paramedic yelled, "Officer, look at this!"

Officer Gerry had been trying to get a statement from Darin. He had a muscular build, stood six-feet-one, and had curly red hair. Today he wore tiger-striped jeans that looked out of place. As Officer Gerry turned to see what was happening, the paramedic showed him the cotton swab and pointed to Cynthia's arm. He swiped his finger across Cynthia's other burn, and she screamed. Officer Gerry looked at his finger to see that it had turned red and asked in an angry voice, "Did you put red makeup all over yourself?"

Cynthia protested her innocence and accused Officer Gerry of assault. Darin hollered, "You attacked my wife!" Officer Gerry then touched Darin's arm, and again his finger turned red. He hollered "police brutality" louder than I had ever heard anybody yell.

Officer Gerry threw them into the back of his police car with two big thuds. This display of strength impressed me. Three minutes later, Craig returned with Julius, and Officer Gerry talked with him while writing notes. Then, another police officer escorted me into their apartment "crime scene."

Cynthia and Darin had pulled out their shower valve, and water had sprayed everywhere. We used all the towels we could find to clean up, and an hour later, the plumber arrived. He suggested taking pictures of the extensive damage, and we got out our phones.

Later, Officer Gerry told me the law required that after Cynthia and Darin made bail, I would have to pay for their hotel until I fixed their apartment. This situation outraged me, and I started the eviction process that night.

The next day, the plumber gave me a bill for $3,121. This expense stretched my credit card right to the limit. Fortunately, it was the end of the month, and I would deposit rent checks soon.

Four days later, I heard a knock at the door during breakfast. While my harvest abilities were practically nonexistent, I occasionally had impressive flashes of clarity and knew what would happen next. So I cheerfully opened the door. "Time for another round of questions?"

Detective Camron started to speak, stopped, and then smiled. He took me to the same filthy interview room and made me wait for two hours. Then a woman and a man came into the room. She wore a fashionable pantsuit and had done an excellent job applying makeup. He was six-feet-four, dressed in a tan business suit, and had a sharp profile.

The woman began, "I'm Detective Dana Carroll of the Las Vegas Police Department. Do you know a Douglas Obrien or a Spencer Weber? Spencer goes by Gabby Walls, Bernard Perry, and Eugene Strickland." I shook my head, and she continued, "We did a lot of digging and found a connection. Do you know what it is?"

"No clue," I said, and then suppressed a chuckle.

"They're missing their pancreas and were murdered!"

Her setup had been too perfect, and I made a wise-ass comment. "It would be impressive if they were alive without their pancreas."

Detective Carroll did not appreciate my flippant humor, and she informed me that Douglas had been a suspect in several sex crimes, but there was never enough evidence to convict him. Five months ago, he died in a violent knife attack. Clues at the screen led investigators to a local drug dealer, but he professed his innocence. This description made me think about the man Grace killed in the first harvest, but she said his name was Gerald Donner.

Then Assistant District Attorney Juan McCormick of Cody, Wyoming, took over the conversation. "Spencer Weber worked as a tabloid writer in the Los Angeles area. A real dirtbag. Also five months ago, we found his body impaled on a cement pillar for a building under construction. Security cameras showed a large man leaving the area in a black car. A witness got the license plate number, and we traced it to a local identity thief named Roderick Stevens. We executed a search warrant and found Spencer Weber's possessions and his identification. Stevens also proclaimed that he had nothing to do with the crime.

"We find it interesting that both cases occurred within two days. Both autopsies revealed unusual burn marks and missing organs, including the pancreas, sections of the kidneys, and the adrenal gland. We considered this evidence to be inconsequential at the time and did not make it public. But there is a striking resemblance to the accounts in your book. What do you have to say about all of this?"

My mind felt foggy, and it took great effort to focus on my present situation. *I should have changed more details in my book! Wait a minute. I took the life of Spencer Weber. Wow! This is real.*

As I thought to myself, I noticed Detective Carroll picked up on my altered expression. I shifted my stance to look at Juan, who looked comfortable interrogating me. However, I also knew they had not placed me under arrest, and these two crimes already had two people in jail. I surmised that somebody had been digging into autopsy reports and found a link. However, I also knew that Grace had superior crime disguising skills.

I asked, "Did Detective Camron tell you I wrote a fictional book based on true crimes?" Detective Carroll looked angry, and I continued, "I used the newspaper database to locate two unrelated crimes. Then I crafted my story around them. I'm sorry you came all this way to figure this out."

Detective Camron said in a bitter voice, "I don't believe you. Your description had too much information that is not in the public domain."

"Ahh, that's correct. However, people talk to reporters, and reporters do lots of digging. That's how I created my book. Trust me. It's purely fiction."

I pasted on my biggest fake smile, and Detective Carroll countered, "All right. Show us everything you collected."

"As a reporter, I enjoy freedom of the press. You cannot force me to provide anything."

"We will see about that!" Detective Camron countered.

The three of them questioned me for 91 minutes, and I continued the same story. Then, reluctantly, they let me go. A police officer drove me home, and when we got there, I saw a police car in my driveway. When I got out, Officer Bradley introduced himself and asked, "Are you James Kimble?"

"Ahh, yeah," I answered with deep hesitation.

"Owner of the apartment complex on Eighth Street?"

"No. I'm the manager. The Hallstead-Reevy Corporation owns the property."

At that moment, I felt relieved because I'd had the foresight to put my apartment complex under a corporation with no direct ties to me.

Officer Bradley continued. "There has been an incident, and we need a statement." He drove me to a police station near the apartment building and then showed me pictures of burn marks on Julius.

I put my hand over my mouth and asked in a choked-up voice, "Are these real?"

"Yes, they are as real as the sky is blue!"

"How? How did this happen?" I stuttered.

"You don't know?" Officer Bradley asked in confusion.

"Know what?"

"About the faulty shower incident."

"When?" I asked in horror.

"Two days ago."

"What? I don't understand."

Consulting his notes, Officer Bradley said, "We took statements from Mrs. Cynthia Kara Evans and Mr. Darin Ronald Evans. Their son, Julius Paul Evans, was in the shower when the water burned him. Darin had no option but to break down the water heater door to shut the water off."

"What the heck?!" I yelled. "Two days ago?! No, no, no! They are the ones who destroyed the water heater and shower valve. After that, the fools faked injuries with red makeup. Julius was playing soccer at a nearby field and was fully healthy. We have pictures of all of it, including their fake burns. The police were there when this all went down and they saw Julius. He was healthy!"

"I'm unaware of any other report."

"Did you talk to Officer Gerry? He can tell you what happened. You must believe me. Please believe me!"

Officer Bradley looked suspicious, and I continued, "He gave me his card. Here, I have it in my wallet. Please call him. Please!"

I took the card out and gave it to Officer Bradley. He then stepped outside the room. Eighteen minutes later, Officer Bradley returned and said, "I spoke with Gerry, and he confirmed Julius had been in good health during the incident. With this recent information, I will further question Julius. Off the record, I overheard Cynthia stating she would take you to court for all you are worth. I see no reason to keep you here, and you are free to go."

At that moment, I felt weak and had to sit down. I knew Cynthia or Darin had burned little Julius to make a buck off of me. All because of their cold shower. I covered my face and wept while thinking about little Julius crying out in pain as they burned him.

That evening, Dave, Craig, and I went to the hospital. We located Julius in the children's ward and saw the bandages covering his arms. He managed a faint smile when we approached. Dave brought a new soccer ball and gently handed it to him. Julius looked at me, and tears formed. Finally, he mustered up a lot of courage to whisper, "Sorry, guys."

I felt heartbroken and could not speak. Craig turned to me, and tears were streaming down his face. Then, suddenly, we heard a commotion behind us, and Cynthia screamed, "Stay away from my child! You heartless bastard!"

I turned to see who had shouted, and I will never forget that moment for as long as I live. Her eyes contained more evil than I could comprehend. The white parts had become dull gray, and the pupils were inky-black. There before me stood the source of all malevolence—the absolute cold wrath of a woman who had burned her child. As I stared into the hollow eyes of a woman without a soul, I fell into a tranquil state.

As she yelled, Dave and Craig held her back from attacking me. I found myself entranced by her evil aura and could not move a muscle or take a breath. I had never known that so much hate could exist in a person, and now, I stared into its bottomless depths. One would think the appropriate response would be fear. But, instead, I experienced a deep fascination as I looked into the reflection of Satan himself.

Cynthia continued to yell and scream. I knew two security guards were pulling her away in my spellbound daze, but that did not matter. Darin ran in from a side door and joined the ruckus. When I turned to look at him, I saw the same evil energy. His eyes were cold, dark, and full of hate. At that moment, time slowed down. People exchanged angry words, landed punches, and threw hospital equipment. All while Julius cried his heart out and the other children tried to dodge flying objects. My harvest abilities allowed me to appreciate the entire emotional spectrum.

The adults continued to struggle, and then more security guards arrived. Together, they dragged Cynthia and Darin out of the children's ward while they continued to kick and scream. I looked down at Julius to see tears streaming. He reached out his little bandaged arms toward his parents. I knew despite his injuries, Julius still loved them.

I left the hospital in a complete daze with Dave driving. Craig insisted on staying behind in case Cynthia or Darin returned. Dave tried to make conversation, but I could not comprehend his words. I only thought about Cynthia and Darin's eyes. *How could these horrible people have such a beautiful child? Why did they burn him? He must have felt so much pain. Why?!* The awful experience left a permanent scar in my heart, and I knew that my life would never be the same. I fell asleep sobbing.

The following day, I woke up in a foul mood. The area around my incision itched badly, and my arm hurt from sleeping in the wrong position. After breakfast, I went to the door and knew somebody was on the other side. I opened it and said, "Hi, detective. Another round of questions?"

He tilted his head back with an angry smile. I sighed and asked, "Time for handcuffs?"

Detective Camron nodded and read me my rights. On the way to jail, he confirmed they had charged me with the murder of Spencer Weber and conspiracy to murder Douglas Obrien. At the police station, officers fingerprinted me, then took my photograph and personal possessions. Unfortunately, I had been holding my laptop, and they took it.

Afterward, the officers permitted me one phone call, and I called my divorce attorney, Nicholas Berry. He was a friendly individual with a broad forehead and a handlebar mustache. Coincidentally, I had sent Nicholas my last check to pay for my divorce the previous week. He had never loaned money (for his services) to another client, and he appreciated my prompt payments. Two hours later, Nicholas arrived, and we went over the charges. Then, he left, and I spent the morning in jail.

That afternoon, at the courthouse arraignment, Nicholas began, "Your Honor, I have been speaking with the district attorney, and he charged my client with two crimes that have jury-rendered convictions. They were open-and-shut cases based on solid evidence. There has been no attempt to overturn said convictions.

"The district attorney is fully aware that my client's book is a publicity stunt. All factual information contained within my client's book was obtained while working as a reporter. This arrest is an attempt to gain his fingerprints and laptop. I request you dismiss all charges, return my client's property, and destroy the information recovered from my client's laptop."

The judge looked at the district attorney and asked, "How about it?"

"My team prepared a solid case," the district attorney answered with confidence.

"Is all your evidence from the book?"

The district attorney looked away and muttered, "Yes."

"Can you directly link the defendant to the crime?"

"Not directly."

"Do you have any other evidence?" the judge asked.

"We have a solid theory."

"Solid theories are not evidence! Therefore, Mr. Kimble, I am dismissing the charges and ordering the return of your property. Mr. District Attorney, you are to delete all laptop data you may have recovered."

The judge banged his gavel, and the district attorney requested, "We reserve the ability to recharge Mr. Kimble at a later time."

"So noted."

I felt ecstatic until Nicholas handed me the bill. Another $2,000 debt. Nicholas then told me the reason for the arrest was to get the information on my laptop. They kept a copy and would later try to claim an inevitable discovery. However, the judge had ordered them to destroy the data, which was a powerful legal argument. I rested all hope on my use of powerful encryption software.

FOUR

The drama surrounding Cynthia and Darin combined with my close call in court wiped me out. The police released my possessions two days later, and Dave got his gaming computer back. Unfortunately, it no longer worked because they took it apart to remove the hard drive. Also, the police had ripped all the pages out of my *Dawson's Creek* notebook and returned them out of order. The $2,000 I owed Nicholas put me up to my eyeballs in debt, and I could no longer feel the harvest abilities.

I decided that my life needed perspective, and it seemed logical to go back to where all my troubles began. So that Saturday morning, I packed a lunch and started driving. An hour and a half later, I turned down the dirt road to Grace's old house. Somebody had put up "No Trespassing" signs and a notice stating the Corbans Corporation (an East Coast logistics company) owned the property. I came to a stop in front of her house and saw that it had been unoccupied for several months.

I noticed the once immaculate lawn had weeds, and the apple trees needed trimming. However, the porch still looked comforting, and I sat down on the steps while gazing upon the beautiful woods. As I smelled the crisp air, the only sound came from the wind, and the experience brought back many memories. While I appreciated my decision to drive to this distant location, I still felt my life lacked direction, and sitting on the steps was not helping.

I wanted to get back the feeling that Grace's pet mountain lion, Heathcliff, had given me. That cat frightened and comforted me at the same time. She was an enigma I would never understand. Without logic, I began walking toward the woods where Heathcliff had taken me on a fantastic journey through her world. Unfortunately, I had not brought hiking shoes, a compass, or water. Eight minutes into my trek, I had lost my sense of direction, and blind instinct took over.

A faint animal trail came into view seven minutes later, and I recognized a few rocky landmarks. An hour later, I stumbled into the same meadow Heathcliff had taken me to. It seemed inconceivable that I had located this beautiful location again. I picked up the stick that Heathcliff enjoyed biting and looked at the deep teeth marks while wondering if I should throw it or hold it. The moment did not seem right to throw it, and I placed it back exactly where I had found it.

Needing more clarity, I walked over to the area where Heathcliff had her lookout. I sat on a nearby rock while looking at the surroundings. As I contemplated the beautiful landscape, untouched by man, I understood that my body had taken me to this place to reflect. I knew the answers had to be all around, and I only needed to absorb them. In that effort, I closed my eyes, danced, punched the air, threw rocks, smelled, asked questions out loud, picked leaves off trees, and appreciated the wind.

My complex reflection provided a sense of personal growth, but no answers materialized. So, I climbed up to the spot where Heathcliff had her lookout. As I maneuvered into her perch, I looked out toward her fantastic view and appreciated her mastery of this little corner of the world. Unfortunately, I was still no closer to getting my life back on track, and I eased myself down onto the ground. As I did so, something caught my attention. I picked up a penny inside a paper coin holder. It was stamped 1969, and seeing it wrapped in a protective holder made me think it was valuable.

Finding the coin inspired me to sit on another rock and contemplate my existence for 68 minutes. Still, no answers came, and I calculated the time to be 4:32 p.m. I knew my return journey would be difficult with the setting sun. As I walked back in the dim light, I ran into many branches and tripped over rocks. Now the terrain looked different, and I did not see previous landmarks.

Three hours later, I stumbled across the road that led to Grace's former property. I absolutely cannot explain how I achieved this navigational feat. So I walked back to her house and went to where we buried Heathcliff. Using the flashlight function on my phone, I saw that the flowers I placed there months ago had rotted, and

I removed them. Next, I walked around the house, gathered new flowers, and put them at the marker. I then thanked Heathcliff's spirit for helping me navigate the dense forest.

Ten minutes later, I began driving home. Again, my mind drifted to thoughts of Grace. I knew her to be an astute and worldly individual, and I wanted to ask her questions. Specifically, what I should do with my life. However, I knew it would be impossible to locate a wealthy person with a deep desire to remain secluded.

As I drove, the impossible logistics of locating Grace sank in. It occurred to me that this new goal would have to be a low priority, and I should not waste money on it.

Two days later, I got a certified letter informing me that Cynthia and Darin had filed a $500,000 lawsuit for injuring their child. I could not believe the court system would allow this outrageous accusation when they were in jail for the same crime. So, I called Nicholas, and he agreed (for a generous fee) to represent me in this matter.

The thought of more debt and a criminal trial over the murder of Spencer Weber kept me up that night. The next day, Lloyd yelled at me for submitting a lousy article about the city repairing potholes. He threw me out of his office with, "Kid, you're losing your edge. Keep this up, and you'll no longer have a job!"

On top of these problems, my constantly itching incision annoyed me. On the way to work the following day, I got so distraught that I had to pull over. I got out of my Toyota and began punching the air in frustration. I am sure the passing motorists found my comical display amusing.

After my outburst, I sat on a nearby curb and looked at my beat-up blue Toyota while wondering what the heck I should do with my life. As I pondered, I remembered I needed to sell my spare tire to help pay the gas and electric bill.

I continued to look at my rusty bumper and began musing. *Grace would know how to handle this. She would say: You are overthinking this situation. Do blank, and everything will fall into place.* This whimsical sidetrack did not help. Angry thoughts of Cynthia and Darin continued to cloud my mind. The worst part was that they'd brought their lawsuit against me instead of my corporation. Of course, they could sue my corporation or me until the cows came home without getting a dime. As I looked at my worthless car, I realized that the sum of my life contained only minor accomplishments. This epiphany further spiraled me into depression.

I began concentrating on Julius. He was so amazing, and I could not imagine anyone ever harming him. It seemed inconceivable that such horrible people could be blessed with a healthy and outgoing child. *Who the heck burns their son to extort money from a guy that cannot even afford a spare tire?!* I continued to muse while staring at my Toyota's bumper. Finally, I looked up to see my cracked rear window reflecting a nearby beer advertisement showing a family cookout.

As I stared at the image, I had an epiphany. *Wait a minute. I could harvest Cynthia. That would solve several problems.* Of course, this concept seemed outrageous. *Who the heck would do such a thing? Charles Manson? You're such a jerk!* Before, when Grace forced me to harvest, I did not have a choice. Now, I had a choice, and I knew Detective Camron would have me under his watchful eye. He had read my book and knew that I needed to harvest every six months. I became angry at myself for thinking of this horrible idea. *Killing a woman! How absurd! You're complete ass! Man the heck up and face your problems! Mom and Dad raised you better!*

I stood and drove to work with crazy thoughts rattling through my mind. That afternoon, I interviewed a local grocer about a new proposed tax. He said that while the tax would hurt, it would help the community. I appreciated his perspective, and Lloyd liked the piece. A great wave of relief washed over me, knowing I could keep my job a little longer.

That evening, I ate an unrewarding pasta dinner, went to bed early, and tried to fall asleep. Instead, I rolled around, and thought about Heathcliff, Julius, Grace, Cynthia, and Darin. In the morning, as I ate bland cornflakes without milk for breakfast, I had not come to any revelations—a phone call from Nicholas shook me out of my funk. Cynthia and Darin hired an ambulance-chasing lawyer, and they wanted to settle out of court for $100,000. Nicholas told them I did not have that kind of money, but they countered, "A well-known published author has money to burn."

Now, everything made sense. Cynthia and Darin had planned to sue me before they broke their shower. This revelation made me so mad that I had to stop driving on my way to work at the same spot. I punched the wind and screamed as loud as I could. A blue Nissan SUV with a blond-haired girl in the back drove by while she pointed at me. *Not amusing.*

I sat on the curb and again stared at my rusty Toyota bumper. As I looked deep into the corrosion, I realized I could see all the way through in many areas. *My car is a pile of crap.* I fell into a deep spell of depression, and then the same epiphany came right back. *I need to harvest Cynthia.* The thought of Julius growing up in an environment without an evil mother dominated my thoughts and eased my tension.

So I jumped back into my car with big harvest dreams and began planning my dreadful act. But, right as I pulled into the *Portland Tribune* parking lot, I realized I had made a horrific decision, and I firmly changed my mind. *Nobody has the right to take a life, even if the jerk deserves it.*

I felt a deep sense of personal shame for my callous thoughts. Plus, a harvest would leave Julius without a mother. *What the heck?! You're not even trying to be a good person! Didn't you learn from the last harvest?! You're so selfish! You promised to stop!*

That night, I tried to sleep, but that awful concept kept popping back into my head. Finally, at 2:07 a.m., I stopped arguing with myself, sat up, and firmly decided to harvest. This choice brought great relief, which reverted to great shame. I changed my mind many times during the night and committed myself in the early morning. To make matters worse, after my big decision, I also chose to take Darin's life. I concluded Julius needed to be free of these horrible people to have a chance at happiness.

Since that fateful moment, I have had a lot of time to reflect upon my gruesome decision. I had reasoned that a single harvest would allow Julius to have a better life. Of course, the harvest side benefit would enable me to locate Grace. I hoped she could help me answer my deep questions and get me back on a better path. After I learned from her wisdom, I would no longer harvest because I would know how to solve my problems.

You obviously see my flawed logic. The principal short-coming is that ending a mother's life was abhorrently selfish and illegal. Another is that the proposed "good outcome" was uncertain. *Who could predict whether my harvest would improve Julius's life? Cynthia and Darin are definitely going to jail. Perhaps a few months behind bars and counseling could turn Cynthia into the mother of the year?* And finally, I was seeking out a woman who selfishly tortured people to death with the vague hope that she could help me get onto the right path. *Why would she want to help me? It would be logical for her to kill me for seeking her out.*

At the time of my decision, I felt entirely in control of my emotions. However, it's clear that my mind subconsciously put me under a lot of pressure, although I had many *logical* justifications. Still, as I pointed out to Grace in *Interviewing Immortality,* "We have an entire court system with laws, judges, and defense attorneys. You bypass all of that and pronounce your own harsh sentence." This was exactly what I was doing.

I had gone from a person in control to a passenger, with the harvest in the driver's seat. At the time, I did not appreciate the significance of my choice. Now, you, deserve more detail about my decision, and the best I can come up with is a similar situation that I experienced.

At age fifteen, I tried marijuana. It had the effect of making me feel supremely mellow, like a warm blanket of escape. Unfortunately, my father's job required us to move, and I could not locate a dealer at my new school. At that same time, my

English teacher took a liking to me, and she encouraged me to explore writing. A new creative chapter opened in my life, but a small part of me always wanted to get high. I still have a powerful memory of those mellow feelings and the physical desire to continue down a drug-filled existence.

The desire to harvest had a similar primal pull, but it affected me differently. It's not a physical desire; instead, it's a mental challenge to be a worthy person. For example, my mind opened up to discover classical music. The absolute discipline of a 90-musician symphony is almost an other-worldly experience. Before the harvest, I felt that the only people who listened to classical music had parents who hated rock-and-roll. Now, I listen to classical music for at least an hour a day and deeply appreciate the fantastic conductor John Barbirolli.

I equate this feeling to an auto mechanic who works hard on a car and refuses to stop working until it runs. Why? So that he can enjoy driving it. That same drive exists within me, and I now understand it results from the massive fight within my body. In this peculiar mental war, thoughts and morals get profoundly altered.

Late the next morning, I began forming the perfect harvest. My first task would be to get cobra venom. After several calls and internet searches, I learned that the only places where snakes existed in the Portland areas were zoos. Unsurprisingly, the zoos were not interested in allowing me to milk their snakes for a newspaper article. Last year, a coworker interviewed a local "snake guy," but I learned he was in Australia buying more snakes.

I searched the internet for companies that sold exotic snakes. Unfortunately, they all required licenses I did not possess. However, the online company Venom SA sold freeze-dried Egyptian cobra venom for $392 per gram. Grace told me that African cobra venom worked better, but Venom SA did not have that type in stock. So, I ordered two one-gram vials of the Egyptian venom. My logic for getting two covered the possibility that one might get damaged. In retrospect, my logic was clearly leading me down a different path.

Venom SA emailed me an hour later, informing me that my credit card had been declined. I had forgotten about all my plumbing bills. By the time I finished reading the email, I remembered the coin. I had it on my desk and took it to a nearby coin dealer on my lunch break.

On my way, I noticed a sharply dressed woman taking her trash to the curb. That day the *Portland Tribune* ran a great article about internet neutrality, and I thought she would make the perfect interview topic. I gave her the basic facts on the subject, and she provided an eloquent balanced opinion. Her wonderful smile made an impressive picture, which complemented another great article. *Bam! I can still write.*

The dealer almost fell over when I handed him the coin. I had a mint condition 1969 S double die obverse penny with a unique error. He checked his price reference book and wrote me a check for $12,192! I could not believe my luck and suspected that Grace had left the coin there for me to find. Two days after depositing the check, the two tiny one-gram vials of powdered cobra venom arrived. The datasheet revealed that each vial contained three milkings.

After studying maps and driving around, I planned to lure Cynthia and Darin to an alley in a bad part of town. Once there, I would use a stun gun on both of them. First, I would harvest Cynthia and then kill Darin to make it look as though they had been victims of a street robbery. However, when I walked around the alley and saw people looking at me, I realized this was an awful concept. *Back to the drawing board.*

My new plan was to allow Cynthia and Darin back into the apartment. Two days later, I would let myself in, plant some red herring evidence, knock Cynthia out when she entered, and secure Darin. Afterward, I would drag their bodies to a local park and harvest them in seclusion. Hopefully, the resulting crime scene would look as if they attacked each other with knives.

I called Nicholas, and he arranged through their attorney to allow them to reside in the apartment for six months. He thought this olive branch would help my case. Nicholas then informed me that Julius would be at the hospital for another week to clear up an infection. He said their attorney *presumed* I would pay his medical bill.

Nicholas also told me that a nurse had come forward to the police. She overheard Cynthia apologizing to Julius for burning him with hot water from a tea kettle. This evidence should have brought relief, but it further fueled my desire to harvest one last time.

Part of my plan required me to learn how to do a sleeper hold. That evening, I went to my karate class and asked my instructor to demonstrate this technique. He added it to the night's routine, along with moves to break out of the hold.

I also inquired about a fireman's carry, which would allow a person to carry a limp body with relative ease. My karate teacher was amused by my second request and joked that "a *famous* author shouldn't have difficulty getting dates." Our last exercise was "bone hardening, to make sure James knows what will happen if he tries to get dates using sleeper holds." This statement translated to "everybody punches James." My karate teacher is a retired police officer with strong ethics.

The following day, I woke up bruised. After a bland breakfast, I retrieved the harvest tools and mint oil from my corporate safe deposit box. In the afternoon, I wrote an excellent article on what had become my favorite topic: how to solve the homeless problem. My local butcher shop owner had great ideas about reducing the minimum wage and tax cuts for hiring homeless people. Lloyd liked the flow of the article and the picture of the owner holding a broom.

I left work early and drove to the local adult bookstore, Pump You Up. My plan required using "love cuffs," of which there are two types. One is metal handcuffs that have fake pink fur glued to them. The second type has padded Velcro restraints and is designed for true sadomasochism enthusiasts because it allows participants to be firmly restrained without damaging their skin. I also purchased two "ball gags" of the same type used in the movie *Pulp Fiction*. These would prevent Cynthia and Darin from screaming. Afterward, I purchased an excellent video baby monitor.

As I headed to the apartment, I remembered the most crucial part of a harvest, an alibi. I had planned the perfect crime that would lead the authorities directly to me. *How could I have been so stupid? Didn't I remember a single thing that Grace told me?*

When I opened the door, Craig looked at me with a funny expression. He had noticed a big red Pump You Up bag, and I said with a sheepish grin, "It's for an article."

"Yeah. An article," Craig mocked, and then we both laughed.

That evening, I worked on inventing a secondary motive and an alibi. The first step would involve purchasing drugs from a local dealer whom I had interviewed several times. Then, I planned to plant the drugs on Darin to make it seem as if he got caught up in a drug-related murder.

I asked Dave about his Friday night plans, and he told me about a party. He called up the host and asked if I could attend. I planned to slip in unnoticed and pretend I had been there all night.

Grace insisted that every harvest should have at least three red herrings. A few weeks prior, I found a BlackBerry cell phone in the park, and over the years, I had collected several business cards. As an added measure, I retrieved cigarette butts from an ashtray outside the *Portland Tribune*. I planned to spread this red herring evidence around the apartment to show alleged third-party involvement.

The next day, I requested another interview from a local drug dealer, Mercedes (obviously not his actual name, but he liked this nickname for newspaper articles). Mercedes's standard interview fee was a tasty pulled pork sandwich and a tall craft beer from a local restaurant.

Mercedes is an extraordinary individual, six-feet-four, with straight black hair, a chiseled jaw, and built like a tank. He speaks in a soft voice that always conveys extreme intent, and yet there is a curious twinkle in his brown eyes. Mercedes flawlessly articulates his thoughts and insights into Portland's drug problems. My readers appreciated his solid viewpoint and general take on life. I even got a few emails asking about his relationship status.

Mercedes was in his second year of college as an architect when his mother got cancer. She did not have medical insurance, and he began selling marijuana to pay for her treatment. After she died, Mercedes stopped dealing, and after graduating, he worked for a prestigious architectural firm. Two years later, Portland's construction slowed down, and the firm let him go. To pay rent and student loans, Mercedes returned to dealing, which eventually became his primary income.

At the restaurant, we made some small talk for a few minutes. "What's the story?" Mercedes wanted to know.

"Actually, I want to buy drugs."

Mercedes looked at me for thirteen seconds with a harsh stare. "Mmm. Really?" He asked in an accusing voice.

"I want to try some for an article."

"Mmm. What kind?" Mercedes asked with a suspicious look.

"The usual. You know. Cocaine, heroin, and crack."

Mercedes stared deeply into me for eighteen seconds with his probing eyes. "I don't believe you," he threatened. "Why would a big-time author want to get into this dirty business? You know what it does to people! This poison destroys everything and everybody!"

As I stared into Mercedes's intense eyes, I realized I had made a profound mistake; I underestimated his intelligence, which put me in an awkward position. But, with no other ideas, I was honest. "I need to frame somebody. Planting drugs seems to be a good idea."

"Mmm. Why?"

Recently, a coworker and I worked on an article that inspired me to lie. "We got a tip about the city roads department, and I began working undercover. My investigation confirmed that for every 25 potholes taxpayers pay for, one gets fixed. Millions of dollars are being stolen and—"

"I thought you only did puff pieces," Mercedes cut me off.

"Correct. But I've been trying to do more serious work."

"Mmm. I see," Mercedes said as he sized me up.

"Anyway, I posed as a file clerk to access the city records. An employee caught me taking pictures of the confidential documents. Even though I am a reporter, I still broke the law. This guy wants a hundred grand to keep quiet, and I do not have that kind of dough. My plan is to keep him in jail until my story comes out. Then the pothole investigation will consume him."

Mercedes did not look convinced. "People will kill to keep this secret," I continued. "He made that very clear. So I'm in a tight spot."

Mercedes thought for 22 seconds before breaking into a crafty smile. "Perhaps we can help each other out," he said. "Let's go for a walk."

I paid the bill, and we left the restaurant. "This has nothing to do with potholes. Does it?" Mercedes asked.

"I'm sorry for not giving you the facts. I am trying to protect both of us."

"Mmm."

I could not believe Mercedes's ability to see through my well-planned deception. We turned three corners and walked up to a beautiful house. He led me inside and asked, "You realize what's happening now?"

"You are trusting me, and if I fail your trust, somebody will kill me," I answered in a shaky voice.

"Very perceptive and very true."

Mercedes nodded with a smile, which gave me a chill. He walked over to a heater vent and opened it. Mercedes took out a small bag that contained five tablespoons of white power. "This is heroin," he informed me. "More than enough to get your perp thrown in jail. The problem is that the idiot I bought it from cut it with laundry detergent instead of baking soda or sugar. Afterward, I beat the crap out of him.

"A less reputable dealer would sell it without a care in the world, but not me. What's worse is I sold a hit to one of my regulars before I knew what it was. It made him sick as a dog, and the hospital bills cost me twelve grand."

I found it remarkable that Mercedes had the integrity to help one of his clients. He then took out a Ziploc bag that contained a small handgun and a thin black notebook. "Use this to frame your perp," he said with confidence. "Don't touch, and don't read!"

"Understood."

"One of my rivals has been messing with me. Doing this favor will help me out. What about you? This thing? Do you need an alibi?"

Without thinking, I nodded. Mercedes worked his phone, then sent me a video. "Every Friday night, the Goofy Brothers put on a rave," he continued. "I used to deal there, but now, not so much. This week, it will be at a warehouse on Jeffrey Street. Study the video and get a feel for what's going on. See this guy with the spiky blond hair? The bouncer's name is Big Dan, and the cute redhead bartender is Cindy Glen. Here's a used ecstasy baggie. If anybody asks, tell them you were there Friday and took a hit. If the cops give you the business, tell them you bought your junk from Danny-O in the left bathroom. Then, nobody will question your alibi."

I profusely thanked Mercedes for his help. Then, as I left, he said with narrow eyes and extreme intent, "I'm counting on you. You know that."

I looked into his eyes, and I could see the threat. "You can count on me," I said because I had committed myself.

"You're in that big a jam?" Mercedes asked. I nodded, and he continued, "Tell me. Is all that stuff in your book true?"

"I changed a few things, but the majority is true."

"Is she actually 500 years old?"

"Yes," I confirmed.

"Mmm. Does this trouble you're in have to do with the stuff in your book?"

Unexpectedly, I nodded, and Mercedes flashed a wicked smile. "We'll talk about all this next week," he said. "You now owe me a favor. That favor will be to do a puff piece on how the idiots of this city cannot dress themselves. Sound good?"

"You bet!"

"All right. Off you go."

That evening, I got everything ready, and when I opened my car door, I saw a flat front left tire. Dave came out of the house and asked, "Still planning to go to the party?"

"I'm not going anywhere with this," I answered.

"How many times have I told you to buy a spare? Hang on a sec."

He opened his brown Ford Ranger pickup, reached under the front seat, and pulled out a can of Fix-a-Flat. I screwed it into the tire stem and pressed the button. Miraculously, the tire inflated. "That will last the evening, but you need to get your tire fixed tomorrow," Dave warned.

"You saved my bacon."

"Remember that when I'm late on rent."

"I will," I said with a smile.

"You going to be there?"

"I'll try, but I found out about a killer rave, and I want to check it out for an article."

"Bring earplugs, and don't do any dope," he cautioned.

"Message received. I'm not planning on staying for long. I only want to get a feel for the place."

"Whatever."

"See you tonight."

I drove to the apartment and used my master key to enter Cynthia and Darin's unit. So far, my plan had gone perfectly, which gave me confidence. After putting on latex gloves, I placed the gun in a sock drawer, put the notebook in another drawer, and looked for a suitable hiding place for the heroin. In a moment of inspiration, I threw the bag against the wall. It burst, and white powder flew all over the tile floor. To further the ruse, I put the cigarette butts on the counter and three ripped-up business cards. I then realized that I had forgotten to bring the BlackBerry cell phone. *Dang!*

Looking around the apartment, I felt satisfied that I had thought of everything. So, I stood behind the door and waited. Eighteen minutes later, I heard soft footsteps and the sound of a key. The door opened, Cynthia walked in, and I applied the sleeper hold from behind. She dropped instantly, and I tried to close the door, but her foot was in the way.

When I looked down, I could not believe what I had done. The sight of her unconscious body filled me with tremendous guilt, and I felt disconnected from reality. Then, a car door slammed, and I reacted by moving Cynthia's limp body away from the door, which allowed it to close. I tried to put the love cuffs on her, but loud footsteps approached. I got behind the door just as it swung open. "What the heck?!" Darin yelled.

Darin's body faced the wrong direction for a sleeper hold, and my karate training kicked in. I gave him a sharp punch in the face and expected him to go down hard. However, Darin is a sizable man, and my well-placed punch did not affect him. Instead, he grabbed my neck with his muscular hands. I could not believe his lightning-quick reflexes and superior strength.

My training allowed me to break Darin's grip with an upward thrust. I tried to spin him around to apply the sleeper hold, but he punched me hard in my gut. As I doubled over in pain, I tried to do a long kick to his head. Unfortunately, being off-balance caused my kick to miss wildly, and Darin landed a solid punch on my left cheek. His well-placed blow left me in a daze.

My "spin Darin around and do the sleeper hold" plan had failed, and I swept his leg out from under him. Darin fell with a massive crash. I then pinned his arm back, and we struggled. "I'm going to kill you!" he yelled.

I waited for the exact right moment to apply the sleeper hold. Darin struggled to stand, and it took eleven agonizing seconds for him to go down. When I looked to my left, I noticed Cynthia had sat up. I jumped off Darin and gave her another sleeper hold. Since the effect would only last a few seconds, I rapidly put the ball gag and love cuffs on Darin. When he looked secure, I did the same to Cynthia.

As I glanced around, I realized that my well-thought-out plan had gone wildly astray, and I contemplated calling the whole thing off. In that brief instant, I stopped moving and listened. The silence brought comfort and confidence.

Darin's movement brought me out of my moment of tranquility. His eyes suddenly opened, and I saw the reflection of evil. It looked hot, angry, and devoid of life. At that moment, the devil himself stared right into my soul. Without thinking, I walked to the kitchen, selected their biggest knife, and stabbed Darin in the chest as far as the blade would go. Then, as I knelt in front of him, I silently watched the life leaving those horrifically evil eyes.

Upon reflection, I'm unsure how much control I had over my actions. Clearly, the prominent driving force behind killing Darin was my fear of what he would do if he broke out of his restraints. However, I must admit that I enjoyed being the one to remove a small amount of malevolence from our wonderful world.

Unfortunately, my plan to drag the pair out of the apartment failed because blood was everywhere. It was apparent that I needed to perform the harvest on the floor. As I turned to Cynthia, she stared at me with hate-filled eyes. I expected her to be afraid, but she looked at me with confident rage. I took that opportunity to study her stare for a full 56 seconds.

Cynthia's evil had become obscure, and I briefly wondered what she was thinking in her last moments of life. It then occurred to me that an angry mother and wife sat before me. I again wondered if I should kill her. As I turned to see Darin's dead body with a knife handle sticking out and the heroin powder on the tile floor, I knew I had committed myself.

I opened my harvest kit, placed a plastic drop cloth on the floor, and put on a disposable painter's uniform. Then, I walked over to Cynthia and dragged her by the hair to the plastic. Along the way, she kicked me with all her might, and even with the love cuffs securing her ankles, she managed several well-placed blows. "Do you understand how evil you are?" I asked in a low voice.

Cynthia looked at me in deep anger. "You burned your only child to get money from me," I continued. "Money that I never had and never will have. Don't you get it? I'm broke. I don't even have insurance for this place."

Cynthia shook her head in anger while staring daggers at me. "You don't understand what's important," I continued. "You burned little Julius! How could you do such a thing?! He is such a sweet little boy. Well, this is going to hurt. Prepare yourself."

Grace had used a Swiss soldering iron to torture her victims, but I wanted nothing to do with that level of aggression. So I walked over to the stove and put on a tea kettle. While the water boiled, I kneeled to take one last look into her eyes. Without a word, I splashed her in the face. She tried to shriek, but the ball gag reduced the noise. She began taking dramatic breaths through her nose, making a loud whistling sound. "That is what you did to Julius!" I yelled. "This is how he felt!"

Her face began turning red as she glared with rage. Then it happened again; the devil looked right back at me. Cynthia's expression held a horrific amount of evil. While her malevolent look should have horrified me, I found her vile soul fascinating.

A moment later, I realized I needed to improvise an alternative harvest plan. As I looked around the apartment, I noticed a long wooden pepper grinder. Without a word, I grabbed it and smashed Cynthia in the temple. Her body slumped to the side, and her eyes fluttered.

At that moment, I became very focused. I selected a scalpel, turned Cynthia so that her back faced up, and began cutting. Recently, I spent time in the coroner's office for a pancreatic cancer article. My newfound medical knowledge allowed me to rapidly extract her pancreas, a section of the kidney, and adrenal gland. I placed the organs into three pre-sterilized teacups I brought along.

First, I used two blue sticks with pin cushion ends to apply mint oil to the kidney. Next, I worked the adrenal gland with a round black stick and a second V-shaped stick to produce liquid. I then opened my tiny vial of freeze-dried snake venom to see several clumps of yellowish-white material.

Using the blue stick, I crushed the snake venom into a fine powder. Next, I mixed approximately one-sixth of the powder into the adrenal liquid. The mixture began congealing exactly like fresh venom in blood. Satisfied, I mixed in the mint solution to make a gooey, yellow-pink paste. Finally, I trimmed the excess tissue away from the pancreas.

I placed the baby monitor on a table and moved its wireless camera to provide a well-focused view of my right shoulder.

As you may recall, I did not reveal the actual location of the procedure. However, for reading consistency, I will continue to refer to this secret body area as the shoulder.

With an unobstructed view, I used a different scalpel to open my existing shoulder harvest incision. I used a copper spoon to lift the old pancreas out. It appeared black and shriveled, which led me to believe that I only had a few days left before it would fail. I placed Cynthia's pancreas in my shoulder using a different copper spoon and then applied the yellow-pink paste. As before, the liquid made the incision feel better. I then made two sutures and applied an antiseptic and a bandage. The incision hurt, but not as much as the last time.

With the procedure done, I turned my attention to Cynthia. To disguise my crime, I jabbed her abdomen several times with the same kitchen knife. Her body continued to wither, and I checked her pulse. It felt weak, and I decided not to injure her any further.

The apartment looked bloody, and I started my cleanup by removing the drop cloth and restraints. I grasped the knife handle with Cynthia's hand, then threw it at the wall near the heroin. When it hit, it left a bloody mark.

I placed Darin's hand around the pepper grinder to make him appear guilty by transferring fingerprints and blood. I then pulled out Cynthia's organs, cut them up on a butcher block with a different knife, and put them into the garbage disposal. The swirling blood in the drain looked horrific, and the sudden motor sound made me flip the switch off quickly. I hoped the investigators would conclude that somebody tried to dispose of the body down the drain and that they would overlook the missing pancreas.

After packing up my harvest kit and taking off the painter's uniform, I checked Cynthia's pulse; it confirmed her death. At that moment, I only felt relief and did a last check. Satisfied, I left their door ajar, walked down the stairs, got to my car, and took off my gloves.

At a nearby park, I placed the drop cloth, gloves, painter's uniform, and shriveled pancreas into a fire ring. I used alcohol to clean off the harvest tools and dumped the remainder on the pile. After setting the fire, I nervously watched all the evidence burn. Seven minutes later, I drove to the rave warehouse. To my great relief, I saw a big guy standing outside a door with wild blue hair and dressed in a black tank top. There were many cars along the streets, and I heard loud techno music.

I walked up to Big Dan, who wanted $20 to let me in. He gave me a hard stare for fifteen seconds and then handed me a purple wristband. I suspect I did not look like someone who usually attended this type of event, which was the reason for the intense glare. Six minutes of slam-dancing later, I dance-walked to the bar and pretended to be drunk. Cindy poured a dark brew into a red plastic cup. I put a $10 bill on the bar, drank a sip, and winked at Cindy. As I dance-walked away, she looked at me as if I were another drunk partier. After fifteen more minutes of slam-dancing, I walked to the back door, threw my drink into the trash, and left.

My ears rang, and my arms hurt as I drove to the next party. I entered through the back door and ran into Dave nine minutes later.

"How long have you been here?" Dave asked.

"Over an hour," I lied. "Where were you?"

"Right here."

"Really? I walked right by this table at least three times and didn't see you," I lied again.

"Been right here all evening. What did you think of the rave?"

"Loud, loud, loud! That is all I have to say about that place."

"Get enough for your story?"

"Yeah."

"Cool," Dave said with a big grin.

I then realized that I would have to write a story about a rave. For the next two hours, I chatted with a funny redhead from Ireland. She told me an amusing story about her cat playing with Christmas lights. I got home at 2:13 a.m., and immediately fell asleep.

FIVE

The following day, I woke up feeling tremendous, and my urine did not smell too bad because of the discarded plaque. After breakfast, I walked to my car and saw a flat tire. Fortunately, the Fix-a-Flat canister still had some tire-sealing goop.

On my drive to work, I reflected on the experience. The knowledge that Julius would grow up without his parents hit me the hardest. *You are so selfish! What were you thinking?* I thought over and over.

Once again, I found myself on the side of the road staring at my rusty bumper. After punching the air and yelling, I decided I could not undo my actions, and I vowed never to harvest again.

After more punching, I got back into my car and drove away in a depressed mood. My cell phone rang as I pulled into the *Portland Tribune* parking lot. One of my apartment tenants informed me about the incident. After pretending to be in shock, I told her I would drive right over. On a whim, I ran up to the office and grabbed a reporter, Robyn. She was a crazy-funny woman, and we always had a good laugh. Today Robyn wore a Portland Trail Blazers basketball shirt and faded blue jeans.

At the scene, we met the same police officer, Gerry. Robyn began taking pictures and speaking to the other apartment tenants. "It is a mess in there, but I'm glad you're here," Officer Gerry told us.

The police secured the area with caution tape and took statements from everybody. When Officer Gerry turned his attention to me, I informed him about my previous disagreements with the victims. Then, reluctantly, I confessed to Officer Gerry that I purchased drugs from Danny-O, and handed him my empty ecstasy baggie to prove my alibi. I then described Dave's party and the redheaded girl. Officer Gerry diligently wrote my information in his notebook. Then he cut off my purple wristband, took the empty baggie, and placed both in an evidence bag.

Officer Gerry thanked me for being honest and implied that the crime appeared to be drug-related. I pretended to be shocked and told him Darin and Cynthia did not seem like criminals.

Forty-three minutes later, Officer Gerry allowed me to view the crime scene. I asked permission to clean up the blood to prevent stains. He said that the crime scene investigators had already taken pictures, and under close supervision, he would permit my request. Robyn offered to help, and together we used a towel from the bathroom to remove most of the blood.

After cleaning, I walked to my car to see the tire was flat again. Officer Gerry called a tow truck, which took my car to a garage around the corner. Sixty-six minutes later, they patched up my tire, and we drove back to the *Portland Tribune*. Robyn filed the story, and I felt a great sense of relief.

Over the next two weeks, Julius's injuries healed enough to leave the hospital, and he stayed with his grandmother. I dropped by to say hi and told his grandmother that I would like to provide any help that she would allow. She thanked me and said Julius would move in with his Aunt Laura and Uncle Willard. While they were older, she felt they would make wonderful parents. I saw Julius's sadness as we talked, but he looked forward to living with his relatives. As I left, it occurred to me that this awful situation might have a positive outcome.

That night, I put together a plan to locate Grace. A big part included going over my finances. I owed my parents, friends, former Best Buy coworkers, credit card companies, and Nicholas $15,244. With checks from the coin dealer, publisher, and rent, I paid off all my immediate debts, with $2,831 remaining. Then I booked a discount round-trip ticket from Portland to Moscow for $1,303.

Dave had a backpack, tent, and camping gear that he let me borrow in exchange for a computer gaming night. *Easy trade!*

Using Google Maps, I found Grace's small town of Valdai to be about 400 kilometers away from Moscow and Google Maps computed a five-hour journey. With a lot of research, I learned that the cheapest way to travel to Valdai started with a train ride followed by a bus to the modest town of Vypolzovo, and finally locating somebody to drive me into Valdai. I read everything I could about Valdai, but the Google-translated web pages were difficult to understand.

Meanwhile, the Darin and Cynthia story continued to unfold. The police arrested a local criminal named Lee Underwood because the gun recovered at the crime scene had his fingerprints. Ballistics matched the weapon to four unsolved homicides. Through my contacts at the paper, I learned the police also recovered a notebook that tied him to additional crimes. I hoped this evidence would deflect the investigation far away from me.

Before leaving work, I informed Lloyd that a Russian book conference had invited me to attend a signing, and I asked permission to interview Russian people about the same topics I used in Portland. He thought this would be a great idea and even gave me a stipend of $100 per day. *Bonus!*

◆ ◆ ◆

When the plane landed, I found every sign was in Russian. A big red sign seemed important, and I reached for my translation book. When I could not find it, I realized I had left it at home. *Bonehead!* My trip had gotten off to an inauspicious start.

After mentally yelling at myself, I walked up to the customs agent, and he inquired about the purpose of my trip. I told him I was a tourist and a writer. This answer did not convince him, but I had the foresight to bring a copy of *Grime: The Big Hate*. In the past, I had used my book to get interviews and smooth over adverse situations. He looked at my picture on the back with some amusement, stamped the forms, and waved me on. A nearby clock read 8:31 a.m.

With tremendous effort and wrong turns, I found the correct train and hopped on. During the trip, I recalled passing two bookstores at the airport, and I should have purchased a translation book. *Bonehead!* Three stops later, I got off and located the bus to Vypolzovo, which dropped me at a small bus stop. Inside the open cement structure was a fantastic tile mural of Soviet cosmonaut Yuri Gagarin and his spacecraft. He looked confident and proud about his incredible accomplishment. There were two nearby people, and I asked, "Valdai? Valdai?"

They looked at me in confusion, and a young man said a word that sounded like Valdai. He made a call on his cell phone, hung up, and smiled. Apparently, I needed to wait, so I sat on the only bench.

It was a chilly day, and 43 minutes later, a beat-up car with a picture of bread on the door drove up. An old man wearing a thick fur jacket got out, and I asked him, "Valdai?" The man nodded, and he motioned me to the passenger seat. I noticed the back seat had wooden boxes with pictures of broccoli. We drove for an hour, and the scenery changed from bleak wasteland to farmland and beautiful forests.

When we turned a corner, I saw the sign for Valdai. When we stopped, I handed the driver 2,000 rubles (about $40). He looked at me, and he held up two fingers and then made three zeros. So, I gave him an additional 2,000 rubles, which pleased him.

Valdai was a small, quaint town that was well maintained. As I walked down the empty main street, I understood that my plan to locate Grace had serious flaws. I now realized that I had come all this way just to see a splendid Russian town. My only clue was that Grace told me her family's home was a "day's ride away," which did not translate into map coordinates or even a direction. My thoughts were, *Why on earth am I trying to locate the woman who captured me, tortured people, and killed people?* As I reverse analyzed my situation, the pieces came together.

A subconscious part of my mind desperately wanted to keep harvesting. This hidden agenda invented an impossible task that could only be solved with harvest abilities. I suddenly realized I had fallen into a perfect mental trap and felt as if somebody had yelled the word "checkmate." *Why didn't I see it? I'm so selfish!*

After violently punching the air for three minutes, I sat down on a weathered wooden bench in defeat. The wind gently moving the nearby plants briefly distracted me, and I watched their faded purple flowers floating away. While contemplating my recent poor choices, I wondered what type of plants they were.

At that desperate moment, I came to an epiphany. *I might as well look for her old family's house. After all, I'm here.* I looked at my watch and confirmed the local time as 4:09 p.m. Knowing it would be dark soon, I walked the length of the town, attempting to locate a place to spend the night. Finally, I saw a well-kept monastery in the distance with red trim and walked up to it. Two men in religious clothing greeted me, and I asked, "Hotel? Room? Food?"

One man seemed to understand some of my words. He nodded and pointed toward a chair. Not knowing what else to do, I sat down and read a tour book from my backpack. An hour and a half later, a different man motioned for me to follow him to a table where several men were sitting. The lead man pointed toward an empty seat. I sat down to three minutes of uncomfortable silence. Finally, another man walked in, set down plates, and served us meat stew with a healthy chunk of dark brown bread.

All at once, the men bowed. I bowed, and the man at the head of the table spoke solemn Russian words for two minutes. Afterward, everybody ate in silence. While the food looked plain, it tasted superb.

After dinner, they led me to a sparse room with a small bed. It had a glass oil lamp which reminded me of Grace's house. They pointed down the hallway to a toilet, and I used the small sink to wash up. Fortunately, the bed felt comfortable, and I slept soundly.

The following day, I woke up confused because of jet lag. After dressing and shaving, I tried to find somebody to pay for my stay. A man I had not met before greeted me, and I offered him money. He did not accept my offer, but as I walked out, I noticed the donation box and put in 8,000 rubles.

A nearby clock read 8:15, and I walked around town search-ing for a person to be my local guide. Unfortunately, nobody spoke English, and by noon, I found myself in a small room that served tea. As I sipped, I again contemplated my recent poor choices and then turned my attention to the task at hand.

It took seventeen minutes to come up with a better plan. I would locate a translation book, a good map, a local guide, and we would search the surrounding forests along old roads. My first step was to get to a larger town and find a bookstore.

As I paid for my tea, a man in his late twenties with a crazy haircut and torn jeans walked up to me. The guy was at least six-feet-five and had to be a bodybuilder. "Hey, you," he asked in heavily accented English. "American. What you do?!"

Hearing English brought relief. "I'm looking for a local guide," I answered.

"Why?"

"Well, this will sound silly, but I'm trying to locate the remains of a nearby farm. It's a day's ride on a horse from here."

The man looked at me with a funny expression. "You seek the farm of the forever woman?" he asked.

"What?"

"The famous farm in the woods? With the apple tree?"

"Ahh, yes." I answered in utter disbelief.

"Tour in half hour. You stay."

The man hastened away, and I could not believe what he had told me. It then dawned on me he might try to scam me, but I could not ignore this spectacular opportunity.

Forty-seven minutes later, a pieced-together vehicle pulled up to a screeching stop. It looked as if it had once belonged to the military, and every panel had a different paint color. The same man sat in the driver's seat, with eight people crammed together in the rest of the vehicle. They looked annoyed that another person would join the tour. "15,000 rubles," the man yelled over the loud exhaust. "Half now."

I paid him 7,500 rubles and squeezed in between two women. The man drove away in a burst of speed. At first, we traveled along a well-maintained road, which turned into a rutty road, and then he turned directly into the forest without roads. The man drove with great skill but hit many branches, making loud *thump* sounds. Every time, I was sure the windshield would shatter and send sharp glass everywhere.

As we were driving, I tried to converse with the passengers, but only one spoke English, and he was not interested in talking. I dared not speak to the driver as I did not want to break his concentration.

Eight minutes later, I began noticing two passengers staring at me. When I smiled, they whispered to each other in Russian. One of them pulled out something from his bag and passed it to the other passenger without allowing me to see what they were doing. It appeared they were doing something illegal from the way they were acting. I tried my best to figure out what was going on without being too obvious. They noticed my interest, and went far out of their way to keep their secret.

Soon, everybody began whispering and looking at me. Finally, the driver asked, "Hey, you American. You, *Anitchka's Apple Tree* book?"

"What?"

The two people that had been acting mysterious handed me a book. It had big red Cyrillic words on the front cover, and I recognized the artwork from *Interviewing Immortality*. When I turned it over, I saw my picture. The sight caught me completely off guard and it took me 21 seconds to answer, "Um, yes. I'm James Kimble. It appears they changed the title to *Anitchka's Apple Tree*."

The driver slammed on the brakes, and the vehicle abruptly stopped. The action threw the passengers forward, and two crashed into the steel dashboard. "You do *Anitchka's Apple Tree*?!" he asked excitedly.

"Ahh, yes."

"You met Anitchka?!" the driver asked, while waving his finger at me.

"Ahh, yes."

Everybody understood I wrote the book without a translation, and they began talking excitedly. "You not before been Russia?" The driver asked after speaking to the passengers.

"No, I've never traveled here. But I like the forest, and the people are nice."

"Anitchka prison you?"

"Ahh, yes."

"Wonderful!" the driver said in a joy-filled voice.

"I didn't find it wonderful."

The driver laughed. "You kill man, get long life?" he asked.

"Well—kind of," I stammered.

"Good! Very good! This is a good day!"

The driver smiled, said something happy in Russian, and threw the vehicle into gear with a loud crunch. We took off with a jolt, and the woman next to me yelled what I thought was a curse word. "In Russia, always rumor of forever woman," he continued. "She near Valdai. She many secret power. All child know story. When *Anitchka's Apple Tree*, everybody know it about our forever woman. Ermolaev, old Valdai name. Over 500 year."

We came to a big meadow, and the driver circled to the south side. On the left, we saw four trucks and 30 people milling about. They all had cameras and were taking pictures.

We got out, and the driver began shouting. Suddenly, everybody ran over to me and took my picture.

I smiled, put my arm around somebody, and somebody else took our picture. As this went on, people began asking me Russian questions (well, I think they were questions). "Look here," the driver said to me as he pulled my arm. "Look here."

The driver pointed to dilapidated buildings surrounded by a recently installed fence. I saw a gnarly apple tree about twenty feet high with two small green apples forming. Grace told me her father planted an apple tree on the spot where she was born, and I was sure this was it. *Knock me over with a feather,* I thought.

Nearby, I saw the remains of a fence and a stable. The ground looked as though crops used to grow on it. Toward the center, we saw the remains of a house. A hundred feet away, we could see the distinct remains of a road. *This has to be Grace's road,* I thought. *We are a day's ride from Valdai.* Then I saw an old handmade sign with Cyrillic letters and an arrow. *This has to be Grace's "a day's ride to Valdai" sign.* The entire experience left me stunned. I touched the sign to reassure myself that the sight before me was real.

The driver liked my reaction. "This it?!" he asked in an excited voice. "This Anitchka Ermolaev's family house?!"

It had to be. There could not be any other explanation. She told me the absolute truth. Wow! I nodded while deep in thought. The crowd now became excited, and they continued to ask me questions. Finally, the driver translated one of them, "When last time Anitchka in Valdai?"

"I'm not sure," I answered. "She didn't tell me about her history from 1963 to today."

The driver translated, and I realized I did not know his name. "Sir," I asked, "what's your name?"

"Ujarak, like Anitchka's half-brother. Where Anitchka now?"

"I don't know. I'm trying to find her."

"New Anitchka book?" Ujarak asked.

"I'm not planning to write another book."

"You ask Anitchka relatives? My sister marries Dementy Ermolaev. He close most to Anitchka."

I felt overwhelmed and said, "Ujarak, I would like to take a few pictures."

Ujarak led me back to his vehicle. I took out my backpack and retrieved my camera. "You show us gathering?" Ujarak wondered.

"Gathering?"

"The take body inside and put in shoulder?"

"The harvest?" I asked in confusion.

"Yes, harvest. Same word."

Clearly, the Russian translation of *Interviewing Immortality* had a few flaws. "Anitchka asked me not to reveal her secret," I answered.

Ujarak nodded. "Wise woman," he confirmed with a nod.

I took a bunch of pictures for the next nine minutes. Afterward, Ujarak gathered the people together to continue the tour. He told us that a larger road bypassed this area, and people no longer travel here. I also learned that our next stop would be the waterfall near the small lake where Cleopatra met Grace.

Now that I had a guide who spoke some English, I formed a new plan. I would first ask Ujarak to locate Grace's relatives, then ask them if they knew her whereabouts or contact information.

As we got ready to leave, I noticed two out-of-place Asian men staring at me intently. They were both the same five-feet-six and wore faded tan khakis. "Ujarak, what is the deal with those two guys?"

"Oh, them! Always here! Stupid men!"

"I see."

Ujarak continued to ask questions, most of which I did not have the answers to. As we got to his vehicle, I noticed the left Asian man using a strange radio that looked like an over-sized '80s cell phone. This activity concerned me, and I began thinking deeply about my security. The man then put his radio away and spoke to his companion, who nodded.

Suddenly, the Asian men pulled large guns out of their bags and began advancing toward us with the barrels pointed right at me.

Ujarak yelled at the two men, but they continued advancing. I planned to let them get closer, and I would spin the left man around, use him as a shield, and then go after the right man. I had perfected this move in my karate class and placed my feet in the best position to be effective. The right man reached into his bag and took out two pairs of handcuffs. He threw them, and they landed at my feet. I looked deep into their eyes and read the intent.

Reluctantly, I put one pair on my wrists, and the right man gestured to my feet with his gun. With little choice, I put the second pair on my ankles. The left Asian man tossed me a hood. I put the hood on, and my world turned black. I found it amusing that I still had my backpack on even though I was now cuffed. One man grabbed my right arm and led me away. Because of the ankle cuffs, I had to take small steps.

I still heard Ujarak yelling, and it briefly occurred to me he might want his 7,500 rubles. Above the yelling, I heard cameras taking pictures. *This will be front-page news in Russia,* I thought. One of the men pulled off my backpack and I surmised he must have cut the straps. They pushed me inside a vehicle, and we rapidly drove away.

SIX

attempted small talk with my captors three times, but they clearly did not desire conversation. The vehicle stopped three hours and 43 minutes later, and they pulled me out. I suspected we were at an airport because of the powerful smell of jet fuel. When my captors took off my hood, I found myself in a sparse bathroom with two Asian men. It seemed logical to relieve myself and wash my arms and face. Finally, they put my hood back on and led me to what seemed like an aircraft.

The men moved me to an uncomfortable seat without padding and tightly cinched the seatbelts. I suspected it was a cargo aircraft. Eight minutes later, the plane started its loud engines. I tried to put my arms over my ears, but the restraints restricted my movement. Then, somebody placed hearing protection over my hood.

"Thanks," I said.

"Mmm."

I took that "mmm" sound to mean "you're welcome."

The plane took off on the uneven runway, and I did my best to sleep.

Nine hours and 31 minutes later, somebody nudged me awake. I felt a bump, and the plane landed. They removed my hearing protection, unbuckled my seatbelt, and I stood. One man led me off the plane to a car with fine leather seats and a pleasant floral smell. The ride felt flawless, and this gave me hope that my situation would improve.

Forty-nine minutes later, the car came to a gentle stop. Somebody guided me out of the car and took my hood off. After my eyes adjusted to the light, I saw the opulent doors of a grand palace. I could not believe the size and beauty of my new surroundings. Then, I noticed Chinese writing in golden letters on three signs.

The person guiding me was a well-dressed Asian man, and he looked at me with a pleasant smile. When we got to the doors, two guards opened them, and the massive entryway overwhelmed me. Inside, I saw many tasteful paintings, gold statues, and exquisite stone carvings. As I looked at them in awe, I wondered what I had gotten myself into.

As I stared, one of my captors removed my handcuffs, and I stretched. A man in a black suit walked up with a silver tray that contained a wet, blue towel. He motioned to my face in a circular pattern. I used the cloth to clean my face and hands. The man smiled, made a quick bow, and departed.

Two gorgeous Chinese women in black cheongsam (fine silk) dresses walked up, and each took an arm. Then, they began leading me away with two guards closely following. As we went through the entryway, I appreciated the incredible artwork. At one point, I stopped to look closer at a massive painting depicting an Asian battle scene. It contained astounding detail and must have taken the artist ten years to create.

The women led me to an elegant room with a long dining table. I saw two place settings across from each other, and the women guided me to sit at the nearest one. My place setting had a fork and silver chopsticks with embedded emeralds. The women left while the two security men stood with their arms crossed behind me. I had an uncomfortable feeling they were armed.

With nothing else to do, I looked at the elegant artwork on the walls. I then noticed the spotless plate in front of me with its exquisite dragon engravings surrounded by gold inlay. This entire experience reminded me of my first meal with Grace.

Three minutes later, a large door opened, and an older man slowly entered, assisted by three people. I estimated his height at five-feet-two, and he wore a traditional gray robe. As he came closer, I was shocked by his grotesque appearance. His arms and face had multiple inch-long scars. There were eight bandages covering fresh injuries. The man's unhealthy complexion had gray bumps and flaking skin. His hair was black tufts mixed with patches of white and bald spots. Overall, the man's head looked like an angry barber had attacked a skunk with shears. *Do you know how bad you look? You're beyond repulsive!* I thought, while doing my best to remain pleasant.

As he got closer, our eyes met. He stopped, and we stared at each other. I immediately knew that this man was immortal. He attempted to intimidate me with a crafty, piercing stare. I stood firm and would not allow my concentration to falter. Our intense interaction continued for an intriguing 68 seconds. Finally, the man smirked, straightened himself, and bit his upper lip with a questioning expression. He made a thin, evil smile and continued toward his place setting. I then noticed his ears and nose had undergone surgery recently.

The helpers eased the man into his chair, and they left. Just then, a man in a perfectly tailored black suit walked in. The old man said something in Chinese, and the man asked in flawless English, "You are James? The immortality author?"

I nodded, and the older man appeared deep in thought for 37 seconds. Then, he made a motion, and the translator left. The old man cleared his throat and said in heavily accented English, "The woman whom you refer to as Grace provided the immortality secret?"

"Um. Yes. She told me about it," I answered with caution.

The man said something in Chinese that sounded like, "Ahh, sasha, sasha." Later, I tried unsuccessfully to look up that phrase, and my only guess from the context is that it meant "interesting."

"Are you aware of her location?" He asked.

"I have been searching for her without success. Now, I have no more leads to follow."

The man seemed content with my answer. Thirty-one seconds later, he leaned back and asked, "In your book, the woman you call Grace informed you that the immortality secret came from Pharaoh Cleopatra?"

"That's what she told me."

"Cleopatra learned the secret from me. I am the original creator of what you term 'the harvest.'"

I'm speaking to the original harvester! Wow! My thoughts went wild, and I had so many questions. "You knew Cleopatra?" I blurted out. "That's so cool!"

The man nodded, and I realized I had said something stupid. I straightened up and said in a reserved voice, "Sir, I'm sorry for my outburst. Unfortunately, I got caught up in the moment of meeting such an extraordinary individual. Please forgive my rudeness."

"Your excitement is understandable," the man said with a grin. "I am also excited about meeting someone who also knows of the process."

"I have questions."

"As do I. Ahh, sasha, sasha. Dinner first."

"Thank you."

The man gestured, and four servants came in with silver trays. The first course was vegetables with beef in oyster sauce. It tasted astounding, and I took great care to eat slowly while appreciating the fabulous flavor. The man seemed content that I enjoyed the food. He ate tiny bites, almost like a bird.

The servers cleared our plates and brought out lobster-filled phyllo triangles, followed by frothy ground duck over long grain rice. Each dish was flawlessly prepared, fantastically arranged, and tasted heavenly. I did my best to smile and act pleasant while enjoying this superb food. Our dining experience concluded with a mango crème pastry that was delicious beyond description.

Throughout the meal, the man remained silent and only nodded when I complimented the chef. He clearly did not wish to speak and, instead, wanted to study me. After dessert, the two women guided me to a tastefully decorated library filled with artwork, and I sat on an immaculate vermilion sofa that had a detailed gold inlay. The two security men silently stood behind me the entire time.

The same three people helped the man out of his dining chair and led him to an oversized comfortable chair across from me. He looked at me with a crafty expression and said, "My name is Quan Wuhan."

"James Kimble," I said with my most pleasant voice. "Nice to meet you."

"Do you know why I have summoned you to my presence?"

"I suspect you wish to know what I know."

"I do," Quan said with a nod.

"Can I learn more about you first?"

"Ahh, sasha, sasha. An interesting request." Fifteen seconds later, he continued, "I choose to answer your curiosity. Allow me to begin at the beginning. I was born in what we now know as the Gobi Desert. Well, it is a desert now. Modern calendars record 71 BC as my birth and—"

"Mr. Wuhan, sir?" I interrupted.

"Yes?"

"Would it be all right if I wrote our conversation down in my notebook?" Quan looked upset, and I continued, "What you're saying is important."

"Are you planning another book?"

"No."

"Why do you require the use of your notebook?"

I did not know why, but the little voice in my head screamed that I needed to record everything. I thought about tactfully answering his question and came up with, "I'm more intelligent when I write. That's how my mind works."

"Ahh, sasha, sasha. I see."

Quan said something in Chinese to the man behind me, who spoke into the cuff of his suit. Forty-eight seconds later, a young man arrived with my backpack. I zipped it open and extracted my *Dawson's Creek* notebook. I still could not believe that I used the same notebook. My workplace had been throwing them out, and I rescued 20. The worst part was a goofy picture of the lead character on the cover with "Tiger Bae" written in orange and pink letters. It also had "Is Pacey the best sex you've ever had? Take the quiz!" I hated these notebooks, but I was too cheap to buy something decent.

Quan looked at me with amusement, shook his head, and continued, "Ahh, sasha, sasha. I came into being amid a family of travelers. We now call this class of people 'nomads.' We were fortunate because my father picked the best routes, and this circumstance exposed me to many wise people.

"I desired to become a healer from a young age, and my father used his connections to get me an apprenticeship with the best healer in all the land. His name was Master Buyantu. During my fifteen years of study, I attained the ability to set broken bones, cure infections, treat illnesses, and even perform simple surgeries. I also accumulated a wide range of rudimentary medications.

"As my reputation spread, the young leader whom you call Cleopatra was informed of my abilities. She summoned me to her far-off land so that I could improve her health.

"I arrived at a glorious city with sculptures, gardens, and people from many nations. You must understand that up to this point, the largest gathering I had witnessed comprised fewer than 100 people. The experience of so many well-dressed citizens in one location was surreal, and an amazing woman stood at the center of their society. The history books correctly record her striking appearance and a strong sense of vanity. After introductions and a party in my honor, she put forth her request. I would use all my abilities to help her become the most beautiful woman in all the land.

"Ahh, sasha, sasha. Because I did not speak her language, she located a bright Chinese translator named Jank. With his help, Cleopatra outlined the services she expected me to perform. I was to use any means necessary to develop cosmetic enhancements. Her most important request concerned age reduction. This task proved daunting, as we did not have modern laboratories or chemical analysis. However, I possessed a major advantage over modern science: an endless supply of slaves for medical experimentation."

Quan said the last sentence calmly, which sent a deep chill up my spine. He continued, "I began by improving what women now call face cream. To accomplish this feat, I invented alternative methods of extracting and refining plant and animal oils. For pigmentation, I mixed plant extracts with highly refined clays. This fine paste allowed users to enhance or suppress facial features.

"Cleopatra appreciated my efforts but still sought more variety. So, I ordered teams of traders to scour faraway lands for exotic plants and pigments. Meanwhile, I continued my makeup experiment to provide enhancements in every color of the rainbow.

"Every day, Cleopatra tastefully applied my latest creations in different combinations to enhance her beauty. The result impressed everybody she encountered, which fueled her desire for more variety. You may not know that my creations became the literal foundation for the modern makeup industry," Quan said with great pride and raised eyebrows.

"Ahh, sasha, sasha. Jank took over makeup development while I focused on combating the aging process. My vast medical knowledge led me to believe that I needed to work from inside the body to make skin appear younger.

"While searching for potential solutions, I sought a wise healer, Biming Lau. He could remove deep arrowheads and heal the severe cuts. However, his most significant advancement was using a clean operating environment long before Western medicine. Using his knowledge as a starting point, I began experimenting. My first step was to dissect slaves to understand how their organs functioned."

The thought of living people getting dissected horrified me. It is hard to comprehend that a person could be so cruel and yet still speak pleasantly. But, of course, I kept my terrifying thoughts to myself.

"I explored the different parts of the brain and how they affected the thinking process while taking careful notes of my findings," Quan continued. "I then learned how the heart pumped blood and the lungs processed air. Later, I explored the functions behind the kidneys, spleen, and liver.

"As I developed my theories, I began wondering what would happen if a person had multiple organs. It seemed reasonable that a body would function better with duplicates. Thus,

I performed the first human transplants. But, the concept of organ rejection was far beyond my knowledge and resulted in immediate death or terminal infection.

"My breakthrough in the life-giving process occurred when I did my first pancreas transplant. Most slaves died, but a few experienced a brief period of good health. This slight improvement intrigued me.

"I began experimenting with different methods to increase the slave's life. Eventually, I understood that transplant preparation was the key to solving the riddle of longer life. It took three years to learn that adrenal gland extract combined with snake venom prolonged a person's health. This combination is not as strange as it may seem. The adrenal gland produces a stimulant, and snake venom acts as a congealing stabilizer.

"However, the beneficial effect only lasted five days. My experimentation revealed that I could prolong the effect by waiting two days and performing another transplant. To my amazement, the slaves not only survived, but they also indeed looked younger, had more energy, and greater mental ability. Cleopatra appreciated my success and encouraged me to refine the process.

"I altered the pancreas location, tried different stabilizers, and introduced binding oils. Eventually, I developed a procedure that would last a month before the slave required another transplant. Only then did I apply the process to myself. Ahh, sasha, sasha. The results were astounding. My mind worked better, and I appeared ten years younger.

"When Cleopatra saw I trusted the procedure enough to apply it to myself, she studied every aspect. Her diligence included observing many transplants and suggesting insightful experiments. Several months later, I achieved consistent results and applied the procedure to her. Cleopatra was astounded and demanded even more improvements.

"Ahh, sasha, sasha. Unfortunately, Cleopatra became obsessed with my technique, and she stopped focusing on being a ruler. While I voiced my concerns, she had no use for opinions from a lowly healer.

"Her son, Caesarion, led the inevitable revolt. One night, guards surrounded the royal palace, and they killed Cleopatra by savagely striking her in the head. Afterward, Caesarion informed the masses she induced a snake to bite her. Later, he killed Mark Antony because they hated each other. The crime was disguised to look like a suicide pact. Dates were then changed to coincide with besieging Alexandria to give Caesarion an alibi. Ahh, sasha, sasha. As I had witnessed her battered body, I had no reason to think she could have survived. Only after reading your book did I suspect otherwise.

"Two days after the revolt, Caesarion sent guards to my domicile. When I saw them approach, I threw my notes into the fire. The guards broke down the door, and Jank fought to protect me. In the struggle, they stabbed him to death.

"The guards led me away, but a crowd had formed to see what had happened. When they observed the guards restraining me, they came to my aid. 'Why?' you might ask. You must understand that as a healer, I helped many of them, even assisting in their birth. In this moment of confusion, I struck a guard to make my escape. Without money, I returned to my nomadic existence, and my skills allowed me to attain wealth.

"Many years ago, I traveled across a vast tract of land suitable for farming and built this dwelling. Over time, the leaders desired wealth, and I sacrificed much to maintain my land. And then, the communist revolution took my nation by storm. As a person of means, the leaders singled me out as an aristocrat. Fortunately, I hoarded gold, which allowed me to bribe the worthless bureaucrats. But, even today, my solitude requires a high price, and each generation wants more.

"Ahh, sasha, sasha. The vast lands of China have undergone so many changes. And now, I am outraged at how much pollution is present in the once sweet air. I long for a simpler time."

Quan leaned back for 78 seconds, and I could see his exhaustion. "Our discussion has taken its toll, and I grow weary," he continued. "In the remaining time, I have a request. Please provide the notes about your encounter with the woman you call Grace."

As Quan revealed his extensive history, I had been writing every word. Then, when he stopped speaking, I looked up to see his curious expression. As I stared into his eyes, I understood that his polite request was a direct order with dire consequences if I were to refuse.

At that moment, I thought about the implications of revealing Grace's information and realized that her secrets were useless to Quan. My notes did not contain the harvest details, and Grace's experiences were only a descriptive slice of history. "Yes, of course," I answered in my best cheerful voice. "If you would provide me a printer or a memory stick, I'll make you a copy. However, I must warn you …"

As soon as I spoke those last words, I realized Quan did not appreciate my direct tone. So I gulped and continued, "Mr. Wuhan, sir, I wrote my notes for myself, and I am sure they aren't up to your excellent literary standards. Mr. Wuhan, sir."

Quan looked at me with amusement for 22 seconds. Finally, he took a sip of tea and said, "In your book, you wrote that the woman you called Grace experienced moments of delight in your presence. I now see why she expressed this opinion. Your demeanor follows an exact path. Ahh, sasha, sasha. Concerning your writing, it is understandable that your notes are not of quality. A servant will provide a memory device. Good evening."

"Good evening, Mr. Wuhan, sir."

I felt a massive wave of relief as three servants appeared and helped Quan up. I stood, and they assisted his departure. Two different women with matching dark blue cheongsam dresses escorted me to an opulent room with an enormous bed. The left woman opened the door to reveal a tastefully decorated bathroom, and the right woman showed me a closet full of sharp clothing in my size. They smiled and left while two guards remained outside. Two minutes later, a man appeared with my laptop and a memory stick on a silver tray.

I set my laptop on an immaculate dark oak desk with gold inlay and turned it on. After entering my password, I copied several files onto the memory stick. Inside, I laughed because I knew how bad my chaotic note-taking system was. *Quan will be in for the surprise of his life when he tries to understand my gobbledygook.* I thought, as I asked the man with the tray, "Is it all right if I type in some notes?"

The man clearly did not speak English, but the guard overheard me, spoke into his cuff, and 87 seconds later, he nodded. I began typing up my experience with the apple tree tour and then my dinner with Quan. When I looked out a nearby window, I noticed the sun had set. So I set my note-taking aside, and I took a bath.

Afterward, I came out to see that somebody had placed my backpack on the bed. I found it amusing that somebody had repaired what I had assumed were cut straps. While it was still early, I fell asleep thinking about what had recently happened.

The following day, I awoke to see two new attractive women wearing matching pink cheongsams staring at me with funny expressions. Then, they motioned toward a tan three-piece suit, giggled, and left. I got out of bed, shaved, and put on the suit. It fit perfectly and made me realize I had not looked this good since Grace's house.

The women led me to the dining room, where I ate a breakfast of rice porridge, steamed buns, and strawberry pastries. The food tasted exquisite, and the meal concluded with a delicious oolong tea. *I could get used to this,* I thought, as the women led me to an unfamiliar room with modern oil paintings and two sofas facing each other. The entire artwork theme was the same, a mother tiger playing with her cubs. *Quan has exquisite taste in artwork and decoration,* I thought while studying the sights before me.

Next to the bookcase, I noticed a large window with a superb view. I looked outside, and a picturesque garden greeted me. It must have been over 50 acres of fountains, manicured bushes, sculptures, flowers of every color, and pruned trees without a single brown leaf.

Two minutes later, a voice behind me asked, "Are you enjoying my garden?" Quan had snuck up behind me. "It's i-i-i-impressive," I stammered. "Quite spectacular."

"I am glad my garden pleases you. Please sit."

I walked to the sofa and sat while two guards stood behind me. Quan looked at me somewhat angrily. "Ahh, sasha, sasha. You were correct to warn me," he said. "Your notes were in a sorry state."

"I'm not that organized when I take notes."

"Did you have a merry laugh as you handed the memory device to my servant?"

"May I be honest?" I asked with hesitation.

"Yes."

"It took every ounce of strength not to laugh out loud."

Quan smiled, and I shook my head with a big grin. He leaned back for 51 seconds while sizing me up and tilted his head. "I read your book," he said, again with some anger.

"What did you think of it, may I ask?"

"You had no right to reveal my procedure! It is mine! Not yours! To worsen matters, your creation lacked substance. And finally. I dislike first-person works!"

This condemnation upset me. *Everybody is a critic!* I thought. *Writing a book is hard!* It made me want to yell, "Hey, try to write your own damn book and then feel the pain as every online idiot publicly slams you! Plus, my book was about what happened to me, so writing a book in anything other than the first person would be stupid."

But, of course, I knew such a statement would not be welcome, and I did my best to nod in understanding. Although I acted pleasant, I sensed Quan had discerned my thoughts.

Quan looked at me harshly for eighteen seconds and seemed to rethink his last statement. "Perhaps I spoke harshly. If I were to improve on what you presented, I would have emphasized the immortality procedure and the history of the woman you call Grace. No author should emphasize their glorious failures."

"I put in as much of her history as I could. Normal readers only tolerate small amounts of violence. Otherwise, my book would get categorized as a gore novel, and those have limited marketability."

"I see."

"I hoped readers would appreciate a character who directly experienced a harvest. To me, that was the central part of the story. Grace encouraged me to be honest about my life's failures, and I did not want to displease her."

Quan seemed uncertain, and I'm not sure my defense worked. He leaned back for 38 seconds, and I could tell he wanted to know something important. Then he folded his hands and said in a monotone voice, "Your notes did not provide the information necessary to perform the life-giving procedure."

"I did not include that detail in my notes in case somebody stole my laptop."

"Ahh, sasha, sasha. A wise precaution."

Quan seemed to wait for me to say something, so I asked, "I have many questions about you. Would now be a good time?"

"Questions of what kind?"

"About your life, world history, how you do the harvesting procedure, and where you see the world going."

Quan looked at me with an unyielding expression for eleven seconds. I still found it challenging to remain pleasant while looking at his dreadful features.

"Yes, let us discuss the life-giving procedure," he coldly replied.

Quan made a motion, and three servants appeared. They gently helped him stand. I stood and watched as they led him out of the room. We traveled at a snail's pace for six minutes. During this time, I appreciated the many paintings adorning the walls. *It's nice to be wealthy,* I concluded to myself.

We ended up in a bizarre room, and they placed Quan in an oversized comfortable chair. Two guards grasped my arms and bound me with leather restraints to a steel chair bolted to the floor. I was terrified. The experience reminded me of my first harvest.

As I looked around the sterile white room, I realized Quan used it to harvest. A spotless stainless steel table dominated the center. It appeared to be the type that a coroner would use, with long troughs along the edges to allow fluids to collect in a bucket. He had added thick black leather straps to hold down the donor body. A grand wooden cabinet with chemical jars was on the left, and on the right stood a silver tray that contained gold-plated medical tools. The two guards left us alone.

"I am going to perform the life-giving procedure," Quan said in a menacing tone. "Then we will discuss your method."

Quan took off his shirt to reveal over a hundred disgusting scars. Many were fresh, with bandages over them. The sight repulsed me, and I had to turn away.

When I turned back, Quan pressed a button, and the door on the other side opened. Two powerful men entered while holding a boy in restraints. He was about thirteen years old and was dressed in tattered clothes. When he saw the table, he screamed at the top of his lungs.

Seeing the terror in the child's eyes enraged me, and I yelled over the screams, "What the heck are you doing?!"

"My procedure," Quan calmly replied. "You should recognize this."

"No, no, no! You cannot do this! The child deserves to live!" Quan made an evil grin and continued. I had to save the boy's life and yelled, "Grace told me that young people have unpredictable results!"

Quan seemed perplexed and said, "I read this description in your terrible book. It made no sense. Elders always yield bad outcomes!"

The boy continued to scream, which made it difficult to hear. "Will you take the boy away so we can talk?!" I yelled.

Quan made a hand gesture, and the powerful men removed the boy. Seeing that the boy would at least be alive for a little while was a tremendous relief. "Would you please explain your procedure first?" I asked, hoping to gain some time to think up a way to save the boy's life. "We can compare notes."

Quan looked upset and took a deep breath to calm down. Then, eight seconds later, he said, "The boys must be healthy and between the ages of eight and ten. Obtaining subjects is a straightforward process as I have an agreement with the Xinjiang district ministry of health. They provide boys from notoriously seditious families."

"That's repulsive."

"What you must understand is that we come from vastly different societies. In your culture, the government encourages freedom. In China, we choose conformity."

I wanted to argue, but I knew my efforts would be pointless. Quan took a sip of tea and continued, "Ahh, sasha, sasha. I begin by extracting the adrenal gland and pancreas. Next, I press the gland to extract its liquids. I combine this liquid with eastern Egyptian cobra venom, crushed rosemary extract, and saffron. Lastly, I add minke whale oil.

"At the location, I make a three-centimeter-long incision that is two centimeters deep. It must be near a large muscle and follow its outer contours. The incision may never enter the body cavity, and the location must be precisely 20 millimeters away from the last procedure.

"I place a prepared pancreas in the new incision along with the liquid. After suturing the wound, I apply an antiseptic made with Mojave Desert honey and yarrow root. The yarrow also aids in scar reduction.

"Ten days later, I must remove the previous pancreas. My procedure lasts eight to eleven days, but I remember when it regularly lasted 67 days. You will explain your procedure!"

It seemed incomprehensible that this man took three boys' lives every month and had done so for over 2,000 years. I needed to put my repulsive thought aside, and changed the subject to give the boy more time. "Wait a minute. What is the purpose of rosemary, saffron, and whale oil?"

Quan became upset again and took a deep breath. "I pulverize the rosemary into a fine paste. This prevents rejection," he answered in an annoyed voice. "I grind saffron into a fine paste, and it provides special nutrients that prolong and enhance the harvest. Minke oil is a binding agent that the body does not reject. Now, explain your procedure!"

"Why do you have all these scars? The harvest should heal scars."

Quan looked as if he'd had enough questions and sipped tea. "The procedure used to heal all my scars," he answered with controlled anger. "Alas, my aged body no longer operates as it once did. Now, I must find alternative locations for the incision. Your procedure! Now!"

"Did you try to improve the procedure?"

Quan again took a sip of tea. "I made many improvements," he continued in a forced, calm voice. "For example, I began with goat renderings, and now I use whale oil. Rosemary and saffron were later additions."

"Did you have scientists examine the procedure to see how it worked?"

"They came to the same conclusion listed in your book."

Quan took another sip of tea and again said in a forced, calm voice, "I went to great lengths to replicate the procedure presented in your book. But my results were unsuccessful."

"I altered the procedure to prevent the world from turning into a killing circus."

"Ahh, sasha, sasha. A reasonable course of action. You will explain the differences now!"

I knew Quan would not allow another question, and I began, "All right, let's start with the harvest subject."

Quan began taking notes. "It doesn't matter if the harvest subject is male or female," I continued. "They should be between 20 and 45 years old. The subject must have evil deep in their heart."

"Why?"

While Grace had implied differently, I suspected the harvest subject did not need to be evil, but I objected to killing innocent people. So, I made something up. "An evil soul fights harder, which leads to a longer harvest effect."

"Ahh, sasha, sasha. I see."

"You must then arouse the harvest subject to a heightened state of anger. As I understand, this entices the adrenaline gland to produce fresh fluid. Grace used a soldering iron."

Quan produced a Swiss kerosene soldering iron from a drawer. I could not believe he held the same type that Grace used. With an evil grin, he asked, "Like this?"

"Um. Yeah, that's the one. Anyway. After burning the harvest subject to a heightened state, you stun them and extract the pancreas, adrenal gland, and kidney."

"You described a procedure that went through the back?"

"It is faster, with less blood. After the extraction, you must process the organs with mint oil and snake venom. I have tried freeze-dried snake venom, and it also works."

"Freeze-dried? Most fascinating."

"Now, the most important part is the correct location. If the incision is a millimeter off, then it will not work."

"I see. What is the purpose of mint oil? Anti-rejection, I assume."

"I believe that's the purpose."

"And the changes you made in your book?"

"There are four major differences."

I provided a detailed explanation, and Quan looked pleased. "Cleopatra made many improvements since I shared the secret with her," he said. "You will demonstrate this improved procedure on yourself. Now!"

"Wait, that's not what we discussed."

"You will perform the procedure!" Quan said forcefully.

"I did a harvest a few days ago, and I don't know what would happen if I did another so soon."

Quan did not appear convinced, and I had him lift my shirt so he could see the fresh scar. So, he leaned back, looking deflated. "Very well," Quan said with a huff. "You will perform the procedure on me. If you fail, you will die."

"Well, um, here's the thing. I'm not too confident about the initial incision. I've never tried it on another person, and I've only done one harvest by myself."

"You will succeed!"

"Alright, but there's one other thing. After your first harvest, did your body drive you to do another one?"

"I read your immediate drive description but experienced no such pull the first time I performed the procedure."

"I think it will happen this time because this improved procedure is more effective. But, I'm not sure. Anyway, I wanted to warn you."

"Thank you."

Quan made a dismissive gesture, stood, and made a telephone call. Then, he sat back down, sipped tea, lit the soldering iron, and clearly did not desire conversation.

Eight minutes later, the same two men came into the room with a bruised adult male in restraints. He looked enraged, and his powerful arms had many ghoulish tattoos. They strapped him to the stainless-steel table, face up. The two men glared at me hard for eight seconds and left.

Quan began yelling at the man, and his words threw the man into a rage. With surprising agility, he stood and burned the man with the soldering iron. The disgusting smoke in this confined room made me want to vomit. The taunting and burning went on for seven repulsive minutes. Meanwhile, I desperately wanted to cover my ears.

"Enough?" Quan casually asked.

I nodded vigorously. Without hesitation, Quan struck the man in the temple with a thin hammer. It looked smaller than the one I described in my book, and I could not believe that Quan had gone to the effort to fabricate this tool.

As I looked at the blood dripping off the hammer, I realized that another person had died. At that moment, I wondered if I would ever escape the merciless killing that surrounded the harvest. Quan began undoing my restraints.

"Just as the woman who called herself Grace admonished you," he cautioned. "Do not attempt an assault on my person. You are not fast enough!"

I looked at Quan in terror and did my best to eagerly nod. He undid the restraints, and I flipped the man over. The sound of his labored breathing reminded me that he was still alive.

Quan turned to me with an encouraging gesture, and I looked at the tray's surgical instruments. He moved to the other side of the table to get a better view and made the same encouraging gesture. I selected a medium-sized scalpel and studied the man's muscles. When I found the correct location, I cut into him and retrieved the pancreas with two snips from surgical scissors. Quan handed me a white teacup, and I placed the pancreas inside. Next, I removed the adrenal gland with two snips, and then sniped away a kidney section.

"Your technique is fast," Quan commented. "I'm impressed with what I'm seeing. Ahh, sasha, sasha."

Quan made additional notes, and I looked at him solemnly. Then, he nodded, selected a chisel-shaped knife, and turned to me with a stony expression. "This man is a criminal who preys on the elderly," he said. "The people of China will sleep better tonight."

Quan thrust the blade into the base of the man's skull and turned to me with a wicked grin. I again feared for my safety and did my best to nod approval.

I took fifteen seconds to compose myself, selected a fresh pair of surgical scissors, and worked on the adrenal gland and kidney to remove the unnecessary bits. Then, using two bamboo sticks, I extracted their liquid. Quan surprised me by expertly milking a cobra. He pointed to several jars of mint oil, and I selected the brand I had used before. When I mixed everything, the color looked correct.

"The next step?" Quan wanted to know.

"I need to place the pancreas inside you," I answered with hesitation.

"Proceed."

I had Quan sit backward in the same chair his men restrained me in. I then selected a scalpel. "Wait, I cannot see," Quan interrupted. "Hand me that mirror."

I handed Quan the mirror and cautioned, "This will hurt."

"I am familiar with pain. Do it now!"

Quan pulled up his pant leg to reveal many scars and healing incisions. One bandage looked recently applied, and I opened it to see two neat sutures. I cut them away to reveal a bloody infected mass. With little effort, I removed it, cleaned the wound, and applied Quan's antiseptic. Satisfied, I put in two sutures and a fresh bandage.

My attention turned to his right shoulder, and I had to remove three bandages to get an unrestricted view. It took some probing with my fingers to identify what I thought to be the correct location. After taking a deep breath to reassure myself, I made a deep cut, and blood gushed out. A gauze pad allowed me to slow the blood flow and move the muscles. As I peered inside, I realized that I had made the incision in the wrong location.

Quan saw my disapproval and commanded, "Again!"

I probed inside the incision with tweezers to better understand Quan's anatomy. It became apparent that the incision needed to be 10 millimeters higher, 20 millimeters to the left, and deeper. I cut in the new location, and more blood gushed out.

To my surprise, Quan did not react. Instead, he handed me a penlight, and I explored this new incision. Fortunately, I had done a better job and only needed to deepen the cut. Using the mirror, Quan studied the incision with great intensity while I held it open. He then noticed my smile and pointed to the teacups. I mixed the extracts into a single teacup, and the consistency looked correct.

Carefully, I placed the pancreas inside, applied the extract, and sutured both incisions. After cleaning the area with alcohol, I applied Quan's antiseptic and two bandages.

"It's done?" Quan asked with surprise.

"I recognized the muscles, and it looks like I put the pancreas in the right place."

"You know this for a fact?"

"No."

"What's next?" Quan asked.

"If everything goes the way I think it will, tonight, you will feel awful while your body repairs itself. Then, in fifteen to eighteen hours, I think your body will urge your mind to harvest."

Quan nodded, tried to stand up, and sat down.

"Yeah, you'll be weak until after you do another harvest," I commented. "Eat some easy-to-digest food, drink lots of tea, and then try to get some sleep."

"There is nothing else?"

"Nope."

Quan looked dreadful, and it reminded me of my first harvest. It dawned on me that his frail body might not withstand this new harvest method. He pressed a button, and three assistants came in to help him stand. I watched them leave, and two men in suits appeared. "Hi, guys," I cheerfully spoke. "Now what?"

SEVEN

T he guards crossed their arms, and I confidently walked past them. It took five minutes to locate a tastefully decorated study room filled with more exquisite artwork. One wall contained an ornately carved bookshelf, and I thumbed through three books. Twelve minutes later, reading did not seem satisfying. "I would like a tour of the garden," I told the left guard.

They looked at each other, and one of them pointed toward a door that led outside. Up close, the garden was even more impressive than I imagined. Every flower looked perfect, and they impeccably pruned each tree branch. I saw ten gardeners in my immediate vicinity hard at work. The guards followed ten paces behind me.

Forty-nine minutes later, I sat on a wooden bench overlooking a small waterfall. They had crafted the structure from cut blue rocks arranged in a seascape pattern. As I enjoyed the view, two servants appeared carrying silver trays. One tray contained an elaborately decorated plate, napkin, and gold chopsticks, while the other had two black lacquered bowls. The first bowl held chicken with egg noodles, and the second had wafer-thin beef with vegetables and rice in a ginger crème sauce.

My lunch tasted fantastic, and as I ate, one servant poured me a tall glass of green tea with honey. The taste reminded me of Grace's drink, shuduka. When I finished, the other servant produced a small tray of pastries.

Seven minutes later, I continued my self-guided garden tour and eventually returned to the main house. Inside, I explored the many tastefully decorated rooms with the guards three paces behind. Eight minutes later, I located a different study room and after thumbing through many books, I selected a Chinese art book.

At 5:30 p.m., I made an eating motion, and the guards led me to the same dining room. Three waitresses served me a fantastic seven-course meal, and the cucumber salad stood out as superb. After taking a bath, I sat in bed and typed up the day's events while wondering what would happen the next day.

In the middle of the night, somebody shook me awake. I opened my eyes, and two security guards looked at me with angry expressions. They hastily led me along many hallways to a grand room. Inside, I saw a bed big enough to park two cars. Six people stood around Quan as he tossed from side to side in agony. I recognized his harvest experience. "Wow, you look awful," I said, repressing a laugh.

"I cannot sleep," Quan shrieked. "What's happening to me?! Help me! Please!"

"I'm not completely sure what's going on. My only advice is to let everything take its course."

"If this doesn't work, I left orders for my men to kill you!" Quan threatened.

"Yeah, you already made that clear. A man of your age should know that you can attract more flies with honey than with vinegar."

"You must make this stop!" Quan demanded.

"The procedure needs to go through its paces. I'll check back in with you in an hour or two. In the meantime, try to relax."

When I turned to leave, the two guards stood in my way. I looked at them, turned to Quan, turned back, and confidently walked around them. As I headed down the hallway, they followed three paces behind me. Before I closed the bedroom door, I said, "Wake me in two hours. Sound good?"

The guards seemed annoyed and did not answer. So I went back to bed, and 58 minutes later, somebody shook me awake. I opened my eyes to see one guard. "Another hour," I told him in a sleepy voice.

They looked angry and walked away in a huff. I went back to bed, and 52 minutes later, somebody shook me awake. I had enough sense not to push my luck, got dressed, and the guards led me away.

When we came to Quan's bedroom, I noticed a dramatic change. He now sat up, stared at the door with great focus, and did not detect my presence. "Your body is almost ready," I said. "Probably less than two hours. Do you want me to remain here?"

Quan continued to stare, and I took his silence to mean no. "Do you two have names?" I asked the guards.

They stared at me. "All right, fine," I said with a huff. "This is what will happen. At some point, Quan is going to get out of bed. When he does, have somebody help him to the room with the operating table. Sound good?" The right guard nodded. "All right. We can communicate. Well, since I'm awake, I'm going to type up some notes."

The guards stared at me with disdain, and I walked by them. Again they followed me as I returned to my room and got my laptop. We then walked to the room where Quan and I first met. The lights were off, and I asked them to turn them on. The guards looked at me with annoyed expressions. I searched for a light switch and eventually found one. Three hours later, the sun rose, and one guard motioned for me to stand.

We walked to the room with the stainless steel table, and I saw Quan looking miserable. Two people were holding him, and I pointed at the chair. They gingerly helped him to sit, and Quan stared at me with a focused expression. "I can see it in your eyes; you're ready," I said with a nod. "Do you have a bad guy lined up?"

Quan only stared, and I continued. "Well, you will need one because I cannot help with that part."

Quan absently made a telephone call, and the same two enormous men brought in a disheveled woman. Her hands were bound, she shouted angry Chinese words, and the guards struggled to contain her. When our eyes met, I knew she led a despicable life and inflicted pain upon everybody she came across.

The men forcibly restrained the woman to the table, face up, and she continued to yell what I perceived were Chinese obscenities.

"Are you going to let the two security apes watch?" I asked in a friendly voice.

Quan looked at me in rage-filled defiance and motioned them away. As they left, I wondered how much English they understood and if they knew the term "apes." *Probably should not have used that word.*

Quan pointed toward the woman in anger.

"You want me to do it?" I asked. "No, no, no. I have killed too many people already. Do your own dirty work."

"You will do as I command!"

"I showed you the procedure. Let's go!"

While my refusal had made Quan spitting nails angry, he could not do a thing about it. Yet, the little voice in my head screamed repeatedly, "There will be consequences!"

Quan lifted his arm, I helped him stand, and he hobbled over to the bench. He lit the Swiss soldering iron and savagely burned the woman. She swore up a storm, and I held my ears while they traded insults.

When the woman achieved unbridled anger, Quan grasped the same hammer described in my book and struck her in the temple. This callous act disgusted me, and I watched her eyes change from rage to absent fluttering. I helped Quan undo the restraints, flip the woman over, and he expertly extracted her organs.

A minute later, Quan did not hesitate to push the square blade into the base of her skull. He turned to me with that same thin, wicked smile which again sent a chill up my spine. Quan then rapidly prepared the solution and the pancreas.

Quan sat down in the chair, and I held a mirror to help him view the incision. His dexterity surprised me as he quickly snipped away the sutures. Next, Quan extracted the old pancreas and threw it on a tray. It looked dark brown, and an unfamiliar yellow liquid oozed out. I did my best to hide my uncertainty.

Quan pointed to the cups, and I brought over the donor pancreas. He expertly inserted it, applied the solution and three sutures. I then applied the antiseptic and a bandage. The entire procedure had taken less than eight minutes, and Quan looked exhausted. "Your body needs rest," I said in an encouraging voice. "When you awaken, you will feel like a million bucks. Um. Well, for you, a billion."

Quan smiled weakly, and I left the room. The guards were waiting outside and followed me as I walked to the dining room. I ate a tasty poached egg and grilled chicken breakfast while dwelling on recent events. For the rest of the day, I typed, explored, and read. That evening, I went to sleep early and woke up late the next morning. After a delicious roasted ginger pork breakfast, I found another room filled with priceless artwork and read an English illustrated book about 4th-century Chinese history.

At noon, I returned to the dining room, and the servants did not want to serve me. I suspected that Quan was going to join me. Six minutes later, he walked in unassisted and sat across from me with a pleasant expression. Quan looked much healthier and nodded slightly.

Four servants immediately served us lunch on gold platters. Quan began eating with his hands. He took large bites, chewed with an open mouth, belched loudly, and drank big gulps of black tea. I ate like a gentleman while enjoying the exquisite taste of orange-rosemary roasted duck. When the moment seemed appropriate, I said, "Your appetite returned with gusto and your skin looks better."

Quan flashed an annoyed smile and tore off a large piece of duck with his hand.

"How do you feel?" I asked.

"Fine," Quan answered with a dismissive gesture.

"Did your urine smell bad?"

"Ahh, sasha, sasha. The worst ever."

"The smell means the process worked."

"Good."

"It will take your body a few days to adjust," I said in an encouraging voice.

"The procedure you have shown me will last for six months?"

"It's supposed to. With you? Honestly, I don't know. You've done thousands of your versions of the harvest. And I'm not sure how this new procedure will affect you. If I were to guess, I would say two."

"All right."

"What will happen to me?" I asked with hope.

"To what are you referring?"

"Am I free to leave?"

Quan looked at me with a displeased expression, and he returned to eating. He finished eleven minutes later, threw down his napkin, glared at me, and left unassisted.

For the rest of the day, I wandered around the compound with two guards following. They refused to tell me their names, so I called the taller one Bill and the other Ted from the movie *Bill and Ted's Excellent Adventure.* They did not get the reference.

That night, the chef prepared egg noodles right at the table. I made a point of letting her know how much I enjoyed the meal. Afterward, I asked Ted if the house had a television, and he refused to answer.

I washed up and went to bed while thinking about my situation. Quan clearly would not allow me to leave because my harvest knowledge made me too great a liability. However, he had not jailed or killed me. It then occurred to me that Quan was keeping me alive in case the harvest process did not work.

This situation left me with two choices. I could either make the best of my time left or try to escape. I stood, and three armed guards looked up at me when I opened the drapes. Escape clearly would not be possible, and I fell asleep, attempting to figure out a third option.

The following day, I woke up early and got dressed.

"Here is my plan for today," I said to Ted. "This place has horses and a riding area. I have never ridden a horse, and it is high-time to learn. Also, there is a martial arts dojo. After lunch, I will give you two the chance to kick my ass. Sound good?"

They stared at me. "That's a yes," I continued.

After a scrumptious breakfast of thick egg noodles and rosemary salmon, we walked to the stable. I selected a beautiful horse, looked at Bill, and asked, "Where's the saddle?"

They stared at me with blank expressions. "Look, you two," I said with more force. "Either I try this myself and upset the horse, or you can get somebody to help."

Bill motioned, and two men appeared. They brought out a fine black saddle, showed me how to put it on, and helped me up. One man showed me how to guide the horse while the other led us around. For the next four hours, I learned how to ride a horse.

Wow, living here could be extraordinary, I thought.

I walked back to the house with a tender butt. For lunch, I ate a cheese and bacon omelet with fresh mangos and sweet sticky rice.

After letting my food settle for thirty minutes, we headed to the dojo. Once inside, Bill and Ted stared at me with vacant expressions. "Who wants the first punch?" I asked, while sticking out my chin.

They turned to each other with big grins, and this was the first time they seemed happy. Bill made a motion, and an older man entered the room dressed in a karategi outfit (thick white loose-fitting fabric). He held a supremely confident expression and instantly sized me up. I bowed for ten seconds while maintaining eye contact. Then, the man motioned toward a set of drawers, and I found a karategi outfit in my size. He pointed to a side room where I changed. Then, the man motioned to the center of the mat. I went to that spot and stood up straight.

The man flexed, and I positioned myself in a traditional karate stance. "Master," I said and then did a quick bow.

The man nodded and adjusted my arms to be in a better form. As he could not speak English, we went through a training routine in silence. After 35 minutes, the man switched me to the Wing Chun punch trainer (a padded wooden post with protruding sticks that simulate an opponent's arms) for 23 minutes. Occasionally, he corrected my form and taught me two new moves. We then went through a fascinating sparring match where he expertly demonstrated the new moves. After the session, I felt exhausted. The man nodded, and I bowed for 20 seconds. He gave me a thin smile and walked away.

The guards and I headed back to my bedroom, and I took a long hot bath. My muscles ached, and the water felt good.

At dinner, they served me ginger smoked pork over steamed wild rice. Afterward, I wanted to watch television, but instead we went to a study room and I selected a book about modern art. Bill and Ted seemed increasingly annoyed at having to follow me around. When I looked out the window, the sun was setting, and I took a stroll in the garden. A beautiful stone bench seemed appealing, and I sat and contemplated the moment while looking at the peaceful flowers in the dim light. Bill and Ted watched me in silence from ten feet away, and I wondered what they did while I slept and how many suits they owned.

Somehow, Quan crept up behind me and joined me at the bench. I knew enough not to speak, and we stared at the perfect plants for eleven minutes. "Do you know how long it has been since I've taken a stroll in my garden?" Quan asked in a pleasant voice.

"No, sir."

"Ahh, sasha, sasha. It was when your country became embroiled in its independence war."

"Wow. That's a long time. How are you feeling?"

"I am feeling well and considering bedding a woman this evening. My wretched body has prevented me from enjoying the pleasures of the flesh for so very long."

I did not know how to react to this statement and went with a neutral response. "That sounds good."

Quan turned to me with a curious expression. "Xiang informed me of your desire to ride a horse," he said with interest. "Most amusing."

"It was a captivating experience. Thank you for allowing me the use of your stable."

Quan nodded and motioned with his hand in a grand gesture. "This is nice," he said in a pleasant voice.

"I'm enjoying the evening air. The warm weather is perfect, and the flowers smell delightful."

"Master Liang confirmed your martial arts skill," Quan said with a slight smile.

"If I may correct your statement. Master Liang has exceptional skills, and I'm grateful that my clumsiness didn't upset him."

Quan and I laughed for seventeen seconds, and he turned to me. I noticed his scars were fading, and his skin looked much better. He had combed his hair, and his expression held more life.

"Ahh, sasha, sasha. You had asked me what I intended to do with you," Quan said in an amused voice. "What are your thoughts on this matter?"

My harvest abilities allowed me to make magnificent observations and sound decisions. This improved intuition led me to believe that I needed to directly answer Quan's question with great care.

"I would like to thank you for your hospitality," I said in a pleasant voice. Quan nodded, and I continued. "I've had some time to think about my situation, and I understand my place. Simply stated, I know too much about you. That makes me a big liability, and it would be a mistake for you to allow me to leave this wonderful estate."

Quan seemed deep in thought, and I continued, "That leaves two options. There's the obvious choice where I would end up on the harvest table. The other option is be your assistant. This choice has many benefits. For example, I can act as your aide during the procedure. This arrangement would allow us to harvest together and come up with improvements. Plus, you would be free to discuss your history and other topics you dare not share with others. Also, I am an outsider who could provide honest opinions from a different viewpoint. And, finally. I know the harvest secret. This knowledge means I will not accidentally uncover it or try to steal it. In time, I could become a trusted individual."

I looked at Quan. He seemed intrigued by my honesty and leaned back for six minutes. It was so quiet I could hear Quan breathing. As the evening light faded, two women arrived with red paper lanterns. We watched the plants come alive in the flickering light, making the experience feel less dangerous. As we sat in serenity, the air changed, and I smelled the faint scent of honey.

Quan made a "hmm" sound. "Your book came as a surprise," he said in a reserved voice. "At first, I considered it a work of fiction and concluded that you had stumbled upon half-truths. When I focused on the specific historical facts, they confirmed your work. As a result, I sent teams of men to bring you to me. Unfortunately, the customs paperwork took excessive time, and my men failed to capture you in America.

"Then, to my amazement, my men located the apple tree that belonged to the woman you call Grace. Ahh, sasha, sasha.

I ordered them to wait until this woman revealed herself. Instead, my men brought you. And now you sit beside me."

Quan seemed to contemplate the moment, and I knew to remain silent. Seventy-seven seconds later, he continued. "You are an enigma. You comprehend the nature of your position, yet you speak freely. Most unusual. Hmm. Last night, I decided you no longer serve a purpose. Your logic is correct; you stand before me as a great liability."

Quan gently placed his hand on my leg and continued in a soft voice, "When you announced you wished to learn to ride a horse and further your knowledge of self-defense, I found this intriguing. A person in your position should have tried to escape or plead for mercy."

Quan turned away and took a sip of tea. My senses were heightened, yet, I did not know where the tea came from. This action reminded me of the mysterious way that Grace behaved. He took a long breath, held it for a moment, and let it out slowly.

I gulped loudly, and Quan continued, "You accepted your fate with dignity and offered me a unique option. In all my years, I have never uttered a word about the procedure. Even my most trusted servants are unaware. As a precaution, I have killed many who might know too much. And now there is you, a person who knows my deepest secret. Ahh, sasha, sasha."

Quan leaned back for 33 seconds while probing me with his eyes. I hoped he would see my value and did my best to remain pleasant.

"I like the prospect of discussing the procedure without consequences and devising improvements," Quan continued.

"Ahh, sasha, sasha. This prospect makes sense. An assistant would be useful. And, you will explain the method by which you received mental images from the Heathcliff animal as you described in your book."

Quan sipped the rest of his tea, set the cup down, and stood with ease. He turned to his garden and fixated on a blooming plant with thin leaves that appeared to dance in the red light. Thirteen seconds later, he turned to me and said in a menacing voice, "I will try this arrangement—for now. There is much for you to learn. You will start by mastering the Chinese language. From now on, you will work harder than you ever have. Never disappoint me! This warning is your last!"

After Quan's commands, he smiled slightly and blissfully walked away. I noticed him touching plants and bending down to smell flowers. The two women retrieved their red lanterns and followed him at a distance.

The wave of fear lifted, and I took a deep breath. However, I felt like somebody saved me from a burning house by throwing me into a tiger pit. Bill and Ted walked over.

"Now what?" I asked. They looked at each other, and Ted motioned me forward. His demeanor changed, and I understood that I no longer had my privileged status. We began walking, and they led me to a nondescript building with long dreary hallways. Finally, we stopped in front of a door, and they opened it. Inside the small room, I saw my backpack and a thin bedroll.

As I wondered what to do next, Bill said in accented English, "The washroom is down the hall. Your day begins at 5:00."

His statement caught me off guard. I nodded, and Bill made a stern facial expression. Then, he tightly pivoted and walked away. I wondered if he had overheard my conversation with Quan and then recalled I had referred to them as "apes."

I opened my backpack to see that they had taken out my tent and other items. Fortunately, they left my laptop with the charger, shaving kit, and notebook. I walked down the hall and found a small, grubby bathroom. Inside, I looked at a tiny, well-used bathtub. It was difficult to bathe, and the water had a strong sulfur smell.

After my bath, I returned to my room smelling like rotten eggs and noticed somebody had put a small sign next to my door with "James" neatly printed along with Chinese characters. It then dawned on me that my new home might be this tiny room for the rest of my life. This thought depressed me, yet being alive brought relief.

With my watch alarm set for 5:00 a.m., I got under the thin gray blanket while thinking about my situation. From now on, my every action would be under Quan's thorough scrutiny. Plus, I would have to figure out how to share mental images with him. I fell asleep, shivering from the cold with troubled thoughts.

EIGHT

My beeping watch woke me up. I got dressed in the suit I had worn the previous evening and opened the door to see Ted glaring at me. "Not like that!" he yelled. He then tossed me a pile of grubby tan work clothes and left in a huff. After changing into scratchy, well-worn overalls, I realized by his accent that Ted also knew English.

In the hallway, the workers were all walking to the left, and I followed them. They wore the same tan outfits, and when combined with their dreary mood, this made for a depressing scene.

Eventually, we came to a large dining room, and the people sat down at long tables. Two people entered with blue plastic buckets, and they served us overcooked rice and runny eggs. This image reminded me of prison movies because the dirty plates had bits of food from the last meal. A thin man with black square glasses stood on a chair and spoke in Chinese for eight minutes. At one point, I recognized my name, and everybody looked at me with mixed expressions.

When the speech concluded, the people clapped unenthusiastically, and we ate. The food tasted bland; however, my chopstick skills provided some comedy to those around me. Afterward, a man handed me a piece of paper with my name on top. I noticed a large number six in the upper right. When I asked him what the writing meant, he walked away.

The woman next to me pointed to the paper, then to a door, and motioned for me to follow. Two more joined us, and the four of us walked down a dreary corridor to another building with a small classroom. I sat behind a tiny, well-used desk and noticed a beat-up picture-tube television. Five more people came in, and a young man put a VHS tape into an antiquated player.

After the television had warmed up, a woman appeared and began speaking rapid Chinese. Unfortunately, the low-quality image had excessive blue, and the sound hissed. Everybody looked around in boredom, and I wondered what the lesson would be.

The class perked up when the woman said in a high-pitched voice, "I best-ee English professor. You learn from me English good-lee. Begin."

The woman spoke fast Chinese, followed by, "I businessman in hat."

"I businessman in hat," the assembled people droned.

It suddenly dawned on me that I was in an English class. I found the situation comical but understood the need to learn

Chinese. So, I tried my best to repeat the woman's Chinese sentences. Unfortunately, my poor attempts to speak Chinese upset the class, and they got even more upset when I did not repeat the English words. The man sitting beside me poked me in the ribs six sentences later, and I repeated her comical English sentences. However, I repeated them with correct pronunciation and grammar, which further upset the class. *You know, I understand English? This situation is crazy!* I thought.

As I looked at the off-color image and repeated the poor English, I noticed a bookshelf. I walked over to see many well-used books, and after leafing through a few, I found a children's Chinese to English book with pictures. As I read, an older woman stopped the tape, pointed to me, and then my chair. I grinned sheepishly, sat in my chair, and she pressed play.

As I absently babbled improper English phrases, I leafed through the book. Chinese differs substantially from English, but I began understanding the basics. "Hello" sounds like "nee-how" and "cat" sounds like "mao."

Sixty minutes later, the tape ended, and everyone stood. I showed a paper with my schedule to the woman next to me. She turned to the man next to her, and they began an angry diatribe that included the name "James" many times. Finally, he walked over to me, said an angry word, looked at the paper with my schedule, and motioned for me to follow.

I followed him to an area with fifteen gardeners milling about. They did not seem happy to see me. Finally, a muscular six-foot-one man walked up to me, yanked my schedule out of my hand, and studied it. He then began pacing in front of me while lecturing and pointing dramatically. Of course, I did not know what he was saying, which infuriated him. Finally, he halted and asked me what seemed to be a grave question. I smiled and put up my hands to show, "I do not know."

My pleasant attitude infuriated the man, and he angrily pointed to the wooden wheelbarrow with a shovel next to it. I walked over to it, and two men went to their wheelbarrows. Together, we traveled along a long windy path to the stable and then shoveled horse manure into the wheelbarrows. When the wheelbarrows were full, we took them to a compost pile. Along the way, the men whispered to each other. Judging by their tone, I suspected they were complaining. Occasionally they discreetly glanced at me, almost as though they were looking for a reaction.

We loaded horse manure for the next three hours, and I found the experience enjoyable—a significant change from working behind a computer screen.

When we had removed all the manure, we returned to our wheelbarrows. It was then lunchtime, and in the dining room, they served us watery chicken soup with mushy brown rice from the same blue buckets we had eaten from at breakfast. This time, my plate did not have leftover bits of food on it from the previous meals. Afterward, a different man stood on a chair and spoke for eleven minutes. I did my best to look interested and nodded at anyone who looked in my direction. Toward the end, I recognized my name and everybody looked at me. I smiled, which angered three people near me.

When lunch ended, I showed my schedule to the man next to me. He looked at the paper, became upset, pointed to the number six, and yelled angrily. Next, another man motioned to me to follow, leading me to a room full of woodworking tools.

The shop supervisor greeted me with a bow, and I helped him cut wood for two hours. Afterward, he shook my hand warmly. Next, I showed him my schedule, and he walked me to the dojo and again shook my hand. His kindness gave me hope my situation could improve.

Master Liang greeted me along with seven other people who had been stretching. I walked toward the drawer where I had previously picked up my karategi outfit. Master Liang grunted and pointed to a different drawer. Inside, I found several well-worn karategi outfits. I changed in the side room, and we began practicing basic stances for ten minutes. Then, Master Liang gave the signal, and we started sparring.

My partner turned out to be a student from my English class, and he kept punching me in the kidney while yelling "liu." I still did not know what I had done to upset him or what "liu" meant.

Fortunately, the student's insolence did not go over well with Master Liang, and he directed the student to behave respectfully. We switched to Wing Chun punch six minutes later, and then Master Liang demonstrated a standard downward blocking technique. The class perfected this move for eighteen minutes while Master Liang observed and corrected us.

When our session concluded, I bowed to Master Liang. He seemed impressed with my attitude and nodded. However, I noticed the others looked upset that Master Liang did not nod at them. Afterward, I changed back into my work clothes, and a different person led me to the dining room.

They served us a small portion of dried fish in heavy oyster sauce over rice. The taste was far too salty, and I ate little, but everybody else gobbled down their meals with big smiles. After dinner, a woman stood on a chair and talked for twelve minutes. People listened with intense expressions and clapped warmly when she finished.

Afterward, we had free time, and I took a much-needed bath. The manure smell was difficult to remove, and it took a lot of scrubbing to get my body clean. I also washed my work clothes because I noticed other people had their clothes out to dry. Unfortunately, somebody had taken away my nice suit.

For the rest of the evening, I sat in the corner of my room and typed into my laptop. As I reviewed my words, the reality of my new situation settled in. I had become the humble servant of a madman. However, I appreciated the limited benefits of my captive life. Already, a few people accepted me, and I would learn new skills, including the Chinese language. I resolved to make the best of the situation.

At 8:15 p.m., I got ready for bed. Somebody softly knocked on my door and opened it (there were no locks). An attractive, middle-aged woman walked in. She wore a low-cut shirt, tight slacks, and white high heels. The woman closed the door behind her while looking at me with fondness.

"Hello," I said, not understanding why this woman was in my room.

The woman started to take off her shirt.

"What the heck are you doing, lady?!" I yelled.

She looked at me in confusion, reached into her purse, pulled out a tiny book, and searched through it. "You six," she translated. "You one sex week."

What the heck? I thought, and then motioned to her book. She gave it to me, and I located the English section. "Why you do this?" I translated.

She took the book back and translated, "Job."

Wow! A prostitute, I thought in surprise, because I had never met one. Without further ado, the woman caressed my chest in a playful swirling pattern. Her matter-of-fact actions made me uncomfortable, and I shook my head. The woman gave me a coy smile and translated, "You like boy?"

I laughed, which confused her, and translated a lie. "Girlfriend in America."

The woman touched my arm with a smile, nodded, and translated, "Let know when change mind."

The woman left my room, and it then dawned on me that I should have asked her where to get a translation book.

As I lay down, I thought about the encounter and understood that being a "liu" provided certain privileges, including a weekly prostitute visit. When I was a teenager, I dreamed about paying for sex, but my morals have since changed, and this perk held little value. I set my watch alarm for 5:00 a.m. and instantly fell asleep.

❖ ❖ ❖

A thunderous explosion broke my tranquil rest. The force threw my body upward, and I crashed down onto the wooden floor. Instinct took over, and I covered my ears and closed my eyes tightly while waiting for something awful to happen. Eight seconds later, I opened an eye and looked around to see a dark room. It suddenly occurred to me I was now in great danger.

It took eleven seconds to get dressed in my damp work clothing, and I pulled open the door to see Bill's angry face in the dim light. "You!" he yelled. "Stay here!"

Bill ran to my left as people ran past each other, including a naked man. Suddenly, another explosion shattered the chaos. The ground shook, which made me lose my balance. I fell hard to the right and hit my head.

I jumped up and put on my shoes. Sensing impending disaster, I then crammed my notebook and laptop into my backpack. Without thinking, I defied Bill's stern order and began running faster than ever. Because the hallways had only a slight amount of light, I crashed into objects and people. Finally, after bursting through three doors, I found myself outside.

The dead of the night appeared as bright as day. I looked up to see four massive red flares on giant parachutes sending out harsh monochromatic light.

On my left, I saw the remains of the main house going up in flames. I briefly thought about all the fantastic artwork and rare books being destroyed.

On my right, I saw small fires, smoke, and people running around in confusion. There were large pieces of smoldering debris everywhere.

Suddenly, a naked man ran toward a wood pile with a naked woman running after him. I recognized the man as Ted and the woman as the prostitute. In that tumultuous moment, I had to chuckle.

The sound of a jet aircraft shrieking past scared me out of my mind, and I threw myself on the ground, expecting a bomb to drop. After five seconds of nothing happening, the shock of hitting the ground forced me to come up with a plan. I would go to the stables and make my getaway on a horse.

It took only 46 seconds to run to the stable, which was probably a personal record. When I opened an outer door, a horse rushed past me, and I fell backward. When I jumped up and ran to the nearest stall, I saw a black horse. He looked at me with wide eyes, and I opened the door. As I led him outside, he trembled, and I realized I was trembling too. Like a flash, I jumped onto the horse and landed perfectly on its back. This was an incredible feat of coordination because the horse did not have a saddle. Plus, I'd had my first horse ride the day before, and I wore a backpack. The horse bucked me off, and I fell with a big thud. As I looked up, I watched the horse running away to my right. It then occurred to me I should have been gentler.

I selected another horse and recognized him as the same horse I had ridden earlier. He seemed to remember me when our eyes met. As I led him out, I spoke calmly and rubbed his neck. When we got outside, I carefully climbed on his back.

The horse had no reins and instinctively trotted away to our left. It then occurred to me that I did not know which direction would lead us to safety. I heard nearby gunfire, and suddenly, a massive explosion boomed behind us. When I turned around, I saw the dilapidated building I briefly called home erupt upwards into an enormous fireball. Debris began raining down around us. The sudden noise made the horse charge through the trees, and branches began hitting and scratching every part of my exposed body. I did my best to shield my face by leaning forward, which caused the branches to smack me on the top of my head.

As the horse ran with me on his back, a deafening "Dunt-dunt-dunt-dunt-dunt" sound came from the ground our left, followed by a loud "Brrrrrrrrr-rip" in the air. I turned to see miniature explosions followed by plumes of dust. A fighter jet had fired its massive machine gun. *That was so cool!* I thought.

The horse had been going at maximum speed before the machine-gun fire. After the firing sounds, he found a hidden source of energy and charged even faster. We dodged people, flew through bushes, and leaped over hedge walls. These leaps terrified me because I did not know what would be on the other side.

We came to a massive steel wall, and the horse began running parallel with it. Twelve seconds later, we came to a bend where somebody had torn down the wall. The bright light allowed me to see a line of soldiers running through the gap. I held onto my horse's neck for dear life and tried to guide him in the other direction. Unfortunately, he did not follow my gesture, and we charged forward. A few soldiers noticed our rapid approach and raised their weapons. A burst of aircraft machine-gun fire then hit right behind us, and dirt flew everywhere.

As if we weren't already flying through obstacles, the horse found an even deeper energy source and began charging right through the soldiers, sending them flying sideways from the impact of his massive legs. Before I knew it, he leaped through the gap in the wall.

We landed hard, and I saw several soldiers waiting to advance. White light from a flashlight briefly illuminated the area, and I saw soldiers with blue patches on their uniforms.

The horse plowed right through the soldiers, and they went flying from his kicks. Then, I singled out an upside-down flying man. He had a thick brown mustache and a cross tattoo on the back of his hand. This soldier looked utterly shocked when our eyes met.

We bolted through a field, over hedges, and then traveled along a narrow walking path. Fortunately, the stars provided enough light to see the ground. A dirt road appeared, and the horse instinctively ran down the center. His breaths were deep, and each one sent a massive wave of moisture that engulfed me. Behind us, I heard another enormous explosion, followed by several bursts of aircraft machine-gun fire.

After eight minutes, I sensed that the danger had passed and began repeating, "Whoa, horse" to calm him down. After 92 seconds, he slowed down to a trot and, 27 seconds later, he dramatically stopped. I took this as a sign to dismount and eased myself off. As I rubbed his neck, our eyes again met, and I said, "Good job, horse." I swear on my life that he looked at me with an expression that meant, "You too, big guy!" We instantly bonded.

Together we walked slowly, side by side, and 68 minutes later, we came across a farm. I led the horse to a giant water barrel, and he began drinking noisily. This commotion awoke the people in the farmhouse, and an older man came out holding a wooden pitchfork with an angry expression. *Who still uses wooden pitchforks?* I thought, as a mother and three children stared at me with sleepy eyes.

It occurred to me that I should find out where we were. "How far is it to town?" I asked in a pleasant voice. They looked at me in complete confusion, and I decided a more fundamental question would be better. "Road map?" They still looked confused. "Phone?"

I made the hand symbol for a telephone and pretended to talk. A young girl began rapidly speaking, and she ran into their house. She returned with an odd cell phone and proudly handed it to me. I pressed a button, and the display appeared in Chinese.

Who could I call? The local police? My roommates? My parents? The state department? Detective Camron? The thought of calling Detective Camron and telling him I survived a Chinese airstrike made me chuckle.

Out of my crazy side thoughts, I formed a plan to get myself into a better situation. Using a nearby stick, I drew a squiggly shape of China in the dirt. Next, I pointed to the squiggle and said, "China." I then put a dot in the center and pointed to the people. They followed my logic with great interest. I then made a shrinking motion with my hands and pointed to the cell phone. The girl understood my gestures, and she spoke to her parents while using the phone. Soon a map (in Chinese) appeared with a little blue dot. She handed me the phone with pride, and I zoomed around the map until I found the nearest town.

After showing the town to the family, I pointed at the nearby road in both directions. The girl excitedly pointed left with a big smile. I then pointed to my watch, and the older man put up three fingers. I smiled from ear to ear, and they returned my smile.

It was 4:21 a.m. *Well, I might as well ride into town.* I thought, then looked at my horse. He clearly did not have the energy to go anywhere. I motioned to the horse and then to the young girl. The people began speaking harshly with angry expressions. After realizing they misinterpreted my gesture as a trade, I shook my head while waving my hands. Then, I made a grand sweeping gesture from the horse to the young girl with a pushing motion and my best smile.

Suddenly, the girl's eyes lit up, and she hugged the horse's leg. Now, everybody started talking and touching me. At that moment, I deeply regretted not knowing the Chinese words for "You're welcome."

After two minutes, it seemed an appropriate time to leave, and I turned toward the road. The oldest woman tugged at my arm and rushed into the house. She returned with a grubby burlap bag and handed it to me with a toothless grin. I bowed several times, and a tear ran down her face, which left a big impression.

As I walked away, I watched the people gather around the horse. He looked at me with a stare I interpreted as, "What have you gotten me into?" It made me laugh out loud.

Half an hour later, the sun began rising on the lonely road, and I wondered how big the town would be. As I walked, I came up with an alternative plan. Quan's people had taken my wallet and phone, but I had the foresight to keep my passport in my sock. My only possessions were a cheap Casio watch and my old Sony laptop. My backpack had a shaving kit, my *Dawson's Creek* notebook, and a copy of *Grime: The Big Hate*. I decided to contact the US embassy, then contact my bank and convince them to send me money.

By 6:10 a.m., the dirt road had turned into a paved road, and the city had come into view. An hour later, I entered the outskirts of a medium-sized town. People stared at me as I walked, and I suspected they had never seen an American walking around their back streets. Especially one dressed in old Chinese work clothes.

Unfortunately, all the signs were in Chinese, and I did not know where to go. It seemed like a good idea to locate the local police station. However, as I searched for somebody to help me, the traffic became chaotic.

It occurred to me I needed a vantage point to locate a police station, and I found an office building under construction with an outside stairway. At the top, I spotted a building three blocks away that looked like a police station. To my left, I saw a big airport several miles away.

As my stomach grumbled, I opened the burlap bag to see a green leaf wrapped around brown rice and a steel drink can. The sticky brown rice with beef tasted terrific, but the tea flavored drink tasted harsh.

After a ten-minute rest, I climbed down and walked toward the police station. A green military truck pulled up while I was waiting to cross the street. Six soldiers leaped out with blue star patches on their green camouflage uniforms. I found it odd that they were Caucasian.

The soldiers approached the front door and got into a shouting match with a police officer. He put his hand on his gun, and the six men raised their rifles. The police officer raised his hands, and five soldiers pushed their way past the police officer while one soldier kept his gun pointed at the officer.

This scene made me uncomfortable, and I rapidly walked away. I decided that my best option would be to go to the airport and find somebody to contact my bank. My journey took me down sketchy alleys, across big streets with cars that did not stop for pedestrians at intersections, and through backyards. A vast airport came into view two hours later, but only two planes were at the gates. I suspected the other planes had all flown out for the day. Finally, after three wrong turns, I found the main entrance, and the air conditioning felt outstanding.

The airport had only one open ticket counter, and I waited in line. When my turn came, the woman did not understand English. Instead, she pointed to a chair, and I sat. Then, I thought about all that had happened that morning.

After ten minutes, I noticed a group of six twenty-year-olds looking at me with great interest. They would stare, whisper to each other, and then stare more. Their sly interaction continued for four minutes, and I finally said, "Hi." They looked astonished at being spoken to, and a girl giggled. "Hiya," she said in a shy voice.

I ignored them while thinking about how to convince the woman to contact somebody. The group continued to whisper and stare until a boy with a colorful manga shirt walked over to me and asked in a strong Chinese accent, "You are James?"

My jaw must have dropped so far that it hit the ground. "What?" I stammered.

The group became excited, and one girl asked, "*Grime?*"

"What? I mean, yes. I mean, I'm the author of that book."

They all grinned, surrounded me, and chattered with each other. "The Big Hate?" the boy with the manga shirt asked. "I love book! It favorite!"

At that very moment, you could have pushed me over with a feather. *This is so cool! They loved my book in China!* I thought with delight as they pounded me with Chinese questions. As an author of minor fame, people had recognized me in the past. Once, at Best Buy, somebody asked me for my autograph, which was one of the highlights of my life.

I took out my copy of *Grime: The Big Hate*. This action excited them beyond belief, and two of the girls started jumping. "Would you like me to autograph it?" I asked.

The boy with the manga shirt began moving to the side, and I thought he would faint. When I asked his name, he answered in Chinese. I realized I did not have a pen and turned to the ticket counter woman. She had been watching this event with great fascination, and walked over with a pen.

When the ticket counter woman saw my book, she became excited and pointed at me. As I took her pen, I remembered my book contract stipulated my *Grime* series would not be translated into other languages, and it was out of print. *I will be speaking with Bethany about this matter.*

The boy with the manga shirt wrote a Chinese name in my *Dawson's Creek* notebook. The group snickered at the sight. Then, on the back of the front cover of my book, I wrote, "To the biggest Grime fan in the world, (name written in Chinese characters)."

The other six people became excited, and they grabbed my notebook to write their names in it. Even the ticket counter woman joined it. I signed every one of their names, put my signature and the date. I handed my book to the boy with the manga shirt, and he held it as if it was made of gold. The others looked at him in astonishment.

"You? Immortal Woman Grace?" One girl asked. "You read? It last week. I start read!"

I thought the alternative title, "Immortal Woman Grace," sounded funny and answered. "Yes, I have a new book out. That's why I'm here."

In simple English with many gestures, I told the group about going to the apple tree, being kidnapped, and then escaping. The girl translated my words, and by this time, the group had swelled to over 25 people. When I told them about the airstrike, they all spoke at once.

"What is everybody saying?" I kept asking.

After 32 seconds of rapid Chinese discussions, the girl replied, "Near is plantation. Plantation is big. Plantation is long time. Boy have go there. No come back. Very secret. In today, morning, is big gun. Plantation is fire. Now is gun with men, looking people."

Her statement gave me a huge scare.

"Why you, airplane?" The girl asked.

"I'm trying to get home."

"America?"

"Yes."

"How fly?" The girl asked.

"I don't understand?"

"Government is security. Because is plantation. Only few airplane. None is, America, Japan, Europe. We is Switzerland ski. No us fly. Government no tell when next fly."

I did not know what to think about this information. However, I did not have money for a flight anyway.

"Where you fly?" The boy with the manga shirt asked.

"I'm trying to get home, but I lost my wallet. Hopefully, the airline will contact my bank."

"Father have money. I buy ticket."

This windfall stunned me, and I profusely thanked the boy several times while bowing. "Would you put me in book?" He asked.

Of course I will put your name in my next book, and here it is: Huang Bao of Nanchong, China. You are the best book fan ever! You and your dad ROCK!

Huang talked to the ticket agent and gave them his credit card. He then translated for the ticket agent, "You have choice: Panama, Havana, Qatar."

Panama seemed like the closest option to America, and I again thanked Huang several times. After exchanging contact information, it occurred to me I still needed interviews. "Do your friends have some time?" I asked. Of course, they did.

For my typical interview, I give my subject neutral facts about a local or national issue and then ask their opinion. I avoid topics that elicit an emotional response, such as abortion, religion, or political party preference.

Recently, I interviewed a schoolteacher for the *Portland Tribune* about the Terri Schiavo court case where the husband and family got into a disagreement over the right to die. I asked Huang his opinion, "If there is an accident and a married woman's brain can no longer function, which family member should choose when to end her life?"

Huang thought deeply about my question for 21 seconds and gave a well-thought-out answer involving the father and the husband having a private discussion. The result would be an amicable solution that mainly revolved around the father's wishes. I typed his response as he spoke (and people translated).

I then interviewed Huang's five friends on alternative energy, drinking age, best profession to pursue, greatest personal accomplishment, and my favorite topics: best beer to drink while watching a sports game.

Huang's friends provided outstanding Chinese viewpoints, and I rapidly typed my articles. Then, my computer found an unsecured Wi-Fi connection, and I emailed Lloyd. I gave my new friends Lloyd's email address, and they sent him the best photos from their phones.

Twelve seconds after emailing, the laptop battery died. I could not believe my luck. An hour later, I said goodbye and then got on my plane.

On my way to Panama without a single cent! I laughed out loud about this crazy thought and fell asleep.

NINE

The landing announcement woke me up, and seven minutes later, the plane touched down in Beijing. As we exited, security kept a watchful eye on all the passengers. As I was the only American on the flight, they gave me a harsh stare and closely inspected every page of my passport four times. When I walked to my connecting flight, I noticed planes leaving for Chicago, New York, and London. I asked at a nearby information booth about the "travel ban." The man was unaware of any policy, which came as a surprise. Twenty-two minutes later, I boarded the plane and headed for Panama.

On the flight, I tried to fall asleep, but the people sitting on either side of me kept talking to each other in Spanish. While I offered to switch seats *twice*, they seemed content to remain in their assigned seats. *Sometimes, it is difficult to figure people out,* I thought while reading the inflight magazine for the second time.

When the plane landed, I entered the crowded and humid airport. My plan was to go to the US embassy and have them contact my bank. At the customs booth, the officer asked me why I was visiting, and I answered. "I lost my credit card in China and a new friend bought me a ticket to Panama. I will only be here long enough to go to the American embassy to get a replacement credit card. Then I'm going to fly home."

He looked at me with a blank expression and announced, "You're a tourist. Next!"

I could not believe that this outlandish but true story did not even get a raised eyebrow. *Would he allow me an interview?* I thought, while attempting to leave the crowded airport.

People yelled for their rides at the passenger pickup area, and overloaded luggage carts were everywhere. I began asking random people, "Is anybody going to the US embassy?"

This tactic yielded only shaking heads, and after 37 minutes of crowd fighting, I spotted what appeared to be six American tourists. They had made it to the curb and were flagging down a cab. I needed to act fast if I wanted to ask their destination, so I pushed toward them.

Halfway there, three big guys with crew cuts blocked my path, and I could not convince them to get out of my way. Instead, they adopted angry stares and began using their bodies to herd me toward a van. I did not wish to be forced anywhere, so I squeezed around them and dodged a bunch of other passengers to get away. Simultaneously, an attractive woman put her luggage into a taxi and started to get in. The driver took off with screeching tires, and she ran after him. In the process, she crashed into me, and we both fell.

This woman was in her mid-twenties, had black hair with blond tips, and was dressed fashionably. She stood five-feet-four and had a trim build and flawless makeup. I helped the woman up and did my best to smile. She began yelling angrily in Spanish while pointing to where the cab had been. "Sorry," I said.

The woman looked at me in confusion. "You? American?" She asked in broken English.

"Yes."

"You see what car do? I so angry. I chase car. I no hit you. Father car no here."

"It looked like the taxi took off with your stuff."

"My ..."

She looked around and pointed to a woman's purse. "The taxi drove off with your purse?" I guessed. "It looks like the driver planned to rob you."

The woman spoke dramatically and made angry gestures toward the other cabs. As she did so, I noticed that the three big men had disappeared.

"My wallet and cell phone are in China," I said in frustration. "I'm trying to get to America."

The woman laughed. "You?" she asked. "No phone? No money? What do?"

"I'm trying to get somebody to drive me to the US embassy so I can get a credit card."

The woman thought for a moment, nodded, and made a coy expression. She reached into her bra and then produced a folded currency note. The woman smiled and said, "This little money. We take car to um—other family mother house. They pay car. Other family mother son drive you America house."

"Wow, you would do that? Thank you so much. That's very nice."

The woman grinned, and we walked toward a taxi. She rapidly spoke Spanish to the driver, and he yelled back in anger. The scene repeated with the following three taxis. Finally, the woman motioned to me at the fourth, and we jumped in.

The driver wore a sports themed shirt and smoked a thin cigar. He grabbed her money and recklessly sped away. The driver took us through all kinds of side streets and the wrong way on one-way streets. I tried to get a sense of direction while holding onto my backpack for dear life. "I Anna," the woman said as she looked at me with amusement. "What you?"

"James. Nice to meet you, Anna."

"What you do?"

I understood her English skills were lacking, and I used simple sentences. "I'm a writer. I write books. I write for a newspaper."

"You do good English."

"I try."

"I no good English. Father need better," Anna conceded.

"I understand you."

Anna smiled, batted her eyes, and said, "No long now. We go there."

Anna pointed to several beautiful houses in a secluded neighborhood. "Where do you work?" I asked.

Anna laughed and answered. "No work! I shop!" I laughed, and she continued. "Father is big ship company. Lot money."

"You're a lucky girl."

Anna grinned as we pulled up to a large house with a massive iron gate. They spoke in Spanish, and it was clear that the driver was upset. "You. Wait," she said while jumping out of the taxi to press a button on the gate. The taxi driver turned to me and spoke in a threatening tone while pointing his finger like a gun. I looked at him, smiled, and shrugged. From his annoyed expression, I gathered he did not appreciate my smile. The speaker beeped, Anna spoke in Spanish, and a male voice replied.

The gate opened, and Anna jumped back in. We drove up to the main entrance, and I started to get out. The taxi driver yelled at me and grabbed my arm. "You wait," Anna said, she walked toward the house.

A young man opened the front door, and they spoke to each other. He was wearing a nice blue suit with a thin black tie. The man confidently walked over to the taxi and handed the driver money. I got out and looked at the driver. He glared at me, yelled angrily, and then sped off with screeching tires.

"Hello," I said to the young man. He laughed and asked me in excellent English, "You let Anna make you a taxi hostage?"

Anna laughed, then I began laughing. Afterward, he shook my hand and said in a warm voice, "I'm Anna's cousin Evan."

"Ahh, she called you 'other family mother son.' My name is James Kimble. Nice to meet you, Evan."

"Wow, she needs to work on her English. 'Other family mother son?' That's funny."

"Well, her plan worked," I admitted.

"True. What brings you here?"

I explained my tale of researching a book in Russia, being kidnapped, the airstrike, making my way to Panama, and bumping into Anna.

"That's outrageous!" Evan exclaimed. "So that's why you are wearing those crazy clothes. And you don't have any money?"

"No money or credit cards. I'm hoping the US embassy can help."

"All they would do is call your bank. So why not use my phone?"

"Really? That's very nice of you," I said with great relief.

"It's the least I can do."

We walked inside Evan's beautiful house, and he handed me his cell phone. I found the 800 number for my credit card company using an internet search. After endless security questions, they agreed to send me a replacement card to Evan's address in two days.

When the call ended, I felt defeated because I did not want to impose on Evan to let me stay at his house. He had been following the one-sided credit card conversation and offered, "Hey, I got an idea. Anna needs to work on her English. Her father's house has a bunch of rooms. I bet he would let you stay in exchange for teaching her."

"Wow, that's an amazing idea. Anna, do you think your dad would allow me to be your teacher?"

"Evan right. I English help. Father want better. I call."

Anna used Evan's phone to speak to her father and nodded with a big smile.

"Both of you are so nice," I said. "Thank you so much."

"You are the one helping us. Anna needs an education miracle."

"Well, I'm sure we can come up with something. She has the basics down."

"What kinds of books have you written?"

"Well, I'm kind of the author of the *Grime* series. They were modestly popular."

"I do not know that title," Evan admitted.

"I understand. I recently published a book called *Interviewing Immortality*."

"I'm not familiar with that title either."

"It has only been on sale for a few months, so I'm not surprised."

"What is it about?"

"It's about the immortal woman who captured me and forced me to write her story."

"That sounds interesting. Hey, come to think of it, this reminds me of a book I downloaded last night. It's called *The 500-Year Interview*. I only read the first chapter, but I recommend you check it out."

"Really? I hope people do not confuse it with my work."

"Authors will always use similar concepts," Evan offered with a smile. "Consider it a compliment."

"True. Hey, can I get the book information to forward it to my publisher? Maybe they can take them to court or something."

Evan worked his phone, and a book came up in Spanish. As I could not understand the language, I clicked on the author icon and up popped my picture. *What the heck!* I thought. *Somebody in Panama downloaded my latest book in Spanish. How is that possible? Bethany, we are going to have a major conversation when I get back!*

"You write book?" Anna asked with great surprise.

"Yes, but something is wrong. The electronic version is not supposed to be available yet, and I never approved a Spanish translation. Plus, the title is all messed up. This is all wrong."

"My associate recommended this book to me," Evan commented.

"I hope you enjoy it."

"I read the summary. Is it true? Is that woman actually 500 years old?"

"Um, yes," I admitted.

"And that's why you traveled to Russia?" Evan wondered.

"I have been trying to find her again."

"Simply amazing," Even said with awe. "Well, I'm sure Anna had a long day. My driver will take both of you to her house."

Anna and Evan spoke in Spanish as we walked to the front door. A husky man greeted us, and I noticed a big revolver tucked in his belt. I had seen far too many guns in the last few days, and the sight unnerved me. They spoke rapid Spanish, and he briskly walked away. A moment later, he drove up in a beautiful black four-door Mercedes. I thanked Evan profusely, and he waved goodbye. During the drive, Anna seemed nervous, which made me feel uneasy about meeting her father.

We drove for nineteen minutes and arrived at another large estate that occupied the entire side of a hill. The main house had at least 40 rooms and was constructed with red brick and black painted steel. A 20-foot fence with spikes on the top surrounded the property. I spotted over fifteen security cameras, and four of them panned and tilted to follow our approach.

Two guards built like tanks wore heavy body armor and held large assault rifles at the gate. I could tell they recognized the driver, but they still suspiciously watched our approach while nervously holding their guns. When they recognized Anna, she waved, and they opened the gate. We drove up a long driveway, and I saw more security cameras. Finally, when the car came to a gentle stop, Anna jumped out and dashed through the front door. I got out, waved to the driver, and stood at the entrance while holding my backpack.

Two security guards walked toward me and motioned to my backpack. The left guard searched every part with great care, and the right guard frisked my entire body. It felt very uncomfortable getting my balls grabbed by a man. Afterward, they nodded to each other and led me inside.

The entryway contained many paintings and carved stone sculptures. One stunning painting of a noble gentleman caught my eye, and I walked up to it. The shadow capturing technique was breathtakingly realistic. Unfortunately, I did not recognize the signature, but the style followed that of the famous Spanish painter, Diego Velázquez. This grand entryway immediately reminded me of Quan's house, which made me wonder who owned this spectacular mansion. I then got sidetracked with thoughts of the art in my house's entryway, Craig's ripped *Def Leppard* poster. *I've got to work on that.* I thought with a big grin.

A well-dressed man with neatly combed black hair approached me. I estimated him to be in his mid-thirties, five-feet-eight, and of Hispanic descent. He began speaking in an authoritative voice with a slight Spanish accent. "I am Mr. Olmo's personal manager. You may refer to me as Mateo. I understand you are to be Anna's English teacher. Is this correct?"

"For reasons beyond my control, I'm staying in Panama for the next two days. In exchange for helping Anna with her English, her father graciously allowed me to stay. I appreciate this superb opportunity."

"What are your qualifications?"

"I majored in journalism with minors in English and literature from UCLA. I have a daily column in the *Portland Tribune* and have written eight books. My fourth book was the first to be popular, and my last book is selling better than expected."

"Very well," the man said after eleven seconds of studying me. "The agreement Anna brokered requires four hours of English coursework per afternoon. In exchange, you will receive room and board plus 100 US dollars per five-hour session. During your stay, you will occupy your room, the bathroom, the kitchen, or the study room. All other rooms are off-limits. Is that clear?"

"That offer is more than generous. Thank you."

Mateo handed me a cell phone. "Keep this on your person at all times," he said sternly. "I permit 100 minutes of use per day. The Wi-Fi password for your laptop is 'fifteen empanadas,' and your English session begins promptly at 1:00 p.m. Juan will show you to your room and provide you with proper teaching attire. Good day."

Mateo spoke to the two guards in Spanish and hastened away. One of the security guards motioned me to follow, and I assumed he was Juan. We walked through several hallways that all contained outstanding artwork. Afterward, Juan showed me a small study beyond the opulent dining room, and he said with a heavy accent, "School."

I nodded, and he led me through the kitchen and pointed to a small table. I guessed the staff ate here. At all times, I noticed at least one security camera panned and tilted to track our journey. This overt spying felt unnerving, and I wondered who operated the cameras.

We came to a long hallway with doors on each side with numbers. Juan pointed out two large bathrooms. We retraced our steps along the corridor, and he opened door fifteen. Inside, I saw a low bed, desk/dresser, a small television, and a tiny window. Fortunately, the room looked tidy. It reminded me of my freshman UCLA dorm room, and I nodded in approval. Juan gave me a stern look and departed. I did not understand the source of his attitude.

It had been over 36 hours since I got a good rest, and the alarm clock read 3:02 p.m. I set it and my watch alarm (reset to local time) to noon to ensure I did not miss our first class. As I lay down, I reflected that I was bombed out of a servant's quarters three days ago, and now I slept in another servant's quarters across the globe. *The universe has a funny sense of humor,* I thought as I drifted off to sleep.

I woke to the alarm clock blasting Spanish rock music and my watch beeping. The alarm clock read 12:03 p.m., and I could not believe that I had slept for so many hours. Outside the door was a shopping bag with two pairs of tan slacks and two white button-down shirts. After taking a quick shower, I dressed and walked to the study room. Unfortunately, I found that all the books were in Spanish.

I sat down with my laptop, entered the Wi-Fi password, and began reading email. The first one came from Lloyd, who liked the six articles I sent from China. I then emailed my room-mates to tell them what happened and asked them to check on my apartments.

At 1:45 p.m., I started an email to Bethany when Anna walked in. She wore a fashionable blue dress while eating candy with an intense strawberry smell. "We English now?" Anna asked with a smile.

It occurred to me I did not have a lesson plan. "Do you have a dictionary and an English-to-Spanish dictionary?" I asked.

Anna held up her cell phone and waved it. "A printed book?" I asked.

"No English book."

"We will need one."

"We buy," Anna suggested.

"All right, let's begin. Tell me about your life." I encouraged her with a smile.

Anna spoke a sentence in broken English, and I corrected it. She then repeated it back. Sometimes I had Anna repeat the sentence a few times to get the correct pronunciation. Through our interaction, I learned that her mother and father had been in a terrible automobile accident when she was one. The accident claimed her father and older brother and severely injured her mother.

Anna's father had been in business with a man named Arturo Del Olmo. As a matter of honor, Arturo helped Anna's mother recover. During that time, they began a relationship, and he raised Anna as his daughter. She had many wealthy friends and fond childhood memories. Six months ago, her mother died from cancer. Anna was still heartbroken and said she went to her grave every Sunday afternoon.

It took many back-and-forth interactions to learn these basic facts, and by 6:00 p.m., Anna had had enough. She appreciated my help, and I noticed pronunciation improvement. I asked her to watch a movie with English subtitles and the volume muted as a homework assignment. When she came across an unknown word, she would pause the movie and look up the word on her phone. Anna liked her assignment and agreed to do her best. She stood, smiled, and left.

The study provided a magnificent view, and I finished my emails. I then walked to the kitchen, and the cook served excellent chicken empanadas with dill seasoned rice. I found it amusing that the Wi-Fi password matched my meal. Back in my room, I turned on the television, but all the channels were in Spanish. After researching English teaching methods, I went to sleep at 8:00 p.m.

I woke up early, or at least it felt early. My plan for the day included exploring the city and getting an interview. I headed for the kitchen with my *Dawson's Creek* notebook in hand. With nobody to prepare breakfast, I settled for a glass of milk.

As I cleaned the glass, Mateo arrived. "I'm pleased to see Anna's improvement," he said in a surprised voice. "I'm not sure that I approve of her watching *Friday the Thirteenth* as a homework assignment."

"Oh, I asked her to watch a movie with English subtitles and look up words on her phone. I probably should have discussed appropriate titles."

"Very well."

"That brings up a point. I wanted to buy her English books to help our studying. Would you please arrange for somebody to drive me to a bookstore?" I asked with a smile.

"Take the local bus for three stops and then walk two blocks east. There, you will find several stores, including a bookstore," Mateo curtly answered.

"All right. Um, how do I pay for the books?"

Mateo looked annoyed and handed me a $100 bill from his wallet with a huff. Finally, he turned to leave, and I asked, "I'm still getting my bearings. How do I leave the compound without going through the main house?"

Mateo turned and looked at me with a thoughtful expression. "Turn around, three lefts and a right," he answered. "Follow the path to the main gate."

"Thank you."

I followed Mateo's instructions and located the bus stop. From reading the map attached to a nearby pole, the mansion was located in Costa del Este. Twenty-one minutes later, the bus arrived. I hopped on, and the driver took off with a jolt. He pointed to a mechanical coin machine, and I pulled out my $100. He angrily pointed to the coin machine and yelled in Spanish. "This is all I have," I replied.

The driver said something and waved me to the back of the bus. I sat down next to an older woman who was knitting and she did not make eye contact. We drove for three minutes, and I noticed a teenager across from me staring. He had crazy green and red hair, wore a colorful soccer shirt, and said in English with a heavy Spanish accent, "The driver told you to bring the money tomorrow morning."

"Oh, hey, thanks for telling me."

"*Dawson's Creek?*" The boy asked with a grin.

I looked at my notebook and sighed. "I needed a notebook, and my old workplace was throwing a pile of these away."

"What are you doing in Panama?" he asked.

"I'm stranded here for two days and taking the bus to a bookstore."

"Do you need a guide?" The boy asked with raised eyebrows.

"I'm not sure how much I can pay you. I only have this 100 dollar bill, and I need to purchase three books."

The boy's eyes lit up. "I'm your guide!" He said with great enthusiasm.

We got off at the third stop, and the bus driver glared at me. The boy yelled something to him on our way out, and he looked less angry.

On the way to the store, the boy turned to me and introduced himself. "I'm Miguel."

"James," I responded.

"What's your job?"

"For the next two days, I'm an English teacher. Normally, I'm a journalist in Portland, but I ended up here. I plan to buy some books for my English class and interview somebody this morning."

"Who do you want to interview?" Miguel asked with raised eyebrows.

"I like people with amazing personalities. It's hard to describe, but I know a good interview subject when I see one."

"What kinds of questions do you ask?"

"I give people basic facts about a topic and write what they say. It's a natural process."

"I know many amazing people," Miguel said with a big grin.

"Really? That's wonderful."

Miguel led me to a large modern bookstore. There, I purchased a hardcover English dictionary, an English-to-Spanish book, and a Spanish-to-English book. The total only came to $35. *Miguel is going to make out well.* I thought, while he led me down several side streets.

Three minutes later, we came upon a well-dressed man who was watering his garden. He had a piercing gaze, sized me up, and nodded when our eyes met. Miguel had scored!

After introducing myself, I asked (through Miguel) about the consequences surrounding offshore oil drilling. The man

I came to know as Felix Cheucarama gave the matter serious thought. He provided a well-balanced answer centered on responsibility for an oil spill and respecting the environment. He also recommended using ten percent of the oil revenue to develop tidal energy sources. I took a picture of Felix watering his well-manicured plants with my cell phone.

Afterward, I thanked Felix, and I asked Miguel about lunch. He led me to a McDonald's, and I told him, "Let's go somewhere local."

Miguel smiled, led me down sketchy alleys, under three fences, and over a wall to an open dirt lot surrounded by houses. I saw several rusty steel tables, plastic chairs, a small fountain, and a large bucket for dirty dishes. An older woman made meals in her kitchen and served them through her back window. "What do you want?" Miguel asked. "This place is called Viviana's kitchen. It's been here for a long time."

"What are you having?"

"Arroz con pollo y coco and a Coke. That's rice with chicken and coconut milk."

"I will have the same, and bottled water instead of a Coke."

Lunch tasted excellent. Each bite exploded with flavor, and it reminded me of Grace's homemade cooking. Our meal only cost eight dollars, and I think the woman overcharged me. However, for a meal that good, I had scored the bargain of the century. Afterward, we headed back to the bus stop in a good mood. "How much does it cost to ride the bus?" I wondered.

Miguel handed me a coin, and I gave him my remaining cash. "Do you need a guide tomorrow?" he asked with a big smile.

"I have to pay the morning bus driver back, so I will be at the bus stop in the morning. I'm not sure if my employer will pay me today or not, though."

Miguel programmed his number into my cell phone, and we agreed on a $40 fee if I got paid. I walked to the main gate; the guards checked my bags and thoroughly frisked me. Having my balls grabbed again still felt awkward. They waved me through, and when I reached the main door, Mateo asked in an accusing voice, "Did you purchase the required books?"

"They're in the bag."

"The receipt?" Mateo demanded.

"It's in the bag."

"Where is my remaining money?"

I grinned sheepishly and answered, "I gave the rest to my guide."

"You got ripped off."

"I know, but I'm new to the area," I admitted.

"That money will come out of your pay!" Mateo threatened.

"That is fine."

"Are you going to ask me when you will receive payment?"

"I'm thrilled by your generosity, and any time you wish to provide payment would be fine."

Mateo sized me up for eight seconds and said, "Mr. Olmo approved of your efforts. You'll receive payment at the end of each day, minus the amount you spent on your *guide*."

With that curt statement, Mateo briskly walked away. I was unsure what I had done to upset him, and I went to my room feeling disappointed. After getting my laptop, I walked to the study room and typed up my article. Then, I emailed the file to

Lloyd and used the translation book to figure out how to send him the photograph on my cell phone.

Bethany had written me a long email. Sales of *Interviewing Immortality* had skyrocketed, and their marketing department identified Goth readers as the largest buyers. She got nineteen requests for book signing events. Bethany also confirmed that she had arranged to translate my work into several languages and e-book formats. She explained that my contract allowed market expansions after 50,000 sales. *Wait a minute. Did I move 50,000 books? Yes!* This knowledge put me in a great mood.

Bethany also informed me that this month's royalty check would be impressive, putting me in an even better mood. Her most crucial request concerned a "nationwide signing tour" in Russia because my visit to Grace's apple tree "covered the entire internet." Now, everybody wanted to know if my book was a big publicity stunt or a true story.

I replied to Bethany's email and began researching the airstrike in China. The government news agency reported that Falun Dafa (also known as Falun Gong) members had occupied a large estate for many years. "The local police encouraged the misguided worshipers to depart their illegal compound peacefully." However, many questioned the official explanation as the troops were not wearing Chinese military uniforms, and pictures of dead Caucasian soldiers emerged on chat room sites. Fortunately, my name did not appear in the articles.

Craig emailed me that my apartments were doing well, and his friend needed a place to stay. He asked me if I could let him rent out Cynthia and Darin's apartment.

Dave informed me that Detective Camron dropped off a Texas warrant for me to be a material witness in the murder of James McCaw and his deputies. Failure to comply within ten days would lead to my arrest. It seemed inconceivable that he served my house and not me. I forwarded this information to my attorney, Nicholas.

Dave included a link to Cynthia and Darin's murder. The article said that the coroner uncovered several inconsistencies in her body and recommended further investigation. As I was replying, Anna walked in. She wore a stylish black dress with her hair combed up into a tight bun. I noticed she dyed the tips of her hair blue. As I closed my laptop, she asked, "You email wife?"

"No, I was emailing my roommates and publisher."

Anna picked up my phone and asked, "You call wife?"

"The phone is in Spanish, and I haven't figured out how to call America. I no longer have a wife."

"You call girlfriend?"

"No girlfriend."

Anna brightened at this information.

"We should begin," I said. "I hear you watched *Friday the Thirteenth* last night?"

"I watch movie. English hard. I understand most."

"Good. I have purchased these books, and I think they will help."

The sight of the books did not make Anna happy. "We could begin by writing some sentences?" I suggested. She looked away, and I asked, "You're not good at writing English?"

Anna nodded without turning back. "That's all right," I said. "I'm sure you will learn fast."

Anna turned toward me with a smile, and we began our lesson.

By 6:00 p.m., Anna had reached her studying limit, and as she was leaving, I asked, "Would you show me how to text Mateo?"

Anna rapidly went through the phone menus and handed it back to me with a big grin. I saw she had changed the language to English, and I thanked her.

I texted Mateo to request a short meeting and returned to my emails. Seven minutes later, Mateo entered the study with a hard-to-read expression.

"Sir, I recently learned something that I need to inform you about," I began with concern. "The state of Texas issued me a warrant to appear as a material witness. This legal request doesn't mean I've committed a crime, but the Texas state government wants to speak to me. I'm working with my lawyer to get this matter settled."

"Why are you telling me this?" Mateo asked with a stern expression.

"You strike me as the type of man who doesn't like surprises."

"You are correct. Do you wish to inform me of anything else?"

"My last book mentioned several crimes. I linked actual crimes to my story as a publicity stunt. After my book came out, I got arrested, and they dropped the charges because there was no evidence."

Mateo thought for seven seconds and said in a harsh voice, "I am aware of your legal background and read all of your books. The three *Grime* books did not read strong, but your interviewing book was fascinating. Mr. Olmo is aware of my concerns, and he requested I maintain a close watch on you."

This news brought great relief.

"What do you intend to do?"

"I'm waiting to see what my lawyer says. My credit card should arrive soon."

"I see."

Mateo studied me for nine seconds and continued, "Because of your honesty, I will permit more lessons."

"Thank you."

"Is there nothing else?" Mateo asked.

I looked away and then back. "Sir, there is a rather delicate matter I wish to bring up," I said in my most humble voice.

"Anna?"

"She has taken an interest in me."

"I see."

"Today, she asked me about my girlfriend and wife."

"What about them?" Mateo asked with suspicion.

"She wanted to know my relationship status."

"I see."

"Sir, I fully understand that I am your guest. As such, I will keep my behavior professional. You have nothing to worry about."

"Anna is free to date whom she pleases. Including you. However, if you decide to enter a relationship, you will act with honor. I assure you, Mr. Olmo will not tolerate mistreatment."

"I understand. Thank you for clearly explaining this critical matter."

Mateo nodded and briskly departed. It seemed inconceivable that Anna's stepfather would permit a person with my misguided past to instruct and possibly date his daughter. I also wondered why Mr. Olmo did not speak with me in person about this important matter.

An hour later, I finished my emails and got up to leave when Anna unexpectedly walked in. "You talk Mateo about me?" she asked.

"Yes, I wanted to make sure I didn't cross any lines."

"What mean? Cross line?"

"Um, make you uncomfortable."

"Oh. What you do tomorrow?" Anna wanted to know.

"I'm not sure, I planned to go into town, but I don't have any money."

"What you do in town?"

"I wanted to look for someone to interview."

"Interview?" Anna asked, tilting her head.

"Write a story about them."

"Why?"

"That's my job. I write stories about people and put them in a newspaper."

"What kind people?" Anna asked in a playful voice.

"Oh, just ordinary people."

Anna made a coy expression, reached into her bra, and produced a $100. "Use to write story," she said with a smile.

"Thank you. I'll pay you back."

Anna smirked and shook her head. "You help lot. Gift," she said with a laugh.

"Well, thank you."

Anna fluttered her eyes and left. *Wow,* I thought. *It's going to be difficult to be a gentleman around her.*

The following day, I texted Miguel while eating breakfast. The dish was called gallo pinto (spotted rooster) made with rice, beans, and pork. My meal tasted outstanding, and the cook generously made the change for my $100 bill. He explained in broken English that the government uses United States currency and their own Balboa currency.

I gave the bus driver a Decimo (ten cents) coin to pay him back and put a Decimo into the machine. He looked at me with a blank expression and put the coin into his pocket. Then I sat down next to Miguel, and we made small talk.

We rode the bus for several stops and got off in a lower-class neighborhood. I followed Miguel through sketchy side streets, and he knocked on the door of a small house. A woman opened the door with a grand welcome gesture and led us inside. She wore tastefully applied makeup and was dressed in a fashionable blue ruffle dress with a green pillbox hat. The woman I came to know as Valentina Palacio had a million-dollar smile, and I instantly knew Miguel had scored again.

That morning, a suicide bomber struck an Israeli market. With Miguel translating, I asked her about suicide bombers and what the world should do to prevent these tragic events.

Valentina thought for a full minute and told me how sad this incident made her feel. She explained that the drive to become a religious martyr is powerful for many young people and said through Miguel, "The only way that we may prevent martyr incidents is through the freedom of a balanced upbringing. Therefore, the people of the world should do their best to educate the misguided children to show them how much more there is to life than a suicidal act."

Valentina recommended that these lost souls learn about music's healing power and try different ethnic foods to see how enjoyable life could be. I started to take her picture when Miguel stopped me. He had been carrying a bag, and he opened it to reveal an excellent camera. "My brother's old camera," Miguel said with a grin. "A reporter needs a good camera. For you, 40 dollars."

I looked at an excellent Fujifilm Finepix S5. While it was not the latest technology, I knew it cost over $40. "Having this camera will not get me into trouble?"

"No, it belongs to my brother," Miguel answered. "He takes pictures for his job and recently got a better camera. This old one was sitting on a shelf."

"Thank you, and please thank your brother."

I figured out the controls and took a fantastic picture. After thanking Valentina, we walked down more side streets and ended up in a city square surrounded by local shops. Through Miguel, I met several remarkable people and took photos of the neighborhood. Miguel then led me to another out-of-the-way restaurant, where we sat at a well-used wooden table.

"You won't find food like this anywhere else," Miguel told me with a big smile.

We made small talk for five minutes, and a woman came out holding two clay vessels. She broke them on the table corner with a whoosh of steam and poured the contents on a plate. It smelled magnificent, and the woman looked at me with pride. My meal was a ham bone surrounded by yams and a hearty pepper sauce. I could not help myself and rapidly ate. The meat fell off the bone, and the yams tasted out of this world. Lunch with two bottles of water and two Cokes for Miguel cost seven dollars. *What a deal!*

Miguel explained that the same family had been making this dish for many generations, and they refused to share the secret recipe. Afterward, we walked to a local school, and I took more photos. We got back on the bus an hour later, and I informed Miguel that tomorrow would probably be my last day in Panama.

At the house, the guards thoroughly searched me and their firm hands still made me uncomfortable. When I walked to my room, I found a FedEx package with my credit card. It felt great to connect to America, and I took my laptop to the study room.

After writing the article, I figured out how to get the images off my new camera. The quality looked excellent, and Valentina's smile looked even better on the computer screen. However, I found several family pictures in the camera's memory. The older boys had shirts with Chicago Bulls emblems, which meant the camera did not belong to Miguel's brother.

I sent off the article and began reading an email from my attorney, Nicholas. He informed me that the police could not break my laptop encryption. Instead, they had trumped up charges to force me to appear before a Texas judge. Then the prosecutors would ask me questions I could not answer. Afterward, I would be charged with contempt, giving them leverage to obtain my password.

Nicholas filed motions to quash the warrant, and he "strongly advised me" to stay in Panama until he worked things out. I emailed a thank you, and Anna walked in. She had dressed in a slinky pink dress, and we began our English lesson.

Halfway through, Anna left for the restroom, and when she returned, she sat next to me rather than being across. At the end of our session, she asked about my interviews, and I told her about my latest article. Anna read it with quiet fascination and complimented me on the photo. Afterward, she touched my arm, produced another $100 from her bra, and said, "For tomorrow interview." I told Anna that she didn't need to keep giving me money, and she laughed with a big grin.

Over the next twelve days, my life settled into a pattern. I went on interviews with Miguel in the mornings and taught Anna English in the afternoon. My interviews got better, and Anna's dresses got shorter.

TEN

Nicholas was making some progress in quashing my warrant. The Texas prosecutors had expected me to give in without a fight, and instead, Nicholas used every conceivable legal defense.

The following day, my bank granted me online access. I could not believe the $71,036 balance. In my absence, my publisher had deposited a check for $52,816, the *Portland Tribune* had given me a $1,203 bonus (for attracting new readers), and my apartments had made $6,107. As I was not staying at home, I did not spend money on food, gas, or entertainment. Craig emailed me about losing his supermarket cashier job and asked if he could take over running the apartments until I got back. *Of course he could.*

I enjoyed interviewing the people of Panama, and through Miguel, I got to know the city from a unique perspective.

Everybody was friendly with warm demeanors and impressive opinions.

I received positive comments from my Seattle readers and my boss. I also had a wonderful time teaching English. By the third week, Anna's reading had improved, and her basic sentences were better. Even Mateo begrudgingly complimented my progress.

Two days later, Mateo informed me that Mr. Olmo wished to meet. Two heavily armed security guards accompanied him, and I understood his "wish" was a direct order.

The guards escorted me through an unfamiliar part of the house while I appreciated the tasteful artwork. Along the way, I contemplated how odd it was that I did not know what Mr. Olmo looked like even though we lived under the same roof. Finally, we came to two grand hardwood doors with ornate tiger images in gold inlay. Inside, I saw an opulent office and a man standing behind a massive red oak desk.

Mr. Olmo appeared to be in his early seventies and was dressed in a splendid tan suit. He stood five-feet-seven with dark, patchy gray hair and non-Latin features. Mr. Olmo had visible inch-long scars on his arms and a slightly disfigured nose. We began challenging each other with our gaze.

Our focus session lasted for 86 seconds, and I found the experience intense, tricky, and fun. Mr. Olmo was the first to break off our staring contest with a crafty smile. Then, he sat down with a look of contentment.

"Please leave us," I asked the guards.

It did not surprise me when Mr. Olmo nodded, and the doors closed behind me. I sat in a elegant gray leather chair, which felt more comfortable than I expected.

"I'm guessing your actual name is not Arturo Del Olmo," I said with a smile.

Mr. Olmo looked down to touch a scar on his right arm, looked up, and nodded with a grin.

"I suspect you knew a woman named Cleopatra," I continued. He smiled and nodded. "We have a lot to discuss."

"Indeed, we do," Mr. Olmo replied in a strange accent that seemed to be a collection of several languages. "Please call me Arturo."

"May I get my notebook?"

Arturo reached into his desk drawer, produced my *Dawson's Creek* notebook, and looked at me with a humorous expression.

"I need to buy a better notebook," I admitted.

Arturo laughed and said in a warm voice, "That's true. Let us begin with my history, and then we will discuss our mutual interests."

"Sounds good."

Arturo's pleasant attitude was an enormous relief. He leaned back, contemplating the moment, and looked directly at me for eleven seconds. "You must forgive me," he said in a sheepish voice. "I am not used to revealing my true details."

"I understand. This is not my first immortal rodeo."

Arturo chuckled and said, "I suppose there is no harm now in being honest. I came into this world so very long ago. I surmise my given birth occurred in 66 BC, and my father named me Amten. Hmm. So much time has passed since that word rolled over my lips—so much time. My family comprised landowners in what we now call Egypt. From an early age, they groomed me to take a role in the royal court. A prestigious position that held great honor."

Arturo adopted a proud expression as he continued. "At the proper age, I took my place. A new pharaoh assumed power, and history records her name as Cledopart or, as you would pronounce it, Cleopatra. A woman of outstanding personality, intelligence, and stunning beauty. I had the esteemed privilege to be in her presence.

"Cleopatra ruled as all great pharaohs did, with an iron fist. However, from my perspective as an Egyptian citizen, her rule did not stand out. Now take Pharaoh Sera. She expanded the empire, and Pharaoh Katesch brought water to the masses. And yet, Pharaoh Ketet brought eternal shame. Of course, their names are not in history books. Successive leaders often erased everything about their predecessors. Hmm. So many names lost to the sand. And what of Cleopatra?

"Ah, yes. Cleopatra. As her rule grew, my role increased until I became the first assistant. You might consider this to be the equivalent of the American Secretary of State."

Arturo's eyes lit up, and he continued. "I took charge of all palace business, including the royal schedule. A great time in my life, and I got to know her well."

Arturo made a coy expression and whispered, "May I share a secret?"

"Yes, indeed."

Arturo leaned back and said with a grand smile, "Cleopatra bore two children. Her daughter died shortly after birth, and later, she had a son, Caesarion. History records other children, but she secretly adopted them in order to maintain a trim figure. Back to Caesarion.

"We shared many traits, including a curled left toe. To maintain appearances, Cleopatra insisted that Julius Caesar sired her child. However, if you study the dates and know about his health, it is apparent that this man could not have been the father."

"What an honor it must have been to be with her. Thank you for sharing."

"Indeed."

Arturo leaned forward and said with a big grin, "Also, a lot of fun making him."

We both laughed. Arturo looked to the side for a moment and said, "My queen was obsessed with her appearance and began performing gruesome experiments. A man named Quan oversaw the matter. He—"

"I've met Quan," I interrupted.

Arturo looked at me with wide eyes and asked in a low voice, "What did you say?"

"His men kidnapped me in Russia. Then they flew me to his house in China."

"Quan is alive! I find this quite shocking. Quite shocking, indeed. Hmm. Well, your presence in China now makes sense. How is Quan? It has been so very long since we've spoken."

"He's doing much better since I revealed the improved harvest technique. But his house got bombed and then attacked by a private army."

"That is outrageous! Did Quan die in the attack?"

"They blew up his entire house, and I cannot imagine that anybody could have survived. If Quan somehow made it out, I'm sure the soldiers captured him."

Arturo leaned back in his chair and became concerned. Then, 27 seconds later, he asked, "An improved technique, you say?"

"Yes, but first, please tell me more about yourself."

"Of course. Quan had developed, as you call it in your book, the harvest. What you did not record is the horrific cost of refining his procedure. Quan and his assistant, Jank, butchered countless slaves in their lofty pursuit of medical knowledge. I felt their effort was cruel and a waste of good slaves. However, to my great surprise, they made progress. Later, their brutal experiments required children because their bodies provided better organs. Often, their selection fell to me as I supervised all labor requests. I will tell you this. It is an appalling act to take a crying child from their mother's arms. But of course, I dared not voice my concern.

"Back to Caesarion. As he matured, Cleopatra groomed him to be her successor. However, her obsession with beauty distracted her from her leadership duties. I began hearing rumors that Caesarion had gathered a small army of trusted men. When I informed my queen, she ignored my sound recommendations. One night, his men stormed the royal palace and took the guards by surprise. They fought with great tenacity but failed to prevent the revolt.

"At the time, Cleopatra and her personal servant, Thoeris, were trying on new dresses in the royal changing room. I had been standing guard when two attackers burst in. We strug-

gled, and an attacker stabbed Thoeris in the heart as she protected her queen. I killed both men with this very knife."

Arturo reached into his desk drawer and produced an ornate
knife of exceptional craftsmanship. He smiled, put the knife away,
and continued. "Cleopatra began yelling incoherent orders, and I
closed the door to prevent further attacks. However, when I went
to the window, I saw over 30 armed men in fine armor running
toward our location. Clearly, I could not fight them all.

"My queen continued to yell out orders while I attempted to
explain the dire situation. When this effort did not work, I had
to take control. So I removed her royal crown and placed it on
Thoeris. The anger in my queen's eyes! In her mind, there was
no choice but to strike me with all her might. But, of course,
her fists held little energy. To help her understand, I forced her
to the window to see the situation for herself.

"One significant aspect of Cleopatra that history did not
record is her astounding ability to recognize an opportunity.
She immediately grasped the severe nature of our predicament
and understood my plan. So she placed her rings and clothes
on Thoeris's body. Cleopatra had selected Thoeris because
their figures matched, making her an ideal clothing model. I
took a large—um, the object does not have an English translation. Allow me to call it a religious candle holder. I crushed
Thoeris's face so people would conclude she was Cleopatra.

"My queen had a large jewelry chest, and I took it into my
possession. We left the changing room, and I came upon an
attacker. After setting the chest down, I dispatched the man
with my knife. We traveled down the main hallway and entered
the left greeting room.

"Fortunately, six loyal palace guards were present, and together, we fought our way through the kitchen. Once outside, all eight of us crossed a courtyard to a nearby stable, where we met three more loyal guards.

"Cleopatra had never ridden a horse, and she required my help to lift her onto the saddle. I got on in front, and she held on to me with all her might. All of us rode away under the cover of darkness. A magnificent escape, if I say so myself.

"We traveled to the edge of the city and spent the night at a dusty storehouse. Two days later, I traveled to the royal palace disguised as a peasant. During our absence, it had become big news that Cleopatra killed herself by inducing a snake to bite her. Her fascination with snakes was common knowledge, and this circumstance made sense to the masses.

"Later in the morning, I met a trusted friend at his home and learned that Quan had fled. He also informed me that the attackers had stabbed Jank to death. As nothing else could be done, I sold two pieces of jewelry to a local merchant, and our group left the city. Cleopatra decided we needed to settle in a faraway land, and we traveled toward an area now known as Poland. I later learned we ended up in Russia because of a miscommunication.

"Three weeks into our journey, my queen revealed the fact that she knew of an eternal life procedure. I suggested she apply the procedure to the guards. In this way, they would remain loyal because they would need additional treatments.

"Cleopatra applied the procedure to all of us, and we excelled as a group. Having many subjects also allowed her to experiment and improve the process. While she did not share its exact secret, I took great care to discover every aspect.

"As the years passed, Cleopatra's wealth grew, and we went from traveling nomads to lavish-spending tourists. We changed locations every two to six years and excelled as an extended family. However, the reality of being her second-in-command proved difficult. At best, Cleopatra treated me like a loyal servant. I wanted to be a much larger part of her life and receive all the benefits of a wealthy individual. She would not hear of it.

"In the year 980, the pressure became too great. We had a terrible argument one night, and I left Cleopatra's presence. Words cannot describe the pain I endured for abandoning the family that I had known for so many years and my queen, the woman I truly loved.

"Fortunately, I had collected a few coins, and this meager sum was enough to travel to a nearby town, where I began an apprenticeship as a land broker. I used this knowledge to start a business that turned a tidy profit.

"Two hundred years ago, my sailboat hit a reef near Panama. Well, it was still part of Colombia then. As it was being repaired, I came to appreciate the local people and stayed.

"Over the years, I attempted to locate Cleopatra and her men. However, my searches were unsuccessful. So, when I discovered your book, my surprise was so great that I fell out of my chair. Quite amazing. Now, let us discuss what information the woman known as Grace shared with you."

I had been writing like a madman and looked up to see Arturo staring at me with a curious expression. He continued in a voice conveying extreme intent, "Please reveal your harvest technique."

"Wait, a minute. Why am I here?"

"Yes, of course. Let us discuss this key subject. A month ago, I downloaded an electronic book for the first time. I selected your book, as it appeared at the top of the list. Upon reading it, the content shocked me."

"What did you think of it?" I asked with hesitation.

"You created a superb work with great detail and genuine honesty."

"That's a nice compliment. Thank you."

"I had one question about its contents," Arturo said.

"Sure."

"You spent a great deal of time describing Grace's mountain lion, Heathcliff—like the orange cat from the comic strip. Most amusing. Heathcliff sent you an image through her eyes. Did you write the truth?"

"Of course."

"Do you have this ability?" Arturo wondered.

"When I returned home, I tried to send images to my room-mates, but nothing happened. I did lots of research and came up empty. My only guess is that Grace trained Heathcliff to accomplish this feat."

"That's unfortunate," Arturo said sadly.

"I wish I could share images with people."

"Were you able to attempt this ability with Grace?" Arturo wondered.

"I never had an opportunity. If I were to guess, I think the technique only works with a trained mountain lion."

"Hmm. Do you think it would work with an untrained mountain lion?"

"I would be afraid to try, but it might."

"Interesting," Arturo said with a smile.

"Please continue."

"Of course. After reading your book, I sent two men to observe you. It was during this time that you flew to Russia. Unfortunately, they could not locate you, and then you appeared in China, of all places."

"How did you track me?" I wanted to know.

"My men installed sophisticated software within your laptop. But you did not connect your computer to the internet while in Russia."

"That makes sense. Wait a minute. How did you get around my laptop encryption?"

"My computer expert waited outside your house, and when you went to the bathroom, he installed sophisticated software before the password timeout."

"I wouldn't have expected that. Hold on. How did you get me to Panama?"

"Ahh. We observed you in China from a distance. Days later, a great attack occurred at your location."

"Do you know who caused the attack?" I asked.

"I'm not aware, but arranging a full airstrike in a foreign country is a major undertaking and well beyond my meager resources. After the attack, I knew you would survive, and I had my associates convince the officials at the Nanchong airport only to allow flights to Panama."

"The ticket agent said there were also flights to Havana and Qatar. I randomly picked Panama."

"Strange, I told them only Panama," Arturo said in a concerned voice.

"What about Anna? Is she your daughter or an actress?"

"Anna is my adopted daughter."

"She mentioned that her mother passed away," I said in a sympathetic voice.

"Daniella married my dear friend Marcos. Ra blessed them with Anna and her brother Juan. One night, the family got into a terrible car accident. The impact killed Marcos and Juan instantly. By a great miracle of Ra, Anna was unharmed.

"Daniella had severe wounds, and the doctors told me many times that she would not survive. I was duty-bound to Marcos and kept a close watch over Daniella. While I was not looking to start a relationship, she became my wife. And I will tell you this. In all my life, I have only loved two women. I do not expect to find love again."

Arturo looked away, and I knew his sorrow ran deep. He composed himself for nine seconds and continued. "At the airport, Anna had not been aware of you. Only an inconceivable stroke of luck brought you two together.

"I left instructions with my men to pick her up and bring you to me. But there was a big football match, and many spectators flew in for the event. In the confusion, my men thought you went back inside and failed to locate her. My mistake was not sending enough men.

"Then, Anna asked if I would permit an English professor to stay with us. I liked the prospect and agreed to her request. You cannot imagine the surprise of seeing you at my doorstep through my security camera. I took advantage of the opportunity and began observing you."

"It's all a coincidence?" I asked in shock.

"An astounding coincidence."

"Wow."

"You know Anna enjoys your company," Arturo said.

"I'm aware."

"Do you love her?"

"I'm still getting to know her," I stammered.

"I understand. Well, I must confess that I enjoyed reading your interviews with the people of Panama. They certainly have a unique view," Arturo said with a hearty laugh.

"Is Miguel in on this?"

"Who is Miguel?" Arturo asked in confusion.

"He's my local guide."

"I don't know him."

"What about Mateo?" I wondered.

"I told him to keep a close watch over you."

"This is so unexpected."

"I'm the one who is finding all of this unexpected. The revelation that other people know the procedure is enthralling. Now, I would like to learn more about your improved technique."

"May we discuss your technique first?" I asked with hesitation.

"Why not discuss both? It has been several days, and I require another procedure. Let's go down to the treatment room."

"Mr. Olmo," I said in a solemn voice.

"We are friends," Arturo interrupted in a firm voice. "Please call me Arturo."

"Arturo, sir. I've decided not to harvest anymore. I only did one to give me the ability to locate Grace. After the effects wear off, I'm never going to harvest again."

"Why are you acting so formal? You must relax," Arturo said in a friendly voice.

"Well, the immortals I have encountered are used to getting their way," I answered with concern.

"Nonsense, you're like me. We are better than other people. It is curious that you call us immortals. I like this term."

"Mr. Arturo, sir. I'm happy to discuss harvest techniques, but I prefer not to participate."

"I must insist."

Arturo's eyes held a calm, deadly glare, and I knew that any resistance would lead to torture or my death. "Please forgive my next statement. I do not intend to be disrespectful, but I'm helping you against my will," I said in a forced, pleasant voice.

"Nonsense. You will see. Everything will be fine. And please relax. It's plain Arturo. No need to call me sir. Sound good?"

"Sure," I answered without enthusiasm.

We stood and began walking in silence until we came to a steel door with four locks. The security guards looked surprised when Arturo and I entered.

Inside there was a large stainless-steel table and shelves with chemicals and instruments. I noted that this room looked nearly identical to Quan's harvest room. I even saw the same Swiss soldering iron. There were four cages on the left side, and three of them contained boys that looked to be about twelve years old. The left boy was bruised and wore a tattered blue shirt. The right boy had curly hair and only wore shorts. Arturo had restrained them with handcuffs, and they had white tape over their mouths. The boys looked frightened beyond belief and struggled against their restraints.

The horrific sight of children about to be tortured to death made me want to vomit. It took all my self-control to remain composed while Arturo calmly took off his shirt to reveal many ghastly scars. I tried the same excuse I had used with Quan. "Look, this is all wrong," I said. "Children make unpredictable harvest subjects."

"You mentioned that in your book. I tried adults many times without success. However, I assure you that my method works."

"Can we start with you explaining the details?"

"Of course. I begin by removing the adrenal gland and pancreas. Then, the organs get prepared with Egyptian cobra venom and lemongrass oil extracted with supercritical carbon dioxide. I tried mint oil after reading your book, but it yielded no success. Burning the boys also provided no improvement."

"Where do you place the pancreas?"

"Originally, Quan selected a spot near the liver. Cleopatra determined that the left leg provided better results, and I used this location for many years. Now I must use alternate locations because so many procedures are required. The muscles in the shoulder fare no better than the other locations."

I shook my head and explained the technique that Grace had shown me. Arturo took notes as I spoke in a blue notebook, and he appreciated the use of freeze-dried snake venom because snakes had bitten him twice. Arturo agreed to hold off on the harvest until he located "an evil person" and obtained freeze-dried snake venom.

"Now what?" I wondered aloud.

"What do you refer to?"

"I'm aware of your secret, which will prevent me from leaving your house. I assume you will lock me up."

"Nonsense, you are free to come and go as you please."

"I don't understand. You harvest young boys. It must be against the law," I protested.

"Bah! I pay the local police to provide undesirable street thugs. This arrangement works out well for everybody. Now. You mustn't worry as you do. For you see, you cannot tell anybody about me, and I cannot tell anybody about you. We are brothers!" Arturo said with a big smile.

"Are you sure?"

"All is well between us. You will see. Now, this has been a long day, and I grow tired. Please enjoy your dinner and then get a good night's rest. In the morning, why don't you do another interview?"

Arturo smiled and exited the harvest room. The boys turned to me with shocked expressions, and I think they believed I would hurt them. I realized that Arturo would have to kill them anyway because they had seen his face. This thought horrified me, and a massive chill ran down my spine as I locked the door behind me.

Back in my room, I sat on my bed and stared at the wall while gathering my thoughts. *Am I living with another harvester? Why are children always involved?!* Eight minutes later, somebody knocked on the door. I stood, opened it, and Anna smiled. She dressed in the most revealing outfit possible, and it took great effort to force my eyes to behave. "We not have English lesson in afternoon," she said in a seductive voice.

Anna's English had improved, but we had a long way to go.

"I met your stepfather," I replied. "He's an interesting man."

"You not eaten?"

"No."

"Eat with me," Anna said, and then touched my arm. "We practice English better and get to know each other more."

With that, Anna turned away. I needed a distraction and followed her to a tastefully decorated dining room. "We can eat anything," she said, and then threw her hands up in a friendly gesture. "Tell, and I order."

I looked around at this astounding room filled with artwork and understood the chef could prepare every conceivable dish I could imagine. However, I needed to know if Arturo truly trusted me, so I asked, "Do you like chicken?"

Anna nodded, and she motioned to the chef.

"I want to go to a place in town," I said.

"Why outside? Pablo is good food."

"Pablo is an excellent cook, but tonight, I need to go out."

"We go now?" Anna asked in a confused voice.

"Um, sure. But the place I want to take you to is casual. So you cannot wear those clothes."

"I not understand. You not like the way I look?"

"The place I want to take you to is much less formal," I answered. "You know. Regular people. Not high-class people like you."

Anna appreciated my compliment. "I will change," she said with a big smile.

We walked down several hallways until we came to an enormous bedroom. Suddenly, Anna began undressing. I turned around until she asked, "Like this?"

I turned around to see Anna zipping up a revealing fashionable dress. "That's too nice," I answered while wishing I had waited a few more seconds to let her finish.

"You choose."

Anna pointed to a door, and I walked inside. She had a closet over three times the size of my living room that contained every conceivable outfit. I walked down the aisles until I found a pair of gray slacks and a pink shirt.

When I turned around, Anna only wore a white bra and panties. Words cannot describe the extreme effort I used to force my eyes forward in the presence of this seductive woman. She seemed amused by my performance and looked at my clothing selection with disdain. Anna rifled through her clothes, selected a pair of blue slacks and a revealing tight black shirt with pink hearts. Anna looked in the full-length mirror for fourteen seconds and turned to see her back. "Like this?" she wondered, while knowing the answer.

Given the circumstances, I knew she'd selected the best option, and I nodded. We walked out to the car, and through Anna, I told the driver where to go. A few miles later, we came to a stop. "Here?!" She asked in shock.

"Yes."

"This not restaurant. This low-class street!"

"It's a neighborhood. Please tell the driver to pick us up in an hour and a half."

Anna translated, and we began walking through alleys, under fences, and through apartment yards. Eleven minutes later, we arrived in the small square Miguel had taken me to.

I walked over to the kitchen and said to the old woman, "Dos arroz con pollo y coco and dos agua. Por favor."

The older woman looked at me with good humor and began cooking. I turned to see Anna looking at me with great confusion, and she said with a hint of frustration, "Pablo make great arroz con pollo y coco."

"I haven't tried it, but I'm sure it's excellent."

"Why you take me here?" Anna wanted to know.

"To open your eyes."

Seven minutes later, the woman came out with two plates, and we began eating. "This good," Anna complimented between bites. "I not ate like this since I young girl."

"Told you."

After we finished, I ordered two more bottles of water, and we enjoyed them while watching the other people eat. Eight minutes later, the older woman put up gas lanterns, and the yellow-green light added to the cozy atmosphere. "You tell me?" Anna cautiously asked.

"What?"

"You like me?"

"Yes," I admitted.

"I not understand. Why you not kiss? You need kiss you first?" Anna said.

While I had been expecting this conversation, it still made me uncomfortable. I thought about Anna's request for seventeen seconds and answered, "My life is complex, and I don't want to involve you with my problems."

"Because of father?" Anna asked with narrow eyes.

"Your father and I share a similar path."

Anna looked down at the table for 21 seconds. "He kill boys," she said with remorse. "I read your book. It is good book. James? You kill? Like in book?"

Anna's statement caught me off guard, and I needed a distraction. So I took a long sip of water and leaned back in my plastic chair. Anna continued to look at me with an unsure expression as I let out a deep breath. Fifteen seconds later, I leaned in close and answered, "I've committed many horrible acts. A few weeks ago, I killed a man and his wife. They had a child, which means I took away his parents. Even now, I don't know why I ended their lives. But, that's not an excuse or an answer. My priority is to keep you safe."

"You love me?" Anna asked with confidence.

Anna's reaction surprised me. I would have expected her to run away after my abhorrent confession. Instead, she looked at me with curiosity, and I wasn't sure of its source. *What kind of woman would fall in love with a murderer? Is Arturo forcing her to act this way?* I had not planned an intimate conversation or getting close to a woman with an immortal father. Yet, I admitted to myself that I liked Anna. "I care a lot about you, but I am not sure about the word love," I answered warmly.

"Do you want to kiss me now?" Anna asked with a smile.

"I would like to. However, we both need to realize the consequences of a relationship."

Anna looked at me with a confused expression.

"Think of what it would be like to get close to a man like your father. We share a similar path."

"You kill boys?" Anna asked with interest.

"No, I have never killed a child, and I never will. I'm not as bad as your father. But that's not the whole truth. Anna, there's evil inside of me, and I'm not proud of my choices. I am trying to stop going down the wrong path. However, your father wants me to travel to a dark place, and a big part of me wants to join him."

Anna seemed fascinated with the conversation and asked, "You live long time? Like vampire?"

"I can live for hundreds of years, but I choose not to."

"Does father live long time?" Anna wanted to know.

"I think he should be the one to tell you that."

"I know he kill boys. He must live long time."

The statement again surprised me, and I said, "Hmm. I guess you already know his secret. He has been alive for over 2,000 years."

"Wow!" Anna chirped. "That long time. He never tell. Do you think father want me to kill boys to live long time?"

"He doesn't want that. I'm sure of it."

"From book, you send mind picture to big cat. You do with me?" Anna asked with a wink.

"It doesn't work with people."

"I understand. Thank you for explain. I want to be friends if all right."

"I would like to be friends with you."

We finished our water bottles. Anna paid for our meal, and we began walking toward the car. After going under the first fence, Anna began holding my arm. I looked at her, and she smiled warmly.

As we continued through this sketchy part of town, I realized I had powerful feelings for Anna. She was intelligent, attractive, funny, and I liked her forward personality. As I helped Anna over a small fence, I squeezed her hand, and she smiled at me. *Yeah, this could work,* I thought, and smiled back.

We got back to the car and drove home. Mateo met us at the front door, and he did not look happy. Anna smiled, touched my arm, and walked away. I began walking toward my room, and Mateo said in an annoyed voice, "Not that way."

Mateo began leading me down a long hallway. "This is my room, and next door is your room," he said in the same annoyed voice.

Mateo opened the door to reveal a beautiful bedroom. I saw cherrywood furniture, a grand bed with a fluffy comforter, and three suits hanging in the closet. Somebody had placed my backpack in the corner and my laptop on the desk.

"I'll be right next door if you need anything," Mateo informed me. "The builders were instructed to install soundproof walls, but you will soon learn otherwise. Be careful."

Mateo made a hard-to-read expression and walked away. I surmised it was now common knowledge that Anna and I were a couple. I sat down at the desk and typed.

Twelve minutes later, somebody knocked and opened the door. Arturo walked in and sat in a chair. He looked happy and said with pride, "The police detained a local criminal. He takes people for ransom and then sends body parts to the families to prove he has the victim. Is that evil enough?"

"Sure," I answered without enthusiasm.

"You don't sound convinced. But, trust me, your body will tell you what to do, and you will make the right decision. Now enough about that unpleasant subject. My driver informed me he drove you and Anna to town. I understand you both ate arroz con pollo y coco at Viviana's kitchen?"

I wondered how Arturo gathered this detailed information and answered, "We did."

"When I first came to Panama, I went to Viviana's great-grandmother's house at least once a week. Later she turned her backyard into a restaurant. Your ability to locate excellent food is a testament to your superb reporting skills."

"No, it's my good luck in finding a knowledgeable guide," I said with a smile.

"Indeed!" Arturo said with a hearty laugh. "Now, tell me. How did your conversation with Anna go?"

"Um. Anna wanted to be—closer."

"I see."

"I also told her about my complex life and my choices. She took the news better than I thought."

"What exactly did you tell her?" Arturo said.

"She read my book, and I confirmed it was true."

"I did not know she read your book."

"She knows about you."

"What?! What does she know?!" Arturo asked with intense shock.

"That you take the lives of boys to prolong your life. I also told her how old you are. I hope my admission wasn't out of line."

"My daughter has a sharp mind, and I should have antici-pated her discovery," Arturo confessed and then glanced away. "Bah! I went to great lengths to shield her from my misdeeds. Bah! What's done is done."

"My book is probably responsible for her discovery. I'm sorry."

"What happened is unfortunate but an eventuality. I planned to discuss this matter on her 25th birthday. Your presence will make this conversation easier."

"What are you going to tell her?" I wondered.

"I had planned to show her the procedure and discuss its benefits."

"Really?! You wanted her to have an awful future?! You know the harvest devours a person's soul! It's pure evil!"

"It will be her choice."

"It's a terrible life full of murder! Don't make her a part of this. Please!" I begged.

"With the improved procedure, taking the lives of children is no longer required."

"It's an appalling life!"

"I will give her all the facts, and then she can decide."

"It's still a destructive path," I reminded him with some anger.

"With you here, she can learn from our experiences, which will allow her to make an informed decision."

"I'm going to tell her not to harvest. No matter what!"

"I encourage you to be honest."

"Thank you."

Arturo leaned back and asked, "What are your intentions with Anna? She speaks about you with great fondness."

"She wanted me to kiss her, but I refused."

"Why?" Arturo wondered.

"Because of what we are and what we do."

"You informed me you would no longer apply the procedure to yourself."

"True," I said with a laugh. "However, harvesting keeps catching up with me no matter what choices I make."

"Yes, it does, my friend," Arturo said as he joined my laughter. "Now, tell me. What are your intentions?"

"For now, I am going to take things slowly. The last thing I would ever do is hurt her."

"I like your attitude. Now, first thing in the morning, let's do a quick procedure. I promise the man I have selected is of ill repute. The world will be better without him."

At that moment, I again realized I lived with a madman and bent to his wishes. Yet, I wondered if I could ever return to an existence without harvesting.

"That sounds good," I said with a sigh.

"This is all going to work out well for both of us. I'm glad that you're able to relax in my presence. We have so much to talk about, and perhaps I can join you for one of your interview adventures."

"I'd like that, and I would like to learn more about your life."

"That's the spirit. Now, I want you to—"

The sound of automatic weapons firing interrupted us. Instinct took over. I put on my shoes, grabbed my backpack, and threw my laptop inside. Arturo had already run down the hall to the left, and I ran after him twelve seconds later. The lights went out, and I heard Mateo yelling in Spanish. When I came around the corner, a skylight provided enough moonlight to see Mateo pointing a large revolver at Arturo. The two of them were arguing, and Arturo suddenly lunged at Mateo.

The gunfire outside increased, and a bullet sprayed drywall dust onto my hair.

Suddenly I faced a decision. *Should I help a man who murders young boys or the man who wants to rid the world of that murderer? It might be better to let them fight it out.* In that moment of mental debate, I reasoned that Arturo had been kinder to me.

I had enough visibility to land a solid punch on Mateo's jaw. Unfortunately, my aggressive efforts did not deter him as much as I would have expected, but the distraction provided Arturo an opening, and he skillfully wrestled Mateo to the floor.

Anna began yelling from behind us in Spanish. Arturo then used his foot to jam Mateo's hand with the gun to the ground, and I tried to pull it away. He lunged to the left, and the gun fired with a terrific boom. Mateo seemed surprised by the noise, and I used this distraction to pull the gun out of his hand. They continued yelling, punching, and struggling.

Finally, I pushed the gun barrel into Mateo's forehead with substantial force and yelled, "That's enough, you two! Stop!"

Arturo sprang off Mateo and ran behind me. I looked back to see Anna sitting down. Even in the dim light, I noticed a big stain on the wall behind her. She held her hand over her chest and looked at Arturo with a frightened expression.

I turned to Mateo and saw the anger in his eyes. "Arturo is a heartless bastard!" He yelled at me. "He kills innocent children for pleasure! You know this! Why are you helping him?! Are you as big a bastard?!"

Mateo's words forced heart-wrenching pain into my soul. I questioned my decision and understood my actions protected the life of a ruthless mass murderer who selfishly preyed on boys. *What have I done?* I thought to myself.

Mateo saw my hesitation and grabbed for the gun. We struggled, and Mateo's phenomenal skill surprised me. Now, I needed to fight for my life.

As we struggled, Mateo quickly gained the upper hand, which forced me to decide. At the exact right moment, I pulled the trigger. The gun made a big flash, a loud boom, and the force nearly jerked it out of my hand. The back of Mateo's head exploded all over the floor. His body slumped down, and his eyes looked forward with no life.

What had I done? I had killed again! Why is there so much death surrounding me? These thoughts twisted through my tormented soul as I looked at the gun in my hand. There was no choice, and I set it on the floor.

A deep gasp distracted me, and I turned back to look at Anna. I knew the wound was fatal, so I walked over, and got down on my knees. Anna took a dramatic gulping breath while looking at me with more fear than I had ever witnessed. Arturo spoke Spanish to her in a kind voice while Anna looked at him and then at me in utter desperation. Finally, Anna took one last gasping breath, held it, and slowly let it out.

In that dim light, I watched Anna pass. Her final decision had been to look at me instead of her father. I felt deep humility in that dim hallway, and while holding Anna's hand, I whispered, "Thank you for the wonderful time we had together. Be at peace."

Anna's head drooped to the left, and Arturo closed her eyes. He began speaking, but I did not comprehend his words. Finally, Arturo pulled me up by my collar and forced me to walk.

We came to his study; he locked the door with a heavy bolt and pushed a rod into the floor to further secure it. Arturo then pulled back the carpet and began entering a combination to a small floor safe while speaking to me. Next, he took something out of his safe and put it in a small duffel bag. Arturo then grabbed some items from his desk drawers and put them in the bag. I watched the actions without comprehending his words. Next, Arturo began yelling orders, but I could only think about Anna.

Arturo smacked my face and raised my head by grabbing my hair. Finally, he punched me in the gut and yelled something. Arturo then pinched my ear and yelled directly into it, "I need your help! Let's go!"

"What?" I asked in confusion.

"Help me push this desk!" I heard him loud and clear.

I absently helped Arturo push the desk to the center of the room.

"Move the bookshelf! Now!" he yelled.

Together, we pushed the bookshelf, and it fell on top of the desk with a crash. The hail of bullets increased, and one of them grazed my cheek.

Arturo began climbing on top of the fallen bookshelf, and reaching up to the skylight. I helped steady him; he undid a latch and pushed the skylight open. Arturo reached upwards, and I helped lift him through with his duffel bag. For a moment, I was alone and staring at the beautiful stars in the clear night sky. I could hear someone banging against the door with a heavy object.

Suddenly, Arturo's face appeared in the skylight, and he looked down at me. "Let's go!" he yelled.

Instinct took over, and a full load of adrenaline forced me to climb on top of the bookshelf to get closer to the skylight. I grabbed Arturo's hand, and he pulled me up through the opening. We were now on a tile roof, and Arturo rapidly headed toward the south corner. I followed, but the slippery tile made traveling difficult. At the corner, I looked over to see a drainpipe.

Arturo slid down the pipe, and I followed. He kept low, and we zigzagged around the plants until we came to the main entrance. I saw that somebody had forced the big gates open, and there were three large black SUVs. Three men stood twenty feet apart from each other with big assault rifles. I suspected they were there to look for people jumping over the fence.

Arturo pointed to the left man. I snuck up from behind and used a sleeper hold on him. Arturo grabbed the man's gun, checked it, and shot the other two guards right through their left eye. His outstanding marksmanship should have impressed me, but I still had not gotten my head into the game. Arturo began running while I blindly followed. I heard yelling and gunshots behind us, which fueled my physical ability.

We took side streets, leaped over fences, and sprinted along thin paths filled with prickly weeds. When we reached a safe distance, we stopped to catch our breath. "They will be here soon," Arturo cautioned in between gasps.

"Who are those men?"

"I don't know. Mateo betrayed me!"

"Is that what you two were yelling about?"

"I asked him to explain his motives. He insisted I hadn't shown him the proper amount of respect. I treated him better than a brother."

"I shot him."

"He would have killed you."

"I know," I said with remorse.

"You did the right thing."

"It doesn't feel right."

"In time, it will."

"Anna ..."

I looked down, and Arturo put his hand on my shoulder. He raised my head with his other hand and looked into my eyes.

"This life we choose is difficult," Arturo said with conviction. "In the many years I have walked this earth, I have only considered one girl my daughter."

"I cared about her," I admitted.

"I'm aware of your feelings."

"I wish I had gotten to know her better."

"I would have been proud to call you my son."

We could hear voices getting closer, and Arturo said, "Let's go to my customs transfer warehouse and hide in a shipping container. Nobody will locate us. Tomorrow morning, we will sort everything out."

We walked briskly, using the shadows to conceal our movements. "You did all this with your big backpack?" Arturo quietly asked.

"I did," I answered with a quiet laugh. "Didn't I? Kind of amazing. Hey, what's with your bag?"

"It contains a hard drive with an up-to-date copy of my accounts and passwords. I also have 50,000 dollars and my knife."

"That's enough to get us out of here."

"Where is the ..."

ELEVEN

My head hurt, and I tried to sit up, but my body refused to cooperate. To my surprise, my captor had not bound my hands, which comforted me. It took time to focus on my dimly lit surroundings. I first noticed the low ceiling and then a tiny room with damp air and a salty smell. It then occurred to me that the room light did not behave normally. It seemed to dim and then brighten.

Finally, as my eyes focused, I realized it flickered, which seemed familiar. *Where did I see this before? It's an oil lamp!* I realized, and then asked, "Grace?"

"You certainly made a mess of things," a familiar woman's voice spoke.

I turned to my left to see Grace sitting on a chair while holding her legs with her arms. She wore a fashionable striped blue shirt with tan slacks. Grace had tied her soft brown hair

into a braid, and her amazing brown eyes conveyed warm emotions. She smiled at me, and her face remained as beautiful
as I remembered. There had been so many doubts about why
I had undertaken this unforeseeable journey, and that single
smile confirmed I was on the right path.

"You were out for a long spell," Grace observed. "I did not
intend to strike you so hard." Her sweet words still held a
slight Russian accent, and the sound comforted me.

"It's all right," I mumbled. "Did you get another mountain lion?"

Grace laughed, and this beautiful sound made me feel complete. "I must have hit you with too much force," she answered.
"Rest now, and then we will talk."

Grace got out of her chair and left. I felt a wave of relief,
knowing the danger had passed. Then, as I drifted off to sleep,
I wondered what she had planned for me.

◆ ◆ ◆

The sunlight forced my eyes open, and I looked over to see
a porthole.

I must be on a boat, I thought, while looking to the right to see
a pile of clothes neatly tied together with a yellow piece of fabric.

My head hurt when I sat up, and I felt a painful bump near
my left ear. I got out of bed, put on my new clothes, and just as in
my previous experience, Grace had selected an unorthodox outfit
that fit perfectly. This time, a navy-blue ensemble that combined
an '80s New York power executive with a decorated 1800s military general. The reflection in the small mirror confirmed I looked
like a million dollars, with a grin that could charm the world.

I could not locate my shoes, so I put on a pair of comfortable slippers. Outside my cabin was a long hallway. As I looked both ways, I understood the immense size of this boat. I headed left, and the corridor ended at a narrow staircase. At the top, I found a tastefully decorated lounge, and the Midwestern-themed artwork surprised me. It looked good, but it was not the style or quality I expected Grace to have. I proceeded through a beautiful dining room, and then an entertainment room, before I came to a deck with an enormous swimming pool.

The horizon confirmed that we were far away from land, and I realized I was in the aft section. The air felt warm, and the sky was overcast. Somebody walked up.

"Nice boat," I said without turning around.

"So to speak, it's a ship," Grace corrected.

"Must've cost a lot."

"I'm renting it at a low rate. The owner has fallen on hard times."

"You didn't answer my question," I said with humor.

"No, I did not obtain a pet."

I turned to look at Grace. She wore a stylish gray dress with her hair tied up in a bun. Her fashionable black sunglasses complemented her sophisticated appearance. We stared at each other for twelve seconds, and she said, "You have many questions. Breakfast first."

"I'd like that."

We proceeded to the dining area, and I asked, "Where are my shoes?"

"Your shoes had integrated tracking devices, as did your backpack and laptop. A local man drove them to the jungle and dropped them off. I had the foresight to keep the hard drive and remove the tracking software."

"How?"

"How did I know where to locate you? Since our departure, I have kept a close eye on you and the people who took an interest in your activities. Incidentally, the people I hired installed the tracking device in your backpack."

"Hmm."

We arrived in the dining room to see a tasteful assortment of food. A five-foot-five man with neatly combed brown hair motioned for me to sit. I suspected he was from India and was dressed in a white uniform typical of a restaurant server. I found it amusing that the man went far out of his way not to make eye contact. His presence surprised me because I knew Grace liked her privacy. I sat down first, and then Grace sat with a pleasant expression. The man silently served me a tiny bacon quiche, French pastry, sliced bananas, and coffee.

I remembered my lesson from our previous encounter and placed my napkin in my lap while maintaining peaceful eye contact. The man then served smaller portions of the same meal to Grace. We began eating, and I took great care to take small bites, savor the food, and use my silverware to the best of my ability. I found the taste good but not excellent.

The man left, and we continued to eat. Grace occasionally looked at me as if her eyes asked questions and somehow ascertained answers. Six minutes later, she asked, "Are you enjoying your meal?"

Clearly, she was testing me, and I knew we were back to our old game, which meant always telling the truth and acting supremely respectful. My harvest abilities now made this task easier. I thought about the flavor and replied, "The food is delicious by my standards, but I'm not sure it's up to your culinary expectations."

Grace looked satisfied and said in a coy voice, "Indeed."

At that moment, I had a revelation. Because of the harvest, ordinary people had become tedious to Grace. She craved respect and disliked people who did not immediately understand her requests. I looked at her and knew she understood my realization.

"You have taken up a minor interest in cooking," Grace commented.

"You gained this knowledge by looking at the change in my credit card spending."

"Indeed."

Grace formed a thin smile, which brought me comfort. However, it also reminded me that my life had been under her microscope. We continued to eat for another eighteen minutes, and then Grace directed me to a washroom, where I cleaned up. Again, the towels impressed me, and I wondered where she purchased such fine cloth.

Instinctively, I walked into the living room area. Grace sat on the sofa with her legs crossed, wearing a curious expression. I sat down as she reached behind and produced my *Dawson's Creek* notebook. I should have expected her mysterious action by this point in my life, but I started laughing.

Grace looked at me and shook her head with a warm smile. She tossed me the notebook, and I noticed a nice black pen clipped to it.

"I missed our conversations," I began.

"I enjoy your company as well. You have had quite an adventure since we last spoke."

"Adventure is one way of putting it. What have you been up to?"

I sensed I had accidentally crossed a line, because Grace adopted an annoyed expression.

"I've been overcoming business difficulties," she answered angrily.

"I hope the problems weren't too severe."

"They were formidable."

"Oh."

"Tell me. Do you enjoy the harvest gift?" Grace wanted to know.

"It's amazing; I've learned so much and have a fantastic body."

"Your face lost its blemishes, and you have more muscle definition. The harvest has been kind."

"True," I admitted.

"I can also see that you have lost weight and regained hair."

"It lost its gray, and it's thicker."

"Overall, your appearance has improved," Grace said with a thin smile.

"Thanks."

I sensed a change, and I wondered what she had planned for me. While I contemplated my fate, the same man who served us earlier walked in with a silver tray and a fancy silver pitcher. He poured a light-brown liquid into two tall glasses and silently departed. I recognized the same cut glass with a deer theme from our first encounter. As I took a small sip, the delicious taste surprised me. I was drinking birch bark tea with fresh mint, lemon, and agave. I appreciated the refreshing drink and looked over to see Grace smiling.

We both leaned back.

"So to speak, I read your book," Grace mused.

"I knew you would. Did you like it?"

Grace's expression darkened. She straightened up and said in a controlled tone, "I expected you to pen something to a higher standard."

"I'm disappointed that I did not fulfill your request."

"Piz-dets! (I later learned this was Russian for "damn it.") Why did you use the name I provided?!" Grace demanded.

I was not expecting her angry reaction and answered in a hurt voice, "I thought you wanted me to?"

"You publicized every fact about me! I provided that information to you and you alone! What possessed you to act with such insolence?!"

"I did my best," I admitted, and then wondered why, if she had been keeping a close eye on me, she did not stop the publication of the book.

"Alas," Grace said with a deep sigh. "A large part of the blame rests with me. I was well aware of the risk associated with an inexperienced author. I hoped the harvest gift would have provided superior abilities to enable you to choose what topics to include and what to discard."

Grace's harsh criticism of my beloved work felt like a knife piercing my heart. It reminded me of when she forced me to admit I plagiarized my *Grime* books. I knew Grace would punish me for revealing her secrets and looked at the floor in disgrace while contemplating the magnitude of my failure. I now questioned my reasons for undertaking my journey.

"James? — James?" Grace asked.

"Yes?"

"My remarks were uncalled for."

"I am truly sorry for disappointing you," I said in a hurt voice.

I looked up to see Grace's sad expression, which intrigued me. "Your book caused quite a disruption in my life," she said with a weak smile.

"I'm sorry."

"It was I who desired to come forward and did not provide guidance on what content to include. Thus, the blame rests with me and I apologize for my outburst," Grace said in a kind voice.

"I offered to let you review my work," I reminded her.

"That, you did, and I should have been proactive." Grace took a full minute to reflect, and she continued. "As you know, my life had come to a crossroads. In retrospect, I had set an impulsive goal. Part of my motivation came from the passing of my only companion."

"Heathcliff?" I guessed.

"Yes."

"How long did she live?"

"Twenty-two years. That is a long time for her species."

"I thought she lived to be a hundred or something," I suspected.

"I do not know why you invented this foolish notion."

"It seemed natural to think that you applied the harvest procedure to Heathcliff."

"That is an unrealistic concept."

"Then why didn't you correct me when we last met?"

"Putting down my dear friend upset me, and I chose not to discuss the matter."

"Oh. I should've recognized this."

"Indeed," Grace said with a nod.

"May I ask—"

Grace interrupted as if she read my mind, "Yes, I named Heathcliff after the comic strip character. It fit her mischievous personality."

"That makes sense."

Grace looked around the room for a moment, and I wondered what she was thinking. Then, sixteen seconds later, she said, "After your book became available, my well-groomed managers recognized my identity. This forced me to remove many talented people."

"Why?"

"For the same reason as always."

"I don't understand."

"The vermin attempted to take over my businesses," Grace said in a bitter voice. "Foolish men!"

"What did you do?"

Grace adopted a dark expression, and I gulped. She looked at me for fourteen seconds and answered with narrow eyes, "Greed is the common denominator. It blinds us to the truth."

I needed to change the subject and decided to discuss a painful topic.

"You didn't appreciate my book. Is this because the story focused too much on me?"

"So to speak, no," Grace answered in surprise. "I expected you to pen a complete picture of my life."

"I worked hard to develop a rounded story."

"I expected more detail."

"The information you provided had gaps that more questions would have answered."

"In retrospect, I should have spent more time with you. Tell me, why did you not use an alias?"

"I wanted to make sure you identified me as the author," I answered.

"Hmm. I put a lot of pressure on you to succeed."

"That's putting it mildly."

"Perhaps more of the blame rests on my shoulders than I realized. Well, at least you did not give away the exact harvest details."

"I would never do that."

"As I predicted."

I sensed a positive change.

"Tell me," Grace asked, "why did your book not include Van Klinken?"

"The murder in Germany?"

"Yes," Grace answered with a nod.

"There wasn't much to tell. You tracked down a serial killer."

"He took the lives of nineteen babies!" Grace said with measured shock.

"You removed many bad people from society. The only difference is that he acted a little worse than the others."

"But, his death?" Grace said, while being taken aback.

"They all died by your hand. What made that man so special? Oh, I remember. You struck him so hard that his false teeth flew out."

"And you did not include that incident."

"You killed him. You killed them all. The gory details of how they died didn't add to your story."

"Hmm. So to speak, what about my art teacher, Jean-Claude?"

"You were learning how to paint portraits and learned that he took advantage of his models."

"But, he—"

I interrupted, "You respected Jean-Claude, and it hurt you to take his life. Grace, they were all bad people, and I believe that harvesting isn't easy for you. But you need to realize how hard it is to write a book about a woman with your complex history. If I wrote that you killed bad person A, then B, then C up to person ZZZ, it doesn't make for a readable book. An author needs to place every aspect into context. That way, the reader can enjoy the full story without getting bogged down by excessive details."

Grace leaned back and took a long sip of tea. Then, she nodded and said, "Many people have read your book. This morning's sales figures exceed 180,000."

"What?!" I asked in complete shock. "Really?! Bethany told me 56,000."

"Bethany only thinks about her bonus check."

"I'm getting that sense."

Grace took another sip of tea, looked at me for seventeen seconds, and said with a warm smile, "So to speak, I have missed our conversations."

"So have I."

"I must admit that I am not truly upset. You took great care to remain honest and included moments of humor. In retrospect, I placed more anguish upon you than necessary."

"You appreciated my humor?" I wondered aloud.

"Yes."

"That makes me feel better."

"I am glad."

We appreciated the moment for 28 seconds while enjoying the tea. Grace seemed to contemplate taking the conversation in a different direction, and I considered this a good sign.

"I have more questions that I would like to ask. If that's all right?" I ventured.

"I also have questions."

"We could answer each other's questions."

"Indeed," Grace said with a warm smile. "Tell me, when we parted ways, you seemed determined not to harvest. What changed your mind?"

"That's a complex matter. I think my mind got confused, and it made me harvest."

"More."

I looked at Grace and realized how much I missed her ability to challenge me. So I smiled and answered, "I wanted to see you again, and the only way to accomplish this impossible task would be to harvest one last time. Somehow, my mind tricked me into creating the goal of locating you."

"Why did you desire to meet me again?"

"My life became confused. I thought you would be the only person who could get it back on track."

"Have you located the answers you seek?"

"I'm starting to," I admitted with a smile.

"Interesting. So to speak, what event challenged you to harvest?"

I found it uplifting that Grace had such stunning insight into how my mind worked, and I answered, "A woman burned her child to extort money from me. The only solution I came up with was to harvest."

"How much did this decision trouble you?" Grace inquired, and I glanced away.

"I have many regrets."

"Knowing what you know now, would you still proceed down this path?"

I looked at Grace's hard-to-read expression, thought about her question for eleven seconds, and nodded. My actions pleased her, and she took a sip of tea while maintaining a curious stare.

"Why did you choose me?" I wondered. "Did it have something to do with the author I plagiarized?"

Grace looked surprised and answered, "Jack was a talented author, but no, that is not the fundamental reason behind my choice. I saw a lot of myself in your blog writings. You desire to make the world a better place one reader at a time, and I knew your personality would take well to harvesting."

I did not know how to interpret Grace's answer and asked, "What would have happened to me if I hadn't written about you?"

"Nothing."

"Nothing?" I asked in complete surprise. "Really?! You put an awful scare into me."

"So to speak, I felt it was necessary."

"Why did you need to tell your story so badly?"

"As I stated, the harvest is no longer as effective, and I wanted to share my narrative before my demise. Also, I desired to locate the other harvesters so we could compare experiences. My prior attempts had failed, and I required a novel approach. Literally."

I laughed at the pun and asked, "Did it work? I mean, did you locate anybody else?"

"Together, we located two people who harvest along with two and a half more."

"Two and a half?"

"I monitored every sale of your book and researched every buyer. Irregular patterns emerged from a fourth and possibly a fifth. We are now traveling to Thailand to see number three."

"What about the others?" I asked.

"I could not pinpoint their locations. However, I am still pursuing the matter."

"Why do you call one of them a half?"

"From the information I've gathered, I'm not sure if the person is a harvester or a rich individual who desires our secret. This person has gone far out of their way to maintain a private life. That's why I call the unknown person a half." Grace leaned back for 33 seconds and continued. "So to speak, I found your use of freeze-dried snake venom a creative solution."

"It also works better."

"I agree."

Grace always seemed at least one step ahead of me.

"What happened to Amten?" I wondered.

"The harvester from Panama? He used the name Arturo, and I have him in restraints below."

"Wow! He's here?! I guess you captured us as we ran away."

Grace momentarily scowled at my outburst and said, "The

two of you were about to encounter assassins. Therefore, I disabled both of you at the appropriate time."

"Um. Thanks. Hey, I wish you could have met Quan. He was brutal but interesting."

"He is also below."

"What?! No way!" I said in shock, and then realized I had made another silly assumption and should have used better language.

"He escaped through a tunnel, and I detained him."

I was glad Grace was not upset by my second outburst and said, "I thought he died in the airstrike."

"Quan slept in a secure room located deep within his compound," Grace confidently said, as if she knew more than she let on.

"How did you capture him?"

Grace smirked and answered, "The aerial view of his compound revealed the most likely escape exit. He emerged three days after the attack, and I detained him."

"How is he?" I wanted to know.

"He refuses to speak with me."

"Oh."

"He will talk soon," Grace said with a wicked grin.

"Knowing you, he'll say a lot."

"So to speak, that is for certain."

An evil smile spread across Grace's face and left me uncomfortable.

"Do you know who blew up Quan's house and attacked Arturo's house?" I wondered.

Grace leaned back, looked away, shook her head, and answered without looking at me.

"What you must understand is that the attack aircraft flew through Chinese airspace. This journey required efforts to mislead Chinese radar operators and multiple refueling stops. It was an unprecedented accomplishment for a private contractor.

"After the attack, I detained three soldiers who revealed the names of two different contractors. Later, I *inquired* with the firm's owners about the hiring party. Unfortunately, they were unaware of the responsible individual."

When Grace used the word "inquired," it sent a chill up my spine. She turned to me and continued, "I then detained two of the men who attacked Arturo's house. They confessed to being associated with a small organization. When I interrogated the owner, he did not know who paid for the operation."

"Do you have any thoughts about who might be behind the attacks?"

"I have determined that a person who knows the earlier harvest secret would like to learn about the improvements. However, a second possibility exists. A powerful person may desire the secret to cure their declining health. This would add tremendous motivation."

"I see."

Grace shifted her position and asked, "Tell me. Do you enjoy the harvest gifts?"

"I do."

"Which do you value the most?" Grace asked with a curious expression.

"As you predicted, I appreciate the passage of time. Now, I watch people making life choices and observe the long-term results. Also, the harvest opened my eyes to the finer things in life, especially art and music."

"Indeed," Grace said with confidence.

"There is one troubling aspect. I clearly see people getting older. Watching my parents aging hurts the most."

"My parents slipped away right before my eyes. My father's last words to me were, 'Why do you remain so beautiful?' I did not have the heart to tell him the truth. He died in my arms, and I think of his passing often. James, your family has read your book. What information did you reveal to them?"

I looked away and answered without turning back, "They asked if my story is true. I showed them my harvest scar, which confirmed everything. My mother cried and cried. Afterward, she pleaded for me never to take another life. Of course, I agreed. And then ...

"My mother doesn't know that I have recently harvested. But the damage is done. Now, when I see her, she turns away. On the rare occasions when we speak, she mumbles, and I hear the disappointment in every word. My father acts gruff and gets right to the point. Inside, I know he hates me. And my sister ... My dear sister refuses to take my calls. Perhaps in time, I will regain her trust. However, when I tell them I took the lives of two parents, it will crush them."

"You do not have to discuss the topic."

"Yes, I do," I said with conviction. "They deserve the truth."

"So to speak, families forgive."

"I don't know how," I admitted.

"Your heart will figure this out."

"I'd like to believe that."

Our mood had become gloomy, and we sipped tea while looking at the artwork. Two minutes later, I changed the subject. "I have some basic questions, if you are up for more conversation."

"Such as?"

"Do you ever get colds?" I wondered.

"An interesting question," Grace said with a cheerful expression. This change brought relief that we were on to more pleasant topics. "No, I do not. The harvest gift provides an effective means to protect my body, and I have not experienced a full day of sickness in many years. Occasionally, my body rejects a foreign mass, resulting in an abscess. You will become an expert at lancing them."

I felt concerned as I understood her desire for my harvest journey to continue. "What about your teeth?" I wondered. "What if you chipped one?"

"That is a splendid aspect of the harvest. Every fifteen years, a new set appears. Sometimes, a tooth comes in at an odd angle, and it will require extraction."

"Wow, that's unexpected. What if you lost an eye? Would it grow back?"

"I am not sure," Grace admitted. "Many years ago, I lost the tip of my index finger in a knife fight. It grew back over three years. I imagine an eye could grow back."

"May I ask a personal question? It's fine if you choose not to answer it."

"I know the source of your question. Yes, I have a monthly cycle. It is much shorter than before the harvest."

The statement took me aback, and I humbly said, "I wanted to ask a different health question."

"It's fine. Now, to finish your inquiry, I have had some difficulty with kidney stones in the distant past. Switching from mint extract to mint oil eliminated this malady. Otherwise, my body behaves like everybody else's."

"No other health issues?"

"In our first meeting, I discussed growing taller along with ear and nose growth. Oh, yes. There is one topic I failed to reveal. Over the years, my bust increased, but this would not affect you. I will ask Quan and Arturo about changes to their manhood."

"Oh," I said in embarrassment.

"Is this conversation making you uncomfortable?"

"No, I mean yes, I mean ..."

"So to speak, you must relax," Grace said with a chuckle.

I desperately needed to change the subject and said, "I can tell time accurately without a watch. How well can you tell time?"

"Growing up, our household did not have a clock. So, we learned how to tell the time by looking at the sun's shadow."

"Your last sentence took four and three-quarter seconds. It's been two hours and 39 minutes since I woke," I said with confidence.

"That is remarkable!" Grace said, and then pinched her lips with her right hand.

"I assumed all harvesters got that ability."

"So to speak, I cannot tell time with that level of precision. What else can you do?"

"My physical and mental abilities are better, but nothing extraordinary," I admitted.

"Come to think of it, I have one unique ability. I can visualize distance and angles with great accuracy." Grace pointed at a chair and continued. "That object is 2.6 meters from the back wall, and it is pointing at 28 degrees from that bulkhead."

"Wow, that's amazing. Anything else?"

"Before the harvest, my mother tried to teach me to play the flute, and I did not have the ear for the notes. However, after the harvest, I excelled."

"It would be nice to hear you play."

"I will arrange that," Grace said with a warm voice.

"I think I now have some artistic skills, but I haven't attempted a project."

"As a child, I drew basic pictures. You would consider them unremarkable. But, after the harvest, my artistic ability flourished. Come to think of it, I possess another unique ability. I can memorize a hundred items and change the order in my mind."

"Wow, that's impressive," I said in awe. "My memory is much better, but I cannot remember a comprehensive list."

"Did your writing improve?" Grace wondered.

"Oh, yes. Now, I can think quicker, and the words flow right out."

"You wrote that your high school football knee injury went away after your first harvest."

"Yes," I answered with a grin.

"As a young girl, I fell off a horse, resulting in a stiff arm. The harvest eliminated this malady."

"I think it's the same thing."

"Tell me. What did you say to upset the player?"

I took a deep breath and answered, "On the next play, keep your eyes on the ball and not their butts."

"So to speak, those words do not contain wisdom."

"The other players laughed their heads off."

"You have a great sense of humor. Your issue is in the application," Grace said with a smile.

"True. Hey, another question. I noticed my personality changed. I went from a strong liberal to middle-of-the-road."

"My personality also changed. I am now more reserved," Grace said with an amused expression.

"It is interesting that the harvest has affected us differently."

"It is."

Grace smiled at me and took a sip of tea. The uplifting mood allowed me to push the conversation boundary. "Does the harvest gift allow you to communicate images mentally?"

"What?" Grace asked in surprise.

"Heathcliff sent me mental images."

"I found the passage in your book most amusing. It is quite clear that Heathcliff had a high opinion of you."

"Well? Did you do this mental image thing with Heathcliff?"

Grace took a sip as she pondered my question.

I did not know what to do and leaned back on the sofa. Eighty-five seconds later, I probed further, "Can you do that with people? I tried it with some friends, but it didn't work."

Grace continued to stare at her teacup while occasionally taking small sips.

Finally, after two minutes, I knew the subject needed to change, and I casually mentioned, "I got your coin. Thanks."

"What coin?" Grace asked.

"The coin in the paper wrapper you left at Heathcliff's rock."

"I placed no such coin for you to find, and I am unaware of any specific rock associated with her. However, many years ago, I came into possession of a coin collection. Heathcliff wanted to help in the sorting process, and she ran off with a mouthful. You must have found one."

"That's unexpected."

"It appears Heathcliff left you a gift," Grace concluded with a smile.

"Hmm. That's something to think about. May I ask an important question?"

"You are free to do so. Why do you inquire as you do? Are you still intimidated by my presence?" Grace sensed my hesitation, and she tried to put me at ease. "I see," she surmised, "my actions still intimidate you. So to speak, I confess I am not used to speaking with a person who is aware of my past. I will do my best to make you more comfortable. Please relax and ask your question."

As I was thinking, Grace admitted, "I have become more comfortable around you."

"Really?"

"I keep saying, 'So to speak.' This is an old phrase my mother used to say, and it only comes out in casual conversation." Grace smiled broadly.

"What's next?" I wondered aloud.

"This vessel is faster than any other in its class. As a result, on Thursday morning, we will reach the coast of Thailand. Then, you will take a small craft to shore, travel to a remote location, and confront a person who knows the harvest secret."

"You won't be joining me?" I questioned.

"I will keep a close watch over you. But no, I will not accompany you."

"Oh. What do you know about this person?" I wondered.

"This individual is secretive, spends many hours on their computer, and has had a deep interest in you. I also learned they pay local criminals to obtain young boys."

"That makes the person a harvester. Do you know their name?"

"This person uses many names, but I am unaware of their actual name," Grace answered and then changed the subject. "I read many Facebook remarks about me."

"Really? I hope I didn't offend you with some of my answers."

"I would not think they would care," Grace said with a puzzled expression.

"Please consider their perspective. You were present for history. Unfortunately, all us mortals can do is read history books."

"You have a whimsical method of summarizing," Grace said with a hearty chuckle.

"Thank you. Did you ever want to answer any Facebook questions?"

"James, I'm a normal woman. No big surprises. People somehow got this grand idea that I am a wunderkind who resolved the answers to life's important questions and was present for every historical event."

"They're curious," I said with a smile.

"So to speak, I am aware."

"Well, how about this? What's your favorite movie?" I asked with great interest.

"Fair enough. We will play the twenty-question game. But first, please answer an important question. Have you encountered these people who refer to themselves as Goths?"

"There were lots of posts from Goths, and I met several."

"They have taken quite an interest in my life. Three sought me out."

"They located you?!" I exclaimed.

"Yes."

"Wow. How the heck did they do that?" I again caught myself acting boldly and made a mental note to tone down my behavior.

"Upon questioning, they admitted to undertaking an extensive computer search concerning shipping and art transactions. They cross-referenced this information to other data and located a business meeting requiring my attendance."

"That's quite an accomplishment."

"These *Goths* think they have a connection to me. Clearly! They don't!" Grace fumed.

"What did you tell them?"

"I do not appreciate uninvited guests!"

Grace glowered and looked away.

I knew those three wayward Goths did not survive their interrogation, which reminded me that I was in the presence of an extremely dangerous individual.

Eighteen seconds later, without looking at me, Grace continued, "To answer your earlier question, the movie *Dr. Zhivago*. However, not for the reason you think. I appreciated the cinematography. A more recent favorite is *Romancing the Stone*."

"Wow, I wouldn't expect that choice."

"A funny movie. Also, well-filmed," Grace said in a pleasant voice.

"Favorite sports team?"

"So to speak, I do not follow sports. However, I occasionally watch the Toronto Blue Jays."

"How did you vote in the last election?"

"I am not registered to vote. However, if you were to ask my political beliefs, the Libertarian party aligns with my values."

"Do you play video games?" I wondered.

"I occasionally play online chess."

"Many people had questions about your religious beliefs. When we last spoke, you gave me a well-thought-out answer, but how about a more basic question? Do you think there is a heaven and a hell?"

Grace stared down at her hands and answered, "Over the years, I have thought much about this concept. When a person passes, I observe something I interpret to be their soul leaving this world. If the person is evil, their soul seems to fight against an unseen enemy. On the rare occasions when I witness a good person passing, I perceive their soul being welcomed. Hmm. So to speak, you are the only person since my father who brings out my compulsive habit of looking at my hands," she said, looking down at her hands again.

"Really?" I wondered.

"Indeed. I will anticipate your next question. You wish to know what will happen to me when I pass. I have committed many regrettable actions, but overall, I have lived a good life and helped many people. The divine spirits should welcome me because of my charity and removal of evil. Now, I would like to hear your answer."

Grace's profound moral question sat me back on my heels for 27 seconds. Finally, after a deep breath, I answered, "I harvested a mother and father of my own free will. There can be no doubt. My actions were not honorable, and there can be no forgiveness."

"You are not giving yourself enough credit. Were these two people of ill repute?"

"It's still murder."

"Did you see the evil within their eyes?" Grace asked in a probing voice.

"It was so awful; completely dark and devoid of humanity."

"Did you see improvement in the lives of those who surrounded the harvest subjects?"

"The parents had a young boy, and his life will be better," I answered. "That's kind of why I did the harvest."

"So to speak, a benefit of the harvest is that you can see the full result of your efforts. In time, the boy will grow up and have children. The harvest will allow you to observe the long-term result. How much better do you think his life will be?"

"I'm not sure," I admitted. "But I know he will have a full life without terrible parents."

"Do you see? You have brought about a powerful change, and you must trust your decision."

"That's a lot to think about."

I remained silent for 83 seconds, put my head down, and quietly said, "When I last escaped, a man named Mateo worked for Arturo, and they got into a fight. I had to make a choice ... I killed Mateo with his own gun. Before I shot, he called me a bastard for protecting Arturo. I believe he was a good man, and I think he had a family."

"If Mateo had won the struggle, what are the chances that he would have killed you?"

"I don't know," I absently answered. Then, after thinking for thirteen seconds, I said without looking up. "He always acted annoyed around me. Even when we first met, and I never knew why. I guess you're correct. He would have killed me in the blink of an eye."

"So to speak, you made the right choice," Grace said with confidence.

"I don't feel like I made the right choice."

"In time, you will."

I leaned back, sipped my tea, looked up, and thought about the topic for 43 seconds. Then, I needed to change the subject. "I have another question, but it might be too sensitive."

"You remain intimidated?"

"A bit," I admitted.

Grace mused for twelve seconds and said, "I regret my treatment of you when we first met. To be honest, I had not thought through the entire course of events. However, I want to assure you that I mean you no harm. Now, please ask your question, and I promise not to take offense."

This permission put me at ease, and I said, "When I first interviewed you, we covered a lot of ground, but our short time together did not permit me to capture everything. I always wondered if you withheld any information."

Grace leaned back and took a long sip of tea. She stared at her cup and nodded. I patiently waited while she gathered her thoughts for 91 seconds. "Over the years, many men passed through my life. I did not share my relationship details with you because the world does not deserve this knowledge. However, to satisfy your curiosity, I will provide more detail. I got close to a few, but our interaction did not last. As I stated before, I married once, and I only allowed that man into my heart."

Clearly, I had hit a nerve, but I wanted to learn more. "Thank you for revealing more of your history. Would you like to share anything else?"

"I will reveal an additional fact. You once asked if I harvested any celebrities. I provided a truthful but incomplete answer. My complete answer would include taking the lives of two well-known people. They were not harvests, mind you. I chose not to share this information out of respect for those who appreciate their memory."

I desperately wanted to know their identities, but I knew Grace did not wish to provide those details. She turned away and seemed to concentrate on a colorful cat painting on the other side of the room. I did not care for the piece.

After 76 seconds, Grace let out a long breath and said without turning back, "I regret not bringing up one other topic. Allow me to share it now. You are no doubt aware that the harvest provides many benefits. It also has downsides. You see—well—the harvest causes addictive substances to become far more appealing."

Grace turned to me and encouraged me to fill in the blanks, and I finished her thought, "The harvest takes away bad parts of drugs and alcohol?"

"To make matters worse, the harvest enhances the induced feelings."

"Wow," I said in surprise.

"When opium became popular, I underwent three dreadful years. If you study your notes from 1871 to 1874, you will find one harvest every four weeks. I have a strong word of advice. Observe a zero-tolerance policy on all addictive substances."

"That's good to know. I will certainly take your advice."

Grace took a sip of tea, and I asked, "After my book came out, did you feel I should have included another subject?"

Grace looked at her teacup for 46 seconds, glanced up with a smile, and asked, "You viewed my paintings?"

"Of course."

"What did you think of them?" Grace said with a smile.

"You have a true artistic gift; they're very well done."

"By looking at the subject matter and style, what did you think of the artist? What is her personality?"

"She seemed to be a sophisticated woman with a lively personality, but she had a dark streak."

"Exactly," Grace said with confidence.

"Exactly what?"

"Overall, I am a cheerful woman. I like music, I paint, I travel, I read, I cook, I write, and I meet lovely people. As I shared with you in our first encounter, I provide many scholarships, and I often call the recipients to ensure they are cared for. Plus, every one of my workers has a pleasant environment and good management. Twice a year, I take employee satisfaction surveys and read every single comment. I do this because I want everybody who works for me to be happy.

"Your book painted a bleak picture of my life. Harvesting is the dark one percent. I wished your work conveyed more of the uplifting 99 percent. As I think about it, this aspect upset me the most."

I stared into my teacup.

"James?" Grace asked.

"Yes?"

"It's not your fault."

"No, I negatively portrayed your life," I admitted.

"I forced you to interview me, which led to unintended consequences. You must not blame yourself."

"If we had spent more time together, I would have captured more of the 99 percent."

"Circumstances made that impossible," Grace concluded with disappointment.

"I experienced your wonderful cooking, and many people asked about the taste."

"Exactly."

"Something for my next book," I said with a smile.

We laughed. Grace poured more tea. "I'd like to ask another question," I probed.

"It's an important one. Go ahead. Please ask."

"When we last departed. I sensed you withheld the biggest part of your story. You replied, 'some mysteries should remain mysteries.' What part didn't you share? What did that statement mean? I never figured it out."

Grace leaned back for three whole minutes while sipping tea, and I wondered if she would answer. Eventually, she said with obvious sadness, "I will tell you two things. First, the death of Heathcliff took a significant toll on my heart, and our interview turned out to be more difficult than I expected.

"We developed an unexpected *friendship,* and upon your departure, saying goodbye became—*difficult.* That's why I said 'mysteries should remain mysteries.' In retrospect, I acted selfishly by not stating my true feelings; I am sorry for being so vague. That brings up another point. I never properly thanked you for being Heathcliff's friend during her last moments. For that, I will always be grateful.

"Second, I shared my full life's story. Looking back, I made many sincere statements I had not planned to. However, I chose not to share one key aspect. Please understand that I undertook this action for an important reason and still cannot speak about this matter."

"May I make an observation?" I wondered.

"You may."

"I think a fundamental part of you enjoys being mysterious."

"Hmm. Perhaps."

Grace made a crafty smile, and her eyes darted around. I wanted to lighten the mood. "Please share a funny story."

"My, aren't you the inquisitive one? Well, let's see. Oh, I recall a funny family story from my childhood. My mother was teaching me how to bake, and I made berry tarts for the first time. I told everybody to prepare for a wonderful surprise. When dinner came, I went to get the tarts and found an empty plate. My brother Ujarak had eaten them. That may not sound like a funny story, but we recited it often—such simple times.

"Hmm. You might prefer a more recent event with more humor. Well, now. Eight years ago, I attended an after-concert party in an exclusive German hotel. On rare occasions, my stomach becomes unbalanced, and during dinner, I had to excuse myself.

"In the elevator, it became apparent that I needed to vomit. When I got to the door of my room, I felt dreadful, and, in my haste, I could not get the key to work. Fortunately, a nearby housekeeper let me in. James, I had a ghastly experience resulting in an appalling sight. When I recovered, I noticed a man's suit on the bed."

"It wasn't your room?!" I asked in shock.

"Tragically, no. It turns out that I had gotten off on the wrong floor."

"What did you do?"

"So to speak, I exited in haste and took the elevator to the correct floor."

I rolled in laughter, and Grace shook her head while laughing. Then, when we calmed down, she said, "And now, a funny story from your life."

"Oh, I remember one. My parents, sister, and grandmother all came to visit me at UCLA. As we walked to dinner, my grandmother found a dime, and she found another a few steps later. This discovery excited her, and she told us, 'Look at all these rich students. They throw their money away like water!' Well, I got a crazy idea and bummed some change from my father. I walked ahead and discreetly put coins on the ground. Grandmother could not believe her luck, and she scooped up every single coin like a hawk. Meanwhile, we were doing our best to keep from laughing. Eventually, my mother stopped it all, and Grandma reprimanded me. 'That's a dirty trick. Don't think you're getting your money back!' She said. We laughed and laughed."

"My, aren't you the scamp?" Grace asked with a laugh. "Now, be honest. How much do I intimidate you?"

"It's natural to be cautious around you. However, you must admit that you can be a dangerous individual. How many people have lost their lives since we met? Like those Goths."

"Do you think I would take your life at this moment?" Grace asked in a slightly hurt voice.

"It's clear that I must remain careful around you. I know you have at least one weapon within reach. You even pointed a gun at me in the kitchen. A nine-millimeter, as I recall."

"Yes, I remember."

Grace turned away, and I realized I had unintentionally upset her. So I looked down into my teacup in deep thought. Forty-three seconds later, she asked in a hurt voice, "What specifically have I done to unsettle you?"

I looked up and answered, "You killed a man right in front of me. I even found out his real name, Douglas Obrien. Normal people don't force others to kill."

"I see."

We leaned back, and each took a sip of tea. I did not know how to get the conversation back to a friendly place, and I wondered if I should talk or if Grace desired silence. Ninety-one seconds later, it all became too much, and I spoke my mind, "I understand your motives, and I hold no malice toward you."

Grace looked up and then back into her teacup. Clearly, I needed to mend some fences, and I thought for two minutes. Finally, a childhood memory popped into my mind.

"Growing up, my family moved a lot. Around the age of thirteen, we lived in a house with a forest behind it. On weekends, my father and I went out to collect firewood. He used his big powerful chainsaw to cut up the branches, and I stacked them into the wheelbarrow.

"My dad knew I was afraid of using a chainsaw, and we had talked about it a few times. I thought he understood my position, but, one day, he put the chainsaw down and turned to me. He had left it running and pointed toward a log. Now, a typical father would carefully explain all safety aspects of such a dangerous tool. No, no, no. Not my father. Even the idea of touching that sputtering chainsaw riddled me with fear. After all, I had just witnessed it cut through a massive log in seconds. Imagine what it would do to my arm! So, I refused to move and watched him load logs. Even when I protested, he ignored my pleas.

"Something took hold of me, and I picked up the chainsaw. With extreme care, I revved the engine and cut a thin branch. I was wholly terrified, but somehow, I did it. When the branch hit the ground, I was so relieved. So, I lobbed off some more small branches. After about twenty cuts, I tackled a thicker branch. Halfway through, I thought for sure the chainsaw would buck and cut my leg off or kick up and slice through my forehead. At that moment, I looked over to see my father attentively watching. His thoughtful expression encouraged me to continue, and I cut another. Half an hour later, he took over. My father had this little grin that I will never forget. I often think about that moment, and I now realize that he helped me to grow by challenging my fears. Later in life, I understood this moment held a life-building lesson.

"Now, I knew my father's tool shed contained a chainsaw. When I would go in there alone, I could see it and did not run away. But I would never start it up without him around. I guess what I am saying is that I was not afraid of the chainsaw, but I had tremendous respect for how dangerous it could be.

"You're like my dad's chainsaw, and perhaps the word 'intimidated' isn't the word that I should use to describe my feelings. I have a deep respect for you, and I sought you out. In making this decision, I knew that you would not harm me unless I did something stupid."

Grace looked at me with a piercing expression for 24 seconds and said, "You have a thoughtful perspective."

We mused while enjoying our tea. Seven minutes later, Grace twisted her fingers and said in an uplifting voice, "Now for the 'stop intimidating James plan.' Let's go for a swim."

With that, Grace stood. I stood, and we began walking. "There's a swimsuit in your room," she said without turning around. "Meet me at the pool. I've never used a pool on a ship, and it will be an adventure for both of us."

"Sounds like fun."

To my great relief, the discomfort between us had lessened, and I walked to my room. In the top drawer, I found clothes, including a black Speedo swimsuit. I had never worn a Speedo, and this one fit tightly. As I looked into the mirror, I felt incredibly self-conscious. Until that moment, I did not think the term "skimpy" could apply to men's clothing. I decided, *when in Rome.*

When I arrived at the pool, I sat in an expensive outdoor lounge chair. I still felt embarrassed when Grace came dressed in a fluffy white robe. I remembered another drawer in my room contained a robe and wished I had it on. She laughed and asked, "You put that little thing on?"

Clearly, Grace planned to mess with me, and I laughed in embarrassment. Then, I put on my game face and said, "Thanks to the harvest, I have a body that rocks!"

I stood and did my best muscleman pose with a confident grin. Grace laughed even harder.

"My body rocks better!" She countered.

Grace took off her robe to reveal a breathtaking body. Her purple, white polka-dot bikini fit perfectly. Grace's sculpted figure looked over-the-top gorgeous, and the sight electrified my mind. My jaw must have dropped so far that it should have broken through the ship's hull. She bit her lip, raised her eyebrows, and jumped into the pool.

It took 21 seconds to recover from her sexy image, and I jumped in. She splashed me when my head emerged from the water and rapidly swam away. I reasoned we were now playing catch the leader. But, while I swam my heart out, she was much faster on every lap. We played our chasing game for six agonizing full lengths of the pool, and then she slowed down to swim side by side. "You're quite the little fish," I complimented her in between strokes.

"I'm surprised you put on that little swim suit."

"For you, anything."

Grace laughed, and we continued to swim. After five laps, we got out and rested in the lounge chairs. As I recovered, Grace caught me looking at her several times, and she grinned at me. Of course, I saw Grace checking me out a few times. When she realized I had observed her, she quickly glanced away. I enjoyed briefly intimidating her.

Our interaction made me wonder about what she thought of me and what our future might be. As I pondered my situation, like magic, the man who had served us before silently brought a silver tray with glasses. We enjoyed Grace's apple drink, shuduka, and the taste took me back to our first encounter.

"Tell me about her," Grace unexpectedly said.

"Who?"

"Anna."

"Oh. I hadn't realized that you knew so much about my recent history. Well, as you probably know then, Anna is Arturo's adopted daughter, and I taught her English."

Grace turned toward the sky and said, "She held your arm while looking at you with great fondness."

"You saw that?"

"Yes," Grace confirmed, and then turned back to me.

"Oh. All right. Well, I had known for some time that Anna wanted to start something between us. Over dinner that night, I explained that I led a complex life and that starting a relationship would be challenging. I also confirmed that Arturo harvested. Anna took the news surprisingly well. I think she might have put the pieces together from my book. Anyway, on the way back to the car, Anna began holding my arm. I think she did this to let me know she accepted my life choices while inviting me to be more than a friend if I desired. But I also knew that she could have been manipulating me in order to learn facts about her father. I have never been good at reading women."

"Did she consider this event to be the first date?" Grace asked with a curious stare.

"In her eyes, I'm sure she thought of that night as a first date."

"What was it in your eyes?" Grace probed.

"In retrospect, I guess it was."

"Did you enjoy the evening?"

"We had a wonderful time, but there were awkward moments," I admitted. "Anna was a very forward woman, and I'm not used to that."

"You picked an excellent place to eat. Did you try the mango curry shrimp with brown rice?"

"No."

"Something for you and Anna to experience the next time you see her."

"What?!" I exclaimed.

"You two can return to Viviana's kitchen and appreciate the shrimp entrée."

"Anna's dead!"

"What?! How?!" Grace asked in shock.

"Mateo had a gun pointed at Arturo, and I joined the struggle. His gun—it went off. I turned around and—the bullet—and the bullet—it went right through—it went right through her! I didn't protect her! I could have helped! I should have helped! She bled so much! And she died. She died right there. I watched her die. She looked so scared. So completely terrified! I felt so helpless! I could not save her. It's all my fault! It's all my fault!"

I started crying, and Grace got out of her chair. She moved next to me and said, "Arturo failed to mention her passing. I am so sorry to have brought this subject up. I can see that Anna meant a lot to you."

I had not grieved for Anna, and now I felt the full weight of her loss. I put my hands over my face and cried as hard as I could. Grace put her arm around my shoulders. "Let it out; it's all right," she whispered.

The more I thought about Anna's death, the more I lost control. We were not lovers, but she had a kind heart and cared for me. A large part of me wanted to start a relationship with her. As I spiraled further into my heartache, it became clear that the chain of actions I started directly led to her death. *I should've reacted faster and attacked Mateo harder! I'm fully responsible!*

It took eight agonizing minutes before I could look up at Grace. Then, to my surprise, tears ran down her face.

The somber moment lasted for two minutes as we looked into each other's eyes. I was glad that Grace was with me during this sad moment, and sixteen minutes later, I had recovered enough to stop crying.

"I am touched that you care so much for somebody whom you knew for a short time," Grace soothed. "You are a deeper person than I imagined. Harvesting must be difficult for you."

"I have made my last harvest, and I intend to adhere to that goal."

"I am sure you will accomplish your worthy goal. Now, you have experienced a painful moment. Please rest, and then we will enjoy a pleasant lunch."

"That sounds wonderful," I said weakly.

"What would you like to eat? Anything you want, and I will have the chef make it."

"Something simple."

"I will see to your request."

Grace stood, put on her bathrobe, and walked away. She returned seven minutes later, took her bathrobe off, sat down, and turned to me. At that moment, I did not get what was going on. Grace (at least by her description) is worth over a trillion dollars. She has a stunning mind and a complex personality that begged to be explored. Now she wanted to show off her fantastic body to me. I could not wrap my head around her behavior. *A woman like her could get, well—any man she desired. Why on earth did she choose me? I am a nobody who cannot even afford a spare tire,* I thought, and turned to look at the horizon. I knew Grace continued to watch me, and at that moment, I desperately wanted to know what she thought of me. When I turned back, she turned away.

Suddenly, all the pieces came together. Grace trusted me, and she had not trusted another person in a long time. At that exact moment, I saw a slight smile form on the side of her face and knew she had come to the same conclusion. This revelation lessened my heartache. Thirteen minutes later, I asked without looking at her, "Have you met any nice musicians recently?"

We had previously joked about telling a musician the harvest secret so that Grace would have somebody to date. Thirty-four seconds later, Grace answered, "So to speak, I entertained a gentleman named Paul. He was an executive in the high-end artwork publishing business. That man did not know what to do with a woman like me."

I found this statement funny and asked, "Did you care about him?"

"I prefer my original word, entertain, to describe our relationship."

Anna's passing continued to hurt. I did my best to enjoy the overcast day and the salty air. Our conversation turned to art and classical music. It surprised me to learn that Grace and

I agreed that the composer Niccolò Paganini was overrated. We also discussed my recent history, including the summons to appear in court and additional details about the six Texas Rangers that Grace shot.

An hour later, the time seemed right, and we departed. I walked to my bathroom, and as in my previous encounter, the soap smelled like fresh lavender. I still wondered where she purchased these extravagant items. After my shower, I changed back into my morning clothing and strolled into the dining room. After sitting, we were served baked burgundy chicken. The presentation appeared simple, yet it was delicious.

While eating, Grace kept looking at me with a curious expression, and I wondered about the source of her brief fixations. I was attempting to come up with an intelligent question to explore more of her history when she asked, "We have three days together. What would you like to do with our time?"

In all the time I spent thinking about finding Grace, I hoped that answers to my life's deep questions would magically appear. This concept now seemed utterly foolish. My confused expression must have amused Grace, and she concluded, "It seems you did not have a plan for our time together. Well then. We will explore your defense abilities."

Knowing what would happen next brought relief, and I said, "Sounds good."

We finished lunch, and I changed into a white karategi outfit from the bottom dresser drawer.

Clearly, Grace had planned this activity. She met me in the hallway, and we headed down the stairs. Grace dressed in what I would call "Karate ninja lady meets energetic '80s music video workout dancer."

Her style looked very "Grace." She opened a lower deck door to reveal a modest exercise room and said, "The person who commissioned this vessel was obsessed with fitness."

"It's huge for a ship," I exclaimed.

"Begin!"

One quick punch to my gut, and I found myself on the floor while looking up at the ceiling in pain. This encounter reminded me of our fight at the bookstore parking lot. "Ouch," I said in a forced, pleasant voice.

"Again!"

I stood and faced Grace with a classic karate stance. She made a quick jab, and I successfully dodged left. Unfortunately, this move left me off-balance, and I spun to center myself. Grace did not expect this fundamental response, and while I could not strike her, I pushed her away. To my great surprise, she rolled, flipped back, and delivered a light punch to my gut. I toppled over.

"Again!" Grace commanded.

For the next 71 minutes, I did my best to dodge with an occasional attempt to strike while Grace landed light blows that still hurt. My only victory was elbowing her once in the ribs.

The intense experience left me sweaty and exhausted. Grace paused after a fantastic side punch, and we began working the cardio machines. During labored breaths, she said, "You have improved since our last encounter."

"I feel dead."

"You can still move. So to speak, that is a good sign."

I nodded because I could not talk. I switched to the weight trainer seven minutes later to work my arms, and Grace switched to the elliptical machine. As she exercised, she hummed a tune that I did not recognize. I would have given anything to know her thoughts.

Twenty-one minutes later, my muscles gave out, and I needed to stop. Grace threw me a large white towel and said, "Put this on."

She pointed toward a door, and I opened it to see a small bathroom. I undressed and put the fluffy white towel around my waist. When I emerged, I saw Grace dressed in an oversized white towel. She smirked, and we left the exercise room. I obediently followed her down the hall, and she opened a wooden sauna door. Inside, I closed the door and we sat down. The hot air felt relaxing, and a small light bulb provided the perfect amount of dull yellow light. Grace rested against the wood, and I did the same. The pleasant woody cedar smell eased my mind, and I allowed my thoughts to drift.

While contemplating our exercise, I listened to Grace's soft breathing with my eyes closed. Then, unexpectedly, she lightly nudged me with her knee. I opened my eyes to see her smiling with a playful expression. *Now, I really wonder what she is thinking.* However, I understood her well enough to appreciate that a conversation would disturb our tranquil atmosphere.

Nine minutes later, she stood, then I stood and opened the door. The cold air felt refreshing, and we walked toward the back of the ship. As Grace headed for what I assumed was her cabin, she turned to me, nodded, and walked away.

◆ ◆ ◆

After my shower, I wore a green pin-striped shirt with shiny black pants. It is incredible how the right outfit can provide enormous confidence. I walked to the study and found Grace reading a book with Cyrillic (Russian) letters on the cover. She had dressed in tan pants, a sheer white blouse with hand-sewn red hearts, and a modest gold necklace.

Grace motioned to a book, and I immediately recognized the title: *Mayhem in Hyde Park* by Edmund Summers. I had plagiarized this author to write my *Grime* series, and I sheepishly nodded to let her know I understood the selection. It then occurred to me that Grace brought this book on her journey to mess with me.

As I read, it was clear that Edmund Summers (the pen name of Jack Dunkin) was an excellent author, and I now had a better understanding of the disservice I had done to him. However, we occasionally peeked over our books at each other which confirmed she was not upset with my plagiarism.

When it seemed as if we had both read long enough, we took a short stroll. The ship was at least 150 feet long, and we ended our walk at the bow. When I turned to look up at the bridge, two men looked down at us. One was the server from earlier, and they were talking to each other. I reasoned we were the subject of their conversation.

The light began fading, and the moon was becoming visible through the clouds. Afterward, we walked inside to enjoy a baked crab dinner with red potatoes served in giant clamshells. While enjoying our meal, we discussed new classical music. After the main course, we ate a thin slice of tart apple pie on black glass plates, followed by a small cup of sweet coffee.

Our discussion turned to art, and then Grace led me to the pool. The lounge chairs were moist from the salty air, but we sat down anyway. I wanted to understand so much about her. I started to ask about her favorite books.

"Now is not the time for questions," Grace interrupted.

While I did not want to comply, I said, "All right."

We continued looking at the stars as I contemplated many profound thoughts about Grace, Anna, food, and classical music. Forty-one minutes later, we walked toward the dining room, and Grace departed. After standing there for a moment, I walked to my cabin to find a new Sony Vaio laptop on the desk. When I turned it on, I discovered Grace had installed my old hard drive. After entering the encryption password, I typed in recent events for two hours.

I felt exhausted from exercising earlier, so after changing, I lay down and tried to rest. Unfortunately, my memory of Anna prevented me from falling asleep.

Sixteen minutes later, there was a soft knock at the door. I got out of bed and opened the door to see Grace standing outside. She wore a stylish tan nightgown with her hair tied back. Grace's expression did not betray her thoughts, and I wondered about her motivations.

"You are sad," she whispered, before smiling weakly and turning to walk away.

As I stared at the hallway, it occurred to me to follow. She opened the door to a massive cabin that took up half of the ship's upper deck. I could not believe the luxury of this stunning room and the fact that such an ample space could even exist on a ship. Grace walked over to the bed and looked at me. For the first time, I noticed the vulnerability in her expression. When I got to the bed, she began unbuttoning my shirt. When Grace got to the last button, she made a crafty expression, rapidly yanked off my shirt, and motioned toward the bed.

This afternoon's knocking about left a big impression, and I was unsure of her intentions. I cautiously sat on the bed facing forward, and she sat next to me. Grace pushed me over face down and moved my legs. Her strength and physical dexterity continued to impress me. Grace hopped on my butt and playfully moved her legs. I got the impression that she enjoyed toying with me.

Grace began working my lower back with stunning skills that melted my muscles to oblivion. She knew everything about every fibrous tissue my body possessed. Her touch felt probing, sophisticated, and deeply personal. I became putty in her hands, and my mind switched from being on fire with anxiety to being dead to the world.

Grace worked my lower back, upper back, sides, shoulders, and neck. She then did a scalp massage that penetrated my inner thoughts. Her technique shifted between steady kneading, probing, and firm pressure. It never occurred to me that my body could get transformed to this supreme level of relaxation. My subconscious ability to measure time had ceased, which provided a liberating zen. All my tension drifted to some otherworldly place, and every muscle became a peaceful realm of unity. I briefly wondered if any other human had ever achieved this level of tranquility.

Grace finished with some light swirls and lay next to me. After another unknown amount of time, I used lots of energy to reenable my muscles enough to turn my head. Grace looked at me with a warm smile from about eight inches away. "Your muscles carried excessive stress," she whispered. "Anna's passing placed a substantial burden on your heart."

It took time to reengage my mind enough to comprehend her words and reply. "My body needed that. Thank you."

"At our first meeting, you gave me a massage, and now I returned the favor," Grace said, and then turned away to look up.

"I remember the experience well."

"I appreciated the effort," Grace offered with a deep sigh.

"Clearly, your body needed relief."

"I had been preparing to end Heathcliff's suffering."

"Well, you sensed how much Anna's passing affected me," I admitted.

"True."

Grace paused for thirteen seconds and continued. "In your book, I liked how you described me. 'Complex, but tender.' I have thought about those words many times."

"That's how I felt."

"You know, I didn't have my hand on a 'James Bond button' that would send your body through the roof. Now, be honest.

Did you genuinely have this foolish notion?" Grace asked in a playful voice.

I snickered and rolled over to face her. "I suspected you prepared for something," I replied.

"I will be honest. A weapon was not within my reach."

"Really? That's unexpected."

"I did not expect your massage. Your actions were—brave," Grace said with a hint of apprehension.

"The word 'brave' is an interesting word to use."

"So to speak, it is an appropriate word."

"May I share something about that moment?" I asked, unaware if I was taking the conversation too far.

"Go on."

"In my book, I said that my reasons for massaging you were an apology."

"I read your words and determined you provided an appropriate description of the moment. Did you not speak the truth?"

"Partially. I also wanted to get to know you better, and a massage seemed like a wonderful method." Grace seemed to be intentionally silent. "Would you tell me something about that night?" I asked with great hope.

"I might."

"What were you expecting when you invited me into your room that night?"

"For you to go to sleep."

"And nothing else?"

Clearly, I had pushed the conversation boundaries far beyond Grace's comfort zone, and I went for broke. "What if I had kissed you?"

Grace's breathing changed, and 38 seconds later, she answered in a trembling voice, "Your massage had more of an effect than you may have realized."

"How?"

"I let you get close to me," Grace admitted.

"Our interview got rather personal. But you have been close to other people. What about that Paul guy?"

Grace turned to stare upwards. She took a deep breath, a deeper breath, and replied, "He knew nothing about me—the real me. You got far closer to Anna and wept for her demise. When Paul left my life, I dismissed my emotions."

"Oh. I did not realize how much I affected you."

Grace turned to me for 26 incredible seconds. "Yes, you did," she said with a warm smile. Grace reached for my hand, held it, and whispered, "I hope my efforts to reduce your intimidation have succeeded. Goodnight, James."

"Goodnight, Grace."

We continued to hold hands, and I enjoyed the warm emotion conveyed by Grace's gentle grip. I tried to prolong the moment, but the massage shut my body down.

TWELVE

T he following morning, I realized I was not wearing my pajama shirt. When I turned to the side, Grace was standing next to the bed, and she whispered, "Hi."

"Good morning."

"We will swim and then enjoy breakfast," Grace whispered with a nod.

"I would like that."

I walked to my cabin, shaved, changed into a Speedo, and glanced at the mirror. The reflection provided my confused expression, and I wanted to ask, "Who are you?" When I could not think of the correct answer, I pondered the possibilities and consequences of becoming close to this remarkable woman.

It took three whole minutes to get myself out of my questioning funk. When I got to the pool, I watched Grace take off her bathrobe to reveal a fantastic blue and white striped bikini.

This awe-inspiring sight still mesmerized me. She grinned and jumped in with a tiny splash. I took off my bathrobe, jumped in with a big splash, and we swam laps. Well, I floundered from one end of the pool to the other while Grace controlled her precise strokes as she dashed past me.

In the middle of the sixth lap, Grace dragged me down and pinned me against the bottom of the pool. While struggling for my very life, I awkwardly broke her grip. Our pleasant swimming experience had turned into "advanced underwater combat training." Otherwise known as "See how long James can hold his breath while being punched." Grace continued pulling, pushing, holding, slapping, pinching, and twisting me into submission. As she bashed me about, I figured out some of her techniques and broke three of her basic holds. At one point, I wrestled her head underwater for an astounding six seconds!

After an agonizing fourteen minutes, Grace suddenly stopped pummeling me, made a crafty grin, and we returned to swimming laps. Three laps later, my body could not continue, and I had to get out. Grace did ten more laps and joined me in the lounge chairs. Eight minutes later, I had enough energy to ask, "What the heck did you do that for?"

"You must be ready for action at a moment's notice," Grace confidently answered.

"Still ..."

"You have much to learn. Wash up, and we will eat."

Grace stood, put on her bathrobe, and walked away. *How the heck does she keep her hair so perfect?* I wondered.

After my shower, I dressed in gray and tan trousers and a pale blue long-sleeved shirt. I found Grace in the dining room sipping coffee in a sophisticated high-collared turquoise shirt with dark, blue-toned slacks.

The server came in with a tea pitcher and filled our cups. We made light conversation, and six minutes later, he served me an artichoke and bacon omelet with two slices of recently baked dark rye toast. The butter appeared to have been hand-churned, and it melted quickly. Grace took a smaller cheese omelet with multi-grain toast and blueberry jam. As we ate, I wondered about this man's story. *What's his name? What does he think of Grace? What name does he call Grace? Would he agree to an interview? Will Grace kill him after the cruise?*

After breakfast, we enjoyed fresh blackberry juice.

"I still have many questions," I said.

"There is much to do today."

"There is?"

"On your bed, you will find appropriate clothing."

Grace stood, smiled, and walked away. It still amazed me how much of an outsider I felt around her. I drank the last sip of juice before I walked to my cabin to find gray and blue cotton gym clothes. On top, a neatly written note read, "No underwear." *Amazing handwriting. Wait. Where is this going?*

After putting on my workout clothes, I found a drawer with six pairs of shoes and selected slippers. I exited to the left, and it felt strange to be walking around without underwear. When I got to the end of the hallway, I headed toward the exercise room.

Inside, I saw Grace dressed in similar loose-fitting exercise clothes, and she had shaped her body into something that looked like a pretzel. Of course, I had watched fancy circus shows, and I knew the human body could maneuver into many unbelievable positions, but her body configuration was beyond what I thought possible.

With the precision of an expert watchmaker, Grace unfolded herself and stood with a focused expression. I stood beside her while facing forward as we looked into a large mirror. Grace closed her eyes, began moving her arms, and I did my best to duplicate her movements with my eyes open. As we silently moved, I appreciated the slow rhythm and precise control.

The intricate routine flowed downward as we sat on the floor, and I began pulling my muscles in strange directions. Seven minutes later, Grace stood, and I somehow understood I was to remain still as she walked behind me. She began guiding me into fluid balance moves with subtle hand gestures.

I began understanding that this routine explored my body's ability to adapt to a different center of gravity. I admired Grace's ability to guide me with her eyes closed as if she were listening to my muscles. Clearly, she had mastered her bodily movements at a deep level.

After this series of moves, we sat with our legs crossed while facing each other. Before the harvest, my body could not bend this far. Now, it loosened up enough to tolerate this position. Grace folded her hands together, pointed her fingertips at her chin, and opened her eyes. Her expression held a unique, peaceful focus.

I did my best to clear my thoughts while peacefully looking forward. However, it was difficult for my mind to settle down as it drifted from quiet tranquility to vivid random tangents.

As if by magic, we stood up together while maintaining a peaceful stare. Grace took a step back, and so did I. We closed our eyes and flowed through the identical floor routine in synchronization. I felt giddy to accomplish our harmonious performance without using my eyes to see Grace's position and felt full harvest effects aiding my body. I wanted to shout out my victory, and I hoped that this moment of clarity would never end.

Grace sensed my excitement, and we held the position for twelve seconds. Then, she guided me back to a balanced position, and we held the position for 78 seconds. I perceived this action to be a "casual punishment" for my misdeeds. Grace then guided me back to where we had been in the routine, and we continued. I wanted to apologize for getting excited, but I understood Grace sensed my mistake and forgave me.

I began contemplating my new state of mental calmness and understood that my focus had transcended to an entirely new level. As we continued, Grace added six new moves.

When our routine concluded, I opened my eyes, and Grace stood. We walked to the door, and she nodded. Back at my cabin, I showered and dressed in my tan outfit. As I did so, I understood that I now possessed a better understanding of how my body worked.

When I looked out the porthole, it was dark, and I found it amusing how much time had passed without my knowledge. I met Grace in the dining room, and we ate a wonderful dinner of thin-sliced tri-tip beef in a lite tarragon sauce with a balsamic vinegar yellow tomato side dish. Clearly, Grace provided cooking tips to the chef. However, to my disappointment, we ate in silence. Afterward, we walked to the bow and looked at the ocean. I saw distant lights from cargo ships and listened to the ship slicing through the waves. As the salt spray hit my face, I wanted to hold her hand, but I did not think she was ready for the bold affection that I had in mind.

As we relaxed and stared at the heavens, I felt myself getting closer to Grace, but I could tell she did not fully trust me. Twenty-six minutes later, we retired to the study. Grace sat across from me and stared at me with an inquisitive expression.

I thought of a neutral question. "What do you call that exercise?"

"It contained a combination of many techniques. We focused on yoga holds, center-point balances, and deep meditation. You learned how to position your body, control your breathing, and focus your mind. For your first attempt, you did well."

"I get the sense there is so much more to learn."

"So to speak, I still have much to learn," Grace said with humility.

"Wow."

"Something for you to look forward to."

"May I ask a question?"

"Of course. Why do you become so formal in these moments?"

"You require a light touch."

"Perhaps. Now ask," Grace said with a smile.

"What do you expect will happen when I meet these other immortals?"

Grace seemed unprepared for this question as she answered while glancing at her hands, "It's all troubling. I am not sure what will occur."

"Did you get any information from Quan or Arturo about them?"

"Quan has no appreciation of the harvest gift and only desires control. Arturo is charming but supremely greedy.

Every single word out of his forked tongue contains a hidden agenda. To answer your question, neither man had contact with the other harvesters."

"I don't understand. I mean, you located Quan and Arturo. So that's why you wanted me to write a book. Right?"

"I hoped to find another," Grace answered with some reservation.

"You wanted to locate Cleopatra?"

Grace looked away and nodded. As she did so, the pieces fell into place. The same mental force that instinctively drove me to find Grace had challenged her to locate Cleopatra. She turned back and said with a weak smile, "Tell me about your recent harvest."

"I didn't plan it properly and got predictable results. Hopefully, I covered my tracks enough not to get caught."

"I see."

"The worst part is the guilt," I admitted.

"Given your present knowledge, would you have undertaken this journey?"

"Of course."

My admission pleased Grace, and she made an embarrassed smile. Clearly, I needed to change the subject to make her more comfortable. "Let's have breakfast with Arturo and discuss his history."

As soon as I uttered these words, I realized I had made a substantial mistake. Grace's pleasant expression changed to anger, and I felt our communication bridges collapse.

It still amazed me that the vastly powerful and confident Grace had a fragile side. "I'm sorry," I said.

It then occurred to me that I should have remained silent. Grace picked up a book and began reading. I sensed she wanted me to read as well. So I selected *Mayhem in Hyde Park*. Three chapters later, we silently departed.

I took a shower and dressed in pajamas, but when I got to my cabin door, I stopped, turned, and walked to Grace's cabin. Outside, I took a deep breath, knocked, and entered. Grace had turned the oil lamps down, and she sat up in her bed while looking at me with a concerned expression. I saw her right hand reaching down, and I suspected it grasped a weapon. I walked over, sat down next to her, and faced forward.

Three minutes later, I turned to Grace, who turned to me with an annoyed expression. I could only think of one thing to help mend the bridges. "Please lie down," I whispered. "I'd like to give you a massage if that is all right."

Grace bit her lip as if she were making an important decision, nodded, and lay down on her stomach. I preferred that she remove her top, but I knew she would not appreciate my forward request. I sat on her butt and began working her mid-back. As I massaged, I tried to remember the moves that Grace performed the previous evening. As I worked her muscles, I understood which ones needed attention and applied the appropriate pressure.

Grace began relaxing, which made me more comfortable. Her muscles flowed in intricate patterns, and they seemed eager to accept my touch. I liked that Grace allowed me to explore her, and I relaxed enough to enjoy the experience.

Nine minutes later, I began working on Grace's neck and shoulders. While feeling her skin, I appreciated the smoothness which allowed my fingers to glide along the muscle contours. Clearly, Grace took pride in her body's appearance. But I felt some vulnerability in this powerful woman, which made me realize she set limits on the amount of personal exposure she would accept.

After six minutes, I eased my body down and worked on Grace's lower back. However, I sensed apprehension and understood my actions were making her uncomfortable. So, I moved upward and worked her scalp with my fingertips.

Grace's hair had a beautiful silky sheen to it. My hands glided over her long strands without bunching up. Four minutes later, I began using my forearms to apply deep pressure over a broad area. Then, I switched to applying pressure for long moments on individual muscles. Grace seemed to appreciate this move the most, as I noticed a slight smile.

After 42 minutes, I got Grace to the most relaxed state my limited massage abilities could provide. Then, I switched to light finger swirls, followed by slight fingernail scratches. I rested next to her while listening to her soft breathing. Seventy-three seconds later, she turned to the side and looked at me with a curious expression.

We looked at each other for 88 seconds, and Grace closed her eyes. Her breathing relaxed three minutes later, and I held her wrist. Her eyes did not open, but I noticed her expression briefly tense. Thirty-six seconds later, Grace moved her hand to hold mine. The moment felt friendly, and our grip confirmed each other's feelings. I thought about the positive and negative consequences of our interaction as we fell asleep.

◆ ◆ ◆

When I opened my eyes the following morning, Grace had her arm firmly around me while snoring deeply. It took all my self-control not to laugh, and I enjoyed the moment for twelve beautiful minutes. When Grace awoke, she immediately noticed where her arm was and rapidly withdrew it. Her expression was beyond priceless, like a kid getting caught with a hand in the cookie jar. "Morning, sleepyhead," I said with a big grin.

Grace looked surprised and then embarrassed. She jumped out of bed and turned to look at me with an unsure expression.

"Shall we take a short swim?" I asked while standing up.

Grace continued to stare and remained silent as I walked past her. In doing so, I intentionally brushed against her arm in my best attempt to put her off guard. As I arrived at my cabin and opened the door, a neat pile of clothes with a green ribbon greeted me. *Checkmate, Grace!* I shaved, put on my Speedo, walked to the pool, and jumped in.

As I swam my heart out, I wondered how long it would take Grace to join me. Then, two laps later, I heard a splash behind me. When she raced by me, I got a quick glimpse of her stunning green and blue bikini. On the fourth lap, I planned to grab her right leg and pull her underwater.

In two seconds, I went from swimming in a straight line to gasping for air at the bottom of the pool. I refused to yield and ducked Grace's head underwater twice. To me, this accomplishment felt worthy of an Olympic medal.

Grace had her revenge by introducing a new technique of kneeing me in the gut. This action forced me to blow out air, which terrified me into thinking I was drowning. Six agonizing minutes later, she seemed satisfied, and we returned to swimming laps. Ten laps later, my arms felt like spaghetti, and I had to get out of the pool.

Grace swam four more laps and lay down in the chair next to mine. She was not even breathing hard from all that physical activity. "That knee into the stomach is a powerful technique," I commented.

"In a fight, you must use every advantage possible."

"I agree."

"Next time, I will pull your hair."

"Hey, that's not fair," I protested.

"So to speak, in any physical conflict, all moves are fair," Grace said with confidence.

"I guess that's true."

"You reacted well to my attacks."

"Um, thanks."

"You have more confidence than you know. As an example, you entered my room last night."

"I needed to mend some fences," I admitted sheepishly.

"In that task, you were successful. On the prior subject, I would like to aid in your confidence and confirm that your massage technique has improved since our last encounter."

"I did my best to learn from you."

"Indeed," Grace said with a warm smile.

"Your body carried lots of stress."

"Hmm. That may be true," Grace admitted.

Wanting to probe, I said, "My visit must be difficult for you."

"This level of honesty requires significant effort," Grace said after an eight-second pause.

"Has it been fun?"

Grace laughed and answered, "Yes, it has been fun."

"What's going on today?" I wondered.

"First, we will eat breakfast and then read. Afterward, we can meditate or perform martial arts. Your choice."

"The thought of you knocking me around is less appealing than meditation."

"James!"

Grace laughed, and we stood. I took a quick shower, dressed, and headed toward the dining room. We ate potato casserole, sliced smoked ham, and soft homemade cheese. It was difficult for me to take small bites of this excellent food, and we made small talk about modern art.

After breakfast, we retired to the reading room. Grace picked up her book, and I picked up *Mayhem in Hyde Park*. Forty-nine minutes later, I started the last chapter, and Grace interrupted my reading.

"Are you truly not going to harvest again?"

I looked up to see Grace staring at me. Then, as I pondered her question, it occurred to me she had asked, "Would you consider a relationship with me?"

I had understood we were getting closer, and I should have been more prepared for Grace's question. However, at that moment, I did not know what to say. I knew I liked her, but she could be over-the-top terrifying. Grace had a core personality that contained a ruthless killer that preyed on people with the selfish goal of prolonging her life. I suspected the military contractors she "questioned" were tortured to death. Plus, Grace probably killed the business managers that betrayed her trust, and I knew those Goth people died by her hand.

I continued to look into Grace's eyes and think about her question. *Did a trace of that brave Russian girl who walked into those woods 500 years ago still exist? What if I started a relationship with Grace and it did not work out? Would she harvest me? Would Grace ever let her guard down enough to let me in? Would she force me to harvest?* Then, it occurred to me that starting a relationship with Grace would profoundly affect my life and the lives of many others.

As I looked into Grace's eyes, her expression softened. It took 84 seconds to compose my thoughts. "As you know, I dislike taking lives. To me, it's the ultimate expression of greed. That being said, I agree that taking evil away from society is a righteous cause. However, we have a legal system, and it's their job to rid society of bad people. Therefore, I don't plan to harvest, and I sincerely feel guilt for the human lives I have taken."

Grace's expression saddened, and I continued, "That being said, I enjoy spending time with you. It's nice getting closer to you, and I like it when that wonderful Russian girl comes out to play. Words cannot express how much I enjoyed your massage and how nice waking up in your arms felt. Only one thing would make me harvest again, and that's your wonderful company."

I looked down at my book and pretended to read while Grace contemplated my statement. It took a lot of effort not to look up as I felt her stare. Over the next ten minutes, it became apparent that I had finally made a worthy impression.

We left the reading room three hours later, dressed in loose-fitting clothes, and began a deep concentration exercise routine. Then, Grace added three new moves and two complex balances. Next, we switched to slow martial arts stances and finished with extended meditation while facing each other. Afterward, I rinsed off and changed into a nice dark-green suit.

We had skipped lunch, and for dinner, the server surprised me with pulled pork empanadas with coconut curry rice. I wondered if Grace requested this meal because of my recent Panamanian food experience.

After dinner, we strolled around the ship. I still had many questions but knew Grace desired silence. We found ourselves in the lounge chairs beside the pool, and I looked at the overcast moon. As we stared upward into the sky, I wondered what she thought about me and what our future held.

While it was still early, we headed to bed. When we came to the stairs leading down to my cabin, Grace looked at me with a hard-to-read expression and walked away. I found myself alone in an empty hallway, and I wondered if Grace wanted me to follow. I took a shower and walked back to my cabin. When I got to my door, I continued toward her room and entered without knocking.

Grace had been under the covers and watched as I joined her. We turned to face each other, and she wore another hard-to-read expression. Then, instinctively, I reached with my left hand to hold her hand.

Eighty-eight seconds later, I switched positions and put my right arm under the pillow. Grace moved to the same position. I stopped holding her hand and put it on her waist. She scooted closer until our faces were four inches apart. Grace put her right hand on my shoulder, and our other hands touched under the pillows. As I stared into her amazing eyes, I wondered if she would kiss me or if I should boldly kiss her.

The moment did not seem right to kiss, and I began intensely studying her eyes. Before, when we played our eye-dagger battles, we each tried to gain the upper hand. An appropriate way to describe this action would be antagonistic eye chess. Now, the game changed, and we looked at each other in a challenging friendship. It occurred to me that Grace had used similar rhythms in the pool and our exercise routine. She began leading, and I followed. This fascinating puzzle required deep concentration, and eventually, I anticipated her moves.

It took three and a half minutes to figure out how to lead. I found the experience incredibly challenging and rewarding. Two minutes later, Grace unexpectedly brought our game to a standstill, and without breaking the stare, she moved my left hand away from her waist and held it below her chin. The feelings between us changed to a new comfort level, and her eyes became inviting. As I stared, a strange sensation came over me that reminded me of Heathcliff's visual communications.

Grace gently guided me in an intricate eye movement, and I began *feeling* the image of her apple tree within my mind. Unlike a photo, this image did not have edges. The color appeared crisp, and the details were vivid. I even knew that the apples were juicy and tasted slightly sour. The sudden picture surprised me so much that I nearly lost focus.

As I thought about the content, I appreciated the emotional element. It felt pride-filled, personal, and meaningful as if the apple trees were the primary connection to her former home. The emotional content reminded me of my deep family sentiment.

Grace seemed happy, and she *felt* (sent) me an image of her father working at his forge. He looked handsome, proud, and self-confident. I realized she had great respect for his values, and he was more than a father; he was her role model. I felt humbled to directly experience her inner source of strength.

It took lots of focus, and I eventually felt Grace the image of my car. I chose this image because I had spent a lot of time in it and knew it well. My success startled Grace. However, I could tell that she enjoyed getting an image, and appreciated that my humble car was an essential part of my life.

It is difficult to explain this intimate communication method. What I can say for certain is that this transfer is not mental telepathy, where a mental picture magically pops into my mind. Instead, it is an optical illusion between two people with disciplined eyes.

My best scientific explanation is that one person moves their eyes to trick (distort) the other eyes into "seeing" an image not physically present. I know this method obeyed the laws of physics and had a sound biological mechanism. However, I could not locate any literature about this technique, and the eye doctor I spoke to dismissed the concept as impossible. Heathcliff's ability to send a moving image is a complete mystery. During our interaction, Grace confirmed that she could not duplicate this feat.

My only theory about conveying emotions is that the mind combines visual information with emotions. Because the images get directly transferred, the sentiment does not get removed. Heathcliff's images only contained modest emotional content because humans are more emotionally complex.

While this communication method is vastly incredible, it has limitations. For example, it does not allow one to ask questions or communicate words. Also, I could only send images that I directly experienced and recalled with great clarity.

Most images had a precise meaning, but a few required additional information. For this, we whispered to each other. For example, in Grace's second image, she whispered, "my father."

Together we undertook a fantastic journey and learned a great deal about each other's life. Rural Russia had been a fun place for a girl to grow up. Grace's art appreciation spanned an eternity, and her life experiences were astounding.

Before our exchange, if asked, I would've described Grace as a unique and complex woman. However, the fantastic images I felt revealed an entirely new side. Grace has an ocean of knowledge and a vast perspective. I felt honored to participate in the exchange and explore her extensive history.

◆ ◆ ◆

Our interaction took enormous concentration and effort. I do not remember falling asleep, but I awoke alone. The dark room was disappointing, and I wondered where Grace had gone. When I opened the door, she stood with an intense expression. Grace was dressed in a crisp white long-sleeve starched shirt and trim gray pants. This outfit was not her style, and her demeanor seemed gruff. "Last night was amazing," I began in a pleasant voice. "Thank you so much for sharing. I would like to talk about how it worked."

"You will find an outfit in your cabin along with a backpack. Now, go!"

Grace turned away in anger, which left me feeling hurt. I suspected that our intimate communication crossed an invisible line or I did not take the experience far enough. I changed into drab blue slacks and a tan shirt. My new smaller backpack contained two changes of clothes, my shaving kit, Thai currency, a two-way radio, and a new *Dawson's Creek* notebook. Unfortunately, she omitted my laptop.

When I arrived at the dining room, I noticed Arturo sitting at the table. His legs and left arm were bound, and he did not look healthy. I suspected he desperately needed to harvest. It amused me that Grace used the same restraints on him as she did on me during our first encounter. She sat across from him while eating a fluffy egg soufflé and sipping tea.

When Arturo turned to look at me, my presence startled him. He looked back at Grace, and she nodded. "I'm so glad to see you," he said. "You cannot possibly know what has happened to me."

"I have a pretty good idea."

Grace smiled. I sat down and began eating my soufflé while Arturo cautiously took small bites. After Grace finished, she dabbed her mouth with a napkin, and said in a commanding tone, "You two will use an inflatable boat to get ashore and follow the highlighted map route. If you encounter anything beyond your means, you may use the radio I provided."

Grace's tone suggested the conversation was over. After finishing my meal, I stood, used the restroom, walked to my cabin, and picked up my backpack. When I opened the door, Grace walked inside and closed the door.

We stared at each other, I put my hand on Grace's upper arm, and she did the same to me. I moved my head close, and we looked into each other's eyes. She felt me a sharp image of cooking her first apple pie. The image contained warm and confident emotions. I then felt her the image of getting my first royalty check from a local magazine. Grace squeezed my shoulder and smiled. Clearly, she had become a much larger part of my life. "Time to go," Grace said with a soft voice. "Return safe and soon."

"I care about you."

"Likewise."

Grace smiled, and I wanted to kiss her, but I sensed this gesture wasn't appropriate. I settled for a light squeeze on her arm. Grace turned to leave and asked without eye contact, "Did you find your answers?"

"Yes. Yes, I did."

"That's good," Grace said in a voice that trailed off.

At that moment, I wanted to spend a lot more time with her, but I realized my journey to seek out Grace had ended. She opened the door, and I followed her to the stern. The same two men held a gray two-person Zodiac inflatable boat, with Arturo holding the outboard engine throttle. I stepped in, sat down, and turned to Grace. She had her arms crossed and stared at me with a concerned expression. The two men released the Zodiac, and I turned to see Arturo looking unhappy.

THIRTEEN

Arturo applied full throttle on the small outboard motor, and when we were 200 feet away, he asked, "Do you know what that woman did to me?!"

"I find it best to fulfill her requests without argument."

"I'm a great fighter, and she tossed me around like a rag doll. Then she left me tied up! I was helpless!"

"I remember that feeling."

"She used my hard drive to access all my accounts. Now, she has complete control over my entire shipping operation. Then, she showed me evidence of police payoffs! How did she obtain that information?!"

"That's Grace for you."

"She told me that if this mission was not a success, I could expect a fate worse than death," Arturo said in a panic.

"That's most likely true."

"How did you tame that vile woman?"

"I didn't tame her!" I yelled. "Instead, I listened and did my best to do as she asked. Also, I would never refer to her as 'vile,' and I would appreciate it if you would not use that word."

"Bah!"

Arturo threw up his left hand and continued to pilot the Zodiac. We followed the compass, and 71 minutes later, the shore came into view. As the sun rose, we saw structures along the shoreline. Finally, we arrived at a poorly constructed dock, and Arturo stopped the engine. A young boy had been watching us approach with fascination. When I handed him the rope, he smiled.

"Why are you giving him the boat?" Arturo wondered. "We might need it for our return trip."

"Look around you. These people are desperate, and the boat will not be here when we return. Might as well give it to him."

"You have a generous nature, and I understand why Anna liked you."

I laughed, and we walked ashore on a rickety bamboo platform. After meandering around several shanty houses, we found a poorly maintained dirt road and headed north.

"Before we go any further, you must tell me your relationship with that woman," Arturo demanded.

"I'm still figuring that out," I answered with a wink.

"The way she looked at you."

"What?"

"You know," Arturo hinted in a coy voice.

"Know what?"

"She has you in her heart."

"That might be true."

"Did you sleep with her?" Arturo challenged.

"Four times," I answered with a bashful grin.

"I find it unlikely that she allowed anybody to touch her."

"You read my book, right?"

"Yes," Arturo confirmed.

"You read how I slept with her. Right?"

"In your book, you did not become intimate."

"Exactly," I said with a smile. "I slept with her four times, and nothing untoward happened. We have never kissed."

"Then, what happened? I require details."

"Something amazing," I answered with a big grin.

"I don't understand."

"Neither do I."

We both laughed and continued walking.

Forty-three minutes later, we came to a small town, and Arturo located a man with a vehicle. It had once been a motor-cycle, and somebody had converted it into a wooden contrap-tion that held two passengers. He showed the driver the map, and he shook his head. The man pointed on the map to a location ten miles north of our destination and nodded. We got into the vehicle, and when the driver started the engine, there was a thundering noise because it lacked a muffler.

We traveled much faster than I would have preferred, and I held on for dear life. Thankfully, the road ended after an hour journey, and we paid for our trip. I think the driver said some-thing that translated to "Why on earth would you want to go there?" The driver shook his head and rapidly departed while leaving us in a cloud of dust and two-stroke exhaust.

Arturo spotted a thin trail, and we descended into the dense forest. Unfortunately, it had rained recently, and the slippery terrain proved difficult. As we traveled, I grew concerned because there were no people, and I was unsure if we were heading in the correct direction.

Four hours later, we came to a clearing and saw an old stone structure in the distance. An hour later, the light had faded, it was cold, and I wished we had brought food. I could tell that the lack of a harvest had left Arturo weak, and I knew this need dominated his thoughts.

When we arrived, we saw twenty-foot stone walls surrounding four stone buildings. The only entrance was a massive red wooden door with no latch on the outside. Overall, the place looked sorely in need of repairs, and in the back of my mind, I wondered if the disheveled appearance had been intentional.

Arturo walked up to the door and pulled at a tattered rope. I expected a bell to ring, but nothing happened. He pulled it again and began yelling in different languages. We pressed our ears against the door and heard nothing. "Now what?" I wondered.

"We wait," Arturo answered with a huff.

"I hope they let us in before it gets dark."

"Observing us sleep would be the most prudent course of action. Let's not forget that I scrutinized you for three weeks."

"True. How are you feeling?" I asked with concern.

"Bad."

"How long do you think you can survive without a harvest?"

"Perhaps a month. Probably less," Arturo admitted. "Normally, I require the procedure every two weeks."

"We should rest and save our strength," I suggested.

"Agreed."

We sat down with our backs against the door as I contemplated what could be behind them. Eleven minutes later, Arturo appeared unable to relax. "Tell me," he said with a hint of anger. "Why does this vile woman not do her own dirty work?"

"I told you to stop calling her vile!" I retorted.

"You did, and for that, I am sorry. Answer my question."

"You still don't get it, do you? All right. Two things. One. This place may seem like nothing, but I am sure the people inside are watching us closely. They might even have big rifles pointed at us. It requires a light touch when you deal with immortals. They dislike surprises and constantly think about their security. Trust me, any army that attempts to get close to this place would get slaughtered. Also, let me remind you that Grace wants direct communication. If she came here with bodyguards and guns, the people inside would shoot them.

"Two. You immortals are all about making money, and keeping a low profile. The harvest forces you to build huge emotional walls and actual physical walls. Being outside your walls is terrifying. Grace is not here because she is well aware of how dangerous a first approach is. Now, I know she can defend herself, but this is different. Right now, she needs to be in control of her safety."

Arturo contemplated my revelation for two minutes and asked, "Then why are you here?"

I was not prepared for his question, and after 32 seconds of deep thought, I answered, "Because she asked me to do this."

"You are not honest with yourself. Why do you risk your life for her?"

"I'm also concerned about her safety," I answered without being entirely sure I had spoken the truth.

"It's clear that you care for her and undertake this task because she occupies your heart."

This apparent reason caught me off guard, and I quietly replied, "That's a lot to take in. Well, let's try to get some rest. Want to take the first watch?"

"Every two hours?"

"Sounds good."

I lay down and put my head on my backpack while Arturo sat nearby. As I fell asleep, I thought about Arturo's question and realized that my feelings for Grace clouded my judgment. It also dawned on me that the reporter inside me wondered what kind of immortal awaited us behind these walls.

Two hours later, Arturo shook me awake and then went to sleep. At 8:30 a.m., we walked to a nearby stream and washed. As I relieved myself on a nearby tree, a young boy unexpectedly spoke. His appearance startled me, and I quickly zipped up.

Arturo tried to talk with the boy, but he did not know any of Arturo's languages, and he walked away. We returned to the stone structure and waited. At 10:34 a.m., we discussed hiking back to buy food and decided to leave at 2:00 p.m. Twenty minutes later, we heard footsteps and then the sound of latches being undone. The red door opened, and ten men pointed rifles at us. Behind them, we saw a modest courtyard surrounded by four stone buildings. I raised my hands, and Arturo looked at the men with a confident expression without raising his. Then, the leftmost man yelled angry words, further frightening me, and I raised my hands even higher.

We stared at the men, and they stared back. It then occurred to me that they did not have a plan after opening the door. The man on the left began speaking in guarded tones, and he ran toward the rightmost building. I looked at Arturo and wished he would put his hands up. Finally, the man returned with a book, and I recognized the cover, *Grime: At the End*. I could not believe the sight.

Arturo laughed, and the men started talking all at once. They kept pointing at my picture on the back of the book and then at me. However, I did not take any chances and continued to hold my hands up. Thirty-seven seconds later, the man on the right lowered his rifle. The others looked at him, lowered their rifles, and the man in the center motioned us forward. We walked to the rightmost building, and he motioned for us to sit at a table. As I sat, they placed a large bowl of rice in front of us and stared at us with questioning expressions.

The rice tasted bland but was filling, which seemed to please our hosts. After taking away our bowls, one man produced a small black book, and he searched through it. Two minutes later, he said with a heavy Thai accent, "Hello."

I motioned toward the book and found the English section. It took some time to translate, and I enunciated every word, "We—look—responsible—man."

After the translation, they looked concerned, and the man translated, "You meet house master?"

Arturo and I nodded yes. Then the men huddled together, and they whispered for 45 seconds. The left most man motioned toward our backpacks. I took mine off and extracted my *Dawson's Creek* notebook. They looked at my notebook with great amusement and then spoke to each other joyfully. "We need to get you a better notebook," Arturo said with a hearty laugh. "Even people in this remote location understand how silly it is to have a *Dawson's Creek* notebook. This is embarrassing."

"Yeah, I really need to get a new one."

The men then patted us down and led us back outside. We stopped in front of a massive iron door at the largest building. A man tapped on the door in a musical rhythm and waited with his ear pressed against it. Then, he nodded and stood back.

The door clicked, and the men pulled it open. When I saw their expression, they looked scared to death, which in turn frightened me. We walked into a dimly lit stone room that was twenty feet by ten feet, by seven feet high. The men closed the door behind us with a loud crunch. The awful smell forced me to hold my nose, and I said, "Hello? Anybody home?"

Nobody answered, and as our eyes adjusted, I looked to my left to see a table used for harvesting. On my right, a cage contained two Asian boys who looked terrified. One appeared to be nine years old and the other ten. They were dressed in tattered clothes and looked as if they had not had a meal in days. The sight sickened me. *Why the heck do I keep getting involved with these insane immortals? Don't they know how wrong it is to take the life of an innocent child!* I turned to Arturo, who looked disgusted as he held his nose. We continued walking toward an open door, which was the only light source.

Inside, we saw a modest office with a man sitting behind a small, well-used wooden desk of modest quality. The word hideous could not possibly describe this dreadful being. He wore black shorts and a loose tan shirt. Every segment of exposed skin had irregular inch-long scars. Many of them were fresh, with oozing blood and pus. The sight and smell made me want to vomit, and it took every ounce of strength not to leave the room.

"Open a window to let out this stench!" Arturo demanded.

The man stood, walked up to me, and looked into my eyes. He attempted to stare me down, but his skill was not up to my level. He then walked over to Arturo and gave him a hard stare with no effect.

The man seemed annoyed and sat down. Then, he cleared his throat and said in heavily accented English, "Amten, that is no way to speak to your old friend, Jank."

"Jank!" Arturo exclaimed with great surprise. "You are alive! It's been so long."

"Yes, it has," Jank said with a crafty expression.

Jank made a crackly laugh, stood, and walked out of the room. We stopped at a small iron door, and he opened it. Outside, a tiny courtyard surrounded by high stone walls greeted us. Words cannot describe how good the fresh air felt.

Jank sat in a well-used black leather chair and spoke whimsically. "I am sorry that my odor offends you. As you can see, my body is falling apart, and there is little I can do about it."

"Several trusted people informed me of your passing," Arturo said with concern.

"Caesarion watched as guards stabbed me in the abdomen four times. He then ordered them to drag me to a pile of sharp rocks. I withheld my life-prolonging treatment knowledge for two tortured-filled hours and then relented."

"What happened to Caesarion?" I wondered.

"That fool?!" Jank yelled and then pounded his chair with his fist. "Weeks later, Octavian killed Caesarion in Alexandria. I wish I had witnessed that man's death! But, with Caesarion gone, I gained my freedom, traveled far from Egypt, and ended up here. Unfortunately, my body has decayed to a sorry state, and I require two or more treatments per week. Now, you will answer my questions."

"You want to know the harvesting improvements that Grace came up with?" I guessed.

"I do," Jank confirmed.

"And if I do not tell you, then you will torture me?"

"I will."

I turned to Arturo and said, "You were much nicer about asking."

Arturo grinned, and Jank said, "As part of my request, you will also show me how to send mental images."

While I could send images to Grace, I knew it would be impossible to get comfortable enough around Jank to teach him. I had to be careful with my answer, as I perceived Jank was an astute individual who would see through any lie. "I experimented with my friends and could not replicate what Heathcliff had done."

"You will show me!" Jank demanded.

"I do not know what to tell you. When I tried my friends, nothing happened. We just stared at each other. Heathcliff did or had something special."

"The moment I have recovered from the improved process, we will see what you are capable of!" Jank yelled.

"We can try, but no guarantees."

"Very well." I felt a wave of relief, and Jank commanded, "You will explain your procedure now!"

"May I ask some questions first?" I interrupted.

"Why?!"

"To exchange information."

"Because you are a reporter?"

"I am a person with direct experience who desires knowledge."

Jank made a "hmm" sound, nodded, and I opened my notebook. "*Dawson's Creek?* You like that show?" He asked with amusement.

Now, I really wished I had brought along another notebook. "They were throwing these away at work, and I rescued ten."

"Did you appreciate Joey Potter?" Jank wondered.

"Who?"

"Katie Holmes played that *Dawson's Creek* character."

Arturo let out a hearty laugh, and I shook my head. When the laughter died down, I asked, "Will you please explain your harvest procedure?"

"Are you writing another book?"

"No. I just think better when I'm writing."

"That's an illogical statement. Why are you writing another book?!" Jank demanded with narrow eyes.

"Trust me; writing another harvesting book is the last thing I would ever want."

"Very well. I will address your curiosity. My procedure begins with extracting a young boy's pancreas and adrenal gland. He must be between eight and ten years old and in good health. The adrenal gland juice is mixed with snake venom and crushed rosemary extract with almond oil. I place the prepared pancreas into a thick muscle incision. It must be at least 20 millimeters away from the last procedure. Lastly, I sew up the incision and apply a sulfa-silver antiseptic."

"You killed two boys per week for the last 2,000 years?" I asked in horror. "Do you know how wrong that is?!"

"In time, your morals will adjust."

I realized I should not have pushed Jank so far and nodded. He seemed amused and continued, "I used to kidnap the children directly. Now I pay poor families for their unwanted. What you must understand is that Thailand is a poverty-stricken country, and my arrangement works well for all concerned."

"I'm appalled!"

"The benefits of the procedure are impossible to resist, and you will soon follow our path. Now! Describe the procedure."

"What did you think of my book?" I asked to deflect the conversation.

"Your work did not focus on the subject's attributes. If you are seeking a compliment, the plagiarizing admission was amusing."

This observation fascinated me, but his harsh opinion brought disappointment. Jank's expression told me I needed to describe the procedure immediately. As I revealed the secret, Jank hung on my every word and wrote in a small black notebook. Afterward, Jank leaned back. "I will arrange for an 'evil person' as you so described to be provided," he said while nodding. "You will then perform your technique."

"I would also like the procedure," Arturo said with a wink.

"Why?"

"I'm overdue."

"Why would I allow this?"

Arturo's eyes held tremendous fear as he answered, "A favor to an old friend?"

It was apparent that Arturo had never asked an immortal for a favor, and I enjoyed watching him squirm.

Jank became angry and shook his head. Arturo thought deeply for eight seconds, and he said with a crafty expression, "James may have lied, and if he performs the procedure on me, you could observe its success. So think of me as a test subject."

I immediately appreciated this shrewd argument and watched Jank nodding in approval. He then said, "We will try it your way."

As promised, the iron door opened eight minutes later, and the men brought in two angry men with many tattoos. The men took the boys away, placed one prisoner into a cell, and strapped another to a table. Jank looked at me with a "let's go" expression. "Oh no," I said while shaking my head. "That's not how this works. I will tell you how, but you have to do the dirty work. I'm not killing anybody."

"You will begin!" Jank commanded,

"You begin. What's the first step?"

"You must anger the subject."

"Well? Anger him!"

Jank looked intensely angry for seven seconds, and he awkwardly walked over to a table. He took a Swiss soldering iron out of a set of drawers and handed it to Arturo, who lit it with a wicked smile. I thought, *There must be a store for these antique Swiss soldering irons,* as Arturo burned the man while Jank insulted him.

I covered my ears because the confined space intensified the screams. In between burns, Jank explained, "This man steals motorcycles. For many families, a motorcycle is their most treasured possession."

I nodded slowly while wanting to leave the room. Jank produced a hammer that looked indistinguishable from the one that Grace's father had made so long ago. Arturo continued burning, and when the man seemed in maximum pain, Jank hit him on the side of the head. He must have cut an artery because blood sprayed everywhere, and it took all my strength to remain still.

"Show me what's next!" Jank demanded.

"All right, all right."

Arturo and I rolled the body over onto its stomach, and I selected an appropriate scalpel. As they watched in riveted fascination, I extracted the pancreas, kidney, and adrenal gland. I turned to Jank and looked at him. He produced a long black dagger and jabbed it into the base of the man's skull. This callous action horrified me, and Jank flashed a wicked smile. I turned to Arturo, and he looked excited, as if he was about to receive a precious gift.

"Proceed!" Jank commanded.

I prepared the organs, made the liquids, and Jank removed a giant hissing cobra from its cage. Arturo expertly handled the snake and milked it into a golden cup. Next, I instructed Arturo to sit in a chair facing backward and take off his shirt. He pointed to a fresh incision in his upper arm. After peeling away the puss-filled bandages, I removed the pancreas. Satisfied, I cleaned his incision, sutured it closed, and applied sulfa-silver antiseptic with a fresh bandage.

"This will hurt," I warned Arturo.

"Hand me that mirror!"

I handed Arturo the mirror and made an incision. Blood spouted out, and I used a gauze pad to widen it. A penlight helped me see the muscles, and I felt relieved that I had located the proper location. After extending the incision with scissors, I inserted the prepared pancreas and applied the liquid. I then made three sutures, applied an antiseptic, and covered the wound with a bandage. "Is that all?" Jank wondered. "It's so simple."

"Arturo will be sick for the next few hours. Then the drive to harvest will build."

"Are you sure?"

"I'm not sure how you immortals are even alive," I admitted. "But I recently did this procedure on Quan, and it worked."

"Quan is alive?!" Jank marveled.

"Somebody attacked his compound, and he's now being held as a prisoner."

"The air assault outside of Nanchong?"

"Yes," I answered.

"We will discuss this event in great detail at a later time."

"We have many topics to discuss. That's why we are here."

"I see. Well, our interaction has taken a great toll, and I must retire."

Jank walked to the enormous iron door, tapped twice, and opened it. Arturo looked miserable, and I had to help him stand. Then, we walked through the door together, where two astonished men greeted us. I do not think they expected us to come out alive. They directed us to a room where Arturo collapsed onto a simple bamboo cot.

With nothing else to do, I walked around the small compound with three men in tow. Three minutes later, I went inside the first building. The men sat down at a small table and looked at me with quiet fascination. The accommodations were sparse, and I picked up a book with a red cover and found it written in an unfamiliar language.

Ten minutes later, one man motioned to me as if he were about to reveal a big secret. We walked to the back room, and I saw four tiny cots and a single dresser with four drawers. In the center was an enormous television. He turned it on, and a paused fighting-themed video game appeared. Seeing this big screen made me wonder where the electricity came from. He handed me an Xbox controller, and we began playing.

I could not read the words, but I knew how to play a fighting game. Soon all the men came into the room, and they cheered each time one of us made a hit. We stopped playing two hours and 31 minutes later and ate white rice with dried fish. I did not like the strong fishy flavor, but the meal satisfied my hunger. Afterward, I walked over to see Arturo. He looked miserable and reached out to me in desperation. "It will be a few hours," I told him. "They made rice, and I will bring back a bowl. In the meantime, try to get some rest."

I returned three minutes later with a small hand-carved wooden bowl, and Arturo gobbled it down. For the rest of the day, I sat on the outside stone steps contemplating life and enjoying the sun. After a dinner of white rice and bland chicken, I rested next to Arturo. In the late evening as he moaned and began shaking. I could only ease his suffering by covering him with a blanket.

Three hours later, Arturo entered a calm state with a focused expression. Twenty-three minutes after the change, he sat up, looked around, and then stood. I led him to a chair and asked him to sit.

I walked to the first building and saw the men had brought out cots to sleep on. When I came in, my movements startled the men awake, and I led them back to Arturo. Together, we walked to the metal door, and the men looked deeply frightened when I pointed to it. The man on the left started to tap when the locks unexpectedly clicked. Arturo began vigorously pulling at the heavy door, and he pushed his way past Jank to get inside. Again, the smell repulsed me, and I had to hold my nose. When I looked around in the dim light, I could see Arturo grabbing at a large man with tattoos. He was firmly secured with restraints in a cage and looked confused by being grabbed at.

"He's too big," I observed. "The moment you undo the restraints, that guy will beat the crap out of us. We need to harvest him in the cage."

Arturo glared at me with wild eyes as Jank picked up the Swiss soldering iron. He calmly lit it and passed it to Arturo, who looked at the flame with a wicked grin. Arturo licked his fingers and touched the tip to confirm it was hot enough. The sizzling sound sent chills up my spine, and then he burned the man vigorously while Jank insulted him. The enormous man howled in pain as I held my ears and smelled his flesh burning.

This torture continued for five agonizing minutes until Arturo put the soldering iron down. He grabbed the hammer and tried to swing at the man's head, but the blow impacted the stone wall with a thud. The man struggled against his restraints, and Arturo swung again, clumsily hitting the man in the forearm. The next three blows shattered more rock off the wall.

Arturo cursed in Spanish and swung again. His hammer glanced off the man's skull, which left him stunned. Now the man could no longer dodge hammer blows, and Arturo took careful aim. This time, he struck the man squarely in the temple.

I undid the man's restraints, and he flopped to the ground. Arturo and I dragged him toward the table, but we could not lift him onto it. This effort would have been funny in another situation, but I remained horrified.

Arturo and I rolled the man on his back, and he retrieved a scalpel. He then began wildly cutting into the body and crudely retrieving the organs. Jank handed Arturo the same black dagger, and he rapidly ended the man's life without any emotion. As he did so, I wondered what misdeeds this man had done to end up dying in a foul-smelling harvest chamber.

Arturo hastily prepared the organs and milked the snake. Afterward, he made the solution and then sat in the chair. Arturo used a mirror to remove the old pancreas and threw it on the floor. Then, without hesitation, he inserted the prepared pancreas, sutured himself, and let out a massive sigh of relief. The harvest took less than four minutes.

I turned to see Jank smiling and nodding. Arturo looked exhausted as he turned to me with a lifeless expression. He motioned toward the door, and it took a lot of effort to help him walk over to it. We found the men outside, and they again looked surprised to see us alive. Together, we helped Arturo walk to his cot, where he sat down and stared ahead with a blank expression. Thirty-one seconds later, he gulped down a cup of tea and instantly fell asleep. I lay down on the cot next to him while wondering what would happen the next day.

I awoke in the early morning to unusual music, and I walked outside to see the men dressed in long ornate green robes. They played traditional flutes and a string instrument while one man sang. As I listened to the beautiful music, I wondered what the song was about.

Twenty-eight minutes later, the concert ended, and we ate sweet rice with stewed vegetables. My meal tasted fantastic, and we played video games until dinner. Two hours later, the men gathered on the stone steps to smoke a long pipe. Because of the harvest, I had developed an aversion to tobacco smoke, so I sat nearby.

The weather felt pleasant, and I allowed my mind to drift. *What was Grace doing at this moment? Was she thinking about me?* I imagined her resting on that mega-ship in the comfortable lounge chair while looking at the same stars I was. It also occurred to me she might be looking at my head through the crosshairs of a high-powered rifle scope.

It had gotten late, and I lay down next to Arturo. His breathing became erratic, and his face twitched. So, I put my blanket over him and fell asleep.

At 7:31 a.m., a noise awoke me, and I saw Arturo in a restless sleep. Thirty-eight minutes later, he suddenly stood and looked at me with an urgent expression. "The outhouse is to your left," I informed him. "Your pee will smell horrible."

As Arturo quickly walked away, I grabbed his blankets and fell back asleep. When I woke, I noticed Arturo reading a magazine in a chair. "This new procedure is amazing!" He exclaimed. "How wonderful!"

"I remember that feeling," I said in a sleepy voice.

"No, you don't understand. I have never felt this good. Not even at a young age!"

"I know. Trust me. I know."

"Should we tell Jank?" Arturo asked with concern.

"He is probably spying on us right now with a secret camera or something."

"Perhaps."

"We need to talk," I said with conviction.

"Later."

"Sooner would be better," I pleaded.

"Bah! Get it out! What's on your mind?"

"One of two things is going to happen next. Jank is going to harvest us and then kill us. Or somebody is going to attack this compound. So we need a plan."

"Jank would never hurt us," Arturo said while shaking his head.

"Why?"

"Because we know his secrets."

"He will kill us because we know his secrets. Please think of the situation from his perspective."

"Bah! He will want to learn more from us."

"Jank isn't the conversational type," I observed bitterly.

"Nobody will find this place."

"Grace located this compound."

"She did, didn't she?" Arturo admitted while nodding.

"They have video games and electrical power. We aren't that isolated."

"Interesting. We must speak to Jank."

"Let me be honest. You're not good with immortals. So let me do the talking."

"What are you going to say?"

"That he is in danger and needs to take precautions. I will then ask him if he knows anything about the other immortals. But first, he probably wants to do a harvest."

Arturo and I walked to the iron door, and the clicking latches did not surprise me. I pulled the door open to a wave of awful smells. We walked in to see Jank waiting, and he looked upset. It was then that I saw a man firmly secured to the table. When our eyes met, I saw unbridled evil. Even though the man had multiple restraints, I felt profound fear.

I took a deep breath and said, "Jank, sir. May we discuss something with you before the procedure?"

"Tell me!" Jank demanded. "The procedure worked as promised?!"

"I have never felt so good," Arturo pleasantly replied.

"The procedure will last for six months?"

"I don't know how your body will react to this new procedure," I answered. "You have been doing the other treatment for so long; it's difficult to say. But, sir, there are several topics that we need to discuss."

"You will help with the procedure. Now!"

I wondered what Jank would do if Arturo and I attacked him. He seemed to read my mind, and I noticed the bulge in one of his pockets that could be a gun. Jank looked at me with confident anger.

"All right," I relented. "We'll help, but I ask you to listen to my concerns during the procedure."

Jank lit the flame on the soldering iron and began vigorously burning the man. While I knew the victim was a terrible man, the torture still deeply upset me. However, I put these feelings aside and yelled in between the man's screams, "There is a real possibility that somebody will attack you. It would be a good idea to change locations."

"Nonsense. Only the locals know of this place."

"Grace found you, and we walked right up to the front door. Others will do the same."

Jank stopped burning and glared at me. He then picked up the hammer and, with surprising agility, hit the man in the temple. We undid the restraints and then flipped the man. Next, Jank grabbed a scalpel and began working with excellent technique. After he removed the organs, he thrust the black dagger into the base of the man's skull. Jank turned to me with a wicked smile and then prepared the organs.

Less than a minute after the man had passed, Jank sat in a chair, rapidly took off his shirt, and handed me a scalpel. I could not believe how many ghastly oozing sores his body contained. As I got close, the smell became unbearable. He directed me to a bandage on his upper arm, and I removed the old pancreas. I found it to be in excellent condition and wondered how long ago it had been harvested. After cleaning the open wound, I applied sutures, antiseptic, and a bandage.

Jank picked up a mirror, and I probed along his right shoulder with my left pointer finger to locate the proper location. Jank did not flinch when I cut into him. Arturo watched with great intensity as I moved the muscles around to ensure I had located the correct area. I nodded, which pleased Jank, and he took over. After inserting the prepared pancreas and liquid, he sutured himself, and applied an antiseptic with a bandage. The entire procedure only took two and a half minutes.

Jank looked at me with a big grin, and I pleaded, "Sir, you must consider what I'm warning you about. We're all in danger."

"We're not in any danger. What you cannot see is the hundreds of loyal men who surround my compound. They report every person who approaches and are more than capable of eliminating any threat."

"Sir, may I remind you that somebody did a full airstrike in China, followed by an attack by a private army. Think of the resources required to pull that off."

Jank tried to stand up, sat back down, and glared at me. "I equipped my men with the latest beam-riding Starstreak ground-to-air missiles. They will obliterate any aircraft that dares to approach this compound. We're safe."

Jank waved us away.

"Sir, please reconsider," I begged.

"Leave!"

"Well, let us know when you are ready for the next harvest."

"I require no more assistance. Away! Now!"

Clearly, we were no longer welcome, so we exited through the iron door. The clean outside air felt refreshing. "What do you think will happen to us?" Arturo wondered.

"I already told you what I think. In the meantime, have you ever played Grand Theft Auto?"

Arturo laughed, and we played video games for the rest of the day. In the early evening, we ate an excellent curry chicken dinner with brown rice. Later, we talked more about Panama and then went to sleep.

At 4:42 in the morning, Arturo shook me awake. "What's going on?" I asked in a sleepy voice.

"They want us."

"Jank?"

"Probably."

I stood, and we walked toward the iron door. "Why are you bringing your notebook?" Arturo asked.

"I have a feeling."

"Ignore your feelings. Trust me, after the harvest, Jank will welcome us with open arms."

"Now isn't the time to relax."

When we got to the iron door, it was open. Inside, we saw a bloody man on the harvest table. Jank sat on the floor, looking exhausted. As I closed the iron door, Arturo looked over the body and said, "This man is dead, and Jank did not complete the procedure."

"We need to help him."

Arturo finished extracting the organs, and I prepared them. We then helped Jank to a chair, and Arturo removed the old pancreas. He then placed the new one in and applied sutures.

"Eat something easy to get down, drink a little water, and get lots of rest," I said in a soothing voice. "When you wake up, you will feel a lot better. Then we are going to have a long talk."

Jank looked at us weakly and awkwardly motioned toward a red wooden door. Inside was a modest bedroom, and we helped him to bed. I looked at Arturo, shrugged, and we walked to the iron door. When it opened, we heard distant noises. "Mortars," Arturo confirmed, while squinting in the darkness. "By the sound, 110 millimeter. This is the first salvo in a surprise assault, and soldiers will be here soon. We must immediately depart."

We walked back inside and went to the bedroom. "We're under attack!" I said in a raised voice to Jank. "Time to go."

Jank did not respond, and we nudged him. Finally, his eyes briefly opened, and he whispered in a weak voice, "Red button. Left wall."

"What does it do?"

We shook him to no avail. "What do you think the button does?" I asked Arturo.

"It's probably a distress call. I say, push it."

"I agree."

When I pressed the button, the iron door slammed shut with a loud bang. It sizzled, and acidic smoke came from the edges. I looked at Arturo in horror and said, "We can exit through the courtyard and climb—"

Sixteen sequenced muffled explosions interrupted me. The stone walls shuddered, and dust fell from the ceiling. We instinctively covered our heads, and I looked at Arturo in shock. Fifteen seconds later, it was apparent the stone roof would not collapse and we pushed against the big iron door, but it felt hot and refused to budge. When we tried to open the courtyard door, it did not open. The only other door revealed a sophisticated computer room. "Wow, that is impressive," I said with a low whistle. "This is how Grace found us. She tracked his computer."

"We cannot escape through the computer, but perhaps we can send a message."

"I wish I had brought my backpack with the radio."

I sat down, moved the mouse, and a password request appeared. "So much for that," I said, and then threw up my hands.

"Jank must have some way out of this smelly place. Look for a trapdoor."

We searched the floors and found a steel door with a sophisticated combination lock under the carpet. I sat down in defeat and said, "Well, all we can do is wait for the old sleepyhead to recover."

The computer room had the best smell, and we closed the door. Fortunately, it contained a small bathroom. With nothing else to do, I flipped through the only magazine, *Time*, dated February 1, 1988. There were ten books on a tiny steel bookshelf, and Arturo selected *Grime: The Big Hate*. I found his choice amusing, and we discussed the plot.

Three hours later, we ate the only food available, a dense rice cake wrapped in red wax paper, and we shared a bottle of mineral water. Afterward, Arturo revealed more of his history. He led a captivating life and told me a remarkable story about meeting Teddy Roosevelt in Panama. They were both interested in animal conservation and state economics.

Ten hours later, we heard pounding noises through the stone walls and surmised soldiers were using construction equipment to remove the explosion debris. Again, I tried to wake up Jank without success.

I asked Arturo to try opening the combination lock, and two hours later, he gave up. Three hours later, the noises changed to pounding against the iron door. Forty-five minutes later, the sound switched to loud saws. This noise forced me to shake Jank hard. Fortunately, he stirred, opened his eyes, and smiled.

"We have to go! Now!" I yelled.

"Are they at the main entrance?" Jank asked in a sleepy voice.

"Yes!"

"Hmm."

Jank stretched, stood, walked over to a small dresser, and took out a well-used iPad from under the clothes. He then entered a password and tapped icons. A live picture of the compound from a great distance appeared on the screen. Military vehicles and yellow construction equipment surrounded our location. Jank zoomed in and saw men in uniforms working hard. "Recognize them?" He asked.

"I think those guys are the same jerks who attacked Quan," I answered angrily.

Jank tapped icons and said, "You were correct; they eliminated all of my men. How dreadful. Hmm. Watching the attackers die will be enjoyable."

Jank switched to a different program, pressed icons, entered a password, and put crosshairs on a group of three men who appeared to be supervising the operation. He pressed a red icon, and a confirm box appeared. Jank entered another password and tapped the confirm icon. The image turned bright white for a second, and it became obscured by smoke. Nine seconds later, I felt a muffled explosion. The smoke cleared, and we could see the three men lying on the ground around smoking dirt.

Jank handed me the iPad and said, "You have 24 shots left. Try to hit the construction equipment and groups of people. Now, I must relieve myself."

"It will smell."

"You warned me already!" Jank said with a hearty laugh.

Jank's casual attitude seemed out of place. I turned to the iPad, lined up shots, and sent off missiles. The experience reminded me of playing a video game, except there was no score. Jank came out of the bathroom seven minutes later and said, "Whew. You were not joking. That didn't smell good. Hey! You ate my food!"

"Sorry," Arturo admitted.

"You guys!" Jank said with another hearty laugh.

Now the pleasant attitude made me wonder if it was an act. I turned back to the iPad and continued sending off missiles until there were no more shots. I then walked to the other room to see Jank using his computer. He appeared to be transferring money, closing accounts, and changing passwords. I noticed an oversized T-shaped aluminum USB drive connected to the main computer with a blinking blue light. Without looking away from the screen, he said, "Click the alternate icon."

A new menu appeared, and I had two batteries remaining. I then moved the crosshairs to the survivors helping the injured. Unfortunately, the missiles did not do as much damage as I had hoped. "Look for the person who took command and blast him," Jank yelled out.

I panned and tilted until I located a jeep with several radio antennas. One missile destroyed the jeep, and I found 24 more targets. Finally, I switched to my last missile battery and waited ten minutes for the men to regroup and begin repairing equipment. Then, I blasted a gathering of men and the largest pieces of equipment. As I did so, I reflected that these were not computer dots but actual people with families.

However, they were trying to kill or capture me, and I desperately wanted to survive.

Jank looked at my iPad screen and said, "You took revenge to a new level. And this procedure. Woo-hoo! I have never felt this good. I will look 25 soon!"

"We have to go," I said with urgency.

"Transferring the files will take at least an hour. Let's celebrate your missile strikes. I put a special bottle of water in that box, and now seems like the perfect occasion to open it."

"Err, we drank it," Arturo sheepishly admitted.

"You did? You guys!" Jank cheered with a big grin.

I still had great difficulty accepting Jank's new pleasant attitude. *You threatened to kill me yesterday! What the heck?* I thought.

For the next 58 minutes, the attackers pounded the door with hammers, and I saw large cracks appearing in the stone surrounding the door. "Ten more minutes," Jank casually said. "The door will hold. So do not be so worried."

Jank's calming efforts did not help, and Arturo looked ready to tear his hair out. Jank diligently worked for the next seventeen minutes and then shut down his computer. He looked at it with great sadness and muttered, "My only friend. Sorry to see you go, old chum."

Jank grabbed the USB drive and attached it to a lanyard around his neck. He led us to the steel door in the floor, entered the combination, and said to me, "Close the door behind you and lock it."

I picked up my notebook and watched Jank and Arturo enter the tunnel. When I entered, there was just enough light passing through the edges to lock the door from the inside. Now, in total darkness, I felt my way down a narrow rocky slope. The passage led to an excavated area, and Jank cracked a chemical light stick.

We began walking while Jank hummed an unknown tune. The cavern appeared natural in some parts and carved out in others. Thirty-one minutes later, we came to a rung ladder, and Jank climbed up. At the top, I saw a manhole cover with six combination locks around the edge. Jank opened each lock and used a pry bar attached to the ladder with a rope to move the manhole cover. His strength surprised me, and he flashed me a funny expression before exiting.

I followed Arturo through the manhole into a disused storeroom. We moved boxes, and walked into a garage to see a car under a dusty cover. When Jank pulled it away, we saw a new Land Rover. He looked at me with a big grin and began working on his iPad. A long-distance view of his compound appeared, and I saw ten men hard at work at the iron door and over a hundred standing around the remains of the compound. Jank pressed several buttons and entered a password. A confirmation box appeared, and he asked Arturo, "Will you do the honors?"

"I will enjoy sending those bastards to hell!"

Arturo tapped the red icon, smiled wickedly, and four seconds later, the compound rose out of the ground in a massive fireball. Three seconds after that, we heard a thunderous explosion. "That's epic!" I hooted. "How amazing was that?!"

"Nobody attacks me and lives to talk about it! Well, my friends, we have some choices. I propose taking a plane to the Bahamas.

It has been a long time since my body was well enough to handle the ladies," Jank said as he danced side to side.

"You read my mind," Arturo said with a big grin.

"That is an expected move," I interrupted. "You guys are thinking with your little heads and not your big heads."

"Our little heads?" Arturo asked with a laugh. "How amusing! I haven't been with a woman for over 200 years, and I want to go to the Bahamas."

"What about Anna's mother?" I wondered.

"The accident injured her womanhood, and she never fully recovered. Therefore, it worked well between us."

Jank looked annoyed and said, "We have won. They're all dead."

"You don't get it," I said in a forced, pleasant voice. "Armed men with unlimited resources are now hunting the three of us. Think about it. Where would they look for people trying to escape? The airport? The coast? The highway? We need to keep a low profile."

"Bah!" Arturo said with a dismissive hand gesture. "You watched the explosion. They're all dead."

"I want to bed a girl," Jank hooted. "Here is $10,000. Do whatever you want."

"Look, you two," I challenged. "Let's have a little bet. I say you will get caught at the airport. If we see each other again, the loser has to do the tiger dance."

"What's the tiger dance?" Arturo asked.

"It's from the Calvin and Hobbes comic strip. You dance around while singing, 'Tigers are mean! Tigers are fierce! Tigers have teeth and claws that pierce!'"

Jank laughed and asked, "The tiger dance? You're crazy. Now, see here. The danger has passed. Trust me."

"No. You trust me. Both of you are going to be prisoners before sunset."

"Impossible!" Jank hooted. "Well, we are off. I enjoyed meeting you, and thank you for sharing the procedure secret."

"It has been a pleasure to have made your acquaintance," Arturo said. "I will always remember the man who interviewed Panama. Take care."

Jank looked at Arturo in confusion and said, "I've never driven."

"Bah! I'll drive," Arturo said, waving his hand. "Do you know the way to the nearest airport?"

"Of course," Jank answered. Then he turned to me. "James, you will find a motorcycle under that tarp. Remember, time unused is the longest time, and forgiveness is the attribute of the strong."

Without another word, they drove off, leaving me in a cloud of dust. I then realized that I should have asked for directions. After pacing for a minute, I sat on a wooden box with pictures of carrots on the side and formed a plan.

Jank gave me lots of cash, enabling me to keep a low profile in this inexpensive country. Plus, I had my passport and credit card in my sock. It then dawned on me that my passport and credit card would lead my enemies to me. Then, a crazy thought entered my mind: *English teacher?*

I laughed and took off the tarp to reveal a Honda 125 in excellent condition. The bike had no fuel, but I found a five-gallon container nearby. It kicked over on the first try, and I revved the engine with a whiny roar. *Left or right?* I chose left and took off like a shot.

Thailand is a staggeringly beautiful country. There are endless mountains next to deep green valleys. Everybody rode motorcycles, and I blended right in. With no destination in mind, I appreciated the drive and located a small restaurant 20 miles from my starting location. Inside, the only person was an amused cook who clearly wondered why a person like me had ended up in his establishment. "What's your best dish?" I asked.

The cook looked at me in confusion. When I realized he did not understand English, I handed him $10 and pointed to a fish on a poster. He smiled and began cooking. Seventeen minutes later, I enjoyed sweet lemongrass whitefish while we watched football (soccer) on a beat-up widescreen television. While I could not understand a single word, I had the time of my life, and I could tell the cook also enjoyed watching football. When the game ended two hours later, I thanked the cook, and he walked me to the door.

Outside, I saw four tourists studying a map on the hood of their big white SUV. I got on my Honda, and the man on the left asked, "James?"

How cool is this?! Another Grime fan! "Would you like an autograph?" I asked.

Then I realized that these "tourists" were all well-built men with tattoos. So I sighed and asked, "Are we going on a trip?"

They nodded, and I looked at the ground while shaking my head. There, a rusty Coca-Cola bottle cap caught my attention. When I looked up, three men surrounded me with their arms crossed. One man stood by the open car door while pointing inside, and I said, "Wait a sec."

The man on my left yelled, "Now!"

"Just wait."

I got off my bike and walked it to the restaurant while the three men escorted me. The cook had been watching this event with concern, and I handed my bike and keys to him. He looked confused and then became overjoyed. As I turned to leave, I turned back to give him my cash because I knew the men would take it. The cook almost fainted as he held my hand, bowed, and spouted tear-filled words. I bowed to him several times while my captors looked at me with concern. The three men then escorted me to the SUV, where I sat in the back seat, with one man on each side.

FOURTEEN

While I worried about being captured, I felt comfortable because the men did not search me or put me in hand-cuffs. On the trip, the driver occasionally whispered in English to the man in the passenger seat about directions. His accent sounded Arabic, but it could have been African.

We arrived at a large airport an hour and 31 minutes later, and I whimsically expected to see Jank and Arturo. At the outer gate, the armed security guards demanded to inspect everybody's passports. This request upset my captors, and I could see that a gun battle would erupt. The opportunity opened up the possibility of escape during the chaos, but I decided not to push my luck. So, I pulled out my passport. My captors seemed relieved and did the same. The security guards took down our information, and one of my captors muttered, "Thanks."

"Glad to help," I cheerfully replied.

They drove to a corner of the airport where I saw four large, identical twin-engine business jets. This site looked impressive, and I wondered who would be on board. The men escorted me to the stairs on the leftmost plane, and I walked inside.

An attractive flight attendant with red hair led me through the empty plane to the bathroom in the back. It was spacious (for a plane) and even had a tiny shower. She measured me, suggested I clean up, and walked away. As I rinsed the dirt off from crawling around the tunnel, I reflected on the moment. In one week, I'd eaten exquisite meals, showered on a private plane, and swum on a yacht. This was definitely not how I expected my week to go.

Somebody briefly opened the door and hung a nice black suit on the coat hook. I put it on, and the flight attendant escorted me to a beautiful leather seat. Then, she asked if I needed anything. "Some champagne would be nice," I answered with a smile. After all, people should make extravagant requests like this on a private plane.

The flight attendant returned with a tall flute and a small plate of appetizers. One minor harvest side effect is an aversion to alcohol, and I only took a small sip. Nine minutes later, the pilot said over the intercom that we would take off in five minutes. I leaned back and enjoyed my new surroundings.

We were soon airborne to who-knows-where. Two security men kept a close watch over me as they silently read the same newspaper many times. Well, I assumed they were security men. They might have been mercenaries, bounty hunters, or hired goons. They were not talking, and I stopped trying to make conversation. I located a video monitor at the back of the plane and switched it to the CNN feed. Not much was happening in the news, and I turned it off twenty minutes later.

Eight hours later, the plane landed and refueled. While we waited, the flight attendant departed and returned with a superb meal of grilled steak, potatoes au gratin, crab cakes, and fresh fruit. She served the two security men hamburgers and fries. Since I had a full plate, I offered them my fruit, but they refused.

We took off, and two hours later, it became dark. The flight attendant reclined my seat to make a comfortable bed, and I fell asleep while wondering what would happen upon arrival. When I woke, the flight attendant informed me that the plane would land in two hours. So I shaved and ate an excellent continental breakfast with croissants, brie cheese, and assorted lunch meats.

Through the cabin window, the view was endless desert, and I wondered which country we were landing in as the plane began its descent. The flight attendant opened the door right after the engines stopped, and I felt a tremendous blast of hot air.

On the tarmac, I saw a large hangar and a single-lane road leading away from the sparse airport. The security men escorted me to a stretch limousine and opened the door. I got in and found myself alone while wondering why the security men stayed behind. It then dawned on me that there was nowhere to escape.

The limousine whooshed away, and thirty-eight minutes later, we arrived at a massive iron gate. Inside, we drove through luscious gardens with exotic animals, fountains, and immaculate buildings. Everything looked over-the-top beautiful and made me think I was on an expensive movie set.

We continued for two minutes, and the limousine came to a gentle stop in front of a marble-faced mansion. A well-dressed man opened the door, and two drop-dead gorgeous Arabic women dressed in identical blue and yellow dresses escorted me up the marble stairs. *This is going to be interesting,* I thought, as they led me through the main doors.

Quan's entryway had blown me away with all its fantastic art and sculptures. This entryway was ten times more opulent. I had no choice but to stop and look at the nearest statue. An impressive four-foot black marble lion stood over four iridescent blue granite sheep. I was impressed with the setting, technique, and fine muscle detail. Twenty-two seconds later, I turned to see the nearest painting. An exquisite Rembrandt! This fantastic sight captivated me for 27 seconds as I studied every brush stroke. *What technique! What color! Extraordinary!*

The women tugged at me, and I could not help myself—an immaculate Pollock stood before me. I had appreciated Pollock's paintings, and this tremendous example of his work looked beyond stunning—such a perfect integration of colors and shadows. The women tugged hard at me, and I yielded. We came to a door, and I spotted her. The sculpture of Madonna holding a pitcher had to be a Michelangelo. This flawless white marble example stood six feet tall, and I have never witnessed such a spectacular piece of artwork in person. The women tugged at me harder, and I reluctantly followed. They escorted me down a flight of marble steps through two massive black ebony doors with detailed wood floral carvings.

Inside, I found a vast room with gold inlay on every surface. Miniature lamps of different colors reflected off every golden surface to highlight the perfect craftsmanship. The effect was breathtaking, and it seemed as if I had entered a dream. At the end of the room, two immaculate black granite sphinx sculptures with red jewel eyes surrounded a grand throne. I immediately recognized the picturesque woman who was seated.

Each long strand of black hair on Cleopatra's regal head was combed perfectly. She wore a gold crown made with sparkling blue jewels with a two-inch cobra that looked ready to strike. Cleopatra's light caramel skin had a smooth complexion without a single imperfection. She wore a hint of blush on top of her overall foundation.

Cleopatra had applied glossy red lipstick and pressed her lips together to form a thin, confident smile. Her ears had three elongated gold hoops with blue jewels. Cleopatra's eyes stood out as her most striking feature. They were deep blue with turquoise shadowing under neatly shaped black eyebrows. Of course, she had applied eyeliner in the classic ancient Egyptian elongated shape.

Cleopatra wore a trim white silk dress with an embroidered green star pattern. Each star had blue jewels woven into the outer part of the pattern, and the perfectly tailored dress framed her flawless body without a single seam visible. The cut revealed a tasteful amount of well-toned leg and cleavage. She wore glossy white peep-toe pumps with matching blue jewels. Her adorable toes had tiny blue jewels glued to each toenail.

Cleopatra folded her hands together, and I noticed each finger-nail also had blue jewels.

I have looked at women in magazines, movies, and books. I even met the actress who played Wonder Woman, Lynda Carter at a charity event. However, the astounding woman before me was undoubtedly the best of the best.

I began walking toward her, and her presence became even more sophisticated, infectious, and sexy. Her overwhelming confidence and charisma intimidated me to the maximum. My knees weakened, and it became difficult to walk. My mouth must have been hanging open as I awkwardly advanced. When I stopped a few feet away, she still had not moved a muscle. I could not help myself from staring. Every aspect of her held something new, something fantastic. Even her elbows were perfect. How can elbows be perfect? Cleopatra's were flawless, and she knew this undeniable fact with 100 percent certainty!

This sculpture of a woman raised her faultless head and blinked. I must have been drooling as I stammered, "Um—errr—hi."

"James."

Wow, Cleopatra's voice sounded fantastic when she called my name. She had a slight Arabic accent that dazzled my ears like the fantastic taste of Grace's cooking. *She knows my name. How cool is that? Say it again. James. I love how your voice sounds. James, James, James.*

Cleopatra looked at me with amusement, and I asked, "Um. Mam, is it Cledopart or Cleopatra?"

"You are indeed charming. Like your dear friend Anitchka, you may call me Cleo. Come, we have much to discuss."

"Um—errr, thank you, Miss Cleo."

Cleopatra stood and walked away from her throne. She stood five-feet-five with a trim athletic build with the outline of a skilled dancer. As she walked, she took each step with confident precision, and her two-inch high-heeled footsteps did not make the slightest sound against the marble floors. As I followed, I appreciated my view of her butt gently swaying from side to side. The hypnotic motion made it difficult for me to concentrate on the mechanics of making my feet work.

Even the back of her head looked stunning, and I began getting a whiff of her scent—a sweet mixture of jasmine, lilac, and honey. The combination was breathtaking, and I started taking deep breaths to inhale her fragrance.

We entered an opulent room with an unobstructed view of the surrounding garden and desert. Wonderful jungle-themed paintings and sculptures surrounded us. Cleopatra looked at me, tilted her head, and then sat on an embroidered lion theme sofa. She motioned for me to sit across from her on a similar sofa. The security guards departed, leaving me wondering what would happen next. I did my best to remain pleasant and smiled. She looked at me for 43 seconds while sizing me up, and I could not help but continue to gaze upon her. The little voice inside my head yelled at me to act more respectfully. Of course, I did not listen, and it screamed louder.

I eventually straightened my posture and said in my most confident voice, "Cleo, I'm sorry for my inappropriate stare. Please forgive my rudeness."

Cleopatra tipped her head to the side and smiled. This simple gesture brightened the room like a floodlight. Her teeth were perfect white pearls, and her lips magically caressed them. My little voice now screamed at the highest level ever to get my act together.

I straightened up even more and asked in my most pleasant voice, "How may I be of service?"

Cleopatra continued to study me, which made me wonder about her motives. However, I liked to think that we had gotten off to a pleasant start. She looked upwards slightly and again spoke in her fantastic voice, "I read your book." Her eyes changed to convey frustration, which saddened me.

"I hope you found your description flattering," I optimistically replied.

Cleopatra's expression darkened. She leaned back, glaring as I wondered how bad this situation would get. Finally, she crossed her hands and said in a menacing voice, "I did not expect Anitchka to share the process. I provided that gift for her and her alone."

"I see."

"Her choice of recipient surprised me."

"Me too."

Cleopatra tilted her head for six seconds and laughed. The sound was priceless and lifted my heart to a better place because I made her smile. Then, Cleopatra paused for twelve seconds and asked in an amused voice, "Do you understand why I requested your presence?"

"Cleo, I am here because you wished me to be here. I suspect you would like to learn more about the other harvesters, and I am happy to provide any information you request."

"I see why Anitchka chose you. You're charming."

"Thank you."

Cleopatra turned to the side, then back, and said, "You speak in a reserved voice."

"Recent experience taught me to be respectful toward immortals."

"Indeed."

"May I ask a question?"

"You may," Cleopatra answered with a positive change of expression.

"Did you orchestrate the attack on Quan, Arturo, and Jank?"

Cleopatra became apprehensive, and I continued, "The attackers might want to harm you too."

"I did not instigate the attack, and we are not in danger."

"Please forgive my forward attitude in advance, but the attackers struck three immortals."

"Quan sent men to all corners of the world and directly called each one on his personal cell phone. Amten installed absurd commercial software on your computer that communicated directly to his home computer. How utterly reckless. And that fool, Jank, performed every conceivable search from his only computer. His location stood out like a lighthouse on a moonless night. I assure you, I have kept my location a secret."

"May I ask if Grace found you?"

"Anitchka learned about the others, but she did not discover my location."

"Did the others search for you?"

"They focused on you and were unaware of my existence."

I found it amusing that Cleopatra used the name Anitchka. "Grace informed me that there might be one other," I said in a reserved tone.

"My son, Caesarion, lives outside of Rome."

"What?!" I exclaimed.

"His computer search was far more sophisticated."

"Really? Caesarion's alive?! Wow, that's so cool!" I caught myself acting too excited, straightened up, and continued, "I'm sorry for my last remark. Again, please forgive my rude behavior."

"Hmm. Anitchka did indeed see something in you. I'm also troubled by these unknown aggressions. As for my safety, I have taken appropriate precautions. On to important matters. I have brought you here for a reason I will reveal at a later time."

"Do you want me to ask Caesarion about the attacks?" I asked with a smile.

Cleopatra's jaw dropped as she looked at me with wide eyes for nine seconds. "Indeed," she said after quickly composing herself. "Before we discuss how you will execute this task, we need to conclude prior business." She clapped her hands twice, and six huge guards came in with three men under hoods.

I recognized Quan, Arturo, and Jank. Somebody had dressed them in black jumpsuits without shoes, and this sight briefly reminded me of a punk band I watched in college.

Cleopatra stood, straightened herself, motioned, and the guards removed their hoods. The look on the three men's faces could have set the surprise world record. They looked at each other in confusion and then at me sitting on a beautiful sofa. I loved every second of their utter shock. Then, I noticed Quan's and Jank's skin had significantly improved, and the scars had faded.

Arturo dropped to his knees and said something I interpreted to mean "my queen." I appreciated his ability to show loyalty. Then, the large men that held Arturo pulled him up to a standing position.

Cleopatra walked over to the three of them and stared at each one for 70 to 90 seconds. They all struggled against her stare and then yielded. Cleopatra then asked each man six questions in languages I did not understand, then stared deeply into them until they answered. I recognized the same dagger-shooting stare from my time with Grace, and it impressed me that Cleopatra had superior abilities. After one question, Quan broke down and began babbling.

The interrogation continued for 53 minutes until Cleopatra sat down in exhaustion. "Perhaps a beverage would be appropriate?" I suggested.

Cleopatra made a fluttering gesture; a servant rushed away and returned with a silver pitcher with tall glasses on a silver tray. She drank a sizable amount of liquid from the pitcher in a non-ladylike fashion, which raised a few eyebrows from the guards. Cleopatra then looked at me with a tired expression. "They have not revealed the procedure to anybody," she confirmed.

"Besides Grace, I am unaware of any other immortals."

"Two guards, Humai and Khalid, escaped my presence many years ago. I suspect they may know the details."

"Wow, there might be two other immortals?" I asked, and then regretted my dull question.

"Yes."

"May I ask what questions you asked the three men?"

"They were already interrogated, but I wanted to ensure the results were effective. Quan revealed an additional bank account."

"I see."

Cleopatra studied me for 21 seconds and said, "I have a surprise for you."

Cleopatra clapped her hands twice, and Grace walked in. She wore a stylish green dress with her hair combed up. I surprised myself by standing up and hugging her while saying, "I thought I would never see you again."

Grace became obviously apprehensive. She hugged me back lightly and sat next to Cleopatra. I returned to my sofa, and they smiled at me with humorous expressions. This made me wonder what they discussed beforehand.

As they looked at me, I realized Grace had changed since we last met. She looked more youthful, and I suspected that she had recently harvested. "How long have you been here?"

Grace answered in her fantastic voice, "Cleo observed my ship dropping you off, and I arranged an introduction. We have spent the last two days catching up."

"I would like to have been a part of that conversation."

"We spoke of you several times."

I caught myself feeling embarrassed and asked, "Grace, have you met Jank?"

Cleopatra answered in a bitter voice, "Anitchka supervised his interrogation."

The angry demeanor sent a chill up my spine, and I again straightened my posture. "Cleo, I became distracted and asked a less than perfect question. For that, I am sorry," I said in an apologetic voice.

Cleopatra said to Grace, "He is charming."

"Look at how polite he becomes after a mistake," Grace said with a smile.

"You trained him well."

"So to speak, it took significant effort."

I wondered if they were serious. Then, suddenly, Cleopatra's expression turned stern. "James?" she asked in a calm, authoritarian voice.

"Yes, Cleo."

"Quan has outlived his usefulness."

Quan began yelling, and a guard clamped down on his head with strong arms. This action frightened me, and I asked, "What are you requesting?"

Cleopatra looked at me, and I saw death in her eyes. Her actions horrified me, and I knew my survival depended on choosing my next words with extreme care. "You wish me to— end his life? Here? Now?"

Cleopatra nodded with a stone-cold expression. I instantly knew that I would have to kill this man if I wanted to live. When I turned to Grace, she looked at me with the same expression. I made a big gulp, thought for thirteen seconds, and asked, "Cleo, madame. Please know in advance that I do not intend my next question to upset you. May I ask why this man should be put down?"

"Quan killed countless boys to further his worthless life. In return, he did nothing to enrich our world. The drive within you should recognize the evil contained within his soul."

A million thoughts raced through my head, and I wanted to yell, "You've done much worse!" However, I held my opinions in check. Yet, I could not kill a person who had not wronged me, and I came up with a distraction. "I'm sure there's much more to learn from him. His business contacts might be useful. Maybe you could ask about his history. It might fill in some blanks."

"They revealed all the information I required."

Cleopatra's words crushed me, and I thought up an excuse. "Am I to—kill him—in front of all these witnesses?"

Cleopatra nodded. I took a deep breath and stammered, "I see."

My mind searched for something to say, and I knew my fourteen second pause upset her. "How would you like me to accomplish your request?" I asked in defeat and then stood.

Quan had been struggling while his strong captor kept him contained. Then, somebody handed me a straight razor with a black handle. To this day, I cannot remember what they looked like or how they approached me undetected. I continued to rack my brain to develop a way out of this situation.

The guards rolled out clear plastic and forced Quan to kneel in the center. His expression became terrified. I walked over to Quan, turned to Cleopatra, and said, "Cleo, madame. Again, I do not intend to offend you, and I hold you in the highest regard. However, I am complying with your request under protest."

Cleopatra looked at me for an angry moment, nodded, and I turned back to Quan. While I had no choice, I could not bring myself to kill a man because she asked me. At that moment, I realized only Grace could help me. However, when I turned to her, I saw death in her eyes, and it saddened me to realize she would not offer any help. It briefly occurred to me I could drop the razor and plead for his life. This thought lasted eleven seconds, as I understood my actions would be pointless.

When I turned back to Quan, I closed my eyes and considered the coward I had become. *How can I justify exchanging his life for mine? What kind of person would force another to do something so awful?* Then, after taking a deep breath to gather my thoughts, I opened my eyes while looking down at the immaculate blue tiles.

A small chip briefly distracted me, and I somehow hoped that this sight would get me out of my dilemma. However, the straight razor felt heavy in my hand, and I knew my delays annoyed Cleopatra. I then got sidetracked by realizing that I had never held a straight razor.

Out of my sidetrack, I looked into Quan's eyes for nineteen seconds and saw his deep fear. However, I knew he would not give up without a fight, although his death was inevitable. As I continued to stare, I saw Quan's cunning mind at work, and he made a thin smile. I suspected he thought up an angle to get out of this situation. The deeper I looked, the more I knew this man had a bitter heart. At that moment, my decision to take his life became final.

I motioned, and the guards released their grip while remaining behind Quan. He looked relieved, and I did not want to prolong the moment. I uncomfortably cleared my throat. "You're an amazing individual, and I wish that I could have learned more from you. I'm sorry to be the one who takes your life, and I take no pleasure in this action. Yet, I take comfort in knowing that you walked an evil path for centuries while failing to understand how wrong it was to murder children. If you believe in the concept of hell, you are about to meet the devil."

"I spared your life!" Quan pleaded. "You now must spare my life in order to remain a man of honor. If you fail my request, you will join me in the dark bowels of the afterlife!"

Quan had certainly thought up a brilliant plan by attempting to guilt me into saving his life. *Did he forget that he recently wanted to end my life? Only my cunningness saved me.* As I thought about this concept, his words only strengthened my resolve. It then occurred to me he might have made this request to ensure a quick death.

As I looked into his eyes, they became confident, making me think, *No, you are not trying to send me on a guilt trip.* As I opened the straight razor, I said, "I'm unable to honor your request. Please forgive my actions."

Quan looked crushed, and I knew he was formulating a new argument. Nine short seconds later, he said, "You—" My blade interrupted his words with a swift cut across his neck. Blood gushed out six inches with each heartbeat. I took a step back and watched in horror as he slumped down. Blood pooled on the plastic as he took his last gurgling breath. *What have I done?* I wondered in horror.

In that tragic moment, I saw a slight visual flutter, and it occurred to me that this optical anomaly could be Quan's soul leaving, as Grace described. While I contemplated, I realized I had killed the oldest person in the world, and a vast resource of firsthand knowledge had disappeared by my hand. My knees buckled, my balance faltered, and it took all my strength to remain standing.

As I looked into his lifeless eyes for sixteen seconds, I wondered how I would ever forgive myself. Cleopatra said something I did not comprehend, and I turned to her. She wore a look of honed commitment along with a strange joy and demanded, "Now, Jank!"

Cleopatra's words crushed me, and I could not believe what she had ordered. My eyes again fell to the floor as I wondered what to do. The same chipped tile distracted me, and I tried to concentrate on it. When I looked up, Jank struggled as the guards moved Quan's body away. They rolled out new plastic and forced him to kneel. I knew he was full of fear and would die soon. A huge part of me wanted to tell Cleopatra that I acted under protest, but I knew my words would fall on deaf ears.

Grace wore an expression of contentment. She briefly nodded, and I looked down at the bloody razor with deep thoughts. *Did I really kill a man? What would have happened if I had refused? Why is this happening to me?*

When I turned back to Jank, I saw the fear in his eyes, and I knew he would also die by my hand. *What had I done to deserve this?* It again occurred to me to drop my razor and run away.

It took thirteen seconds to build up enough resolve to wave at the guards to remove their grip on Jank's shoulders. Then, he took a moment to compose himself and said in a fear-filled voice, "We were becoming friends. I need to do the tiger dance to honor our wager."

"Honoring our wager will not be possible."

"I can see this task is making you uncomfortable. So let's overcome our differences. You have a choice in this matter."

"Like Quan, you tortured and then killed boys for your preservation. I am sorry to be the one who takes your life, and I sincerely wish that I could have learned from your vast experience. Please allow me to thank you for the motorcycle. I enjoyed riding it around Thailand and gave it to a cook. You cannot imagine how happy your precious gift made him."

I turned to Cleopatra, and she nodded. Grace also made a slight nod that I understood to be an encouragement. When I turned back to Jank, I knew he would make another attempt to save his life. He said in a choked-up voice while attempting not to cry, "Your books prove your fantastic writing ability. I have so much to share with you. Let's write a book together. I know it will be a best-seller."

"And I would enjoy recording your story. I'm sorry that I cannot fulfill your request."

I cut a deep gash across Jank's neck without waiting for him to speak. Blood spurted out, and I needed to take a step back. Unlike Quan, Jank fought with every ounce of strength to live one second longer by trying to stop the bleeding with his hands. Then, he reached out both bloody hands for my help. His last gesture tugged deeply at my soul, and I will remember those begging eyes until my dying day.

As Jank's life drained onto the plastic, his skin color faded, and his body slumped forward. The sight of his bright red blood against the immaculate blue tile sickened me. I desperately wanted to curl up on the floor and cry my heart out. But, in that heartbreaking moment, Cleopatra's stern voice wrenched me out of my pitiful thoughts. "Now, Amten!"

Even though I anticipated the request, her words destroyed me. My body shook, and it took considerable effort not to collapse. Finally, the guards rolled out clear plastic in front of Arturo and exchanged the razor for something else. I looked down to recognize Arturo's ceremonial knife and gripped it in anger. *How can I kill a man with his own sacred blade?*

After composing my thoughts for 34 seconds, I approached Arturo, and we locked eyes. *Why does Cleopatra want me to kill him? He revealed his loyalty to her. Yes, he killed boys, but I liked the man. We had some fun, right? Plus, he saved my life during the attack on his house.* This deep contemplation made me realize he was indeed a friend.

A fresh wave of shame overcame me as I understood I would again have to kill a living person for somebody else's pleasure. When I turned back to Cleopatra, I saw something different in her expression. A kind of longing or curiosity. Clearly, she is a far crueler individual than I thought. Grace now looked upset, and I wondered why.

As we held eye contact, I again wondered if Grace would help. Three seconds later, she changed her position and folded her hands. Grace's actions crushed me, and it took eleven seconds to regain enough composure to look into Arturo's eyes. They were apprehensive but held a certain amount of acceptance.

After I motioned, the guards released Arturo, and he said in a shaky voice, "I am sorry that my circumstances prevent me from honoring our wager. A man always fulfills his debts. I am also sorry you are the one to end my regretful life. I, too, took the lives of many children who had committed no crime. Therefore, you can take comfort in performing a necessary service to the people of this world. Plus, you are truly a great writer, and I wish I could share my vast wisdom and history with you. And finally, you would have made a splendid husband for Anna, and I would have been proud to call you son."

This sentiment raised me up and simultaneously crushed me. I felt utterly empty, and my mind could not hold a single thought. Arturo turned to Cleopatra, smiled, and said, "My queen. Words cannot describe the happiness that I feel at this moment. Your presence brings me true exhilaration, and I'm again captivated by your beauty. Now that I have experienced the wonderful gift of seeing you one last time, my life is complete. Thank you for allowing me this great privilege, and I hope that my death will bring you closure. You have always been and always will be my queen—and my lover."

Cleopatra nodded, which pleased Arturo. He warmly smiled at her, looked up at me, and said in an encouraging voice, "You're going to be fine. Please do not waste your tears. I'm glad to have had the honor of meeting you. Now, make this quick."

"Arturo, you are my friend. So please forgive me for what I am about to do."

"I forgive your actions in advance. My brother, be at peace and live a long life."

I watched Arturo close his eyes and prepare himself. This action pulled so profoundly at my soul that I could not breathe. Tears were flowing as I gripped his knife with all my strength.

Arturo looked up at me one last time. His eyes held a certain level of contentment, which surprised me. Arturo made a slight nod, followed by a brief smile. He closed his eyes, and moved his lips in what I suspect was a silent prayer. I felt so terrible as I realized that his last action was to make the moment as painless as possible for me. His powerful gesture nearly destroyed all the drive I had developed, and I again wanted to drop his knife. It took all my effort not to beg Cleopatra to spare both of us. Twenty-one seconds later, I weakly raised Arturo's knife and took a deep breath.

Cleopatra yelled, "Stop!" I nearly fainted. She dramatically stood, walked over to Arturo, stared down at him for six seconds, and demanded, "Why did you leave me?!"

Arturo opened his eyes in stunned surprise and stammered, "My queen, that moment stands out as the most painful decision of my life."

"Why?! You will tell me!"

"My queen, it was impossibly difficult to be with such a magnificent woman and not ..."

"Not what?!"

Arturo looked around and whispered, "Have sex with you."

Cleopatra straightened herself and looked at the assembled people in embarrassment. She then awkwardly cleared her throat. At that moment, I discreetly looked at Grace to see her puzzled expression. "I could no longer bear the extreme torture," Arturo confessed with confident resolve. "I needed to leave or kill myself, and I have regretted my dastardly mistake every minute since I left your splendid presence."

Cleopatra seemed unsure what to do next as she looked around the room and then back at Arturo. Twelve seconds later, she straightened her dress and demanded, "Do you pledge loyalty to your queen?!"

"It is unnecessary to repledge my loyalty. You have always had my loyalty—and my love. My feelings for you have never wavered. Not for one second. And my loyalty will never stop! Even death cannot make my sincere devotion fade into nothingness!"

His last words echoed in the dead silent room. Cleopatra stared deeply into Arturo for 24 seconds and walked back to the sofa. Arturo's knife remained firmly in my grasp as she commanded, "You know what to do."

Cleopatra's order crushed me. Arturo had openly pledged his love, and now I had to kill him. I do not know how I found the strength to raise Arturo's knife again. In that dire moment, I hated Cleopatra with all my heart!

When I looked down at Arturo one last time, he unexpectedly appeared happy and touched his arms together. "I serve only you," he said in a confident voice.

Arturo smiled, stood, bowed, turned around, and began walking away. "Stop!" Cleopatra commanded.

I knew Arturo had drastically misread Cleopatra's intentions, and he would die by my hand. When I turned to her, she stared directly at Arturo in anger. He nodded, walked over to me, and whispered, "Tell me. How do you do the dance?"

It took eight seconds to comprehend that somebody had spoken. "What?" I stammered. "The what?"

"The tiger dance? You know. The winning prize in our wager."

I looked at Arturo in confusion and mumbled, "Um. You kind of um, wave your arms, dance, and sing."

Arturo nodded, took two steps back, and said in a louder-than-conversation voice, "Security apprehended us at the airport as you predicted. As a result, I am duty-bound to fulfill the agreed-upon debt."

Arturo cleared his throat and began waving his arms while dancing and singing, "Tigers are mean! Tigers are fierce! Tigers have teeth and claws that pierce!"

Arturo sang three verses while comically dancing. Finally, he bowed to me, then Cleopatra, and briskly walked away. In another time or place, I would have been rolling with laughter. However, at that moment, I could barely stand. From behind, Cleopatra and Grace's snickering brought me back to reality. I turned to face the two women, and Grace asked Cleopatra, "You did not intend to kill him? Did you?"

"Of course not. I wanted to see if he still cared for me."

"You put an awful scare into him," Grace chided.

"I felt it necessary to ascertain the truth. Also, his departure saddened me for a long time."

"He has a nice butt," Grace observed with a smirk.

"Indeed."

The two women looked at me, and Grace laughed. Cleopatra warmly smiled and said, "You have experienced a painful event. Please wash and then join us."

These pleasant words took fifteen seconds to comprehend, and I managed to stammer, "I must ask—"

Cleopatra interrupted, "Why did I ask you to kill? You have some wisdom. Answer your question."

I thought about the topic and said, "You spoke with Grace about me, but you needed to see for yourself what kind of man I am. What did Ronald Reagan say? Trust, but verify."

"You surprise me, and that's indeed rare," Cleopatra said while nodding.

"May I ask another question?"

"Yes, I would have taken your life if you did not immediately comply with my request."

I gulped.

"She's teasing," Grace said with a big grin.

I did not know who to believe when I looked into Cleopatra's eyes.

FIFTEEN

Two women escorted me to a bathroom far away from the incident. When I closed the door, I noticed Arturo's knife clasped in my hand. This sight horrified me, and I set it down on the counter and stared at it for nine seconds while contemplating recent events. When I looked into the mirror, I saw blood spattered all over my clothes, arms, hands, and face.

Am I in a dream? I wondered in silence for 21 seconds. Then, I realized I could not bring those men back to life and took a shower. The sight of bloody water flowing down the drain sickened me. Twenty-one minutes of firm scrubbing later, I turned off the shower, knowing that while I had removed the blood, I had not eradicated the stain on my soul.

Meanwhile, someone had removed Arturo's knife, taken my clothes, and hung up a nice pin-striped suit. After dressing, my reflection looked sophisticated, but my expression was empty. *I just killed the two oldest people there have ever been. Why didn't I try to save their lives?* I thought while staring deep into my reflection; it stared back without answering my heartbreaking questions.

When I returned to the sitting room, I noticed the plastic was gone and the floors were spotless. Grace and Cleopatra were talking in an unfamiliar language. When they saw me, Grace's face lit up, and Cleopatra grinned. I did not understand the source of their joy and sat down across from them while trying to look pleasant.

Cleopatra looked at me with amusement for sixteen seconds, folded her hands, and said, "I put you through an unpleasant experience. However, keep in mind that you dispatched two terrible men and proved your loyalty. For that, I am indeed grateful. Now, relax. The danger has passed."

Cleopatra's expression held some regret. But my experience had been too much, and I remained silent.

"We may have upset James more than necessary," Grace admitted.

"You may be correct," Cleopatra concluded. "How do we cheer him up?"

"He likes to swim."

"James, would you like to go swimming?"

My outlook improved with the thought of seeing these picturesque women in swimsuits. However, that positive feeling did not overcome my overwhelming emotions, so I came up with a distraction. "I have questions," I blurted out.

"Questions?" Cleopatra asked with raised eyebrows.

"At my heart, I am a writer, and there is a great opportunity here. I mean, how can I pass up the chance to speak with a pharaoh who ruled the ancient world? That's every writer's dream. Heck, that is every historian's dream as well."

Grace looked at Cleopatra, and they both began laughing. The sound was uplifting, and I did my best to join in. Cleopatra opened a nearby drawer and pulled out my *Dawson's Creek* notebook with a nice blue pen clipped into it. I should have expected her action, but I shook my head in disbelief. Cleopatra said to Grace, "He has moments of clarity. James, I grant an interview."

I began writing and said, "Please describe meeting Grace."

"Most curious that you begin with this question," Cleopatra said with a smile. "For me, Grace will always be Anitchka. Hmm. I often think of that long-ago event. This fierce young girl came into our presence with so much determination. She stood proud, bold, and fearless. I wanted to learn more about her, and through a book of poetry written in many languages, we conducted a basic conversation. Anitchka impressed me with her drive and intelligence.

"She reminded me of myself, and sharing my secret seemed appropriate. The next day we broke camp where we had been four years and traveled to what you now call Sweden. Since that time, I wondered what became of that young girl and was astonished to come across your book."

"What did you think of it?" I asked.

Cleopatra leaned back, turned to Grace, turned back to me, and answered. "Anitchka and I discussed your work at length. She described the immense pressure her request placed upon you and its unintended consequences. However, the most troubling aspect was your choice to reveal my presence. You had no right to do this!"

Cleopatra pointed her finger at me for three seconds and then studied me with an upset expression for seventeen seconds. I did my best to remain pleasant. Finally, she briefly turned away and continued, "We discussed the motives behind her choices and came to an understanding. While I disapprove of the methods, I now feel the actions might have been necessary.

"You asked my opinion of your work. Anitchka demanded you pen her story, and you fulfilled her request. There is honor in your actions. My criticism is that you revealed too much about the procedure. My compliment is that you presented Anitchka's complex life in a format that readers could comprehend."

Cleopatra smiled, and her answer uplifted my spirits. Unfortunately, I got caught up in my happiness and asked a dull question, "What was it like to lead Egypt?"

Cleopatra looked disappointed. "History books recorded my rule as if I were a rock star signing autographs. The reality of leading a nation is more mundane. Little has changed from the leaders of old to the leaders of today. I collected taxes, organized projects, brokered deals, and went to great lengths to ensure my people's happiness."

"What about the pyramids?" I wondered. "I thought they built those giant structures to honor you."

"You are incorrect. Look at your last American election— consider all those people who voted for Mr. Obama. So many people connected to the man and danced in the streets to his victory. Others became appalled and demanded his removal before taking office.

"The difference between your president's rule and being pharaoh is the level of commitment and devotion. If you took my rule forward in time, it would be indistinguishable from today's leaders."

"May I say something contradictory?"

"You may," Cleopatra approved.

"Arturo worships you."

"Yes, he worships me because he cares for me. You might find this difficult to believe, but I also care for him."

"How were the pyramids constructed?" I wondered.

"I do not understand your question."

"Scientists have several theories. They include ramps, ropes, levers, and some even think the builders made the blocks out of cement."

Cleopatra made a fluttering gesture and answered, "The construction holds no mystery. We used long ramps and simple tools. The only technique the archeologists have failed to appreciate is the use of small canals.

"And another misconception. We did not use slaves for construction. Only devoted followers were permitted to set foot on the sacred ground. It may surprise you to learn that I also took part in the construction of a temple that has long since been dismantled. Yes, indeed. I pounded the enormous stones for hours, and I'm proud of my contribution. It saddens me to see these magnificent testaments to Ra reduced to shameful tourist attractions."

"I have a question about the harvest."

"Proceed," Cleopatra encouraged.

"Because of my harvest, I can tell time with great accuracy. For example, it's been seven minutes and 31 seconds since I sat down."

"That's extraordinary. What else?" Cleopatra asked while pinching her lower lip.

"I have improved physical and mental abilities, but nothing astounding. Grace informed me of her ability to accurately judge distances and angles."

"Is this true?"

"So to speak, this room is six meters by 4.5 meters," Grace answered with pride.

"How remarkable," Cleopatra said with great fascination.

"Do you have unique abilities?" I wondered.

"I must confess that my senses of smell and taste are far above average. With them, I can accurately deconstruct a meal to its specific ingredients. Oh yes. I also can track a person by their scent. Do you two not have this ability?"

We both shook our heads, and then I made a stupid remark, "It's too bad we cannot ask Jank or Quan about their abilities."

Stupid, stupid! They looked annoyed, and I quickly changed the subject. "What have you been up to lately?"

"Let me see. I will reveal my brief history. When we left, I had 21 men under my command. Under Ra, 21 is a sacred number. We settled our first camp in a small village, and while not my palace, it proved suitable. However, there was a problem. Without an empire, there was no reason for the men to stay. I applied the harvest gift to keep them in line but was careful not to reveal the details. This gesture kept them healthy, strong, and fiercely loyal. Amten became my second-in-command, and our community thrived.

"Every few years, we moved from one location to another. Mainly Western and Northern Europe. When navigation became reliable, we traveled to the Americas and the East.

"As the time passed, I sensed Amten's disappointment, and I did my best to appease him. However, my rule needed to be absolute in order to keep the men in line, and I couldn't give Amten the attention he requested.

"After he left, we experienced a gradual decline in the ranks. Some men died in accidents or met their fate acquiring subjects. Four were insubordinate, and three took their own life. And, as mentioned earlier, two men may have escaped."

"Escaped?!" Graced exclaimed.

"My guards assured me they died, but I now have doubts. It is possible they know the secret."

"Troubling," Grace said, while looking intently at Cleopatra.

"Indeed. My last devoted man, Aaheru, lost his life fighting an angry merchant in the summer of 1938."

"What are your plans now?" I wondered.

"Before your publication, I had intended to continue my pattern of moving from one palace to another. However, maintaining a low profile has become difficult. And now, I fear I must live in the open. Perhaps this is a good occurrence. Hmm, I have one uncompleted goal."

"What's that?"

"Returning to my former role," Cleopatra answered with confidence.

"Leader of Egypt?!" I asked louder than I should have.

"Indeed."

"Wow. That's difficult."

"I feel it to be a simple transition. Why do you assume otherwise?"

"Um. How about this? What is the most important issue facing the people of Egypt?"

"I don't understand."

"Is it water, poverty, taxes, religion, energy, food, war, employment, or something else?"

"James, you are acting naïve," Cleopatra said while shaking her head. "The great Nile always provides for the people, and our cotton is the envy of every nation. As for religion, Ra will show the way."

Cleopatra looked supremely confident, and Grace rolled her eyes.

"Do you want to take this one?" I asked Grace.

"No, I would like to hear your evaluation," Grace encouraged. "Please, continue."

"Cleo, please understand that I hold you in high regard, and I know little about the great nation of Egypt. However, right now, people are facing enormous problems. The Nile is polluted, nobody wants to pay for fine cotton, and the different religious groups violently oppose each other."

"James, you are not thinking like a leader," Cleopatra said with a fluttering gesture. "Take the Nile. You simply behead those who pollute its waters."

"All right, that's what I'm talking about. People will not vote for you if you casually talk about beheading them."

Cleopatra looked confused. I stood and asked, "How about a kiss?" I turned my cheek and walked over to her.

"What are you doing?!" she demanded. "You will stop your advance!"

"I will vote for you if you give me a kiss."

"Stop this!" Cleopatra commanded.

I knew I had made my point. So I returned to the couch and said in a pleasant voice, "A politician must connect with the voters. Now don't get me wrong. You're an amazing individual, and I suspect you have astounding leadership abilities, but you need to be one of the voters if you want their confidence."

Cleopatra looked befuddled and asked, "What if I use my money to raise Egypt to the level it should be?"

"That's called buying votes. I understand that you probably have more money than I can comprehend, but your plan will not work in the long term."

"What are you referring to?" Cleopatra wondered.

"There is that old saying of giving a man a fish or teaching him how to fish. Taking Egypt back to being the jewel of the Nile will be a long process. It starts with basic infrastructure improvements, developing new businesses, funding schools, and cleaning up the environment. Now, if you used your wealth to help the process, perhaps in time, the public will accept your commitment."

Cleopatra leaned back pouting, and eight seconds later, she offered in a cheerful voice, "They have election consultants."

"You couldn't plant one kiss on me. Trust me. I am the world's largest pussycat compared to the media monsters. They would rip your beheading attitude to shreds. You need a new goal."

"You've given me a lot to think about," Cleopatra admitted.

"May I make an observation?"

"If you think the effort is worthy of my attention," Cleopatra answered with caution.

"You seem to be out of touch with the present society. I think it would help if you interacted more with normal people."

"You risk your well-being by potentially offending me?" Cleopatra asked with concern.

"I took the risk."

"What is your true motivation?"

"May I offer you a personal observation?" I asked.

"You may."

"The difference between a friend and a true friend is that a true friend will risk everything to point out your mistakes. This action may even end the friendship, and it happened to me when my best friend, Joey, warned me to stop seeing the woman I was dating. He said she was too selfish. After I got married, Joey drifted out of my life. But he was right, and he risked ending our friendship to prove it."

"Are you conveying this information intending to become my loyal friend?"

"I would like to be your friend. However, building a deep friendship takes time. I am trying to point out that honest people are your most valuable possessions. The hardest task in a friendship is to be honest when it's much easier not to be. To formally answer your question, I revealed my opinion because I dislike deception."

"Hmm."

"May I make another observation?" I asked in a humble voice.

"You may."

"I have found that immortals distrust yes-men more than anything."

"Yes-men?" Cleopatra questioned.

"A person who will only tell you what they think you want to hear."

"Indeed."

"His essence contains worthy attributes," Grace offered.

"You may be correct," Cleopatra said with a slight smile, and then stood. I instinctively stood, and then Grace rose. We began walking away, and I wondered why our interview had ended. *I have a thousand more questions!*

When we came to a door, Cleopatra instructed, "Get dressed."

As they walked away, I continued to be captivated by Cleopatra's body. *How can legs move with such elegance? They just do,* I thought, as I opened the door to see a grand bedroom at least three times larger than all the rooms in my house combined. I looked to my left and saw a miniature Johannes Vermeer painting tastefully displayed in a gold frame. It captured a young woman sitting in a chair with a flamboyant hat. I studied this timeless treasure for 84 seconds in utter awe. The sight made me wonder if Cleopatra had somehow learned that I liked Vermeer. With her discernment, it would not be impossible.

As I looked around, I wondered what occasion I should be dressing for. I walked to the closet to see it filled with expensive clothing. Then, I saw it. Somebody had placed a gold Speedo on a rosewood chair.

I let out an enormous sigh and put it on. I then found a blue silk bathrobe and left the bedroom. Two women were waiting, and they guided me to an opulent dining room. *It's lunchtime. How could I have been so foolish?!* I thought about this while they snickered and walked away.

Grace and Cleopatra walked up to me dressed in matching pink and blue exercise clothes. They both laughed at my appearance. "You were to dress for fitness," Grace said with a big grin.

"The joke is on me. I'll go change."

"We will show you the way," Cleopatra said with a laugh.

The three of us walked away, and 38 seconds later, Cleopatra opened the door to a large indoor pool. *What the heck?* I thought in complete confusion.

The pool room had walls that curved upwards with highly detailed frescoes. The effect made it seem like mountains and clouds surrounded the pool in a natural setting. When I turned around, they giggled. Cleopatra closed the door and yanked my bathrobe off. "I told you he would put that tiny thing on!" Grace said in a giddy voice.

They laughed harder, and I did my best to join in the fun. Thirty-six seconds later, I said, "You two change, and I'll test the water."

Grace looked at Cleopatra, and they removed their exercise clothes to reveal silver and black bikinis. They stood side by side, and the coordinated silver pattern flowed from the upper part of Grace's swimsuit to the lower part of Cleopatra's.

Grace was a striking example of beauty and fitness. Her sculpted body molded perfectly to every thread of her swimsuit. Cleopatra's flawless body blew my mind. Her caramel skin glowed with radiance while complementing well-toned muscles. Together they were sexier than my harvest-filled mind could comprehend, and my jaw probably dropped to the center of the earth.

Cleopatra made a thin smile and said, "I think he likes us."

It occurred to me that I had tented, and put my hands down to cover my shame. *It's like high school. How embarrassing!* I thought as Grace laughed and then commented, "A new record."

Cleopatra playfully pushed me aside as she walked past me. Grace grinned and then walked to the pool. I heard a splash behind me and then another. It took an agonizing eighteen seconds to calm down my excitement, and I jumped in too. Cleopatra rapidly swam past me while Grace attempted to catch her. Meanwhile, I tried to perform basic strokes without large splashes.

Two laps later, my harvest-powered mind let me know I would soon get pinned to the bottom of the pool by one of them. On the next lap, Cleopatra pulled me down by my arm in a lightning-quick move. I could not believe her strength and incredible dexterity.

For six agonizing minutes, they took turns abusing me, only allowing me occasional gasps of air. However, I managed one minor victory when I awkwardly shoved Cleopatra's shoulder. Her head did not go underwater, but I felt like superman.

After our advanced water combat, we swam leisurely laps for seven minutes until my body gave out. I swam to the steps and watched them chase each other while I recovered.

Eight competitive laps later, they sat next to me. It was then that I noticed Cleopatra had two thin harvest scars. The second scar puzzled me, and I discreetly looked to see if Grace had a second. But unfortunately, her position did not allow me to ascertain the answer.

"He performed better than expected," Cleopatra commented. "You taught him well. Let's retire to the dining room."

We got out of the pool, toweled off, and Cleopatra asked in a casual voice, "Join me for a bath?"

The question stunned me beyond belief, and my jaw must have dropped through the center of the earth and popped out the other side. Cleopatra grinned, threw her towel at me, and walked away.

I turned to Grace and asked, "Was she serious?"

"So to speak, her offer appeared sincere," Grace said with a smirk. Then she threw her towel at me and walked away.

I could not believe the bold offer and Grace's accepting attitude. It took an entire minute to regain my composure. Then, after I put on my bathrobe, the two women escorted me back to my room. To the left was a bathroom large enough to park a motorhome, and after taking a ten-minute shower, I selected a nice tan suit.

Of course, the same two women escorted me to the dining room, where I saw an elegant walnut table with white porcelain place settings and orange flower arrangements. The walls were adorned with a series of nature-themed charcoal sketches. The overall effect was friendly and sophisticated.

Grace a minute later, and she sat across from me. She wore a stylish turquoise cocktail dress and had her hair combed up. Next, Cleopatra arrived wearing an elegant black shirt and blue slacks complemented with a gold belt. She nodded to me and sat at the head of the table.

A server dressed in a crisp black suit brought us smoked lamb. The chef had wrapped the meat with red and white phyllo dough, making it look like a firecracker. Surrounding the entrée was a mustard honey sauce that had been applied artistically in an explosion pattern. I felt it was a shame to destroy this creative presentation by taking a bite. It tasted superb, and I struggled to eat small portions while remaining polite. Seventy-four seconds later, Grace elegantly put down her fork and commented, "Our meal reminds me of meeting James."

"Look at him," Cleopatra said. "He's trying so hard to behave. Please relax. Have some tea."

"Thank you."

I smiled and took a small sip. It tasted outstanding and familiar. I looked at Grace in astonishment to see if she would recognize the flavor. She took a sip, looked at Cleopatra with a surprised expression, and asked, "Laalamani made a batch for you?"

"No. A tea merchant located an unopened tin," Cleopatra answered with a thin smile and darting eyes. "It was dated 1947."

"It is pleasing that we have similar tastes."

"Indeed."

When Grace and I first met, she brewed a pot of tea made by the same man who grew special tea for the Indian leader, Mahatma Gandhi. I wrote this detail in my last book, and it surprised me that Cleopatra made such an effort to obtain this special drink for our enjoyment. Grace looked impressed and tilted her head to Cleopatra in acknowledgment.

We made small talk, and seven minutes later, the server set down the second course of seared sea bass with a light lemon crème sauce. The meat was tied together with green scallions to look like a net, and the sauce was artistically applied to look like a fisherman. The flavor was outstanding, and Grace commented about the use of tarragon, which pleased Cleopatra.

Next, the server then brought poached artichoke hearts seasoned with red chili and capers. The chef arranged the artichokes and sauce to look like sunflowers. Again, it tasted exceptional, and I continued to use extreme effort to remain composed. Next, he brought out eight cheese portions cut into different shapes to look like a king of spades playing card. The third one seemed to explode with pepper flavor, and I almost blurted out, "Wow!"

Then the server brought us thin slices of braised beef accompanied by a basil dipping sauce. The chili-themed bowls had small lemon-scented candles underneath to maintain the temperature. The meat fell apart without chewing. *Simply amazing,* I thought, while wondering how it was possible to make beef taste so good.

The dessert stood out as unique. My best description would be sweet cilantro cream-filled crepe pastries with tart lime sauce. The outside of the crepes had a chocolate spiderweb drizzle with a single raspberry as the spider—culinary heaven.

We finished our meal with excellent, rich coffee. "I can see that you appreciated my cuisine," Cleopatra said with a smile.

"It tasted outstanding."

"Did my chef prepare the best meal you have ever tasted?" Cleopatra asked with pride.

I thought for 25 seconds while still tasting the coffee and answered, "My first meal with Grace stands out as my best culinary encounter."

"Why?"

"Cleo, this evening's meal may be the best meal I have ever enjoyed. However, I don't have a sophisticated palate to compare the two. What sets Grace's meal apart from your meal is the experience. Before that time, I was a burger-and-potato-chips kind of guy. However, she opened my eyes to truly exceptional food. I guess I cherish that eye-opening memory more."

"You don't give yourself enough credit. Let us appreciate the moment," Cleopatra said in a soft voice as Grace looked at me with a warm smile.

SIXTEEN

We retired to a room filled with fine artwork and books. Grace selected a book with a red cover, and Cleopatra began using an iPad covered in jewels. I looked at the many titles and selected a book based on its fine green leather binding. When I opened it, I found the subject was plants, in a language I did not recognize, so I leafed through it, and then picked another one written in English. It was a fascinating read about building the Panama Canal. I had no idea that the French had started the project, and their failure nearly bankrupted the nation.

Eighty-one minutes later, Cleopatra spoke up, "There is something we should discuss."

"Yes, of course," I answered with a smile and softly closed my book.

"Your future."

"I see."

"What are your plans?" Cleopatra wondered.

"All of this is so unexpected."

"You must have some idea."

"I have a summons in Texas," I admitted.

"You can avoid that trivial legal matter."

"I know, but it's something I must do."

"A man of honor. Rare," Cleopatra observed with a curious expression.

"Thanks."

"After this legal distraction gets settled?"

"Well, I had not thought about my future."

"Are you going to write another book?" Cleopatra asked with suspicion.

"I learned my lesson."

"Meaning?"

"It is unlikely that I will write another book. The last one nearly killed me," I admitted with a chuckle.

"Good," Cleopatra affirmed.

"Tell him," Grace said with finality.

"I place no obligation over your freedom. Do as you will."

"Thank you," I said with relief.

Cleopatra looked at Grace, then me, and said, "The person behind these attacks is of great concern. The evidence points to the leader of a nation or a wealthy individual who wishes to uncover our secrets."

"That's disturbing," I commented, while contemplating the possibility.

"It's likely that the individual is in ill health, which would make them obsessed with survival. Therefore, you will require our protection."

"I would appreciate your help."

Grace took over the conversation. "Cleo extensively studied the harvest process and improved upon it. She's made astounding progress. Tell him."

Cleopatra leaned back and looked at me with her amazing eyes for thirteen seconds and began. "Anitchka informed me about your freeze-dried snake venom improvement. Most intriguing." She looked around to ensure we were alone and whispered, "As you know, the procedure I perfected requires a single incision on the left side of the body."

Cleopatra adopted a thoughtful expression as if she were waiting for me to connect the dots. I thought about her second scar and asked, "What if you placed a second pancreas on the right side?"

"And what if you refrigerated the prepared liquid and applied it once a week? What would that change accomplish?" Cleopatra asked in encouragement.

"Would it sustain the pancreas for a longer time?" I guessed.

"I recently used this improved procedure," Grace added. "The result is an entirely new experience, and Cleo says it prolongs the harvest for over nine months."

"That would change everything. I mean, you thought the procedure would eventually no longer work at all. And now that's all gone?!" I gushed in amazement.

"As you say, all gone," Cleopatra said with pride.

"Wow!"

"You must consider this procedure for yourself," Grace recommended.

"I've made up my mind. I don't want to kill."

Grace looked disappointed, and I knew I had hurt her feelings. "You have a strong will, and I respect your conviction," Cleopatra offered. "However, we ask you to consider this possibility."

"You've given me a lot to think about. Thank you for sharing."

"He needs to know," Grace interjected. "Tell him what you told me."

"Oh, that. He will discover that truth in time."

"We should spare him the pain."

"The knowledge will give him pain," Cleopatra concluded.

"Please tell him."

"Very well. As Anitchka informed you, she investigated the procedure with great diligence. Her scientists completed a thorough analysis, and their conclusions were accurate. Recently, new scientific instruments have become available, and I used this technology to conduct detailed research.

"My investigation revealed that the immune system interaction is far more complex than Anitchka's scientist understood. As you know, all humans contain many types of viruses, bacteria, and microbes. The principal aspect of the life-giving process is providing our immune system with the drive to obliterate harmful parasites. Without this rubbish, our bodies may perform repairs at will. You directly observed success by the foul urine odor. The smell comes from discarded plaque that restricts blood flow within your veins."

"That explains a lot," I said in amazement.

"Did you lose weight?"

"About 30 pounds."

"Attribute that loss entirely to the discarded parasites," Cleopatra said with a smile.

"Wow, that's a lot of dead bugs."

"You must understand that when the body is no longer fighting off these invaders, it radically changes. I studied my transformation at great length and concluded that we are different at the cellular level."

"How big is the change?"

"A basic DNA analysis will reveal we are not human."

"Wow," I exclaimed, while thinking about the ramifications of this concept.

"One result of this change is that I cannot bear children. I have also studied this circumstance and come to two conclusions. The first is that I'm not compatible with a human seed. The second is that my body will aggressively fight an incompatible baby.

"A male who harvests cannot father a healthy child because of his altered seed. There were many *incidents* involving women who spent time with my men. Avoid this horror."

"Thank you for sharing."

"Please tell him the rest," Grace encouraged.

"I was about to. I discovered another aspect of the procedure that is of great concern. The few remaining parasites lie in a dormant state. As the procedure wears off, these aggressive parasites multiply and overwhelm the host. I'm sorry to say that once the body has undergone a single procedure, it must continue or perish. For Anitchka and myself, I estimate we can last six months beyond the deadline. James, you informed me of your weight loss. By my understanding, this loss shows your body has passed the point of no return. I'm truly sorry."

"I'll die if I don't harvest?!" I asked in horror.

"You will," Cleopatra confirmed with a sad expression.

"That's a lot to take in."

"I understand."

It felt like somebody had punched me in the gut, and I looked down in sorrow. When I looked up 32 seconds later, Cleopatra again seemed to struggle internally, and she turned away when I tried to make eye contact. Grace and I looked at each other in confusion. Fifty-one seconds later, Cleopatra uncomfortably cleared her throat, turned back, and said, "I have another disturbing revelation."

"What?" Grace asked and then tilted her head back to indicate shock.

"Are you aware there are bacteria within the brain?"

"I read an article nine months ago about that subject," Grace answered. "The strain belongs to the gut bacteria family."

Cleopatra nodded and said, "When my last devoted man, Aaheru, passed away, I had his body dissected and preserved. I came across that same article, which made me wonder how the procedure would interact with the brain bacteria. Therefore, I studied Aaheru's brain in great detail. But unfortunately, the results were negative."

"Meaning?"

"Because our minds only have minuscule amounts of bacteria, they operate differently than humans without the procedure. I believe this is the reason we are wiser, think faster, and are more perceptive. Have you noticed mental improvements?"

"Yes," I answered.

"Has your personality changed?" Cleopatra asked.

"I see many changes."

"Paranoia?"

"Oh, yeah," I answered with a nod.

"I believe that to be a side effect of missing bacteria."

"I see."

"Is the harvest drive related to the bacteria loss?" Grace wondered.

"I came to that conclusion."

"I suspected a biological mechanism at play."

Grace looked at Cleopatra for a long moment, and I knew there was more. When the time seemed right, I asked, "What else?"

"When a person stops the procedure, my research suggests the remaining mind bacteria would rapidly multiply."

"What does that mean?" I asked, knowing I would not like the answer.

Cleopatra looked at me with narrow eyes and answered, "Meaning you will perform the procedure or go insane."

I needed to cover my face for 48 seconds, and when I looked up, Grace also appeared to be in shock. Cleopatra let us wallow for a full minute, let out a long breath, and said in a forced, pleasant voice, "Enough of this serious topic. Tomorrow, you will be off to Rome to see my son. Then, you will contact us with good news. As it is still early, let us undergo a quick exercise."

I appreciated the distraction and sat upright. "It's really exercising, right?" I asked Cleopatra with a smile. "No tossing me in the pool?"

"He can be funny."

Grace laughed, and I did my best to join in the fun. However, my mind was filled with horrific thoughts about my future. The twins escorted me back to my room, and I changed. As I looked into the mirror, I contemplated my fate. *Would I die in six months? Or go crazy? Why can't I have a normal life? Why is this dreaded harvest consuming me? I hate all the death! It's not fair!* I sat on the corner of the bed while thinking about my new reality for eight pain-filled minutes.

I stood without answers, and the two women guided me to a surprisingly dull gym. Grace and Cleopatra appeared to have been there for a while and were stretching. They wore matching pink and yellow exercise outfits and appeared in a good mood. Finally, Cleopatra motioned, and we stood in front of a mirror.

As I looked into Cleopatra's stunning eyes, we began the same routine Grace taught me, with Cleopatra leading. She moved with exquisite precision, and I applied significant effort to duplicate her movements while maintaining a peaceful outlook. Our routine proceeded through martial arts stances, stretches, and single position holds.

After three full routines, we sat on the floor facing each other in an isosceles triangle pattern. As I looked into Cleopatra's eyes, I felt a deep sense of honor to be in her presence. Later, we stood up in harmony, proceeded through the same routine but much slower, and ended with a cool-down routine.

Grace and Cleopatra nodded and walked out. For a casual workout, my clothes were drenched with perspiration. The two women guided me back to my lavish bedroom, where I took a shower. Afterward, I put on pajamas and got under the covers of my enormous bed. When I looked to the left, I saw a painting of ancient Rome that reminded me of the movie *Ben-Hur*.

It had been a stressful day, and my mind raced with many thoughts. *Why did Cleopatra force me to kill those two? I should have saved their lives. But they were bad, so I get a pass, right?* My cop-out excuse made me feel even worse.

As I considered everything that happened, it occurred to me I should be much more upset with Cleopatra. She put me through an awful test, and at least in her mind, I had passed. My logical reaction should have been anger or fear. But I felt more drawn to Cleopatra than ever. *Do I appreciate her power, beauty, or something else?*

My sense of time had returned, and after 28 minutes, I decided to take a walk to clear my head. *Perhaps I would locate Grace's bedroom in the process? After all, I had undertaken this crazy journey to answer my life's questions.* When I opened the door, two muscular men glared at me. I grinned sheepishly and closed the door.

Back in bed, I tried to sleep but found it frustrating. As if by magic, nine minutes later, somebody held my hand. When I opened my eyes, I saw Grace looking down at me. She wore a two-piece light-green silk nightgown. I briefly wondered how she had entered the room without making a sound. I moved the covers aside, and Grace continued to look at me. Sixteen seconds later, she whispered, "You're troubled," and tugged me out of bed. The lack of guards surprised me as we walked through several hallways and came to two grand doors. Grace opened them and then closed them after we entered.

When my eyes adjusted to the dim light, I saw a smaller-than-expected bedroom lit with oil lamps. The decoration theme was ancient Rome, and there were gold sculptures with intricately cut turquoise stones.

A four-post bed with a black frame and purple sheets dominated the room. Cleopatra sat upright, staring at me with a concerned expression. She wore a stylish gray silk nightgown with embroidered gold thread in a daisy pattern. Grace led me over to the bed, where I sat on the left side. Cleopatra motioned toward the center, and I shuffled over. Then, I looked forwards to avoid uncomfortable eye contact.

Grace slipped under the covers next to me and sat up. My mind now raced with every conceivable sexy thought. "Lie down," she said with a nod.

I got under the covers and faced upward to see the ceiling painted like a cloudy sunset. Grace and Cleopatra then eased back to rest on the silk pillows. While I tried to attain a peaceful state, my mind surged with thoughts about these two immensely powerful and beautiful women. *Am I really in bed with the actual Pharaoh Cleopatra and the 500-year-old Grace? Nobody will believe this!*

"You told me he would relax," Cleopatra whispered.

"You offered to bathe with him. Imagine his lascivious desires," Grace reminded her.

"You initiated his desire by suggesting matching swimwear."

"You may be correct. James, please calm your thoughts."

"It's kind of hard," I stammered.

"This effort will be difficult without your focus."

"I'm doing my best," I pleaded.

Grace grunted and said, "He's faking insecurity to get a massage. Is this your intent?"

"I'm ... I'm not sure what's going on."

"He wrote fondly of your massage," Cleopatra stated.

"So to speak, we had a pleasant moment," Grace admitted.

"It's clear he is attempting to repeat the experience."

"I believe you are correct."

"James, are you attempting to repeat your prior experience?" Cleopatra firmly demanded.

"Um, I don't know," I admitted.

While the harvest provided me with vastly improved mental abilities, I have never been good at understanding women. Also, Grace and Cleopatra are wildly unpredictable. At that moment, I swear on my life that despite the obvious, I did not know what was happening.

"Are you refusing to relax?" Cleopatra demanded.

"I'm trying my best."

"Enough!" Cleopatra said in frustration. "A relaxed mind is required. Remove his shirt and roll him over."

"Very well," Grace said with a huff.

In six seconds, Grace unbuttoned my pajama shirt and pulled it off. Together, they flipped me over in one fluid motion. Cleopatra's strength and dexterity again surprised me.

Grace tugged me downward and then sat on top of my butt. Cleopatra moved my arms and used her knees to cradle my head. Grace began working my lower back while Cleopatra focused on my shoulders. *Were the two most astounding women in the world giving me a massage? Gahhh!* Their skill was unprecedented, and then they began coordinating motions. My mind transitioned from being on fire with lusty thoughts to melting into peaceful oblivion.

Some amount of time later, Cleopatra said, "Hep!" Grace took her arms away, and Cleopatra hit me with her fist in the center of my back. My spinal joints cracked in succession, and I felt a satisfying wave of relief as my body seemed to collapse inwards. Next, Grace began working my sides while Cleopatra focused on my neck. Occasionally, one would locate a tight muscle and apply the perfect motion to eliminate my tension.

While my mind struggled to remain awake, I compared their superb techniques. Cleopatra's movements contained some curiosity and warmth. Overall, I would describe her intent as probing and cautious. Grace's actions felt similar to our time on the ship, but they now had more kindness and intensity.

Cleopatra switched to working my scalp while Grace applied deep muscle pressure. I applied maximum effort to stay awake and knew I was losing the battle. They finished with light coordinated swirls as if their fingernails danced to unheard music.

Am I snoring? I thought, while wondering if I was the most relaxed man in history. Then they lay down next to me, and I was incapable of doing anything.

"Is he out?" Grace whispered.

"His eyes flicker. He remains awake," Cleopatra concluded.

"Give him a moment of contemplation, and we will begin."

"Agreed."

Some amount of time later, they rolled me over. Being next to these two amazing women felt peaceful as I appreciated their soft breathing. As my mind regained focus, I wondered if they would each attempt to feel (send) me images. It then occurred to me that Grace now held my left hand, which made the moment feel even better.

I then realized Cleopatra was holding my other hand. Her skin felt soft, and her grip conveyed a remarkable presence. I moved my fingers to feel the gems embedded in her fingernails and became lost in thought. *The perfect moment became even better. Am I dreaming? It must be a dream. I hope my snoring doesn't upset them.*

As my thoughts swirled, I realized we had achieved a new level of harmony, and I felt honored to be the central conduit. I grasped their hands to signal my appreciation of being together.

As I relished the intimacy, Grace moved above me and looked down with a kind expression. The moment seemed right, and I wondered if she would kiss me, but instead, she felt me the image of our first dinner. The action surprised me, and I do not understand why I misread the situation so badly, but I enjoyed the emotional intensity of the image.

When the moment seemed correct, I felt Grace's image of her apple trees as their flowers danced in the wind. I then realized this exchange had reached a new level of intimacy because I had been holding Cleopatra's hand. The feeling between us seemed to signal that she wanted to appreciate our moment.

To my surprise, Grace lay down, and then Cleopatra moved above me. Her spectacular blue eyes held some trepidation, and I sensed she was unsure about sending images. Our eyes began dancing, and I immediately understood that Cleopatra was a brilliant woman when she flawlessly copied my complex technique. However, she did not possess Grace's eye skills, and it took a lot of effort to follow her eye movements and then lead them. To my amazement, I found the experience contained humor.

When our focus seemed right, I felt an image of Heathcliff to Cleopatra. She reacted with great surprise, and I knew she liked the warm emotion attached to the image. At that moment, I also felt Grace's desire to share in the experience.

Cleopatra worked her eye movements to feel me an Egyptian pyramid in pristine condition. Her success came as a surprise, and I nearly lost concentration. The image content astounded me. Every description of ancient Egypt I had read implied a strict environment with bleak people ruled by heartless individuals. Instead, her image presented pleasant subjects who appreciated a society full of bold sculptures, lavish gardens, and friendly rulers. They all worked together to make an energetic and progressive community. The emotional image content held great pride, and I knew Cleopatra deeply enjoyed contributing to her nation's success.

At that instant, I understood Pharaoh Cleopatra was not a vain, power-hungry ruler. Instead, she stood out as a magnificent leader of a cherished empire. Cleopatra held a deep respect for her followers, and they worshiped her because she earned their respect.

Cleopatra then felt me an image of ancient Rome. This image also shattered my harsh beliefs of a power-hungry nation. Instead, the atmosphere stood out as progressive, fun, and exciting. Everybody knew they were part of a robust democratic revolution that would take the world by storm.

Cleopatra paused and then felt me the image of Quan's death. Her emotion conveyed duty, anger, and sadness. As I worked through the image, I understood Cleopatra regretted putting me through this awful experience. However, this experience answered my questions about her motives. She hated people who murdered children more than I did. The surprising revelation made me more comfortable with her choice.

Cleopatra appeared content, and she moved to the side. Now, both women looked into my eyes, and I realized we would attempt simultaneous communication. I worked hard to succeed, but focusing on these two amazing women immediately overwhelmed my concentration. Finally, they sensed my trepidation and lowered their interaction until I regained focus.

I began chasing Grace's eyes and moved to chase Cleopatra's. This effort spiraled into wild confusion. I then focused on one woman for a long moment and then concentrated on the other. However, no matter how hard I tried, my mind could not interact with both women simultaneously.

As the experience continued, our interaction worsened, and we got annoyed. "Do not try so hard," Grace whispered. "Send me an image."

I closed my eyes to focus, looked into Grace, and felt her the starry bedroom ceiling image from her former residence. She enjoyed the moment, and I attempted to feel the same image to Cleopatra. However, our rhythms were off, and we played the eye dance game until I succeeded. I then tried to keep the same rhythm with Grace. Unfortunately, my efforts did not succeed, and I closed my eyes again to regain focus. I then felt her the image of a spectacular mountain in Thailand.

Our interaction switched between sending and receiving while I experimented with different rhythms. After five attempts, I tried actively leading their eye movements together rather than having them passively follow my movements or have them actively lead me. Finally, I could tell we were on the right track, and it took six more tries to simultaneously feel the image of Heathcliff's rock. *What a relief,* I thought, knowing they also appreciated our success.

I then sent an image of my first book cover, my childhood bike, and my sister. With this success, we focused on trying to allow Grace to lead both of us. This was quite a challenge, and we lost focus three times, but soon, we both experienced the image of her mother.

Natalya stood out as an incredible individual, and Grace still maintained a deep respect. Simultaneously, I knew Cleopatra also appreciated the positive image, and she enjoyed Grace's pride. Grace then shared an image of her brother riding a horse.

Afterward, I knew Cleopatra wanted to share an image with us, and it took seven tries. The image she sent was her mother (also named Cleopatra), teaching her how to sew. Grace's appreciation of sewing reflected a prideful feeling, and this shared kind gesture further heightened the moment.

With a simultaneous communication method established, we began a profound journey through our life experiences. We shared family members, notable events, painful moments, personal victories, and our reactions to each other. Each image increased our trust, which challenged us to send more personal moments.

Our voyage took many unexpected twists. Grace and I were surprised to learn that Cleopatra had been married three times. Also, she loved riding motorcycles and eating popcorn mixed with gummy bears. Grace despised spiders and knew exactly how many she had killed (12,659). She briefly sang in the female '60s rock band, the Vamps, and loved the Beatles.

Cleopatra and Grace found it amusing that I had never tried eggplant (because I refuse to eat anything purple) and enjoyed the movie *Caddyshack* because of the dancing gopher. Learning my favorite color was orange surprised them. Grace expected my favorite color to be blue, and Cleopatra knew for certain I enjoyed black. I am not sure why they felt so strongly about my color preference.

The death of Cleopatra's father felt heartbreaking, and we took a long time to reflect upon her sorrow. Our interaction revealed her deep soul still contained a large wound.

Grace revealed that she had a dear childhood friend, Kozlova. Then, one day, she disappeared, and local people searched for two weeks. Months later, Grace took a shortcut through the woods and found her scattered remains. A bear had killed Kozlova, and that tragic memory remained powerful.

I shared the image of my father's disapproval of writing as a profession. Both Grace and Cleopatra empathized with my shame. Afterward, they offered support, and both felt regret for having criticized my books.

Overall, I would describe Cleopatra's personality as cautious and confident. However, she had a strong sense of order, control, and vanity. Yet I understood Cleopatra's focus on beauty resulted from the logical desire to control those around her.

Grace's interaction also took on a new level. In our previous efforts, she held certain feelings in check. Interacting with two people removed this trepidation, revealing her inner person. Grace had an emotional core that loved challenges and making her workers happy. Yet, under all her protective layers, that wonderful girl from rural Russia still wanted to play.

The entire experience felt overwhelming, profoundly satis-fying, and deeply intimate. However, being so focused took its toll, and I knew our session needed to end. The last image I sent revealed Grace and Cleopatra in their matching swim-suits. This moment filled them with excitement and embar-rassment. In doing so, I announced my deep attraction to these amazing women and my inner desire to get closer.

The feelings they returned felt passionate, thrilling, and bold. However, I felt some jealousy, insecurity, and trepida-tion. As a final gesture, Grace whispered to Cleopatra, "We will share James."

I found this statement surprising and exciting, but I did not know the definition of, "share James." Plus, having multiple relationships stood far outside of my morals.

An exhausted Cleopatra lay down next to me, and Grace did the same. We continued to hold hands as we drifted off to sleep. The moment continued to feel magical, and words cannot express how privileged I felt to be a part of the experi-ence. The last thing I remember is our breathing synchronized.

SEVENTEEN

When I opened my eyes, Grace had an arm tightly around me, and so did Cleopatra. As I turned to the side, Cleopatra's warm smile greeted me as she peacefully slept. At that moment, it occurred to me that might be the best possible circumstance that any man had ever woken up to. This thought comforted me as I found it hilarious that they both snored louder than freight trains. I wanted to laugh my head off, but I remained silent as I savored the experience.

Eight glorious minutes later, Grace stirred and said, "ohh" and then removed her arm. The sound woke Cleopatra, and she said "ahh" and then lifted her arm. I turned from one to the other and asked, "Breakfast?"

They looked at me in shock, and I got out of bed without looking back. As I walked toward my room, I would have given anything to know what they were thinking. The mirror reflected a confident expression, and I dressed in a comfortable gray shirt and black pants.

For breakfast, we ate a wonderful meal of poached eggs, grilled eel, and almond pastries. The mood seemed unusually quiet, and I enjoyed relentlessly intimidating Grace and Cleopatra with my smile. Watching them suddenly turn away gave me a big thrill. Remember, Grace is the same woman who once provoked so much fear in me that I could not move or breathe.

When I felt I had intimidated them enough, I said, "Last night was special."

Grace looked at Cleopatra and quietly murmured, "Um."

"I was not expecting to share images with you two."

Cleopatra quietly said, "Um ... I did not expect—um—to share so much."

"What did you expect?"

Cleopatra looked unsure and quietly mumbled, "Um ... Anitchka revealed the existence of her technique two days ago. Um—she did not explain there would be—um—feelings."

Cleopatra looked away, then back, blinked, and said in a barely audible voice, "Err—my sharing—um—well, I didn't think I could be so ..."

"How are you feeling?" I asked with a confident smile.

Grace looked at me with a bashful expression. Then, Cleopatra answered in her same mumbling voice, "Um—well— your plane will leave soon."

"Not going to tell me. Well, I know what both of you are feeling and thinking."

"What?!" they both chirped at the same time.

"Your expressions told me everything I needed to know," I answered with a big grin. They both looked at me with shocked expressions, and I continued, "I feel the same way."

Grace turned away and then looked down at her hands. Cleopatra also turned away, and when she turned back, I noticed her blushing. While I wanted to learn more about our encounter, I knew this was not the time to ask. Cleopatra straightened herself and said in an authoritative voice, "We are counting on you to successfully contact my son."

"I agree, and that's why I will do this my way," I said with newfound confidence.

"You'll accomplish the task set before you in the manner we instruct!" Cleopatra demanded.

"And where did that get us in the past?"

"You have not worked with me before," Cleopatra reminded me.

"My point exactly. Now let's start with all that you know about Caesarion."

"His compound is—"

"Wait," I interrupted. "Please tell me about raising your son."

Cleopatra looked at me and then dabbed her face with a napkin. She stood, and then Grace stood. I stood, and I wondered why the conversation had stopped. I still felt hungry while I followed the two of them along several hallways. Of course, I still admired Cleopatra's legs. Four turns later, we came to a heavy steel door with three big combination locks. Cleopatra reluctantly unlocked each one, and we entered.

Inside, a small but tasteful office greeted us. The walls and desk had cluttered financial information, books, and printed articles. I noticed three of my newspaper articles tacked to the wall with sentences highlighted in pink. The small, outdated inkjet printer had a large cyan ink smear on the front, and the "out of paper" LED blinked. There was a well-used Kermit the Frog plush toy on the desk, and it took a lot of effort not to grin.

Cleopatra turned to us with an embarrassed expression, uncomfortably cleared her throat, and said, "Please forgive the appearance. Other than one servant, nobody else has been in this room."

Cleopatra pressed a button on the intercom and spoke in a language I did not understand. Thirty-two seconds later, a man brought in two black wooden chairs. She sat down in a well-used tan leather office chair, looked away, and began speaking in a distant voice, "Caesarion is impulsive, untrustworthy, insecure, ruthless, and self-centered. Alas, much of this outcome rests on my shoulders. While growing up, he needed a strict mother and instead got the leader of an empire. My royal court servants raised Caesarion in a sheltered and unchallenged environment. As a result, he never learned from his mistakes and developed a heartless attitude."

Cleopatra leaned back and stared at newspaper clippings while twisting her left pointer finger into her thumb. Then, she looked at Grace and asked, "According to the book, you did not raise a child?"

Grace shook her head, and I sensed a pang of disappointment. Cleopatra let out a long breath and continued, "A woman may have endless love for her child and still end up with a monster. I knew my son required boundaries, but he never got challenges worthy of his soul. I am unaware of what the man is like now, but I can tell you that people do not change their underlying personalities."

"How did you find him?" I wondered.

"I scrutinized every sale of your book," Grace answered. "Somebody purchased an electronic copy with a tourist's stolen credit card and downloaded the file to a secure server in Malta. Afterward, a public domain program on a virtual private machine set up for only this purpose broke the digital rights management and transferred the file to a highly secure server in Kazan. Finally, the file was downloaded by a computer at a house outside of Rome. An investigation confirmed the poor owner did not have computer knowledge.

"Paid men began observing this house, and one day, the owner took the bus to a well-guarded estate. With great effort, I learned the residence belonged to a secretive man named Niniano Del Pizzo. There are no known photographs of him, and he applies great effort to maintain a low profile. However, we confirmed that this man is her son."

"How?" I wondered.

"Caesarion has a distinctive method of conveying his thoughts," Cleopatra answered. "As his mother, I recognized his style."

"Did this surprise you?"

Cleopatra stared deep into me for seventeen seconds and answered, "My son had been dead for so long. James, I nearly fainted."

"Wow, that must have been quite a shock."

"It brought back many emotions."

"Do you want to see him?"

"Of course not! My son tried to kill me. Even though much time has passed, I still harbor anger."

"He's still your child," I offered.

"Hmm." Cleopatra paused for twelve seconds and continued, "Perhaps if your meeting goes well, we will open a dialogue."

"What's he been up to?"

Cleopatra looked at Grace with great concern, and Grace answered. "As I have told you, I attained my wealth through shipping, art, music, and accounting. Cleo concentrated on land, oil, and energy. Quan's wealth came from minerals, technology, and agriculture. Jank dominated insurance and most recently, the stock market. And Arturo made his fortune in shipping and land. It came as a great surprise to me to learn that he was my largest shipping competitor."

"Really? That's unexpected. What about Caesarion?" I wondered.

Cleopatra paused for nine seconds and coldly answered, "James, my son is a reprehensible arms dealer."

This revelation shocked me to my core, and it took me two deep breaths to recover. "I don't mean to speak out of place, but I wondered—"

"I now appreciate why Anitchka chose you," Cleopatra interrupted. "Jank had the largest fortune. He had an incredible talent for picking stocks with long-term value. Now, you know it is rude to inquire about a person's wealth. However, if you were to rank us, it would be Jank, Anitchka, myself, Quan, and Amten."

"What happened to Jank, Quan, and Arturo's money?" I wondered.

"We split it," Grace answered with a big grin.

"Nice! Hey, there are three of us. How about you send a few bucks my way?" I asked with hope.

They laughed, and Cleopatra answered, "You are so amusing. From now on, consider yourself a wealthy individual."

"Hey, just to let you know. My apartments now have nineteen—count them—nineteen paying tenants. So, I'm doing fine."

They were now laughing harder, and I began cracking up. Then, in between laughs, I asked, "What about Caesarion? How much money does he have?"

"That is a puzzling question," Cleopatra answered in a concerned voice. "As far as we could tell, he's on the verge of bankruptcy."

"I don't understand," I said, shaking my head.

"Arms dealing can generate massive profits, but the losses can be tremendous if a business owner is not careful. Clearly, my son has poor economic instincts. Unfortunately, this pressure makes him unpredictable."

"Wait a minute. That makes little sense. I bet you he's hiding his money."

Grace looked at Cleopatra with a coy smile and said, "Very perceptive."

"Where is it?"

"We could not determine the location of his wealth if it exists," Cleopatra answered.

"I find it impressive that he could keep so much information hidden from you."

"Indeed," Cleopatra said with a thin smile.

"How am I getting there?" I wondered.

"We will fly you on a private jet without a flight plan and land along a strip of deserted highway east of his compound," Cleopatra answered. "Then, you will make your way under cover of darkness to a secluded spot on the west side of his compound. You will then climb over the fence unobserved, make your way past the guards, and confront Caesarion. We will provide you with tools and training to defeat the security sensors."

Cleopatra leaned back with a confident expression, and Grace made a crafty smile. "Are you joking?!" I asked in utter disbelief. "Seriously?"

Grace moved her head back and said, "So to speak, it's a good plan."

"Do I look like a special forces commando? All my stealth training came from selling refrigerators. Do you honestly think a person with my limited abilities can defeat the security systems of an arms dealer? And walk past his well-trained guards? Not going to happen!"

Grace looked at me with wide eyes, and I continued, "You two have to think of this from my perspective. Cleo, what would happen if you caught someone sneaking into your compound?"

"They would be disposed of," Cleopatra answered with a scowl.

"No matter what the circumstances?" I continued her line of thinking.

"Of course."

"You immortals don't like surprises, and the thing you value the most is control over your safety. I wouldn't even be able to make it ten miles away from his compound without being captured. So the best outcome of your plan is that Caesarion takes less than a week to torture me to death."

Cleopatra briefly looked away and mused, "I may have made a better choice by selecting you than I initially thought."

"I will take that as a compliment."

"I provided my statement as a compliment," Cleopatra said.

"Thank you. Now, this is my plan. Let's start with me flying out of here on that super-secret jet to some far away airport. That will eliminate any trace of this location. Then, I will buy a commercial airline ticket with my credit card for a flight to Rome. When I land, I will take a taxi to Caesarion's house. He will see me coming from a long way off, and this openness should make him comfortable enough not to shoot me."

"What about the attackers?" Grace inquired.

"They will wait and see what happens. It isn't a trivial matter to attack an arms dealer. Now, once inside, what message would you like me to convey?"

"You are to demand he provides us with all available information about the attackers," Cleopatra answered with narrow eyes.

I snorted and said with a raised voice, "I demand that you leave this room!"

Cleopatra instantly moved into a defensive stance, and I quietly said, "Please forgive my outburst. I performed this callus action to prove that immortals don't react well to demands."

Grace smiled, and Cleopatra nodded. I waited eight seconds for the pleasant mood to return and continued in a calm voice, "My approach will be the same humble approach I used with you. I'll act respectfully, speak the truth, and do anything he asks."

"You will not tell him of my life-giving technique?" Cleopatra wondered.

"If Caesarion is still alive, he already knows how to harvest. I will reveal the same procedure I told Jank, Quan, and Arturo. I will not be informing him of your improved technique, as doing so would be dangerous."

"Dangerous?" Grace questioned with raised eyebrows.

"Yes, for you see, I have only one scar. If I revealed a two-incision procedure, Caesarion wouldn't trust me. When interacting with an immortal, honesty is the most important trait."

Cleopatra and Grace leaned back, and Grace said, "So to speak, I see that we have the right man for the job."

"Thank you. Now, there are a few more things. First, I need a phone number and an email for both of you. I will only use this in an extreme emergency. Second, I need to give Caesarion all the information you two have about the attackers. And finally, I want a positive message from both of you."

"What?!" Cleopatra exclaimed. "I will do no such thing!"

I allowed Cleopatra 22 seconds to calm down and quietly said, "I'm acting as your emissary. If you wish your son to provide information, I need you to pretend to be a loving mother. There must be something positive you remember about his childhood."

Cleopatra looked at me with a pouting expression and then took out an ornate piece of parchment. She began writing with two pens and then lit an unusual red candle. After letting the wax drip on the parchment, Cleopatra pressed an intricately carved brass stamp into the wax. She made an uncharacteristic huff and handed me the parchment with a frown. I looked at the remarkable Egyptian icon symbols with amazement and said, "I obviously cannot read this. I hope it doesn't say, 'Kill the dumb author that gives you this.'"

Grace laughed, and Cleopatra shook her head with a big grin. Grace began writing while Cleopatra used her computer. She handed me a memory stick and said, "This is all the information we have on the attackers. You may give it to my son."

"Thank you," I said with relief.

Grace finished writing her letter and handed it to me. The handwriting was beautiful and appeared to be in Italian. I found it amusing that she had signed it "Barbara." I picked up a large envelope and placed the two letters and the memory stick inside. Then I asked, "What questions should I ask the benevolent Caesarion?"

Cleopatra smiled and answered, "You have excellent tension-defusing skills. I recommend asking him if he wishes our help in this urgent matter. That would be a most diplomatic approach. If he is agreeable, give him the files on the memory device and ask him to examine them. If your exchange is successful, inquire about combining our assets."

"Sounds good," I said with a smile. "Now, the important part. How do I get out of the lion's den?"

Grace looked concerned and answered, "We will arrange for a plane at a nearby airport."

"I would also request an open ticket at the Rome airport along with a few bucks."

"So to speak, a wise precaution," Grace said with a slight smile.

"Which reminds me, you two need to make travel plans."

"We're fine," Cleopatra said with confidence.

"Tell that to Jank, Arturo, and Quan."

Grace turned to Cleopatra. "That's better," I said with a nod. "Now, take a vacation, and don't tell me where. I have a spoiled child to meet."

Cleopatra snickered, and Grace grinned. I started to stand up, sat back down, and asked, "Is there anything else about Caesarion I should know?"

"We know little about my son," Cleopatra answered.

"Would you show me a picture of his home?"

Cleopatra worked on her computer and turned the screen to us. We saw a detailed satellite view of the compound with eight buildings arranged in a circle around a courtyard. The surrounding walls made it look like a military compound. I whistled and asked, "Where is his escape route?"

Grace pointed to three places on the screen. Cleopatra shook her head and pointed to a building. "Anitchka has identified the three underground exits, but this is where he will go," she said with confidence.

"A building?" I asked with confusion.

"Look at this. It is a blast chute. There is a rocket within this building that is large enough to carry three people."

"He is going to escape in a rocket?" I wondered out loud.

"Yes."

"Wow! That's a proper escape."

A pop-up screen began blinking, and I asked, "You like Candy Crush?"

Grace grinned, and Cleopatra looked embarrassed. Then, after suppressing my humor, I said, "Well, I'm going to change and be off."

Grace nodded, and Cleopatra said, "Indeed."

"One more thing. Cleo, do you have a printed copy of my book?"

"Of course."

"I would like to have it for my trip."

"To read?" Grace asked with a frown.

"No. I have used my books to get out of unpleasant situations, and having one is always a good idea."

"You're crazy," Cleopatra said with a chuckle.

"Guilty as charged."

The three of us stood, and I walked to my bedroom without the two women guiding me. I found it encouraging that Cleopatra now trusted me enough to walk around unescorted. Inside, I found a small black backpack with a change of clothes, a cell phone, and a packet of euros. The outer pocket had a new *Dawson's Creek* notebook and a well-used copy of *Grime: Just Cause*. As I searched further, I found a white/green striped Speedo. It made me laugh.

Next to the backpack, I saw a piece of yellow, ruled paper with two phone numbers and two email addresses. pharaohcleo16@aol.com and barbaraed235@compuserve.com. *AOL? CompuServe? Priceless!* After memorizing the information, I destroyed the paper by tearing it to shreds and flushing it down the toilet. I then realized this paper and my book were in the room before I arrived.

After changing into tan slacks, a white shirt, and comfortable shoes, I looked into the mirror. The person who looked back appeared confident, making me feel good about successfully meeting another immortal. At the same time, I wondered what possessed me to leave the safety of this beautiful palace.

When I got to the bedroom door, it opened. Grace walked in and closed it behind her. She looked at me with amazing brown eyes and then put her hands on my waist. I put my hands on her upper arms and moved closer. Our eyes explored each other, and she felt the image of me on the ship when I first wore my Speedo. The emotions attached to the image were passionate and confident. I understood this was the moment she had taken off her bathrobe and revealed her amazing body. The view focused on my Speedo, and clearly, I was excited. *How embarrassing!*

Grace then kissed me on the cheek for eight sensual seconds. *Best eight seconds of my life!* She smiled, turned to leave, stopped, turned back, and quietly said, "Quan discovered saffron extract vastly improves the harvest. Use a ratio of ten parts of mint oil to one part extract. Do not share this information with your new friend, Cleo."

Grace touched my hand, smiled, and I said, "I liked the kiss."

"Likewise."

"Am I ever going to get more than a 'likewise' from you?"

"So to speak, when you return, you'll get that and more," Grace taunted with a bashful expression.

"Are we ever going to talk about these mental pictures? I want to know how it works."

"Maybe."

"Why maybe?" I wondered.

"That depends on you."

Grace made a humorous smile, opened the door, and I said, "Wait."

"Yes?"

"I have a question."

"You wonder how I place packages of clothes in your room without your knowledge?"

"Yes," I answered in surprise.

"You also wonder how I determined your question."

"True," I admitted.

"So to speak, you wrote about that question many times in your book."

"Well? Tell me. How did you put the clothes in my room without me seeing you?"

Grace bit her lip, opened her mouth as if she would speak, and stopped. Then she smiled and slipped out the door. *I'm never going to figure her out*, I thought.

With Grace's mind-blowing kiss deep in my mind, I walked over to the bed and sat on the corner. *She had feelings for me, intense, passionate feelings!* I contemplated this astounding revelation for six full minutes. *What a day!* I stood and left.

The two women were not there to guide me, and I wandered toward the main entrance. Suddenly, a door opened, and somebody pulled me inside. The large room contained racks of household supplies neatly stacked on several shelves.

I somehow knew my captor would be Cleopatra, and she positioned herself face-to-face. She touched my cheek with her left hand, then placed her hands on my shoulders. I lightly put my hands around Cleopatra's waist, and we explored each other's eyes.

Cleopatra's eye skills had improved since our first encounter, and she felt me an image of when she asked me to take a bath. It contained intense, sensual feelings. She smiled, moved back, and looked at me with great intensity. Finally, after eight seconds, Cleopatra squeezed my shoulders and moved closer to kiss me on my lips. This passionate moment lasted for an astounding twelve seconds. *The second best twelve seconds of my life!*

Cleopatra slowly pulled away while looking at me with a fantastic smile and whispered, "Do not repeat what I am about to tell you to anyone, including Anitchka. I discovered many years ago that adding finely pulverized saffron to mint oil enhances the process. Start with a seven percent solution. Now, I want you to be careful around my son."

"I'll do my best," I said in a trembling voice.

Cleopatra smiled, nodded, started to leave, and I asked, "Cleo?"

"Yes."

"This has been special," I said with a warm smile.

Cleopatra studied me for nine seconds and said, "You are not selfish. My life is missing a person with your honest qualities. It has been so long since I—well ... Please return soon so that we can finish what we just started."

Cleopatra touched my cheek, smiled, and turned to leave. "Wait," I said.

Cleopatra turned back and asked, "Yes?"

"Why did you make me kill Quan and Jank?"

"They outlived their usefulness," Cleopatra answered with certainty. "Killing twelve-year-old boys! How abhorrent."

"Our interaction revealed a different side. Tell me the truth."

Cleopatra seemed taken aback. She turned away, opened the door, and said without looking at me, "Anitchka and I talked about you for some time. As you are no doubt aware, she expresses fondness toward you. I wanted to make sure you were worthy of her—of *our*—trust.

"You did as I commanded, which confirmed your loyalty. To further my surprise, you stood up to my wishes while knowing the potential consequences. And I will tell you this. I have known a vast number of people, and I consider you to be— rare. You have a kind soul, a brave soul. I like that. I like that a lot."

Cleopatra left the room without looking back. I noticed her walk looked different; it lacked precision and flow. *Wait a minute. The two most amazing women on the entire planet expressed feelings for me. Incredible, passionate feelings. Wow!* I needed to sit on a nearby step-stool, and it took seven full minutes to compose myself.

I stood, admired the artwork in the entryway for thirteen minutes, and walked outside to a beautiful limousine. As we drove away, I wondered if I would ever see this beautiful palace again. I also wondered what Arturo's role would be in Cleopatra's life. *Were they a couple? Am I their third wheel? Would he be angry with me for kissing her? Yeah, I know that answer.*

EIGHTEEN

boarded the same opulent business jet with my new back-pack and found Arturo staring at me in disbelief. I sat in the seat across from him, and the plane took off. "It appears I'm to be your bodyguard," he said with a grin.

"Do you know where we are heading?" I wondered.

"My queen said Rome. I have not traveled there since 1921."

"It's changed since then."

"True," Arturo admitted with a sigh. "Are you aware of what we will encounter upon arrival?"

"This is going to be interesting," I answered.

"You are aware?"

"Cleo and Grace shared that information."

"And you're choosing not to reveal it to me?" Arturo asked with suspicion.

"I want it to be a surprise."

"I see."

I leaned back while enjoying the flight, and nineteen minutes later, I said in a low voice, "I'm sorry for what happened back at the palace."

"I felt great humiliation during my tiger dance. The terrible memory will haunt me until my dying day."

"You deserved it," I said with a laugh.

"In full disclosure, they apprehended us on the road near the airport. So technically, you lost our wager."

"Darn. Well, a bet is a bet. I will do the tiger dance now."

"I had to do the tiger dance in front of my queen. You will do the tiger dance at a time of my choosing," Arturo said with a chuckle.

"That's fair. Hey, listen. I still owe you an apology. I should have stood up to Cleo. There's no excuse."

"You had no choice."

"I acted cowardly," I admitted, and then looked away.

"The act of a coward would have been to run. Another option would have been to torment us. Instead, you treated the three of us with respect."

"You made it a lot easier. Thank you for what you said back there."

"I spoke the truth," Arturo said with confidence.

"Well then, thanks even more."

I thought about our conversation for seven minutes and then asked, "What happened when they captured you?"

"Do you want to write my answers in your *Dawson's Creek* notebook?" Arturo asked with a hearty laugh.

I joined in the laughter and pulled out my notebook.

"You and your fancy notebook!" Arturo exclaimed. "Let me see. Jank and I drove on backroads to ensure we were not being followed and then headed to the airport. At a stoplight, four men surrounded us. They used tasers to disable us, and despite my skill, we woke on a private plane in handcuffs. Men stood guard over us during the flight and did not permit discussion. When we landed, they took me to a cell, where Grace questioned me for hours. In our first interrogation, I had already revealed all my financial information, contacts, and passwords. This time, she demanded all knowledge about the people who hunt us. Unfortunately, I had nothing to offer. That woman is a master of pain.

"Afterward, I knew my usefulness had ended, and I awaited my fate. After a meal of stale bread, two guards placed me under a hood, and they guided me to my destiny. Only then did I see my one true love.

"At that moment, I silently thanked Ra for the grand opportunity to experience the glory of my queen. Then, I followed protocol and became humble. James, I watched as you killed Quan and then Jank. This dreadful event foreshadowed my demise, and it saddened me to see you would be the one to end my life. Upon this realization, I became determined to die with dignity and serve my queen one last time. And then, by the hand of Ra, my queen permitted me to live."

"Did you get your knife back?" I wondered.

"No, but I know my queen will keep it in a safe location."

"What happened next?"

"I fell back into my old routine. There is a natural order surrounding my queen, and I assisted the kitchen staff. Later, she summoned me to her—um—this word doesn't have an English translation. Let's call it a study room. There, she informed me I would accompany an important person on a dangerous journey. If successful, my status would increase."

I did not feel comfortable with this level of obedience and asked, "What's with you and Cleo? Is this a love thing or a religious thing?"

"It's both, my friend."

"I don't get it. But that's fine."

"You might consider my culture to be dated," Arturo suggested.

"What do you think of her now?"

"My queen is even more beautiful than I remembered."

"I mean, what are your feelings toward her? Do you love her?"

"I spoke the truth," Arturo answered with a nod. "I will never stop loving her."

"Good."

I leaned closer and asked, "May I share a secret?"

"Yes, of course."

"I slept with Cleo."

I leaned back, raised my eyebrows, and Arturo asked, "You slept with my queen?!"

"I slept with both of them at the same time."

Arturo nearly leaped out of his seat and exclaimed, "You slept with both?!"

"Yes!"

"Splendid!" Arturo said with a hearty laugh.

"Not as amazing as the massage they both gave me."

"They gave you a massage?! Together?! James! In a millennium of living with my queen, she never bestowed such kindness!"

"I even had my shirt off."

"Which one did you have first?" Arturo asked while nodding in encouragement.

"I didn't have sex with either of them, but they both kissed me this morning."

"You didn't have sex?" Arturo asked in disbelief.

"Only sleep."

Arturo threw his hands up, sat down, and exclaimed, "Unbelievable!"

"I had the most incredible experience of my life. And I remind you, I escaped a full military airstrike on a horse."

"No sex?" Arturo said while shaking his head.

"No sex. Want to know another secret?"

"Yes."

"They both snore like locomotives!"

Arturo began laughing while slapping his legs, and I laughed so hard that I made my honking sound. When the laughter died down, I asked, "How did you live with a woman like Cleo?"

"She is a handful. And I know you speak the truth. My queen snores like an angry elephant. She's a complex woman, full of passion and thoughtful ideas. For many years, I encouraged her thoughts and provided comfort when her plans failed."

"Do you still want to be the person who comforts her?" I asked, while not entirely wanting to know the answer.

"Of course," Arturo answered with determination.

"Is this going to be an issue between us?"

"There's more than enough of her to go around," Arturo replied, but I did not understand the meaning of his words.

"That is a strange viewpoint."

"In time, you'll understand."

I leaned back to contemplate Arturo's wisdom for three minutes. He seemed to consider an important topic during that time and eventually said, "There is a subject I feel we should discuss. When a man undergoes the procedure, his body changes. The procedure attacks the gonads, which makes it difficult to impregnate a woman. If successful, she will experience a miscarriage, or the child is—*not good.* So it's best if you take precautions. On this same topic. A man can undergo an operation to stop his seed. Don't bother. The body will reverse itself."

"Cleo mentioned that when a person harvests, their body becomes genetically altered. She implied that the procedure affected a man's ability to reproduce."

"Correct," Arturo confirmed, paused, and continued, "The gift does not allow a woman to bear children. After Cleopatra discovered this circumstance, she forbade me from entering her womanhood. To make matters worse, she prevented me from being with the captured women. Of course, Cleopatra still desired womanly pleasure, and I eagerly appeased her, but she did not return any affection. As a man, this denial frustrated me and was the main reason behind my departure.

"Grace also told me that immortal women have difficult miscarriages. Cleo hinted at this."

"My queen had two of them, and they were a shallow point in her life. So never discuss that subject."

I found it crazy that Arturo wanted to coach me on how to act around Cleopatra. *We are rivals for the same woman. Right?* I thought, and then asked, "Were you going to warn me before I got—you know—with Anna?"

"I placed Anna on birth control at an early age. It's part of the Panamanian culture," Arturo answered.

"I see."

"I miss her smile," Arturo said with a long sigh.

"As do I."

Arturo clearly wanted to change topics and said, "Tell me more about Grace."

"All you immortals are the same. Inside, you fear death and will go to any length to protect yourself. From a non-immortal perspective, the most important rule is to act respectfully. Also, you immortals need control, hate giving out personal information, love making money, and don't like surprises. Otherwise, Grace is a normal woman."

"Do you love her?" Arturo asked with raised eyebrows.

"You mean Grace?"

"Yes."

I thought about his question for 34 seconds and answered. "I'm not sure. Um. Yeah, I think so, but it's hard to comprehend a woman like that. I mean, she's so intelligent, so rich and so attractive. I feel completely unworthy around her."

"I have similar feelings toward my queen."

"Hmm."

"Let me reveal what my queen desires the most. Trust. They cut Grace from the same tree, and as long as you try to do as she asks, she will remain loyal."

"Good to know."

"Do you love my queen?" Arturo challenged.

"Kind of the same answer. I hope my admission is all right."

"You *do* love her!" Arturo said with a big grin.

"I'm not sure if 'love' is the correct word. And I wonder if any man could ever get close to either of them. Even when we shared that extraordinary moment, I knew they only revealed a small part of themselves. I bet they could have killed me in the blink of an eye and returned to a peaceful sleep. It's challenging to begin a relationship with that level of danger hanging over your head.

"I mean, both women have forced me to kill people. That's a horrible thing to put somebody through. And also, a relationship is a relationship. You know: doing dishes, painting rooms, setting limits on expenses, crazy relatives, and stupid arguments. I cannot imagine them acting like that. Plus, they hold so many secrets. Even basic conversation is difficult. It's like walking through a verbal minefield every time I open my mouth."

"I'm the only person who understands your circumstances," Arturo agreed, nodding. "Hmm. I wish to bring up a rather delicate question."

"What?"

"On the ship, Grace asked if my phallus grew over the years. I overheard her asking Quan the same question. I got the impression that she asked for your sake."

"Oh."

"Why would she ask such a question?" Arturo wondered.

"Um, well. We were talking, and she mentioned her boobs had gotten bigger. She then wondered if the harvest caused a man's willy to grow."

"What's a willy?" Arturo asked in confusion.

"His phallus."

"Why did you inquire about her bust size?"

"Um, she brought up the topic."

"Really? I cannot imagine such a private woman would openly discuss a personal subject of such magnitude."

"Well, that's what she told me," I offered.

"Grace wouldn't have shared this matter unless you were in her heart."

"Hmm. That's something to think about. Tell me, were Cleo's boobs bigger?"

"Perhaps 40 percent. Of course, I dared not broach this sensitive topic."

"Interesting. Well, let's have it. What did you tell Grace about your willy?"

"Yes, it's larger. Something for you to look forward to," Arturo answered with a playful expression.

I laughed. Arturo rubbed a small scar on his arm, and asked, "Why did you kill Quan and Jank? What was your true motivation?"

"At first, I wanted to stay alive. I mean, Cleo is an immortal. If you want to live, you don't say no to an immortal. But the more I think about it, the less this answer makes sense. Part of my decision may have come from my desire to please her."

"You had feelings for my queen even then?" Arturo asked with raised eyebrows.

"I don't know. But when I looked at this amazing woman, I had a deep desire to make her wishes come true."

"So many people have come under her influence and followed her to the ends of the earth."

"It must have been difficult to leave," I whispered.

"I thought about her every day." Arturo rubbed a different small scar and continued. "Hmm. You don't enjoy disappointing immortals? Did it occur to you that you're an immortal?"

"I'm not in the club yet. Wait 500 years and ask me that question."

"How amusing," Arturo said with a chuckle. "You have a remarkable ability to deal with our kind."

"I've had some training as a reporter. It's kind of the same thing."

"Indeed."

We enjoyed the flight for ten minutes. "You have another question," Arturo said without turning to me.

"I do."

"You wish to learn the motivations behind consuming young subjects for the process."

I remained silent for 45 seconds, and then Arturo took a shallow breath. He let it out slowly and said softly, "At the beginning, I only desired to please my queen. Gathering boys was one task among many. To me, they were like sheep. When the supply in one village became exhausted, we moved to the next. After I left the group, I traveled and began questioning my values. I knew it was a cruel act to take a child away from his family. It is a barbaric thing to take his life. Without my queen to absolve my guilt, my questions grew stronger.

"I still remember the day, July 7, 1752. I came across an average-looking boy walking with his sister. He put up a tremendous fight, and it took all my abilities to restrain him. That night, I readied him for the procedure, and he glared at me with extreme intensity. Finally, when the boy understood his death would be imminent, he yelled, 'Stop! Let me die like a man!'

"I asked about his request, and he wanted to stand firm with his head held high. The honor in the boy's eyes ... It changed me. It changed me forever. Well, there was no choice but to release him.

"James, I did not like the man I had become and vowed to transform myself into a better individual. So, from that moment on, I took great care to select only criminals.

"When I moved to Panama, I paid the local police to round up gangs of street thugs. They liked my no-questions-asked policy, and the result truly improved the community. However, I must confess. The local paper often reported men in black masks breaking down doors of poor homes to take boys away. But, of course, I ignored such rumors.

"The harvest plays tricks on your mind. It gets deep inside and makes taking a child's life seem righteous. To that end, I maintained my sanity by convincing myself that the boys I put down were of ill repute."

"Do you think I can stop?" I asked, fearing the answer.

"The pull of the procedure is very powerful. I certainly don't have the discipline to cease taking lives, and I will commit any unspeakable act to continue my journey. Darn. As I say these words out loud, I sound quite selfish."

We both sat for the next hour in quiet contemplation while staring out our respective windows. Later, we talked about relationships, history, classical music, art, and politics. I found it amusing that the craziness surrounding ancient Roman elections mirrored recent elections.

NINETEEN

We landed in Manila and took a plane to Rome with a stop-over in Istanbul. Cleopatra provided Arturo a passport with the name Fuddy Hedwig Doubledee. *She obviously has a sense of humor.*

At the airport, we hailed a taxi, and the driver drove like a circus clown. We flew over sidewalks at full speed, through parks, against opposing traffic, across a parking lot in reverse, and plowed right through groups of people without using the horn. Before our ride, I wanted to see every sight in this beautiful city, and now, I only wanted to get to our destination alive.

Outside Rome, we barreled down a poorly maintained road. The scenery had changed to farmland, and it occurred to me that few Americans had ever been in this part of Italy. Forty minutes later, a massive compound came into view.

The taxi came to a screeching stop at the gated entrance, and I was grateful to be alive. Six armed guards rapidly approached and began yelling in Italian. I saw three guards inside a cement building with thick glass immediately pick up phones.

We exited the cab, and Arturo threw a wad of cash at the driver, who sped off in a cloud of dust. The guards now had their hands on their guns and looked ready to use them.

I feared for my life and yelled, "Excuse me. Excuse me!" The guards stopped yelling, glared at me, and I continued, "May I please deliver a message to Niniano Del Pizzo? It's important."

The guards now looked even more upset and made it clear that we needed to leave. I tried a different angle, "Everybody, let's calm down. I'm going to remove a book from my pack. It's not a weapon. All right? Don't shoot!"

The guard on my right nodded. I took off my backpack and, with one hand, unzipped it. Slowly, I pulled out *Grime: Just Cause* as the six guards looked at me with great concern. I could see the video cameras, and I held my book in the air to let the people watching get an unrestricted view.

I was confident that we would soon be inside, but the guards again yelled at us to leave. Sensing it would be pointless to continue arguing, we began walking down the road.

"That didn't end the way I expected," Arturo said with a grunt.

"We did fine. See that excuse for a tree? We're going to sit there and stare at them. The guards are trying to soften us up. It was the same thing at Jank's place. You immortals need to do things your way on your timetable."

"You may be correct," Arturo admitted. "We'll wait."

"It's hot, and we will need to drink soon," I said, while fanning myself with my book.

"They are using the heat to weaken us."

"I agree."

We sat under the small tree, and Arturo took off his shirt. We stared at the guards for the next two hours, and they stared back. He eventually became impatient and yelled, "This dreaded heat! Something is bothering me!"

"What?"

"Anna desired you? Yes?"

"Of course."

"And you didn't have her?" Arturo asked.

"I didn't."

"Did you desire her?"

"Of course I did!" I exclaimed in a louder voice.

"You informed me that the reason concerns the long life provided by the procedure. I don't believe this."

"All right, I exaggerated," I admitted. "I feared her father would beat me up or something."

"I've seen how you carry yourself. You would do well in a fight."

"True."

Seventy-eight seconds later, Arturo quietly said, "You knew."

"I strongly suspected."

"Why?"

"That's how my life had been going. Everything had been all too convenient. Plus, you loaded your house with paintings and sculptures. Except for Jank, all you immortals have a deep craving for art."

"I provided my blessing to be with Anna," Arturo reminded me, turning his head to see me better.

"You did."

"Yet, you didn't have her?"

"I didn't."

"Why?!" Arturo demanded. "Anna was attractive."

"You still don't get it. When I first met Grace, I accidentally dropped my napkin. She nearly stabbed me. You immortals are super-sensitive. Plus, the absolute worst offense to any father is a guy who jumps his daughter. So, no, I didn't start a relationship."

"What if she threw herself at you?" Arturo wondered.

"I would have gently discouraged her."

"Because of me?"

"Because of what you are and because I knew it wasn't in her best interest to start a relationship. In time, I would have liked to have known her better."

"Incredible." Arturo threw up his hands and looked at the guards. Then, forty-eight seconds later, he asked, "What about Grace?"

"What about her?"

"Which would you have chosen, Anna or Grace?" Arturo wondered.

"I didn't have to make that decision."

"Who would you choose now?"

"I don't know. Probably Grace."

"Why?" Arturo asked with concern.

"She's amazing."

"Who do you think is prettier? Anna or Grace?"

"They're both beautiful. Maybe Anna or maybe Grace. I don't know. These questions are extremely hypothetical," I said with a dismissive gesture.

"Tell me. You slept with my queen and Grace. Correct?"

"I did," I answered with certainty.

"And you didn't have sex with them?" Arturo asked while waving his hands.

"I didn't."

"If you did, which would you choose?"

"I'm not sure. But the important issue is that I didn't have to decide."

"What if all three desired you?"

"Hmm. I don't know. Cleo and Grace are immortals, and immortals are so unpredictable. Besides, I get nervous around women."

"How gay are you?" Arturo asked with a hearty laugh.

"What?"

"Three gorgeous women want you, and you do nothing. You've got to be the gayest person in history to pass up sex with my queen."

I laughed and said, "That night had nothing to do with sex. Instead, we shared an astounding expression of trust. And I will tell you the experience meant a hundred times more than sex."

"And you say that my queen and Grace only showed you part of their trust?" Arturo wondered while pinching his upper lip.

"They shared more than enough to send my mind to all kinds of crazy places."

"And you didn't desire them."

"Oh, I had a strong desire for them. But, you know, it's strange. At first, I knew all kinds of kinky things were about to happen, but the feeling passed," I said while waving my hand away.

"You don't desire them now?"

"I saw them in matching bikinis. I desire them more than anybody ever desired anything!"

Arturo stood and asked, "You saw them in matching swimsuits?!"

"Yes."

"And then you slept with them?!" Arturo demanded.

"Yes."

"Without sex?!"

"Without sex," I answered while nodding.

"You have more willpower than any other man in history, or you are so far in the closet that you're finding Christmas presents!"

Arturo threw up his hands, and I began laughing so hard that I made my honking noise. Forty-six minutes later, a thin guard with curly black hair ran over and took my book. He studied it, returned it, and ran away.

I told Arturo that we would be inside in fewer than ten minutes. Seven minutes later, the same guard came over and pointed to me. We stood, and he said something in Italian. Arturo and the guard began arguing. "What is it?" I wanted to know.

"They only want you."

"Tell him it has to be both of us."

They argued until the guard ran away. "It's going to take some time," I observed. "Hey. I had another question."

"This dreaded heat!" Arturo yelled. "Enough. Why do you constantly require permission to speak? Ask your hare-brained question!"

"After the harvest, I got good at telling time. For example, 53 minutes ago, we stopped talking about sex."

"Impressive," Arturo said while nodding.

"Do you have any abilities like that?"

"My time-calculating ability is poor. However, after the new procedure, I began accurately estimating distance with my eyes. Quite remarkable."

"Grace has the same ability. She can measure a room to within an inch by looking at it. She can also visualize angles."

"Fascinating. Did my queen mention any abilities?" Arturo asked with interest.

"She has a great sense of smell and taste. She even told me she could track a person by their scent."

"I don't recall her having that ability," Arturo informed.

"I would like to have been able to ask Quan and Jank about improved abilities."

"That would have been revealing."

Six minutes later, the guard came back and motioned to us. Then, he led us to the guardhouse, where they searched us roughly. They took my backpack but allowed me to keep my passport and wallet. I mused during this uncomfortable time that the only sexual action I have received since my wife left was from security guards!

The left guard pulled out my *Dawson's Creek* notebook and looked at me with a funny expression. "I think he is a fan," Arturo said with a big grin.

The guard did not look happy with this brash statement, and eight men in suits put us into separate black SUVs. We drove in a roundabout course through the compound and stopped at a small building.

The men led us inside a sparse room with two well-used steel chairs in front of a modest desk. Behind the desk, we saw an oversized wooden chair with unusual cushions. Six security men stood behind us. One had his hand firmly on my left shoulder while the other had the right. I got the impression that the third man had a weapon pointed at the back of my head. Three were in the same positions behind Arturo, and the remaining two faced us from the other side of the table with their arms in an X pattern with one hand inside their suits. These two men were likely holding their guns as they glared at us for seven uncomfortable minutes.

A door opened, and an overpowering stench blew in. I tried to raise my hand to hold my nose, but the guard forced me not to move. Fifteen seconds later, three people helped a disease-ridden excuse of a man to the chair. He had dreadful scars on every visible part of his body and hundreds of bandages. His hair looked like a patchwork of gray and black tufts with bald spots. The scars made it impossible to determine any facial features. When our eyes met, I knew this wretched individual was an immortal. He tried to stare me down without success and then turned to Arturo for two minutes without either blinking.

When the man seemed satisfied, he reached into his pocket, produced a copy of *Grime: The Big Hate!,* and threw it at me. Then the man then yelled something in an angry voice.

"He called you—" Arturo translated.

"I know what he called me," I interrupted. "Everybody's a critic. Why don't people know that it's hard to write a book?! Geez!"

I leaned back, and stared at the man for 33 seconds while realizing I should not have spoken so forwardly. However, the heat affected me, and I continued without thinking as much as I should have, "It's clear you know who I am. So, tell me. Are we going to have a conversation with the guards listening or not?"

The man nodded. I made an enormous sigh and said, "You immortals have such trust issues. Right now, everybody but us has their hand on a gun, yet, he still thinks there's a danger."

The man got taken aback, and he shook his head. When I turned to Arturo, I saw a trace of a smile and asked without turning to the man, "Are you sure you want these goons hearing what I have to say?"

When I turned back, the man gave me a defiant look, which made me chuckle. I playfully nodded and said, "I bet you will regret hearing what I have to say. It will only take one word."

The man looked angry, shook his head, and I confidently said, "I'll do it. I really will."

The man continued to look defiant. So I stared deep into him for 27 seconds and said, "Caesarion, we need to talk privately."

Caesarion looked stunned, and he shifted back in his chair. He put his hands over his heart and began taking animated, gasping breaths. When I looked at Arturo, he lost his color and shook his head while saying, "Estas muerto." I knew enough Spanish to understand this meant, "You're dead."

The two stared at each other in complete shock. Then, Caesarion took a deep breath and said in heavily accented English, "This meeting has taken an unexpected turn. We have much to discuss outside of my trusted men."

"May we do this in a more comfortable environment?"

"But of course. Come, come."

Three men helped Caesarion stand, and they assisted him out of the room. When the door opened, the fresh air felt fantastic.

Two security men escorted us to a six-person golf cart. The three assistants eased Caesarion into a vehicle designed to hold his damaged body. Next, guards drove us to a small garden, and we sat in beautiful brown chairs with intricate patterns tooled into the leather. Then, assistants helped Caesarion into an oversized chair designed to cradle his damaged body. An attractive middle-aged woman with long black hair brought drinks; lemon honey tea with a hint of pepper. The taste was outstanding, and I found it difficult not to drink my entire glass in one gulp.

The assistants departed, and I wondered how many guards were secretly pointing rifles at us. Caesarion stared at Arturo for 43 seconds, and I said, "I think it is time that you introduced yourself."

"Very well," Arturo said with a grunt. "You probably deduced my given name is Amten."

"Amten, I knew it! I knew it! It's a wonder that you're still alive," Caesarion said with bold hand gestures.

"I go by Arturo now."

"Remarkable," Caesarion said in complete fascination. "According to that rubbish book, my wretched mother is likely alive. This knowledge displeases me more than you can comprehend. Do you know of her?"

"I do," Arturo admitted.

"Tell me!" Caesarion demanded.

"She is well."

"I pissed on that witch's grave!"

I grasped Arturo's arm, and he did not speak. Caesarion seemed amused by my actions; he took a small sip of his drink, composed himself, and said, "This has been enlightening, but our meeting has a purpose."

I spoke respectfully, "Sir, I suspect you wish to learn of my harvest technique, and of course, I will freely share every detail."

"If you fail, you will suffer a fate worse than death!" Caesarion threatened.

"I understand, and of course, I will comply with your every request. Arturo, you were much nicer about asking me."

"In retrospect, I wasn't," Arturo countered. "I regret my earlier behavior."

"The harvest puts a lot of pressure on us."

"That it does."

"Enough!" Caesarion yelled. "Speak!"

After Caesarion learned the secret, I knew that open dialogue would be impossible, so I tried to be diplomatic. "Sir, there are more pressing problems that concern all of us. We are here to discuss these matters."

"There are no other pressing problems. Speak!"

"You're aware of what happened in China?"

"What of China?" Caesarion said with a dismissive hand gesture.

"The airstrike outside of Nanchong?"

"Nanchong? Hmm. A well-executed contract. What does that have to do with me?"

"The estate belonged to a man named Quan," I answered.

"The Quan?!" Caesarion exclaimed in awe. "From so long ago?"

"Yes."

Caesarion leaned back in his chair and asked, "Did the attack kill him?"

"He survived the attack, but he's now dead."

"How do you know of his death?" Caesarion asked with narrow eyes.

"Sir, they forced me to execute him."

Caesarion took a deep breath and looked at me in anger for 33 seconds. Finally, he nodded and asked in a menacing voice, "Forced?"

"Yes. Forced."

"You have killed one of us?!" Caesarion threatened while pointing at me with a shaking finger.

"Regrettably, I did. I wanted to learn so much from him."

"Quan was a repulsive man. A filthy butcher."

"True," I conceded.

Caesarion took another sip and said, "In the inner world of arms dealing, that campaign instantly became a legend. They call it 'the thump.' Very slick and well-financed. The operation involved two contractors: a German outfit, Waffen and Korth, and a Russian group, Tikhiy Gnev, which translates to 'Silent Anger.' Both groups were the absolute best in the business.

"For the operation, they purchased four surplus F16 fighter aircraft. Technicians outfitted the planes with extra drop tanks and stripped out unnecessary weight. On the overflight, they landed on remote roads to refuel. The logistics behind such a coordinated attack boggles the mind.

"But that is not what concerned me. Two days after the attack, all the top men for both organizations went missing.

A single female attacker took one man during a family dinner and shot his wife in the arm."

"That aligns with our information," I said more confidently than I should have.

"It does?"

"We would like to share information with you."

"To what end?" Caesarion asked while scratching at a bandage.

"To determine the identity of those behind these attacks."

"Why would I do this?"

I took six seconds to carefully compose my words, "Sir, please understand, before I answer your question, that I do not wish to come across as disrespectful."

"I understand your intent. Now tell me. Why?!"

"Sir, those same people may intend to cause you harm. We suspect the person behind these attacks is a wealthy individual in poor health. Or this person is another immortal."

"Unlikely. I'm as safe as any man could be. Now, you will provide the procedure details."

"I know three men who did not take me seriously," I countered.

"Who?!" Caesarion demanded.

"Quan, Jank, and Arturo."

"Jank is alive?"

"Are you aware of the attack in Thailand?" I deflected.

Caesarion folded his hands together with a crafty smile and said, "Also a large operation. They secretly prepared loads of equipment far in advance, including ten portable bridges. The operation ended in utter failure when the target fired rockets from cleverly hidden batteries. As a last desperate act, the coward blew himself up. His dramatic suicide killed many fine mercenaries."

"I pressed the button that blew them to hell," Arturo said with a big grin. "We were over a mile away."

"Does this mean that Jank is alive?" Caesarion asked with wide eyes.

"Regrettably, he suffered the same fate as Quan."

"You killed both of them?!" Caesarion boomed as he again pointed at me.

"They forced me to kill them."

"Who?!"

"Sir, may we discuss a partnership first?" I asked in a respectful voice.

"A partnership with that witch and the woman with the apple tree?!"

"Yes, sir."

"They forced you to kill Quan and Jank?!" Caesarion demanded.

"Yes, sir," I answered while hoping he would not be too upset.

"There'll be no agreement. You will describe the procedure."

"Sir, as I have stated, I will describe all aspects of the harvest. However, there are more pressing matters."

"What more could there be?" Caesarion asked while scratching at a scar.

"Arturo, please tell them what happened at your house."

"They attacked my house in Panama and killed my daughter," Arturo answered in an angry voice.

"I am aware of the minor operation in Panama. A new outfit took the contract. The head guy calls his group *The Iron Wolves*. A foolish name with predictable results. No matter."

I had run out of ideas and said to Arturo, "It's time. Please take off your shoe."

Arturo looked at me with raised eyebrows, and Caesarion asked, "What's this about?"

Arturo leaned back for thirteen seconds and said whimsically, "There's something—important that we have in common."

"What could a simpleton like you possibly have in common with me?"

"We share many traits," Arturo answered with a smile.

"Are you claiming to be my father? My father is Julius Caesar, the greatest leader of the most powerful empire in history!"

"When Julius Caesar turned fifteen, a horse kicked him in the groin. His pants only held a little stump. Even if he could get his mutilated pecker up, he didn't have gonads to make you. That's why he had a high voice."

Caesarion looked upset and started to speak. Arturo took off his left shoe to reveal his curled toe. Caesarion was stunned and muttered, "That witch could not keep her legs closed."

"That *woman* is now trying to save your life," I corrected.

I reached into my backpack, pulled out the envelope, and placed its two handwritten pages in front of Caesarion. He began reading, and I wondered what information the letters contained. Eighty-one seconds later, he murmured, "She's scared. They're both scared."

Caesarion dropped the letters, painfully reached down, and picked them up. He then looked off into the distance.

When the time seemed right, I reached into my backpack, pulled out my *Dawson's Creek* notebook, and began writing.

"What are you writing in your absurd notebook? Do you intend to publish another book?!" Caesarion demanded.

"I'm not writing another book. I think better when I take notes."

"No matter. You will tell me about your procedure without delay!" Caesarion again demanded.

"Yes, of course. May I ask about your procedure first?"

"Because of your honesty, I choose to grant this one request. You may not be aware that a plague surrounds us. They call themselves Gypsies, and make no mistake; they do not meet the definition of human. I pay locals to gather boys between eight and ten years old. Sometimes, they bring twenty of the scoundrels.

"I begin by pressing the adrenal gland to produce a liquid. It is mixed with snake venom and almond oil. I then make an incision into my muscles. It must be precisely eight centimeters from my last procedure. I then place the prepared pancreas into the new incision. Two days later, I remove the previous pancreas. As you wrote, the procedure results in prolonged life. Once, so long ago, I used to have boundless energy and impressive looks. But now—but now—it only lasts between five and eight days. Enough! You will explain your procedure!"

It had become clear that I could delay no further, and I explained the harvesting procedure. Caesarion diligently took notes in a fine leather notebook, and afterward, he said, "We will try this update. And if it fails..."

"Yes, I understand what you will do to me. However, please allow me to bring up one more topic? I believe it will benefit both of us."

"Quickly," Caesarion encouraged while gesturing for me to speed up the conversation.

"I know you have taken all the necessary security precautions, but if there is indeed a danger present, then harvesting will leave you physically and mentally unable to coordinate your forces for two days."

"He speaks the truth," Arturo added. "The procedure incapacitated Jank during the attack on his compound. If he had been able-bodied, I am sure the counterattack would have been successful."

"What are you proposing?" Caesarion asked with concern.

"We have brought information for you to look over. Additionally, I ask that you make an extra-deep security check to ensure our safety. Specifically, I request you search for a group capable of attacking your estate."

Caesarion made a "hhh" sound and said eight seconds later, "I have not survived this long by acting foolish. Your logic has merit. Let us retire to my study. Come, come."

Caesarion raised his hand, and three men came over to help him stand. As we departed, I noticed the letters from Cleopatra and Grace remained on the chair. We drove to a small building that contained an elevator. Inside, we traveled down for 71 seconds, and being so close to Caesarion made me want to vomit.

The door opened, and I had to rush out to escape the smell. We walked down a hallway and through two heavy doors to an exquisite office. Despite being buried underground, it had an airy feeling with a tolerable smell. Arturo and I sat in two plush blue chairs while Caesarion sat behind his three large computer screens. I handed him the memory stick, and he put it into a laptop. Caesarion began using a security scanning program while attentively watching it operate.

As Caesarion worked, I looked at the artwork tastefully displayed: a unique combination of the old West and ancient

Rome. I stood to scrutinize a small bronze sculpture of a proud Native American on horseback. The piece had outstanding craftsmanship, and the style reminded me of Frederic Remington. Caesarion looked up from the laptop and commented, "An unknown American artist named Leo Coyle sculpted that piece."

"Excellent technique."

"You have a good eye. Of all my artwork, that's my favorite," Caesarion admitted with pride.

"Thank you for allowing me to view it," I said respectfully.

I sat back down as Caesarion looked amused. Once satisfied that the memory stick did not contain harmful programs, he put it into his desk computer. Our positions prevented us from seeing his screens, but I observed his eyebrows rapidly moving while vigorously using the mouse.

Caesarion said without looking up, "After we finish, you will show me how to send pictures with your eyes."

"I couldn't replicate the process," I answered in my most confident voice, knowing that he could not see my expression as I lied.

"How hard did you try?" Caesarion demanded.

"I asked a bunch of friends to help. We ended up just staring at each other. Are you aware of anybody that can send pictures as I described?"

Caesarion shook his head while continuing to use his computer. Then, a minute later, he whimsically asked, "Are you aware of how I generate wealth?"

"Cleo informed me you are an arms dealer."

"That's a specific term. I provide many services, including arms. It wasn't always so complex. My customers used to require only weapons, men, and information. Today so much more is needed, and yet the same mistakes persist. Armies always forget about water. It's always water. Did she inform you I exhausted my funds?"

"Cleo mentioned you were in great debt."

"You didn't believe her?" Caesarion asked with amusement.

I found this statement astute and answered, "It didn't seem logical that an immortal could remain on the verge of bankruptcy for so many years."

Caesarion stopped typing, looked up, and said, "For any large purchase, the profit is never in the sale."

"You're a banker!"

"I'm *the* banker!" Caesarion corrected with pride. "And I go far out of my way to hide my finances!"

"That's amazing! I would have never guessed."

"In World War II, I tried to sell Mussolini the finest weapons below cost. That fool had other ideas. I ended up financing Russia and made billions. Nobody thought the Russians could win. Even fewer thought they would pay the money back. They always pay because there's always another war. Fear fuels the men who run countries, not common sense. Leaders never see the big picture and act like teenagers with their first credit card."

Caesarion returned to typing, and 84 seconds later, I said, "The history books record that Octavian killed you."

"The people were unhappy, and I saw the inevitable revolt coming. So, I made a deal with Octavian, and in exchange, I became the exclusive arms supplier to the Roman government."

"How did you cover up your murder?" I asked, while knowing I was venturing into a topic that Caesarion might not appreciate.

"Nothing to cover up. Octavian told everybody he killed me, and nobody dared to contradict him."

"Didn't the people see you alive?" I wondered.

"I moved Florence," Caesarion answered without emotion. "You must understand that photographs and newspapers did not exist. Therefore, the locals could not recognize me."

Caesarion abruptly moved back from his computer with a shocked expression for eight seconds. Then, he used his mouse, and a large screen behind him came on. We saw many numbers in columns. "I'm not afraid to admit when I make miscalculations," he said. "Look here."

Caesarion pointed to numbers with his mouse and continued, "I used my high-level financial access to uncover these transactions. Calling those two witches may have been presumptuous. They did indeed discover critical information. Look, look. A $1 billion transfer. And here's another. That's your Chinese airstrike, and that's your Thailand attack. I have never witnessed such aggressive spending! Especially on a private contract. A billion each! Outrageous! Simply outrageous! They didn't even break their payments into partial sums. And look here, look here. Another billion-dollar transfer from the same accounts. This information is indeed troublesome, and you were correct to be concerned. Whoever paid for this attack went directly to the best and paid without argument.

"Look here, look here. The accounts they used are old. Very—old. They did this for an important reason. Old accounts are not in modern electronic databases. I recognize this one; it's related to oil. We may be dealing with a Saudi prince or a United Arab Emirates business executive. That should fit, but something isn't right. Arabs haggle far more than any other ethnicity. Exactly one billion dollars? No, this transaction doesn't seem right. No, not right at all.

"Hmm. How to catch this man? How to catch? Ah, yes! I have it! I will use my Chinese banks to place holds on these accounts. The account owners will, of course, protest. But, my hands will be squeaky clean, and I will watch from the sidelines."

Arturo chuckled when a small pop-up appeared on Caesarion's computer screen, and I asked, "You like Candy Crush?"

Caesarion quickly closed the window and threatened, "You will tell no one!"

"May I share something?"

"I don't see why not," Caesarion answered dismissively.

"Cleo has the same program."

Arturo began laughing, and he asked, "She does? I thought this program only worked on cell phones?"

Caesarion interrupted, "The program comes from their website and will work with Windows. Now! You will not reveal my secret!"

"I won't tell a soul."

"And you won't write of this either!" Caesarion threatened.

"The last thing I would ever do is write another book."

"Very well."

"May I have a copy of the information you discovered?" I asked.

"To give to those two witches?"

"Cleo and Grace are on your side," I reminded him.

"The only side they are on is their own. If your loins did not guide your inferior mind, you would realize this fact!"

Caesarion looked at me for nine seconds, tapped his fingers in anger, clicked his mouse, threw me the memory stick, and said, "See what I care about those two witches. They might make a worthy distraction while I find out who's truly responsible. Now. Tell me about their location."

"I don't have that information," I answered, hoping my response would not upset Caesarion. "After our visit, we were to go to a nearby airport, look for a tail number, and then await instructions from the pilot."

"You do not see it. Those witches convinced you to be the distraction while they hunt me. Typical thinking from my mother. Now, I have indeed taken your advice, and you ..."

Caesarion had been looking at his screen. He frowned, gritted his teeth, and said an angry word. Caesarion stared daggers at me for eighteen seconds and stood with surprising ability. He hobbled toward a steel door, placed his hand on a large plate, and typed numbers into the keypad. The thick door opened, and we followed Caesarion to the end of a short hallway leading to another steel door. Again, he entered a code to a keypad, and we walked through.

Inside, we saw a massive room arranged in a two-level semicircle. There were sixteen large screens arranged around the edge and over thirty men diligently working on sophisticated computers in the center. The screens had maps, satellite images, lists of numbers, news videos, charts, pictures of people, and financial information. The impressive sight reminded me of the NORAD control room from the movie *War Games*.

Caesarion yelled something, and the men began feverously working their computers. Many of the giant screens changed to tactical displays and satellite images. Then, three men ran up to Caesarion and spoke to him simultaneously.

Two minutes later, Arturo quietly said to me, "An attack on this compound is imminent. Caesarion learned this secret because he sold the Italian military a new communication system with a channel that allowed his operators to monitor their communications. He used this back door to intercept an urgent order directing nearby military forces to overrun this compound and capture the leaders. The government believes their soldiers will encounter a heavily armed terrorist camp.

"Caesarion is exceedingly angry with his people and told them that 'an author with the mind of a mule is smarter than all of them combined.'"

I looked at Arturo, and we chuckled.

Caesarion sat down in front of a computer, picked up a phone, and began speaking while typing. Arturo quietly said, "He's now using his contacts to convince the Italian government to stop their advance. He has also placed a call to other world leaders, including your American president."

One man pointed to the center screen, and Caesarion spoke angrily over the phone. Then, he slammed down the phone, switched to a different phone, and we overheard half of the conversation. "General," Caesarion spoke in a deep drawl. "Yessir. I'm in the ole compound. Yessir, there's some sorta misinformation. Lookie here now, this is my summer home. Yessir, from the KH birds it do look like a big ole complex. But iff'n y'all take a closer look, you're gonna see no troops, nuke sigs, chemical sigs, fermentation, an' o' course, no soldiers.

"Why, sure-as-shootin' y'all can send in any ole inspectors. By gosh, I'll show'm all every room personally. No, light arms only. We're all good here. Yessir. What?! No! Course not! Ya can't? Well, there has to be something y'all have on these ole pasta huggers? You do? You'll call? Great to hear! I will personally escort the inspectors myself. I knew I could count on you. Now, general, I certainly owe y'all a big thankee. Say hello to Doreen and the kids!"

Caesarion switched phones and made four more calls in different languages.

The men scrambled for the next 38 minutes, and the mood worsened. Then, Arturo quietly said to me, "I've seen this before. They're panicking. Look at that image. Those are tanks. And those are troop transports."

"Why is the government pushing so hard?" I wondered.

"It's unclear. From what I understand, the government will not stop its advance. Caesarion made many requests to important people, who refused to help. So now, he's warning the Italian government about what will happen when the tanks cross Via Giulia. That's 20 kilometers away."

Our private conversation was interrupted by Caesarion yelling into the phone and slamming the handset down with a crash. He looked around the room for 43 seconds and began walking toward his office with six disappointed men in tow. We followed the group, and Caesarion sat in his chair, looking lost. Finally, one man slammed the door shut.

"You have a decision to make," Arturo said.

"In my wildest dreams, I did not think it would come down to this," Caesarion said in bewilderment.

"What?" I asked.

"A shipping container came into the Port of Anzio loaded with chemical weapons precursors. The manifest listed my address. Then, in Portici, customs officials discovered another container with enough plutonium to make two bombs. That manifest also listed my address.

"Simultaneously, the military intercepted communications which confirmed people from my compound are planning to attack Rome tomorrow morning. And finally, the Italian government and media received a threat from a group calling themselves 'The Great Eastern Brigade.' They are a new terrorist group with many bombings to their credit.

"My government is standing firm in the face of this overwhelming evidence. Whoever planned this certainly did their homework. It must have taken months to set up."

Caesarion leaned back in his chair, folded his hands, and continued, "The fools are sending an armored battalion to this location. What angers me most is I recently sold them those vehicles."

"How bad is it?" I inquired.

"My men have more than enough strength to obliterate armor. But this carnage will enrage the government. They will have no choice but to send a heavy battalion followed by aircraft. Many brave soldiers are about to die."

I understood Caesarion's dilemma. He cared about his country and did not want to destroy the powerful army he'd helped to create. I sensed an opportunity and said, "Send your men through the tunnels and leave the doors open. The soldiers will only find empty buildings. In a few months, you can explain the misunderstanding and return."

"If those soldiers search this compound, they will find more than enough to justify their fears."

A man said something, and Caesarion replied, "They're in range."

"You need to defuse this. Fire a warning shot or something," I suggested.

"Italians do not react well to threats."

"How about a big warning shot?" I asked.

Caesarion chuckled and answered, "I can deploy weapons that will get the world's attention."

"How about you blow up a nearby hill? You need to slow this down."

Two men spoke Italian, and Caesarion rubbed his nose with his eyes closed. My mind drifted, and I wondered how these men put up with his smell. Then, he looked up at me with a whimsical expression and began, "In the '50s, atomic weapons were all the rage. Every nation wanted a huge stockpile, and I did not want to be left behind. British security has always been noteworthy, but their bureaucracy leads them astray. To me, this presented a simple opportunity.

"With one forged requisition, their army ordered 35 Green Grass warheads. Then, a single signature transferred them to the navy. The navy never expected the warheads, and I intercepted the shipment. Imagine that? Thirty-five warheads for free. I placed one warhead under my direct control near capital cities and military interests. However, this secret presented a problem. Nuclear weapons are only useful for preventing wars if world leaders clearly understand their existence."

"True," I said with a nod.

"While those weapons provided great comfort, they began developing problems. What you must understand is that Green Grass weapons utilized first-generation nuclear technology. They required constant repairs and upkeep. All this had to be done in secret at remote locations. Then, British testing revealed yield inconsistencies. It all became too big a bother, and in 1977, I sold the lot to South Africa. After their government fell, I brokered a deal to sell the warheads to Israel. Later, I learned they had no use for the older Green Grass design and recycled the uranium. It would be nice to have them now."

Caesarion scratched a scar on his arm and continued, "The problem is that I have posed as many people. As a result, the leaders do not appreciate who I am. How unexpected."

"What are you going to do?" I asked when the moment seemed right.

"Destroy the country I love or flee."

"An obvious decision."

"We will depart soon."

I felt tremendous relief and asked, "Are you going to take your escape rocket?"

"You know of my rocket?" Caesarion asked with great interest.

"Cleo identified the launch building from a satellite view."

"That witch is smart."

Caesarion stood and hobbled to a different computer, pressed numbers into a keypad, typed several commands, and then spoke to his men in Italian. The men talked into handheld radios for 65 seconds. Then, Caesarion sat back down and said, "It takes nineteen minutes to download essential information and wipe my system. Hmm. My escape rocket? Are you aware of how a person like me obtains the latest technology?"

"No idea."

"Not a class they taught you at UCLA?" Caesarion insulted me, but I still laughed, and he continued. "It seemed a more straightforward prospect to deliver a nuclear warhead on the tip of a rocket. From my previous Green Grass experience, I learned that the most critical feature of a nuclear weapon system is low maintenance. The American Polaris missile proved to be the ideal balance.

"When a man like me wants to obtain a weapon system, I recommend making it better. I ordered one of my companies to write a proposal to extend the Polaris range and improve its accuracy. The US government liked my proposal and provided all the classified designs. My company successfully enhanced the design, and I discreetly made four additional rockets.

"Getting four warheads proved more challenging. At one time, all American nuclear weapons were under the control of the Atomic Energy Commission. Their relationship with the armed forces had always been tumultuous. I sensed an opportunity and quietly drove each military branch to take control of their inventory. While the transfer occurred, I arranged for four suitable warheads to be dropped off the official list. Two weeks later, a truck carried them away without a trace.

"I put the extended-range missiles in the middle of my compound, and nine months later, the problems began. It turns out that this low-maintenance missile system did not live up to its reputation. One Polaris split in half from moisture. Imagine that. A missile for a submarine not capable of getting wet!"

Caesarion shook his head and continued, "The repair efforts grew and grew. Finally, in 1983, I ordered their removal. I sold the missiles to Germany and the warheads to the Chinese. Skilled negotiators, the Chinese. I should have charged them more. Now, that building is empty. Hmm. Given present circumstances, an escape rocket might have been useful."

Caesarion spoke to his men in Italian, and they spoke into handheld radios. Then, he walked to a large steel door, entered a combination, and opened it to reveal a hallway. "Amten, you will accompany me in tunnel two," Caesarion said. "It leads to our departure point."

"And me?" I asked.

"We have had an enlightening discussion, and I would have liked to explore further topics."

Caesarion narrowed his eyes and continued in an icy voice, "Amten knows the procedure well enough, and as disturbing as it may seem, he may be my father." I felt a deep chill run down my spine, and I gulped. He continued, "When you exposed our secret, your fate was sealed."

Caesarion took out a gun and pointed it at me. *Of all places to die, why here?* I wondered in desperation.

"He's useful. Make him a go-between," Arturo interrupted.

"I only deal directly," Caesarion said.

"Let's offer him to those who hurt us. He will make a nice pawn," Arturo suggested with a smile and an encouraging nod.

"Those who hunt me have signed their death warrants. All this man is good for is writing powerful books."

In another time or place, I would have seen this statement as a nice compliment. But, my mind spun out of control, trying to figure out a way to save my life. The sight of six men not paying attention to us, briefly distracted me. *How many people did Caesarion kill in this very office?* It then occurred to me that Arturo had discreetly moved to his left. *He's got a plan!*

I knew Arturo needed time, and I came up with a distraction. "I have more important information."

"What information could a simpleton like you have?" Caesarion asked with a fluttering gesture.

"Cleo's improved procedure," I answered with confidence.

"You already revealed her procedure."

"I told you the procedure that she taught Grace 500 years ago. Cleo made it better."

"Why would that witch reveal her precious secret to you?" Caesarion wondered, scratching a scar on his face.

"I slept with her," I answered with a big grin.

"You're deceitful! She would never lie with a common man!"

"She snores like a freight train."

Caesarion raised his hand without the gun and yelled, "What?! Damn! That witch still cannot keep her legs shut!"

Arturo looked at me for a brief instant and turned away. Caesarion pointed the gun at my head and asked, "What does the procedure do?"

"The effect lasts nine months," I answered with confidence.

"Did you apply the procedure to yourself?"

"She asked me not to share this new procedure with you or Arturo. So I didn't try it yet."

"How does it work?!" Caesarion demanded.

"Escape first. Both of us."

"Very well."

Caesarion lowered the gun, and at that moment, Arturo began lunging at the six men with a small knife. He attacked like a wild beast, and his slashes inflicted long wounds. I used the distraction to punch Caesarion. He cleverly dodged my attack while he tried to point his gun at me with one hand and punch with the other. While Caesarion possessed superb fighting skills, his well-placed punches produced no pain, and when I struck him, I felt bones breaking. One carefully timed punch to the jaw, and he went down hard. So I grabbed his gun, pushed the barrel into his chest, and yelled, "Stop!"

I heard a commotion behind me and yelled louder, "Stop!"

The men continued fighting, and at that dire moment, I had no choice. I shot Caesarion, and the horrific boom reverberated in the small office. Time seemed to slow down as Caesarion's body lunged backward. He looked at me in complete shock. I knew Arturo needed my help, but I continued to deeply stare into Caesarion's eyes. His mouth opened, and he tried to speak. His head then moved to the side as his eyes fluttered.

At that moment, I saw the same flicker and wondered if Caesarion's soul had departed. I tried to understand if he fought something or was being welcomed into a better place. Then, shaking myself out of my sidetrack, I turned around to see two men holding Arturo while a third punched him. I rapidly shot all three of them in the chest.

The bodies fell as Arturo took labored breaths. I felt no emotion from killing three men and briefly wondered if adrenaline was clouding my feelings. However, I did not see a flicker when I looked at the dead men. Arturo broke me out of my moment of contemplation. "Nice work."

"You took out the other three. Where did you find that knife?"

"As you wrote in your book, all us immortals have at least six weapons. This knife is number two. Besides, my queen instructed me to be your bodyguard."

I laughed. Arturo tried to laugh and said, "I didn't fully succeed."

"One of them got you?"

"The thin one. He flashed a blade, and I could not prevent an injury."

"How bad?" I asked with concern. Arturo pulled up his shirt, and I saw a massive gash along his stomach. "We need to get you to the hospital."

"Will you help?"

"Of course. Why would you think otherwise?" I asked in confusion.

"I betrayed you."

"And you tried to sell me out to Jank."

"An old habit," Arturo admitted with a sheepish grin.

"You will not make my Christmas card list if you keep this up."

"Indeed, my friend."

"Let's go."

"Wait. What about his data?"

I looked around and saw lots of activity happening on the desktop computer. Next to it, I noticed a case designed to be carried and said, "This looks like a hard drive container. The screen says two minutes remaining."

"You have the memory stick?"

"It's in my pocket."

"Locate money for travel."

I closed the main steel door, looked around, and found a safe. As I did not know the combination, I searched the bodies. One man had a big wad of cash, and I took it. I opened a desk drawer and found my *Dawson's Creek* notebook. "Really?" I wondered aloud.

Arturo ripped off his shirt and pressed it against his wound. Two and a half minutes later, the progress bar showed completion, and the indicator lights on the case stopped blinking. Next, I disconnected the power and fiber optic cables. After securing the two covers, it took all my strength to get the case off the ground, and then somebody began banging at the steel door. "Don't worry," Arturo said. "If they knew the combination, we would be dead."

"Agreed."

We began walking down the hallway while Arturo held his stomach with one hand and leaned on me for support. His wound made travel excruciatingly slow, and I did not know how long the tunnel was or what we would find at the end. "Did you speak the truth?" Arturo asked in a labored voice.

"Which part?"

"The improved procedure."

"I told the truth, but I haven't tried it."

"Do you plan to?" Arturo asked, clearly in pain.

"I don't want to kill."

"Were you going to tell me about the improved procedure?"

"Cleo should be the one to reveal that information."

"Hmm. I understand your motives."

We walked for eighteen agonizing minutes and found a heavy steel door secured from our side. I pulled the six latches and opened the door to reveal a small freight elevator. When we got in, I pressed the only button on the control panel. After two minutes of slow rising, there was a crashing sound.

The elevator had broken through the floor of a garage. We made our way to an ambulance on our left. Upon close inspection, I found it was an armored vehicle disguised to look like an ambulance. I opened the heavy back door and saw weapons, communication equipment, and military uniforms. I searched for a medical kit and only found basic first aid supplies. "This is supposed to be an ambulance!" I yelled. "Where the heck are the bandages?"

After doing my best to patch Arturo up, he tried to speak, but I could only understand "add one." When I asked him what the phrase meant, he could not explain. His skin had become pale, and he took shallow breaths. As I held his hand, I asked him to conserve his strength and apply pressure on the wound.

After closing the back of the ambulance, I pressed a button to open the large outside doors. I then jumped into the driver's seat, and the engine started on the first try. Unfortunately, the road was full of potholes, making traveling at full speed difficult. Seven minutes later, I saw military vehicles in the distance.

The ambulance had a bunch of switches labeled in Italian. When I pressed the leftmost button, there was a loud machine-gun noise, and I saw the pavement 100 feet in front of me tear up. The next switch turned on the siren, and the next one turned on the flashing lights.

When I got to the military vehicles, I slammed on the brakes and jumped out with my hands up. Ten men came out with assault rifles pointed at me, and I yelled, "Help us! I need to get to a hospital!"

The man on the right with curly brown hair lowered his rifle and said something in Italian, pointing down the road. I thanked them and got back into the ambulance. After driving for 33 minutes, I saw buildings. When I came to one with a person, I screeched to a stop. As I could not roll down the armored window, I jumped out and yelled, "Hospital! Nurse! Doctor!"

The man looked bewildered and pointed down a street. It took five more people to locate a building that looked like a hospital. Unfortunately, a massive parking lot full of cars and a tall fence stood between us. Those obstacles could not stop an armored vehicle, and I crashed through everything like a bull in a china shop, leaving an epic path of destruction.

The hospital staff heard the commotion and came running out. I screeched to a stop in front of the entrance and opened the back doors. Orderlies put Arturo on a stretcher and took him away in a hurry. I noticed raised eyebrows when they saw the pile of weapons.

An agonizing 22 minutes later, a doctor in a white lab coat came to see me with a sad expression. He explained in excellent English that the patient arrived without a pulse, and he did not respond to CPR or defibrillator shocks. When the doctor asked for the deceased man's name, I answered. "Amten. Recently, he changed it to Arturo Del Olmo, and he was my friend."

"Wait here."

I knew it would be unwise to remain, since I had dropped off a dead body and destroyed many cars, so I rapidly drove away.

Several miles later, I pulled into a gas station to get directions to the small civilian Roma Urbe airport. The attendant spoke broken English and asked why I drove an ambulance. I explained it belonged to my brother, which he accepted. The attendant then sold me a map and used a pencil to highlight the route.

An hour later, I drove up to the Roma Urbe airfield. Cleopatra had provided the aircraft's tail number, and I spotted the expensive six-passenger jet from the parking lot. However, when I got closer, I saw three police cars converging on the plane. *How the heck did they figure that out?* I wondered.

After considering my options, I decided to drive to Fiumicino (Leonardo da Vinci) International Airport and navigated with the excellent map. After locating the long-term parking lot, I opened the back doors to see a bloody mess. It again took all my strength to pick up the computer hard drive case.

As I slowly made my way toward the main terminal, a kid appeared with a luggage cart. As I fished through my wad of cash, he grabbed a 50 euro note and took off without the luggage cart. While I wanted to chase the kid, it seemed pointless.

Inside the airport, I located a vast bank of payphones. They all took pre-paid cards, and I found the machine that sold them. The instructions were all in Italian, and the machine happily accepted my money. Unfortunately, I could not figure out which combination of button presses would dispense a card. After inserting four 20 euro notes, I conceded defeat.

As I aimlessly searched for the information desk, I noticed a man arguing with a woman about money in English. When I saw the man waving his iPhone, I asked, "Hey. Can I use your phone? I will pay you 100 euros."

They looked at me with joyful expressions, and the woman hugged me. "Our flight leaves in six hours, and you can use the phone for all six," she said tearfully. "This money means more to us than you will ever know."

"Glad I can help."

We walked to a trendy coffee shop, and I called Grace. To my great surprise, her phone did not answer or go to voice mail. So I texted, "At Rome airport. A and C dead. Please call me. -J."

The phone made an immediate response, "Message Not Delivered."

When I called the number Cleopatra gave me, I heard a harsh beep, ending the call. Texting yielded the same failure message. While I did not want to email from this phone, I felt there was no choice. Unfortunately, both messages bounced with "failure to deliver" messages. The entire event puzzled me, and I leaned back in my chair in defeat. Then, my two new friends noticed my depression, and the woman asked, "Anything we can do?"

"Lunch, my treat?"

"It's dinnertime," the woman corrected with a chuckle.

"Oh. Dinner, my treat?"

We found a nearby restaurant and had an average meal of pasta and steamed vegetables. *I thought Italy had good food? Apparently, not at the airport.* Out of my sidetrack, I absently listened to the couple talk about their problematic vacation.

A pickpocket stole their money and passports. By the time they made it to the Australian embassy, their bank accounts were empty. They had been begging and doing odd jobs for the last two months to save enough money for a flight home. However, after they booked the tickets, the airline imposed an additional 80 euro fee. While I found their story interesting, I did not have the right mindset to interview them.

After dinner, I used their phone to call Nicholas's office. He'd had some luck quashing the Texas warrant but said I would eventually have to appear. I decided to face this issue head-on, and Nicholas told me he would make all the arrangements for my arrival.

My roommate Dave told me that all my apartments were doing well. I left a voice mail with my boss at the *Portland Tribune*, telling him I had a legal matter to clear up and would let him know the outcome. I then thanked my new friends and handed them 200 euros. They asked about my generosity, and I answered. "Think of it as a *graceful* gift." Of course, they did not get my inside joke, but it brightened my mood.

While I searched for the information desk, I found an international shipping company, and they were happy to ship the hard drive box to my house. The helpful clerk started typing on her computer, and I needed to describe the contents for customs. I told her I was a reporter, and the case contained hard drives full of photographs and videos. She accepted this explanation and asked about its value. Caesarion identified himself as "the banker," and I imagined this single case probably contained every banking password in existence. I laughed and answered. "As you can see, this is old computer technology. I guess a thousand dollars. That's probably too high."

The clerk said the package would be at my door in two days. It took another five minutes to locate the information desk.

When I got there, I said to the well-dressed woman, "This may sound strange, but there's supposed to be a package waiting for me. My name is James Kimble."

"Certainly, sir. Here you are."

The woman handed me an envelope with 10,000 euros. However, I expected a note with instructions or new contact information. Then, she used her computer to locate a flight to Texas. I thanked her, walked to the American Airlines ticket counter, and purchased a ticket for a plane scheduled to leave in two hours.

It had been an overwhelming day, and after the security check, I walked to the nearest bar. I wondered what to order as I stared at the various bottles lined up on the shelves. While the harvest made alcohol unappealing and Grace had warned me about addiction issues, I needed a drink. The bartender came over, and I asked him for a rum and Coke. He mixed one up and looked at me with a strange expression. The alcohol sting brought no relief, and it tasted unpleasant. As I contemplated leaving my unfinished ten euro drink behind, the bartender kept staring. Eventually, I asked, "Can I help you with something?"

"You seem familiar."

"I'm an out-of-luck author. And I can't even get that right."

He stared at me with wide eyes and asked, "*Grime*?!"

What are the chances? We talked about all my books until the plane boarded.

TWENTY

I captured all my recent experiences in my *Dawson's Creek* notebook during the flight. So much had happened in a short time. Four of the oldest people in the world had died, and three by my hand. Then, out of the blue, Grace kissed me. *The person who threatened to kill me kissed me!*

On top of that, the actual Pharaoh Cleopatra kissed me. *What the heck were her motives?* And now, I was on my way to answer questions in front of a judge. There was a genuine possibility I would spend what little time I had remaining going crazy in jail. Halfway through the flight, I fell into a deeply troubled sleep.

Twelve hours and ten minutes later, the plane touched down at Dallas/Fort Worth Airport. The customs officer asked me why I had not returned from Russia using my original return ticket. I briefly wondered how she knew this information and answered, "I'm a reporter, and I was following a story."

The agent chuckled and waved me through. Again, I thought about an interview. The taxi trip took a long time because of an accident, and as we were driving, I looked at the people walking around. I saw three men in cowboy hats and boots like in the movies. When I pointed this out to the driver, he laughed, and we talked about men's fashion.

Halfway there, I learned by text message that Nicholas had taken the warrant quashing right to the top of the Texas justice system, and I wondered what his bill would be.

The Dallas County courthouse is a massive building, and after several wrong turns, I located the correct office. The clerk asked me to wait, and with nothing else to do, I began drawing the dying plant in a brown pot. After ten minutes, the excellent results surprised me. *I have artistic talent?*

Eighty-five minutes later, the clerk escorted me into the judge's office. Inside, I was stunned to see Assistant DA McCormick from Wyoming, Detective Camron from Oregon, and Detective Dana from Nevada. Then, I realized they had been talking about the case while I waited outside. When I sat down, Texas State Prosecuting District Attorney Ken Reed joined us.

They refused to answer my questions for the next three minutes and harshly glared at me. Then, Judge Arthur Park came in. He was a tall man with a chiseled jaw and steely gray eyes. I expected a judge would wear a robe, but he was dressed in a nice tweed suit. He sat down behind his grand wooden desk with an intense expression, and a court reporter began typing.

"Your attorney isn't present," Judge Park boomed with a strong Texas accent.

The commanding voice surprised me, and I humbly replied, "My recent schedule has been unpredictable, Your Honor."

"Will this be an issue?"

"Are there charges pending against me?" I asked with concern.

"Not at this time."

This admission was a tremendous relief, and I asked, "So, you only want me to tell my story?"

"Correct," Judge Park answered.

"Then not having my attorney present is fine."

"Very well. Let's get this matter settled."

State Prosecutor Reed looked at his notes and began, "This hearing regards the brutal murder of six Texas Rangers. James Kimble is present because he identified the killer as a woman he refers to as Grace, AKA Barbara Edwards, AKA Anitchka Ermolaev."

Listening to the aliases made me chuckle.

"Six fine young men are dead," Judge Park interrupted in an angry voice. "Do you find this funny?"

I quickly calmed down and humbly answered, "I'm sorry, Your Honor. Perhaps we can get some context. Mr. District Attorney, could you please describe this woman?"

He cleared his throat and answered, "She has a medium build with black or brown hair and—"

"How old would you say this woman is?" I interrupted.

"Um— (Muttered words)."

"I missed that. How old?"

State Prosecutor Reed looked down and muttered louder, "Over 500."

"I see."

Judge Park asked, "Is this a mistake? What the heck is going on here?"

I turned to Judge Park and answered, "Your Honor, they got all their information from my book. A book that I admitted was a complete fiction. There's no such woman as Grace; she's a made-up character, a figment of my imagination. Her 500-year-old age should be proof of my fabrication. All the Texas Ranger information in my book came from a story that my uncle Joe told me. He was a bad-ass Ranger in the '70s."

"Five-hundred-years-old?! I don't like what I'm hearing. This better not be the truth."

"No, Your Honor," State Prosecutor Reed said in a humble voice. "The book contained several descriptions related to actual crimes. Mr. Kimble is a suspect in two."

"Not quite," I interrupted. "They tried to convict me of those crimes. And when nobody could present a shred of evidence, the judge tossed the case out. Now, please tell us the real reason I'm here."

Judge Park became visibly upset, and said with a forced, calm voice, "I put down three quashes to get this man in front of me. Now I find misrepresented evidence. Five-hundred-years-old?! Why is this man here? Let's have it!"

"Your Honor, we have many questions for Mr. Kimble, and this venue is the only method of ascertaining the information we require," State Prosecutor Reed confidently answered.

"Ken, you know how I like direct answers. Why is Mr. Kimble here? Let's hear it."

"I made that clear in my brief."

Judge Park looked at State Prosecutor Reed for eight seconds and boomed, "I did not see any mention of a 500-year-old woman."

"I did not feel those details were relevant."

"You did not feel a 500-year age was important?! This is intolerable! Mr. Kimble, you're free to go. The state will compensate you for your time."

Judge Parks banged his gavel.

"Your Honor, you didn't get your answer," I said.

"No, I did not."

"Mr. Reed, tell him, or I will." State Prosecutor Reed looked defiant, and I continued, "They arrested me in Portland to get my computer files because they couldn't read my awful handwriting in my notebooks. I encrypted my laptop hard drive, and they cannot decode it."

"Hmm," Judge Parks mused as he twisted his gavel.

"I'm here today because they're trying to invent a legal method that forces me to reveal my password. Also, the last judge ordered them to destroy my data. My attorney told me they are going to claim an inevitable discovery."

Judge Park flicked his hand, twisted his gavel, and said, "Ken, this had better not be true. Because if it is ..."

"No, not really, Your Honor," State Prosecutor Reed sheepishly answered.

"Were the aforementioned files deleted?" Eyes began shifting, and Judge Park continued, "Your silence indicates no. Mr. Kimble has stated that a judge handed down an order to destroy the recovered data. Is this true?"

Detective Camron turned away, and Judge Park continued, "I take it that this order didn't get carried out?" The people looked uncomfortable, and he continued, "I order you three to send Mr. Kimble's attorney a letter from the head district attorney from your respective jurisdictions. It will state that you have deleted all recovered data and that no copies remain. Texas justice isn't predicated on back-door bushwhacking! We're done."

"Thank you, Your Honor," I said with a smile. Judge Park stood, and everybody stood. I made one more request to see if I could stop the harassment. "Your Honor, I think it will be possible to clear this up off the record."

"Fine. I have a meeting. Use my office."

Judge Park and the court reporter left. I walked over to the coffee machine, poured myself a cup, sat down, looked at Detective Camron with vacant eyes, and asked, "Did you like my book?"

"It's—hard to believe," Detective Camron stammered.

"Not what I asked."

"I must have read it at least seven times. I was looking for clues, of course. But, hey. I have to ask. Did you really sleep with a mountain lion?"

"Her fur was super thick. It was like a scouring brush. And those enormous paws? Dang! When she spread her claws out, they were the size of dinner plates. I still thank my lucky stars that she didn't tear me to pieces."

"It's all true?" Detective Camron wondered.

"Is this off the record?"

The assembled people shifted their eyes, and Detective Camron nodded.

"As I wrote, I changed the harvest facts to prevent the world from killing itself," I replied. "The rest of the book doesn't contain a single lie."

"What's she like?" Detective Camron asked in amazement.

"She's an astounding woman."

"Did you ever see her again?"

I laughed and answered, "You need to wait for me to write another book to get an answer."

Detective Camron got serious, pointed at me, and said, "You confessed to a murder in your book. But you have an excellent case to explain your actions. So, do yourself a favor and come clean. It's your best move."

I scratched my arm and looked at him for eighteen seconds while wondering if a complete confession would be the best course of action. *So many people are now dead. An entire chain of death for the pursuit of eternal life. And what about Anna? What a tragic loss. She had nothing to do with any of this.*

The thought of Anna's death pulled at my heart, and I needed a distraction. So, I looked at the assembled people and randomly asked Detective Dana, "What did you think of my book?" She did not answer, and I continued, "Be honest."

"I want to meet Grace," Detective Dana confessed.

"She sounds pretty amazing. Right?"

"Oh, yeah."

"My humble words didn't even come close to describing her. But you didn't answer me. Did you like my book?"

Detective Dana turned to Detective Camron and answered, "I'm not sure I liked it, but I read it four times. To check for facts, of course."

"Do you have a family?"

"I don't see why that's important," Detective Dana answered with a hint of anger.

"Family is everything. Do you have one?"

"Yes," Detective Dana admitted with a huff.

"Good."

I composed my thoughts for 22 seconds and began, "Everybody knows the story about the mouse that pulls the thorn out of the lion's paw. In my story, I'm that tiny mouse, but there is a gigantic dragon instead of a lion, and there's no thorn. But the dragon finds me amusing, which is the only thing keeping her from burning me to a crisp. Now, let me first say that I never planned to be that mouse, but the universe somehow picked me."

I continued after brief pause. "Look, I get it. Your job is to fight crime, and I genuinely appreciate all the hard work. Honestly, I do because I have interviewed many cops, and I know your jobs are difficult. Nobody ever thanks you, and your only reward is knowing that your efforts somehow make the world a better place. Your tenacity in dragging me to Texas proves your heart is in the right place. I also understand how much it must anger you when a person flaunts criminal activities.

"So, let me say that I am genuinely sorry for my part in all the crimes. Please understand that I would never intentionally try to make your jobs hard. And I appreciate the fact that you are trying to make things right.

"It's clear that you want to charge Grace with a crime. You don't realize that you're trying to grab the tail of a mighty dragon. This dragon used to be asleep, but now, she's fully awake, mad, frightened, has unlimited resources, and has no qualms about taking lives. Trust me; I have had a front-row seat to her wrath.

"Now, listen up. I will tell you one more thing. There is a second dragon. She is far more powerful than Grace and far more dangerous. Plus, they are working together, which is a force beyond what I can comprehend."

The assembled people were now in shock. I took a deep breath and continued, "About the two dead bodies. Please, drop your investigation. You put real criminals in jail, and that is an impressive accomplishment.

"As for me? I get it. You're trying to pin a murder on me. And believe me, every day, I feel deep regret about what happened. But remember that both dragons like my occasional company. And I cannot talk to them from behind bars. So if you want to stay safe, let go of the dragon's tail. My advice is to go home to your family. Love them and enjoy every moment you have. Now, this jet lag is killing me, and I need some sleep."

Detective Dana asked in an astonished voice, "You found another person who—harvests?"

"Actually, I found five. Four are now dead. But that other dragon. Wow! She is amazing. Yet, she acted more ruthlessly than my worst dreams. Stay out of her way! You cannot comprehend what she's capable of."

Everyone in the room looked at me in complete awe, and Detective Dana asked, "What are they fighting for?"

"Their survival. Recent experience has taught me that survival is the strongest motivation."

I stood and added, "Oh. One more thing about the six deputies. Tell me, Mr. Reed. Around the time those Rangers died, did your research uncover a bunch of violent crimes?"

State Prosecutor Reed looked uncomfortable and answered, "I pulled all the Gladewater files from 1931 to 1938. There were seventeen unsolved cases."

"Did it seem odd that many of the victims were women?"

He looked astonished for twelve seconds and answered, "The files contained some similarities."

"Were all the women sexually assaulted?"

"Where are you going with this?" State Prosecutor Reed asked after switching positions in his chair.

"Please answer my question."

"Well, yes," he answered in a low voice. "That information is in a sealed file. Who told you this?"

I looked at him for fourteen seconds and answered, "The six deputies were a rape gang."

"How do you know all this?!" State Prosecutor Reed again demanded.

"I just do."

"Did you have further contact with Grace?"

"If you bring this to trial, you will end up with egg on your face. No jury will ever convict a woman for taking down a Texas Rangers rape gang. Anything you do will only bring negative publicity for Texas justice. Let the past sins remain in the past."

"Hmm."

"Well, I'm off. Nice meeting all of you."

As I turned to leave, Detective Camron stood and threatened, "We will pursue this matter with every legal means at our disposal!"

His remark made me feel like I'd been hit in the gut, and I sat down feeling defeated. Eighteen seconds later, I sighed and said, "I haven't convinced you. That's discouraging."

BILL CONRAD

My attention faded, and I could not come up with an argument. Then I began staring at Detective Dana while deep in thought. *You look like the newswoman Diane Sawyer.* Twenty-four seconds later, I had a moment of inspiration and asked her, "Based on my book, how smart do you think Grace is? You know, compared to the average woman?"

"I don't know," Detective Dana flatly answered.

"Please take a guess."

"She would need to be smart to make all her money."

"How often do you think she makes mistakes?"

"I don't know," Detective Dana again flatly answered. "Rarely, I guess."

"You still don't get it, do you?"

"Get what?" Detective Dana asked while biting her lip.

"She never makes mistakes."

"I don't understand."

"Why do you think I'm here?" I asked while holding my left hand up as if I were asking a question. "Why do you think all of you are here?" I waved my left hand around.

"What are you saying?" State Prosecutor Reed asked. "She somehow planned this meeting? That's not plausible."

"Think about it."

The assembled people looked at each other, and Detective Camron asked, "To what end?"

"To identify everybody who is pursuing her. And now she knows it all. Your bosses, computers, and family. Everything! You don't realize that all of you stepped on a big land mine. Now, you understand how a land mine works. If you want to live, you need to remain still. Otherwise, boom!"

Everyone now looked scared, and I found it rewarding that I had finally made an impression. However, it still seemed as if the group needed one more push. "Let me try a different angle," I said with a tilted head. "It's safe to assume that all of you understand the power of a nuclear weapon?"

The assembled people looked at each other in confusion, and I continued, "One of the dead immortals had four extended-range nuclear-tipped Polaris missiles in his compound. Also, he had 35 nuclear warheads under his direct control. This psychopath sold them all because they were high maintenance.

"That is the secretive, nut-job you're dealing with! I am their only line of communication! Stop pulling the dragon's tail!"

The assembled people looked shocked, and Detective Camron dropped his pen. I left without another word and took a cab back to the airport.

TWENTY-ONE

I expected to see my house surrounded by SWAT teams, news helicopters, Goth kids, kidnappers, and devoted book fans. Instead, a quiet street greeted me. I lifted the doormat, retrieved the spare key, and walked inside. The computer hard drive case stood in the middle of the room with a DHL box on top.

When I opened the box, I found my Sony laptop, Arturo's knife, and my other *Dawson's Creek* notebook. The last page contained a hand-drawn red heart with "Thinking of you" in flawless handwriting, and it smelled like Cleopatra's perfume. The package's tracking data showed the DHL box was shipped two days ago from a nonexistent Polish address.

My roommates had endless questions, and I told them most of my recent events but left out the details. Dave did not like that I lost his backpack, so I offered him a free month of rent. This trade put him in a better mood.

On the way to work the following day, I passed the spot where I had punched the air in frustration. I laughed, continued driving, and then got sidetracked. *I still need to get a spare tire. Dang! I've got to work on that.* Seeing a homeless person with an enormous hat brought me out of my funk; another insightful interview.

Lloyd was glad I was back and had endless questions. I told him I met many amazing people and had many interviews to write up. However, I did not share any information about immortals because the little voice inside my head told me to keep recent events a secret. So, I typed everything into my laptop and did computer research for the rest of the day.

The Thailand attack was big news. Local hospitals treated 22 survivors, and the authorities recovered 255 bodies. The injured men confessed that a wealthy warlord hired them to attack a rival warlord. However, the dead soldiers were not from Thailand and wore military uniforms with blue patches. The police identified three fingerprints from the dead men who had served in the Russian military.

The official report concluded, "The incident resulted from a territorial dispute between rival militant groups." However, several Thai news outlets disagreed with this explanation. Their prevailing theory suggested that the Thai government attacked a crime lord with Russian mercenaries.

The Italian "terrorist camp" was also big news. The government forces entered the massive compound without firing a shot. Inside, they found an extensive cache of weapons, computers, and valuable artwork.

Seven bodies were recovered from an armored "cocoon," and the government hailed this takedown as "the largest victory in the fight for freedom." I found it amusing that the "largest victory" did not have a single arrest.

There was a side story about one terrorist who escaped in an armored ambulance. After dropping off a fallen comrade, the driver abandoned the vehicle at the airport. I also found an unconfirmed report about somebody stealing the body from the morgue. I used my reporter contacts to inquire further and emailed the coroner who examined the recovered bodies. He described three men who died from knife wounds and three from gunshots. One body was "an unusual specimen with many scars and a foul odor."

Bethany became ecstatic when I called her. *Interviewing Immortality* sales were "through the roof," and she had worldwide interview requests! I confronted her about the doctored sales figures and multiple language translations. Bethany confessed to "minor accounting irregularities" and vowed to "immediately correct them." I may be on the lookout for a new publisher.

I paid all of Nicholas's legal bills and made down payments on three additional apartment buildings from all my rent money and cash from my trip. Craig lost his job at the supermarket and wanted to become my full-time apartment manager. How could I argue with a perfect match?

In my spare time, I began taking meditation, tai chi, gymnastics, painting, and Spanish classes. I also brought props to my karate class such as straitjackets. We experimented with unusual fighting styles under harsh conditions, including trips to the local YMCA swimming pool. At the end of every class, my teacher admonished me not to use these techniques to "get dates." The students never tired of that joke or the opportunity to smack me around.

My ability to communicate pictures and emotions continued to fascinate me. I did extensive research into this phenomenon, including interviewing local psychics. It is now clear that the harvest provides an unknown mental or vision improvement. However, I am no closer to understanding how Heathcliff sent me moving images. My only guess is that her mountain lion physiology provided additional abilities.

While my life had many positives, it also contained large negatives. Mateo's Facebook page had pictures of his five- and six-year-old daughters. His wife's page contained sad messages about his passing.

One could argue that I fought to save my life. However, I find this argument hollow. I alone killed Mateo. I believe he led an honest life, and if I ever met his family, I would tell them how much I regret my actions. But am I going to seek them out to share my heartache? Well, no. The harvest pressure urges me to keep out of trouble. Or am I acting cowardly? Honestly, I can no longer tell the difference.

The six dead men at Caesarion's compound also haunt my memories. They fought to protect their employer against a person with a knife. Perhaps I fought for my life while defending a friend, but I also find this argument hollow. I took careful aim and ended three lives without giving them a chance to surrender. There were so many times that I should have walked away.

My most significant source of mental anguish continues to be the loss of Cynthia and Darin. Since their passing, I firmly decided many times to turn myself in. Yet, when I approach the police station to confess, I turn around in shame.

Sometimes, the only thing that keeps me going is looking after Julius. His life has dramatically improved, and the burns on his arms are healing. On Saturdays, his aunt and uncle allow me to help with his math homework. It is the highlight of my week, and the only time I genuinely feel happy. Yet the thought of Julius discovering what I have done fills me with fear. I do not know what I will tell him.

The deaths of Quan and Jank also weigh heavily on me. I'm still angry at Cleopatra for forcing me to kill them, yet ending their lives brought justice to thousands of slain boys.

Anna's passing also tugs deeply at my soul. I have not forgiven myself for starting a course of action that led to her death. I often wake up thinking of her and what it would have been like to have a relationship. Sometimes, it is not easy to get out of bed with these thoughts.

Another deep concern is Cleopatra's revelation that once a person harvests, they cannot stop. This concept terrifies me more than driving a car toward a cliff without brakes. To make matters worse, the thought of going insane is so terrible that I refuse to confront it. However, I must confess that thoughts of suicide are now less abhorrent. I cannot believe I wrote that last sentence. Truly, I cannot.

Besides all my other troubles, Arturo and Cleopatra told me I could not have children. Having a family has always been a core value, and I think about this hindrance far more than I should.

Three days after I returned home, I told my parents everything. They have always come first and deserved to hear the whole truth. My admission emotionally destroyed them, and their sobs stabbed deep into my heart. They encouraged me to confess my crimes and accept any punishment. When I refused their plea, my parents both said they would go to the police. So far, that has not happened, but I would understand if they did. I feel awful for putting them through so much anguish. No son should ever do that.

Right now, they refuse to speak to me. We have always been close, and perhaps this is my deepest pain. Unfortunately, I do not think our bond will ever recover.

Earlier in this book, I wrote that the harvest gift differs from drug addiction. Through Mercedes's contacts, I interviewed two heroin addicts. To my great surprise, I discovered compelling similarities between our lives. Specifically, our feeling after a fix and the despicable acts we perform to maintain our supply. One told me outright, "Yeah, I would kill to get high if it came to that. And I can see it in your eyes. You would too."

This insight into addiction allowed me to understand that the harvest feelings and abilities are not a chemical escape but instead, a far more powerful "high on life." With this revelation, I had no choice and began attending anonymous meetings for drug users. This experience proved wildly eye-opening, and I now understand that I have a real problem.

In taking a high-level overview of all that has happened to me, it's obvious that somebody is leading me down a specific path. There have been too many perfectly timed and unconnected events. It started with the Chinese men at the apple tree. What are the chances of that randomly happening? Zero! Then, Quan's house gets blown up a few days later. Surviving a military airstrike on a horse? Book fans at the airport?

Arturo's daughter at another airport? Why would Cleopatra send me my laptop and Arturo's knife? Who took Arturo's body from the hospital? It all has to be connected. But how?

The only explanation that makes sense is that a war erupted between the immortals, and I am a pawn in a much larger game. The truly horrific part is that, regrettably, I started the war by writing *Interviewing Immortality*. Imagine that—a nobody author started an entire war. As a result, hundreds of people are dead because of my words.

◆ ◆ ◆

At this point in the story, my adventure should have quietly ended. If anybody asked, I would say that I fabricated everything. The events written in this book should have rattled around my confused mind and stayed in my *Dawson's Creek* notebooks.

Remember those rules at the beginning? No more books! Trust me, I got it! So I came up with a straightforward plan to live a quiet life. In a few months, I would remove my harvested pancreas, and if I died or went crazy, so be it. I felt fully prepared to accept any fate life dished out, even if it meant taking my last breath in an insane asylum.

But not everything in my dull life was negative. I had a giant hard drive box full of bank passwords. I'm not a greedy person; a billion dollars would be enough to buy a few toys.

TWENTY-TWO

Well, my life did not contain a "he lived happily ever after" ending. The universe has its quirks, and it wanted to mess with James Kimble's life one more time.

Three weeks after I returned, I received an elegant letter written on Cleopatra's letterhead in Grace's handwriting:

James,

If you are reading this letter, something has gone terribly wrong. Circumstances forced me to depart from my safe location, and I left instructions to send this letter if I didn't return by a specific time. You are the only parson I trust, and I implore you to use all the resources at your disposal to rescue me. To prove my identity, we affection-ately imagined each other's swimsuits at our last encounter.

Take care, Grace

Every word in this letter was out of place. Grace is a study in precision and would never make such a vague, open-ended request. It also contained a huge red flag. Grace had misspelled "person" as "parson." Mistakes of that magnitude are so far out of her character that I was sure this entire document must be a fake, or Grace was trying to secretly warn me.

The letterhead reminded me of the two letters which were left at Caesarion's compound. I surmised that somebody might have used them to make a forgery. However, the reference to swimsuits puzzled me. I knew Grace would never openly write such deeply personal details.

As I reread the letter a hundred times, I thought of a troubling alternate possibility. *Cleopatra also had swimsuit thoughts about me. Could she be baiting me?*

All of this made no sense. I still lived in the same house, and if somebody wanted to find me, all they needed to do was walk up to my front door. I even found my address posted online several times relating to the *Grime* series.

By the way, readers, if you have a question, feel free to email me. There is no need to send me letters or come to my house. Meeting uninvited guests creeps me out. Not cool!

This entire situation threw my life back into confusion. So, I did what I always did. I punched the air on my way to work, put fresh flowers on Heathcliff's grave, and found myself in her rocky hovel, staring at an empty meadow. The weather had turned cold, and Heathcliff's rock felt uninviting. Like the last time I sat on that rock, there were no answers, but the experience brought comfort.

On my drive back home, I came to the same conclusion I did at the beginning of this book. I would find Grace again.

However, my motivation was different. I admitted to myself that I had fallen in love with her.

Love has been responsible for many crazy decisions in my life. For example, I once tried to impress a girl in high school by dressing up as Michael Jackson and moonwalking to every class. Now love was pushing me down another crazy path, and I would do whatever was necessary (except harvesting) to seek Grace out one more time. This remarkable woman left a colossal impression on me, and I desperately wanted her to be a part of my life. In coming to this conclusion, I also admitted that these same feelings initially influenced my decision to seek her out.

What about Cleopatra? Our time together was brief, but she left an incredible impression on me. I am unsure what part of my heart she occupies, but I would like to see her again.

Thus, my quest began. I started with Caesarion's computer. It undoubtedly contained the means to turn James Kimble into a financial powerhouse who could send vast armies to any corner of the earth! Unfortunately, the computer case contained a basic server computer with 36 high-reliability 500-gigabyte shock-mounted hard drives. This system was designed to interface with other computers through six one-gigabit optical network connections and a single Ethernet port.

To my great surprise, my Sony laptop immediately connected over Ethernet and displayed all the data. I had expected crazy passwords, encryption, and failsafe programs. However, there was a gigantic problem. Caesarion stored the data in proprietary formats. I deduced he intended to take the data from one preconfigured site and move it to another.

To my relief, Caesarion planned for this exact scenario. The hard drive array contained an up-to-date copy of the many programs necessary to access the data and a detailed configuration description. Unfortunately, these programs were not the type that a typical computer user could click "install" and have them up and going. I had some computer knowledge, but this task far exceeded my technical abilities. To make matters worse, I could not ask for outside help, as this would lead my enemies right to me.

Fortunately, I had an ace up my sleeve. My roommate Dave is a computer wizard, and I asked him to help. I explained that people would kill for this information, and once he started down this path, he could not turn back.

Dave agreed on one condition: selfie with Cleopatra. He cracks me up! Dave quit his Information Technology job and moved to an undisclosed location. I am now paying for his expenses while he accesses Caesarion's data. From his initial assessment, this effort will be difficult.

The financial data from the memory stick proved to be more helpful. I tracked down several leads to locate the people responsible for the attacks. However, this is where I hit a financial roadblock, because going any further required trips to foreign countries and private investigators.

I reasoned that only two people could help me: the guards who had escaped from Cleopatra. Despite every conceivable search for these men, I came up empty. Without other options, I would bring them to me. How does an author get attention? Now you know why I wrote this book. Hey, Humai and Khalid. We need to talk!

Many people have asked me if more books are in the pipeline. Honestly, I must be realistic. As these words flow onto my laptop, I feel a strong desire to harvest. However, as stated several times, I choose never to harvest again. Will this decision result in my death? Sadly, my life will end soon and I accept this eventuality.

I do not ask for your sorrow, dear reader. Please recall that I alone chose to continue down the dreadful harvest path. I knew this terrible act would push my soul past the point of forgiveness. However, now I would rather live a short, honest life than a long life fueled by murder.

As a final thought, please allow me to paraphrase Grace. Harvesting is the dark one percent of my life, and the rest has been a grand adventure. Every day I learn about the world, enjoy great food, meet delightful people, and live my life to the fullest. I am deeply privileged to share my story, and I thank all my readers for their generous support.

EPILOGUE

There are some basic rules to writing a sequel that I will now
impart to you.

1) When you commit a crime and want to write about it,
   CHANGE THE FACTS! It's common sense! This time, I
   did a much better job of altering the essential information. The authorities can investigate all they want, and
   they will only find false leads. However, I am giving you,
   the reader, the guts of the actual story.

2) Write lots of books. It's fun.

There is one question that still requires an answer. Would I
have gone to that book signing if I knew Grace would capture
me? I have thought about this question many times and come
to many conclusions. To provide a complete answer, I must
admit that I am profoundly under the harvest influence. My
heart tells me I absolutely would have marched right into that

nasty bookstore and waited a lifetime to meet Grace (if only for one second). How accurate is this statement? Clearly, I can no longer tell.

Would I recommend this journey to others? Absolutely not! The harvest takes ordinary people and turns them into frightened beasts. They become empty shells who fear their own shadows. My journey came at an unimaginably high cost, and my horrific actions have burned my soul.

This book is not about finding immortality. Instead, it is a battlefield where the losing army is my upstanding morality. To put this horrific concept into other terms, this book is an autobiography of a good man becoming a cold-hearted serial killer who would murder in a heartbeat to maintain one more second of a selfish life. Every time I watch the evening news and see the deplorable acts of despicable people, I know my name belongs at the beginning of every newscast. "James Kimble. The worst man in Portland!"

However, there is a paradox. I ended my last book with a boast about not harvesting. And then, in this book, I jumped right back in. I need to state with absolute clarity that I will never harvest again! I have endured a hundred lifetimes worth of death, pain, and torture. My madness over the trivial goal of life extension will come to an end.

What about the person who has pulled at the strings along my journey? I say their actions have resulted in hundreds of deaths, and they should be ashamed of their appalling choices. Take some responsibility!

The humans occupying this world must live a short but magnificent existence. The US Constitution stated this concept flawlessly. "We have the right to pursue happiness." That means we must appreciate the limited time graciously provided to us and peacefully coexist with the wonderful people on this spectacular planet. In the end, we only have each other.

—James Kimble, 1/18/2014

PS: I read several recent news stories about murdered bodies missing the pancreas, kidney, and adrenal glands. Stop it! No matter what you try, it will not work!

PSS: No, I do not own a mountain lion—yet.

PSSS: No, I still have not purchased a spare tire.

ABOUT THE AUTHOR

This project began with me using a completely new writing technique. A story outline allowed me to develop a solid plot with great flow. However, I did not completely follow the outline during the writing process. The Arturo character took on a larger role, and I altered the ending. Initially, I planned a grand reunion, but this conclusion was too idealistic and incompatible with the next book.

Cleopatra was a fun character, and I loved playing with her lack of reality. What an astounding woman, whose memory continues to live in our hearts. It was a great honor to bring her back to life.

I have an excellent story outline for the third book titled *Saving Immortality* and a fantastic follow-up concept which is tentatively titled *Living with Immortality*. Plus, I even have an idea for a fifth book that may unveil another immortal historical figure. But that lofty concept without a title has many bugs to work out. Please check my website for details.

The writing process has undoubtedly improved my spelling and grammar. I can trace my writing spark back to my creative writing class at WPI in Worcester, Massachusetts. There, I received a degree in Electrical Engineering (the best kind of engineering) and a minor in English. The leap into publishing required a *healthy* bout of unemployment to get things going.

What about my details? I grew up in San Diego, California, and still live here without any plans to move. Fortune favored me with an amazing wife, Laurie, and a wonderful daughter, Kayla. Like me, she has a creative side, and you can see her influence in my characters.

Interesting side story. When I showed Kayla *Interviewing Immortality*, she could not believe I had dedicated that book to her. I then showed her one of my father's books, *Advanced Ceramic Manual,* which he dedicated to my sister, Kristin and me. Like father, like son.

—Bill Conrad, May 2023

DEDICATION

Why are book dedications always in the beginning of a book? How does that location help the reader? Do they have the Oscar award thank-you speeches at the beginning of movies? With that in mind, I put my dedication at the end.

I have been fortunate to have had two amazing parents. They were supportive, wonderful, patient beyond words, caring, and loving. Without their support, I would be nothing of consequence. My mother pushed me to keep writing and is my trustworthy beta reader. My father has been an author of many ceramics textbooks and served as an inspiration and role model. My sister is a constant source of encouragement and help. I have been fortunate to have an amazing woman like her in my life.

My wife has been immensely supportive, and without her help and love, this book would not have remained in my mind. And finally, I dedicate this book to my amazing daughter, Kayla. She makes my life complete.

There are two other people I wish to thank. My pen pal from New Zealand, Emily Rayven, and my pen pal, Miriam Yvette have been encouraging and great friends. I am lucky to have met them and read their fantastic stories.

www.ingramcontent.com/pod-product-compliance
Lightning Source LLC
Chambersburg PA
CBHW071633260626
47170CB00001B/83